MACMILLAN CAR

Power Game

Perry Henzell

Macmillan Education
Between Towns Road, Oxford, OX4 3PP
A division of Macmillan Publishers Limited
Companies and representatives throughout the world

www.macmillan-caribbean.com

ISBN: 978-0-2300-2990-3

Typeset by EXPO Holdings, Malaysia
Cover design and illustration by Tim Gravestock

Printed and bound in Hong Kong
2013 2012 2011 2010 2009
10 9 8 7 6 5 4 3 2 1

Part One

The Players

Chapter One

IZion sat in a small canoe and watched as late afternoon turned to dusk, the pink from his wide view of the western sky reflecting off the surface of the sea.

IZion was fishing, but fishing wasn't his living, he made his living in a much more dangerous way than that, and he was thinking that for the danger he faced he shouldn't be poor. So poor that borrowing this lowly craft to leave the city and go to the other side of the harbour for the space and time to think was the one pleasure he could really afford.

He loved to go and sit out there and watch the planes circle and land and rise again from the city's airport. People who could make planes and fly them, buy them and sell them, what kind of world did those people really live in? How did they get that rich? How did they think that big and make it happen? Did they really want to keep poor people poor, or did putting cash in poor people's pockets make them richer because they sold more goods? Who in the city across the bay was really the biggest guy? Was he big enough to make the others bow? For how long?

For IZion these were not idle questions. Whoever was in charge, things weren't going well with him. Whatever was at stake was worth killing for and IZion lived in the firing line. It was one thing to live dangerously and get rich, but to live dangerously and stay poor ... no ... that couldn't go on. He had to find the secret to success, he had to find out what was really going on in the minds of those who controlled his destiny. That's what IZion was thinking as he started paddling back towards the docks in the distance.

The city, downtown, looked much like many others in the Caribbean in the seventies ... Panama, Santo Domingo, Kingston ... sweltered in heat, smothered with smog, square miles of slum rooftops stretching like waves of rusting zinc on an ocean of rotting wood; horizons of poverty unbroken — except for the six dramatically modern high-rise buildings that stood out in the middle of the waterfront, like ocean liners at sea.

The tallest of these buildings was the hotel; the next in height was the Central Bank, and at the top of the Central Bank building stood Winston Bernard looking out across the harbour to the airport for Hugh Clifford's plane.

Winston Bernard was tall, brown, thin in an athletic way, with highly intelligent eyes, the eyes of a mimic, taking everything in.

He had done well enough in the outside world — starting with a Rhodes Scholarship and ending at the World Bank — to feel at ease where he sat at the top of the town. His cousin was prime minister, his brother ran the army, his wife ran the most popular radio station. His father had been the head of the civil service under the British and he'd been knighted for that. But there was relatively little nepotism in the British Colonial Civil Service, everybody got where they were going on their own steam, and because he'd been born into a meritocracy and had surpassed the norm, one might assume that Winston Bernard was comfortable with the idea of being in charge, that he was happy with the assumption that others would look to him for orders in a crisis. He was. Provided that he had full control, provided that he was pursuing a plan of his own choosing, and provided there was nobody blocking his way, because when blocked Winston could be very unhappy indeed, and he'd been blocked now for the last several months.

Winston Bernard and his brother, Mark, came from that generation of leadership in the tropics who were born in the forties and had spent the first ten years of their lives under colonialism; then in the fifties saw the Independence Movement triumph all over the world just as they themselves were coming of age, and, during the sixties, were conscious of the vast resources and enormous riches that were theirs to control now that they controlled the destinies of truly independent nations.

But while the sixties brought independence, the seventies brought the oil shock and an end to innocence. Only ten years had passed since the fireworks lit up the sky for the freedom night celebrations, and already the cupboard was bare.

As the price of oil doubled and doubled and doubled again, those countries who had previously had money in the bank found that their reserves had been wiped out in a few months.

Once more, ministers were expected to go to London and Washington to beg for preferential tariffs, to wait in the same antechambers as their forefathers did during colonial times, accepting the fact that someone else would make their decisions for them. For ten years the former colonies had been banking their own cash, but now everyone who didn't have oil would have to go back into the begging business ... merely back to business as usual for most of those involved, but not for Winston Bernard. He knew the opposition, he had been trained by them and had succeeded in their system, and he was determined to beat them at their own game.

As he walked around the terrace that surrounded his penthouse office, Winston's gaze shifted from the harbour to the hills and mountains that reared up to form the backdrop to the city, disappearing into cloud at seven thousand feet. As he continued his circle to the west, his eyes swept over urban sprawl that stretched for ten miles, ending in the swamp that separated the city from fifty thousand acres of sugar cane. Then he came back round to see the docks, harbour, and airport again, and this time he saw the dot of Hugh Clifford's little jet coming in to land, its wings glinting in the rays of the setting sun.

Winston's mood lightened immediately. If he could swing Hugh Clifford behind him, he stood a chance of winning. Clifford was the only man in the world who could help Winston right now.

As the Lear banked and lined up for landing, Hugh Clifford's wife, Molly, called him over to look at the sunset outside her window.

Molly wasn't one to miss a good sunset. She didn't like missing anything. She hadn't missed much since she first invaded London, as the daughter of a rural Earl, to become deb of the year, 1936.

Hugh Clifford looked out of the window, settled his long frame back into his seat, finished off his scotch and soda, picked up the cards from the game he'd been playing with Molly, and watched as she packed up a wide variety of cassettes and magazines and shoved them into a large leather bag together with her Walkman and the two novels she'd brought along on the trip.

Hugh Clifford was an old man, one of the last of a dying breed. Joe Kennedy, Averell Harriman, Jock Hay Whitney, even the young Howard Hughes, these were his contemporaries at the prime of his life, and he missed them. There were only two classes of people in business as far as Hugh Clifford was concerned: those who could say yes and those who had to ask somebody else. He was bored to find himself, at his age, surrounded by those in government and the corporate world who had to consult with others in endless succession.

Hugh Clifford's father had been one of five railroad barons who'd started it all; got it financed, employed the labour, moved the earth, cut the logs, embedded the sleepers, and laid down on them the lines of steel that crisscrossed North America. He was as rich as such a man would be if he was given the land on either side of the railroad for thousands of miles, and sold off the plots for all the towns along the way. He was as rich as a man could become if he chose where the rails would go and when they would get there, and this was at a time before there were any paved roads or trucks; as rich as such a man would become if he got together with the steel and oil cartels to put competitors out of business with high rail charges, getting a big piece of big oil and big steel for his cooperation. Hugh's father was already as rich as that before Hugh was born to the sole inheritance of all that the old man had accumulated.

Hugh was so rich that throughout his childhood he never heard money discussed. It just didn't come up when his mother was around, and later, when it did, it was always in reference to how much wealth he had, so he didn't think about it, he certainly didn't crave it, and he found the challenges to his ego entirely outside considerations of money altogether.

His skill in sport, for example, was much more important to him than money. How well did he ride? Ski? Play tennis? Dance? What help was money at sixteen when facing a ski slope that could break your legs, or when someone else could simply beat you at a game you were trying to win, or take away the girl you wanted on the dance floor? Right from the start Hugh was brought up to believe that the really important possessions were courage and style, and a taste for the quality that rendered his mother passionate, the quality that money couldn't necessarily buy, either in things or in people, and especially in people.

So all his long life Hugh Clifford had been fascinated by other forms of power. The power of great lovers, of scientists, artists, and politicians. He was fascinated by what they did with their power, and he was even more intrigued by what it did to them. For decades he'd been watching ambitious men climb and seeing them fall, calculating the height at which they would lose their grip and slip, and barely able to hold on, realise that they could climb no further because they were not privy to the secret of success at the highest levels of power—were only now discovering that there were tests to be passed which they had failed, tests which they hadn't even known existed.

The American ambassador was at the airport to meet the Cliffords' plane, and so was the local press.

"Mr Clifford," asked the reporter from the television station, "can you tell us the purpose of your visit?"

"Yes, I think it's time we settled this mining tax issue once and for all, and I'm here to do that for my company."

"Mr Lynch gave out a statement earlier saying that the mining companies were prepared to 'tough it out', as he put it," said the man from the *Morning Daily*, "there seems to be more flexibility in your attitude."

"I'm here to negotiate for my company and Mr Lynch negotiates for the companies that he represents."

"Aren't all the mining companies presenting a united front?"

"Gentlemen," said Hugh, holding up his hands and smiling, "I really don't think I can discuss the negotiations before I've had them."

With that the Cliffords got into the ambassador's car and drove away.

As the big black limousine moved through the boisterous, darkening streets of the city slums towards the hotel, the ambassador handed Hugh Clifford a note and leaned across to switch on the reading light. Molly Clifford handed her husband his glasses. He read the note and grunted.

"Mr Lynch thinks Kass can swing the cabinet against Bernard," said the ambassador.

"What do you think?"

"It's a hard one to call. Percy Sullivan could go either way."

"If Bernard wins in cabinet, he'll be in a strong position."

The ambassador's face tightened. "You'd break ranks with Lynch?"

"Lynch got us into this mess by bluffing, and I don't intend to pay for his mistake. If we pull out, it's going to cost us twice as much to start up somewhere else; and why not come to terms with Bernard? He's got a case."

"You accept Bernard's figures?"

"Well, they're accurate."

"But where did he get them?"

"It doesn't matter where he got the figures; they're reasonable in today's market and I'll go with them rather than sit around 'toughing it out' with Lynch."

"You know, Mr Clifford, Washington feels very strongly that if we don't present a united front here, the rot will spread throughout the entire region."

Hugh Clifford said nothing.

"He's very anxious for a response," continued the ambassador, "he asked that you call him tonight."

"I'll call him when I've made my decision, and tonight we're having dinner with the Bernards."

Winston Bernard and his wife, Michele, lived in the foothills of the mountains that overlooked the lights of the city which stretched across a plain that sloped for ten miles towards the sea.

Cocktails were served by the swimming pool, on a terrace framed at one end by big bushes of flowering bougainvillea, and at the other end by the view.

Laughter drifted through the crowd of twenty, a family of many shades from black to pale brown. Percy Sullivan, the Prime Minister, was there. So was General Mark Bernard, Minister of

Security. Percy was a much married bachelor. Mark had married the daughter of a Latin American ambassador in Washington. He'd met her on one of his many staff courses in the States. Children circulated with trays of hors d'oeuvres, listening to snippets of conversation from the grown-ups, pausing to be introduced to the Cliffords.

"And who's this little sweetie?" Molly Clifford asked Michele Bernard, as a child of six approached, wearing her party dress.

"Mrs Clifford, this is Miranda."

"Good evening, Mrs Clifford."

"Good evening, darling," said Molly, bending down to kiss the top of the child's head.

Molly took an hors d'oeuvre. It was delicious. She liked these people. As a family they were good-looking, talented, hospitable, entertaining, educated, travelled ... there was an atmosphere on the patio, a mixture of confidence and relaxation, that she found strangely familiar.

"I believe we have a mutual friend," said Michele, "Max DeMalaga."

"Oh yes, DeMalaga! Of course I know him," said Molly, "and not only do I know him, but I love him dearly. His mother and I were great friends and I've known him since he was a tot, and my goodness, how he's got on. He really has made millions selling songs you know."

"Oh I know, I'm going to meet him in Antigua tomorrow night because I have a singer that I want him to promote."

"How long have you known him?"

"We were teenagers together, holidays on the north coast. We used to water-ski and go out dancing."

Michele was thirty-five, Lebanese with African and Indian mixed in, her eyes sensual and alert at the same time.

I bet they did more than dance ... DeMalaga couldn't possibly have resisted her at sixteen, thought Molly.

"Well, please give him my fondest love," Molly said to Michele, with a smile.

Winston Bernard and Hugh Clifford were apart from the crowd, talking at the edge of the terrace, looking out over the lights of the city.

"Lynch doesn't want to negotiate," Winston was saying, "he wants to keep control."

"The market will control the price," said Clifford, "not Lynch."

"Yes, but who controls the market?"

"Nobody, not in the long run."

"Well, I hope the run isn't so long that the island runs out of breath in the meantime." Winston turned and looked out over the city. "I'd hate to see all those lights down there start going out, but as far as I'm concerned it's worth the risk of fighting Lynch if I know we have a deal."

"I'll stick to the terms we discussed if you can get the cabinet to stand up to Lynch ..."

He'd said yes? Winston turned back to look at Hugh Clifford, to confirm the moment. *He'd said yes!*

"May I ask you a personal question, Hugh?"

"Sure."

"Why are *you* prepared to fight Lynch on our behalf?"

"I'm not fighting Lynch on your behalf; I'm fighting him because I don't like him. I think he's greedy and stupid, and he's the kind of guy who'll fight even when he hasn't really got an enemy."

"Perhaps that's because what he really wants to do is go on playing the bully."

"Well let's put it this way, he's playing politics and I'm doing business."

A thrill ran through Winston as he realised that the only ally he really needed to push through his plan was the one man he could trust! He instinctively scanned the crowd on the other side of the pool to find Michele, to share the moment, and he saw her ushering the others into the house. Then he turned again towards the old man and smiled right into his eyes.

"Well," said Winston, "it looks as though dinner's on the table."

Often, at the end of the day, Hugh Clifford would lie in bed watching Molly as she moved around the room on a much slower wind down, and they would compare notes. While Hugh was interested in what power did to people, Molly was fascinated by where it would move to next, and over the years she had become so adept at predicting those moves that there were many who, if asked, would have agreed that Molly Clifford was the greatest power groupie of her time.

Her instinct for knowing where the centre of power would lie in any given span had taken Molly around the world many times. She had seen the centre shift from city to city and group to group like a restless spirit, settling on those whose time had come, often for no apparent reason and in ways that no one would have predicted. Over and over Molly had watched as success enveloped an individual or group before they themselves became aware of its arrival, and over and over she had seen the power they once had move on before they knew they'd lost it.

She had seen the magic move from aristocrats to fanatics and from fanatics to warriors and from warriors to scientists and from scientists to stars and from stars to agents and from agents to financiers. She didn't so much watch as listen, because the simplest way of telling who needed whom was by listening for the phone, by knowing who would wait for whose call. Thirty years ago she'd noticed that the most important people in the world would wait for a phone call from Hugh Clifford, and when she got to know him she noticed that he never waited for anybody's call ... until one day he was frantic for a call from her, and they'd been together ever since.

Molly didn't love Hugh because he was powerful in the usual sense; she wasn't a snob in the usual sense because neither she nor Hugh could have cared less about colour or class. But in her special way she was the biggest snob of all, because strictly at a chemical level, the level at which she could tell how she felt about something by the feeling in her stomach, the one thing she could never imagine herself doing was making love with a man who was subservient to anyone else.

Molly couldn't imagine sleeping with a man who would do another man's bidding against his will, and she'd been in love with Hugh for all these years because she'd never seen him bow to anything but his own best judgment. It wasn't the money that had allowed him to do that. What it was, was a secret they shared.

"Who do you think is the strong one?" Hugh asked Molly.

"Do you mean between Winston and Michele?"

"In the family as a whole."

"I've no idea, it's much too early to tell."

"How about between Winston and Percy?"

"Oh, I'd say Winston, wouldn't you? I think Percy's just a narcissist."

"Little bit psycho?"

"Hmm, probably a bit."

People think psychos have no conscience, Molly thought, *but actually they crave forgiveness*. That's what had made them so dangerous for her before she learned that every time they were forgiven they'd take it as a victory and do something even more outrageous until one just couldn't forgive them anymore. Molly climbed into bed with her Walkman, three cassettes, five magazines, and two novels.

"Did you agree to back Winston Bernard against Lynch?"

"If he can swing Percy."

"Are you really in the mood for that kind of fight?"

"I think so." Hugh yawned and closed his eyes. "Somebody has to stand up to that bunch."

"What do you think of Michele?"

"Very beautiful," said Hugh, without opening his eyes.

"She's a friend of Max DeMalaga you know, and DeMalaga ..."

Molly looked over to see that Hugh was fading fast. She kissed him lightly, put on the headphones, switched on the Walkman, and continued reading a novel about the middle of the first millennium when the Roman Empire collapsed and the barbarians sacked Rome.

Chapter Two

Michele lay awake waiting for Winston to come to bed, thinking about sexual magic and how powerful and mysterious it was, and who had it and who didn't. Molly had it, even at her age, and Michele knew that the older woman had recognised it in her immediately ... each had recognised in the other the capacity to inspire passion.

Passion. It was the one drug Michele was addicted to, pure passion, of the cleansing kind. It was the high that set her instincts free, that made her feel sure she was right to follow them. Passion gave her the confidence in her judgment which had made her successful in the theatre because when Michele felt passionately about something her enthusiasm would spread—she had seen it happen time and again.

It was why Michele had earned nearly six figures her last year in New York; why when she called Max DeMalaga he always picked up; why Percy had asked her to take over the running of the government-controlled radio and TV station. The source of Michele's success was in the power of her instincts. All the good things in life shone for Michele when she was in love, and when she wasn't she didn't see the gleam of real quality in anything at all.

Michele had fallen in love twice before she married Winston, each time convinced that the man she was connecting herself to had a link with something that would be fascinating forever; but in both cases she was eventually forced to define boundaries, and when, inevitably, a bored voice in her head said *you can't have everything in life*, or words to that effect, Michele knew she would have to look again.

She was nearly seventeen when she met DeMalaga. He was only a year older, but it was already his avowed intention to set no limitations whatsoever on the amount he could get out of life.

In the days before he lost the fortune that was coming to him, DeMalaga had been a cocky youth.

"Every generation has its challenge," he used to say. "One generation sees who can make the most money and the next generation sees who can have the most fun spending it. As luck would have it I'm a next-generation guy." And indeed his life in those days was a teenaged dream. In the times Michele spent with him she felt he was born carefree, that it was his natural state, and she believed sincerely that if she gave herself over to his life she would feel passionate about him forever, that he *did* have a link with something that could go on renewing itself indefinitely; but DeMalaga had a drunken uncle who was also a gambler, and in one week—when Michele's young boyfriend was in his final year at one of the five most expensive boarding schools in England—his uncle's vices combined to render the entire family, if not poor, certainly no longer rich, and young DeMalaga changed. No longer was Michele the most important thing in his life. Now he was determined to be rich in spite of everything. She discovered that she could no longer distract him long enough to affect his emotions one way or the other, that he and he alone was at the centre of his universe, and the passion of her first love died.

When Michele first met Mark Bernard, Winston's brother, he cut a glamorous figure on the polo field and in his bright red MG sports car. He was twenty-eight and had just returned to the island in triumph, having left as a schoolboy champion and returned with the lead over his contemporaries increased. Now, nobody in the military was even remotely competition for him in combat experience or professional ratings on the international scene, and although he had an outstanding talent for casual friendship there was always a sense, with Mark, of something serious in the background, of a man who was prepared to deal with danger and death on a daily basis. Michele didn't have the feeling he was looking for trouble so much as that if there was any trouble around he'd be drawn to tackle it, as though he was in some way predestined to assume responsibility for others. On the rebound from DeMalaga Michele found that extremely attractive. But while Michele was attracted to the sense of danger in Mark, when he detected the danger in her he didn't find it attractive at all.

There was an independence of mind in Michele that Mark knew he wouldn't be able to live with if they got married; he knew that if she was behind him in what he was doing he would be immensely stronger for it, but he also knew that there would be no guarantee of agreement. His greatest delight in her had been the way in which she had entertained his mind with new ideas outside the military scope of things altogether. But in the final analysis Mark had to marry a woman who would be willing to follow him blindly in a crisis, and when Michele realised what Mark was asking as a condition for marriage she immediately broke off with him and entered a period of fierce independence.

Michele had always been a talented dancer and now she turned her attention to the theatre full-time. She formed her own company and she wrote, produced, and directed a number of plays that established her as a celebrity in the city and as a talent that various people were well aware of both in London and New York. She made enough money to travel frequently, and entertained visitors to the island all the time.

Licensed, by her popularity, to probe, Michele got to know everybody who had "star quality" in a very wide social range, and brought them together frequently. Every day five or six people dropped in for the buffet lunch she served at the theatre. They would sit on into the afternoon, making her theatre the only meeting-place in the city at that time where a cabinet minister could be found talking to a street-side Rasta painter, or a lawyer could be seen reasoning with a musician.

Michele looked everywhere but saw nobody she wanted to make love with. The thought of giving herself to a man, of putting herself physically at the mercy of anyone else's emotions was something she found herself less and less comfortable with. The whole notion of sex became increasingly unlikely and distasteful to her, and slowly the sense of quality that she had always been able to detect started to elude her, first in the work she was doing and then in her appreciation of the work of others.

Four years went by without love, eighteen months without an original idea, six weeks without seeing anything anywhere that she found stimulating, three days with the phone off the hook—then she fled the island as she had often done before. The second night in New York she met Winston.

She saw him across the room at a cocktail party and was instantly aware of how much she already knew about him; she recognised the gestures that he shared with Mark, and those that he inherited from his mother, and she instinctively separated them from the mannerisms that were his own.

She knew within half an hour that he was the man she had been waiting for.

Within six months they were married. For two years they lived between New York, Washington, and Silicon Valley in California; as Winston shuffled his cards in academe, government, and business. Both Winston and Michele felt sure that nothing was more important to them than the fulfilment of each other's dreams, yet even in this first phase of their life together Michele had intimations of the degree to which Winston's concentration could isolate him. Still, the concentration was for relatively short periods of time, the kind of thing she was familiar with from her own work. It wasn't until her pregnancy coincided with Winston's move to the World Bank that Michele came up against a period of total withdrawal which lasted three and a half months. She was tied down, expecting a baby; he was working night and day, usually out of town. He felt secure in the knowledge that she was fulfilling her greatest ambition and that this in turn freed him to work with an intensity that impressed even Robert McNamara. She, on the other hand, was surprised by his abandonment, terrified by her inability to break through the wall of statistics and research that isolated him completely.

Eventually, when she was in her seventh month, Winston had to go to the Western Pacific. He wasn't aware that Michele was upset about his leaving to any dangerous degree, but she was completely baffled that he should disappear at such a time.

When news reached Winston that Michele was frantically trying to contact him, he was within two days of concluding his plan and was working past any capacity he'd ever previously attained. He was so sure that interruption now would be fatal that he ignored her plea for help, the plea that he at least fly to Manila and call her. He reasoned that if he ignored Michele till his work was done she'd never know for sure if he'd got the message and she'd forgive him, whereas if she stymied a project that represented the biggest breakthrough in his career, he'd never forgive her. He had no idea her anguish was so great it could bring on a miscarriage, but when he got back home he realised the real question was: would she ever forgive *him*?

Faced with losing Michele, Winston was appalled at the prospect because he knew that without her his life would lapse back into one dimension, and, when finally he confessed, he begged for her forgiveness.

They made their peace and eventually Michele started to feel passionate about Winston once more, but she resolved never to make the same mistake again, never to find herself without resources when Winston was away, and as he drifted off again, ever deeper into his career, she became more and more involved with the theatre, this time on the international scene.

She did three small productions off-Broadway, she produced plays at theatre festivals in France and Canada, and eventually she got the opportunity to direct the first successful reggae musical in London and then on Broadway.

When the production closed and all that anybody she spoke to ever talked about was "the next one", it seemed much more important to them than it did to her. Michele wasn't interested in another show for Broadway where her work was seen as a look into another world. She wanted her work to be a part of that other world—it was a different quality of buzz in the audience that that produced. So, like other writers away from home, she found herself longing to be back. Back home, where every inflection of either voice or body meant something to her, where the speech of the streets so often made her laugh out loud. So when Percy Sullivan's political campaign took off like a rocket, Michele climbed aboard.

She had never been involved in politics before joining Percy's campaign, but she was immediately caught up in the excitement of it as they swept across the island at the centre of what seemed like a huge and growing celebration party. What fun it was to watch those in power as arrogance turned to apprehension. What a thrill it was to ride the turning of the tide, to feel the strength of the passion in the crowds pushing you forward to take control. The quality of excitement in politics was different from the excitement she had known in the theatre. It wasn't that political campaigning wasn't theatrical—she was repeatedly struck by the similarities—but in the theatre interest was optional whereas politicians starred in a show that had *everybody* for an audience, and even at the height of her excitement Michele wondered how they would avoid anti-climax when they were through with politics and had started to deal with government.

When Percy became prime minister, he was prepared to give Michele unqualified control over the government radio and TV station to keep her by his side, to have as her responsibility the presentation of his image to the world; but Michele had a new fantasy, or rather the old one had returned: she wanted to have a child and make a home, and she didn't want to do it abroad. So when Percy expressed interest in having Winston come back to the island and help him run it, the last piece of Michele's dream fell into place.

Winston was ready too. He came back, they got a house, they travelled the island as they had travelled the world, then after the happiest three months in Michele's life they settled down in the city ... and Winston's meetings started to lengthen into the night.

Michele postponed having a baby. Winston promised that after the first budget was passed there would be time for some home life, he'd set up a computer terminal at home, he'd be there most of the time taking breaks all day... Michele decided to wait and see, she didn't really believe him.

Tonight, she knew, Winston had won a great victory in securing Hugh Clifford's support for his plan, but he hadn't brought the triumph to bed. Michele was not going to share in the celebration, her body would get no thrill from the excitement. No, tonight Winston was celebrating his victory by planning for the battle in cabinet tomorrow; tonight he was sharing his excitement with his computer ... and for Michele things were starting to lose their flavour again ... but now her child-bearing days were numbered ... Three years? A thousand days? Forty months? She'd wait another year. She'd already allowed herself to be seduced onto the career carousel for one more ride, but if after a year Winston still wasn't ready to become a family man then she'd have to think again, *very* hard. In the meantime she was excited by the potential of her job, and as she fell asleep Michele's last thoughts were of Zack and his hit song and the meeting on the morrow that she'd set with Zack and DeMalaga ... and tonight's concert in New York ... as she drifted off she wondered how that was going ...

Chapter Three

In New York City, Zack Clay, reggae prince, was riding high on the applause from the packed theatre as he turned to the band to signal the start of the last song for that night's concert, the last in a tour that had gone around the world and triumphed with a hit.

"Don't be Afraid!" cried out a voice from the crowd.

Zack had been touring for ten years, since he was sixteen. In all that time he had been around world-class musicians, so he had seen hits take off before—he'd even seen a song he himself had written go top twenty in the States for another singer, and he had made fifty thousand dollars in royalties that time—but still he was taken by surprise at the suddenness and size of his own success with "Don't be Afraid".

At the first concert in Boston, Zack had sensed a big buzz around the song, and when he sang it again as an encore the crowd went wild with recognition although they had only heard it once. After the first show in New York, the man from the *Soho News* wrote it up as the high point of the concert and it started to get immediate airplay on WBLS.

Zack went on to play the Palais in Paris with Peter Tosh, Munich with Jimmy Cliff, a TV show in Milan. All the while he was touring Europe, airplay was building in the States, then following on in his wake across the Atlantic. By the time he left Europe for Africa, the tune was in circulation everywhere he had played on the Continent. By the time he arrived in Lagos, there were bookings in Rio, Recife, Toronto, Tokyo, San Francisco, Philadelphia.

When Zack and the band got back to the States from Japan, they picked up the song on the car radio coming in from the airport, and this last gig at the Beacon was packed with kids who were singing and dancing and clapping and shouting and getting high.

The song started, Zack began to sing:

> Don't be afraid
> love casteth out fear
> don't be afraid
> tho' the crisis is near,
>
> Don't be afraid
> give thanks
> and be glad.
> You're still living
> the best life you ever had.

In the seventies, when Carter was president but everybody said the Arabs were in control and nobody seemed sure of anything; when the youth in Europe and North America began to realise that the threat — as well as the promise — of the industrial revolution had finally come to pass, that increasingly the real work would be done by robots and computers, and they, the children of workers, bred for it, begging for it, would find none. Appalled by the prospect of idleness, somehow blaming themselves for their obsolescence, the children of the post-industrial revolution went to hear Zack sing out that it didn't matter that they would have no work to do that couldn't be better done by machines, that it set them free for better things; and when he rejected the guilt they had thus far assumed for their condition with the conviction of a wild young preacher in the style of a Dreadlocks and the vow of the Nazarene, then he felt the waves of acceptance and relief flooding back to him from the crowd, and he knew that the miracle of timing had occurred —

he had been given a message to deliver which vast numbers of people were already waiting to hear.

Don't be afraid
there's more to this life
than Babylon offering
bloodshed and strife,
Jah sets you free
for better things
deal with love, not money
and God, not kings.

Don't be afraid
those who listen will hear,
don't be afraid
Jah will speak in our ear,
follow those who say
that love is the way,
they'll have no fear
on Judgement Day.

The youngsters rocked the Beacon with applause and calls for more, but Zack was exhausted—he embraced the crowds with his arms outstretched and headed offstage, off tour. The next excitement was somewhere else.

When he reached his dressing room it was crowded. A woman reporter from a reggae magazine was set up for an interview.

"So what next?" she asked.

"Straight ahead, no jestering," said Zack, "record an album right away, and tour again behind the album and just ride the wave as the message spread wider, flow deeper."

He suddenly felt very tired of doing interviews.

"What's the toughest part of all this?" asked the reporter.

"Thinking about money and thinking about music at the same time."

"You need someone you can trust," said the reporter.

"That's right," said Zack, and his mind turned to Michele, just as she was falling asleep, thinking of him.

Michele woke up at six the next morning and packed hurriedly but quietly because Winston was still asleep. Everything she was taking with her could fit into one carry-on bag.

As she pulled on a pair of jeans and brushed her hair, she looked in the mirror, aware that once she stepped into the outside world there wouldn't be another chance to look at herself till bedtime, and Michele always felt a little stronger for looking at herself.

Her eyes were the brown eyes of her Parsee grandfather, gentle yet perceptive, able to sparkle in an instant. Michele often looked into them to learn more about herself because she knew they had come to her having already seen more than she would ever know. Her lips were from another world, African and Arab. Her temperament came mostly from an English granny, she felt sure of that, the lady who fell in love with a merchant prince in Bombay at the turn of the century and was never able to return home because she had married him. All Michele's ancestors had crossed great gulfs of ocean and culture to reach each other, and once the original boundaries were crossed they had spread the quest for love even wider, over three generations, evolving a special gift for Michele: a hybrid mix of ancestral experience which enabled her to truly feel that nothing in any culture was so strange as to be incomprehensible. Her ancestors had given her a genetic switchboard, and she had used the gift to take calls on every side, from every direction, from as far away as long distance could reach, without limitations.

Before Michele left the bedroom, she set the timer on the radio to wake Winston in case he overslept. His meeting wasn't till noon, but she set the telephone within easy reach of the bed in case his secretary called in the meantime; she set the dimmer control for the bedside light where Winston would reach for it when he woke up, she checked there was a pad and pen beside the phone, and then she kissed him lightly and headed out into the city and into the day. Feeling full of anticipation and excitement, she hurried her car down the road, dodging in and out between the other vehicles hustling to work, her car radio going full blast: Sun Radio, in the cars and on the minibuses, coming from the speakers of a thousand transistors in the traffic. Sun Radio had the mood of the nation in its tender care twenty-four hours a day, and once Michele had made up her mind to take the challenge of running it she soon found that she was completely absorbed.

When she took over the radio station, the first thing she did was to start treating talent like stars, and the response had been immediate. Within days a vibe had started to run around the passageways, in and out of offices and control rooms and studios, into the canteen. Michele had been able to generate that excitement and carry it around with her because when someone made her laugh, or feel sad, or angry, when she was thrilled by a song, or moved by a movie, or excited by a piece of news, her response came with a clarity that caused other people to see things through her eyes.

By the time Michele swung the car into the car park at the radio station and parked it under the shade of a large lignum vitae tree in full blossom—at that time of year an explosion of bright purple-blue—the music on the radio had given way to a programme in which the public was invited to make calls to the radio psychiatrist, or lawyer, or doctor according to who was featured that day. It was a bright show; nothing for her to worry about there.

Once in her office, she kicked off her sandals, switched on the radio, put a blank cassette in the recorder, ordered a cup of coffee, scanned the mail and phone messages, opened the morning papers, noticed that "Don't Be Afraid" had slipped to three on the charts after fifteen weeks at number one, looked at her horoscope, and then listened to the BBC International newsreel ... 1976. The Shah was firmly in power, the Sandinistas were still in the hills fighting Somoza, nobody had started to worry much about drugs anywhere outside of the inner cities, and Mikhail Gorbachev was running a province from Stavropol, halfway between Moscow and Siberia.

Michele sat in a large swivel chair at a round table which could accommodate ten comfortably. She used the same methods in this office as she'd used when she was producing in the theatre. Anybody who wanted to see her simply walked in and sat down by a phone, going on with their work as they waited till Michele was free.

Her secretary brought her the ticket for the flights to Miami and Antigua, and took notes all the way out to the airport while Michele drove.

On the flight up to Miami, Michele talked with all six of the other passengers in first class, confirmed sponsorship for one show, initiated the idea for another. Once through customs and immigration in Miami, she placed a call to her lawyer in New York about some royalties from a production of the musical in Toronto. Then she bought a stack of magazines and settled down to read them while waiting for Zack to get in from New York, enjoying again the thought of having put together what could be a perfect fit.

DeMalaga was exactly who Zack needed behind him now!

Chapter Four

As Michele sat waiting to make her connection at Miami airport, Winston was driving towards the Prime Minister's office in his new Jaguar, air-conditioned against the heat of the midday traffic. He was thinking about the advantages that had brought him to this point in his life. There were "brains" scattered throughout his family tree like fruit in season: judges, doctors, lawyers, accountants, senior civil-servants. The most successful of the brown middle class had intermarried exclusively among themselves after they left the great houses of their origin, and the family from which Winston's father, Sir Arthur, sprang had become accustomed to being treated with respect for at least two generations.

But the Bernard boys were doubly lucky in their parentage because while Sir Arthur took care of social standing, his influence was stopped short of pomposity by his wife and his wife's family, the Sullivans. For Winston's mother's brother—father of Percy Sullivan, the Prime Minister—was the island's first black millionaire.

Old PJ had started out in betting shops, then had expanded to produce trading—bananas, ginger—then trucking, and finally, real estate. Eventually he owned property worth several million dollars.

In 1962, when the nation got its independence from Britain, life in the colony was divided into definite spheres of control. The English and Canadians owned the banks and controlled the sugar industry. Cattle and bananas were in the hands of the white

29

and brown families who had inherited land. Bakeries, groceries and most supermarkets were owned by the Chinese. The Syrians had a virtual monopoly on all dry goods. The Jewish merchant families controlled rum, the big law firms, real estate, the wharves, the motor-car and hardware agencies, and nearly all manufacturing. The black power base was in the professions — politics, trade unions, and the civil service. As a general rule, successful black people attained status but little actual cash. There was one black man, however, who followed no rule, and he was Percy's father, P.J. Sullivan.

PJ was intensely ambitious in everything he did, and he was determined that his son would shine in something, but the only thing exceptional about Percy was his good looks. As he grew older it became obvious that if he was going to be a star it would be as a lover, and, with unlimited cash and travel at his disposal, by the time Percy was twenty-five he did not go unrecognised at race tracks, on polo fields, and in good restaurants in France, England and even in the USA; with social success on the international scene came a boost to his ego resulting in that arrogance which can come with great force to a serious narcissist when his first fantasies are fulfilled. It can be an aspect of personality which seems so natural, so deeply felt, that it is indistinguishable from self-assurance.

He kept track of his father's real estate, and began to dabble in politics, and he used up twenty women in twelve years. He never came close to loving any of them more than he loved himself, and as the years passed and one after another of the women he had hoped would divert him from himself failed to do so, Percy fell increasingly into the grip of a self-obsession so extreme that he started to lose his sex appeal.

Then the impossible happened — Percy fell in love. He saw a face that surpassed his own in beauty. He couldn't take his eyes off Ada.

She was a young girl from the country who Edna Bernard, Winston's mother, had adopted into her family circle along with Michele and another teenager full of promise named Lucy Anderson.

So startlingly beautiful was Ada that by the time she left school she was already getting offers for modelling jobs in Paris, London, and New York. After five years of that, there wasn't a trace left of her original country girl quality unless she wanted it to show, because right from the very start Edna had never let her forget the strength of her roots, never let her deny her heritage, had taught her to take pride in it, in fact, so when Ada acquired worldwide poise and combined it with local grounding she developed a personality that was able to reconcile all the parts that made her up. She wasn't ashamed of anything, and any hang-ups that Percy may have had with his origins were swept away by Ada's and Edna's sense of destiny and laughter.

The narcissism that had held him captive for so long released its grip on his mind, and, inspired by Ada, Percy seriously went into politics.

When everybody realised that Percy was no longer primarily interested in seducing their wives, Percy's political ambitions became surprisingly practical.

His house filled with people he had never realised before were friends. Within six months he became a rallying point for the opposition movement against a government that had been in power for ten years and was becoming brazenly corrupt and inefficient. There was a ten-year cycle in the politics of the island and it was turning to put Percy in the right place at the right time.

Suddenly, it seemed he could do no wrong. All his decisions taken on instinct were proved correct. His sense of timing constantly surprised him. For the first time in his life, he knew what it was to be joyously free of his egomania, genuinely committed to a scheme of things that superseded his own vanity.

Then, the one women Percy had ever loved more than himself started to die, and he realised what she had been to him; she had brought him happiness and it was happiness that cleared his mind.

Percy knew that without Ada at his side he wouldn't have the strength to campaign, without her he wouldn't be able to trust his instincts; then all those thoughts were lost in grief. Obsessed with her pain, he was drained of everything but love for her. He forgot about his political ambitions. All he could think of was that he had found his soul in this woman, and when she was dead he would have to find a way to maintain contact with her spirit if he was to stay sane.

Then he lost her. Deeply humbled, he went to a place where they had spent holidays together by the beach of an isolated fishing village. He stayed there alone for several weeks, slowly gaining strength, when he found that if he prayed for her spirit to speak with him, she would answer.

When Percy eventually returned to the city, the election campaign was in full swing. He had given up any thought of getting involved, but one afternoon he went to a political meeting, coming in unobtrusively from the back of the crowd. The speaker was chatting crap. As he stood there listening, Percy had an overwhelming feeling that he knew what the people wanted to hear, and nobody was saying it. Percy inched forward in the crowd till the politicians on the platform recognised him. They were glad to see him back. Ever since he had dropped out of the campaign it had lagged. Without him they had not been able to focus on an issue that excited the crowds. The rhetoric was stale: promises of economic development they had heard before. The people were waiting to hear something new, and when the politicians on the platform saw Percy they beckoned to him to come up and join them. In a daze, he went.

When Percy looked out at the upturned faces of the crowd and remembered that Ada had come of humble origins, he recognised her spirit in the people before him. She was the one that got away, but the spirit she carried with her was in front of Percy now, en masse. He thought that he might weep, as he had done almost daily since her death, but he didn't lose his composure on the platform. Instead, a profound confidence that he could reach those people came to him. It was as though Ada spoke through Percy and he repeated a phrase that she had often used.

"Love, love is the key!" were the first words that Percy shouted out with tears in his eyes, and the crowd responded with an outpouring of emotion so great that its roar had echoed constantly in Percy's head ever since.

As Winston turned into the gates of the Prime Minister's office, the sentries on duty recognised him and he passed through without stopping. He parked the car and walked into a modern building set in ten acres of lawn and surrounded by flowering trees and shrubs.

Inside the building there was a sense of polite hush that Winston remembered from his childhood ... the feeling that no matter what happened outside, the atmosphere here would remain calm; the insulation of power was stronger than all those who swore never to put themselves at the mercy of being cut off from the outside world. But to find the outside world all prime ministers had to go outside. It had never intruded here.

Nevertheless, Winston took comfort from a certain detachment that came with the territory. After all he was not the one who'd decide the issue; he'd put his case and then it was up to the politicians to decide; that's what he was prepared for ... it just didn't turn out that way.

Winston found the Prime Minister finishing lunch in his private quarters and ending a meeting with his valet and his tailor. That evening he was to leave on a long journey abroad for conferences, interviews, and speeches.

First there would be the gala performance of the Bolshoi at the Kennedy Centre when he was in Washington. He would need his tails, and he was hoping that the beautiful African princess who was press attaché at her embassy in Washington would look as stunningly elegant as she had when he had last seen her in Paris for the UNESCO conference on intercultural exchange.

Percy was looking remarkably well. Winston, who had seen him two or three times a week since the election, had found him looking better every time. In fact, being in power so agreed with Percy that Winston realised this wasn't a new Percy at all, it was the old Percy from those teenage years when girls and cars were the winning streak. Here he was again, alive and well and ready for a bigger role and a return to arrogance triggered by the release of a deep rooted block to Percy's self-esteem.

All his life, Percy had lived with an intense fear of not being able to live up to his father's accomplishments, but he knew that old PJ in turn had an unrealised ambition to haunt him. PJ had wanted to go from business into politics but he was never able to gain the trust of the masses, whether because they thought he was too ruthless or too black he never found out. In any case, the night Percy was swept to power he had reason to feel he had truly surpassed his father at last, and he lost his humility. When he lost his humility he severed the link with the common people that had put him in power in the first place, but Percy didn't notice — he had his eye on wider horizons.

As the two cousins chatted before going into the cabinet meeting, Winston found that he wasn't able to make Percy focus on the issue at hand at all. Percy was too busy filling Winston in on the role he saw for himself, and Winston realised that from the first moments of his first Barbara Walters interview, Percy was convinced that when it came to the politics of charisma North American audiences had at last met someone from the tropics who they wanted to see more of.

After all, Percy was not in power because he knew about roads, water, and the intricacies of trade; he was in power because he was the superb practitioner of an ancient and honourable art: he was a star orator. He was gifted in his ability to sense what an audience wanted to hear. In front of a crowd, Percy felt as confident of his ability to satisfy its emotional needs with oratory as he felt confident of guessing the mood of a beautiful woman when he wanted to make love to her.

All his life he had known, somehow, that he would be a star without the indignity of having to compete with other actors, and here it was—he was playing one of the most glamorous roles imaginable. The commercials he had made to promote tourism had given him exposure that no film studio could afford to buy for the promotion of any star. Old PJ's investment in giving his son a sense of style had paid off after all, more fully than even the old man could have anticipated.

There were many who agreed with Percy that nothing was more important than the emergence of a figure who could command attention in Europe and America for the cause of the developing nations. At a time when the news of those nations was dominated by the goings on of Amin, Bokassa, Somoza, Gadaffi, Pol Pot and the starving Cambodians, Castro and the Ethiopians, the Ayatollah ... anybody who could break through the stereotyped image of Third World statesmen as dictatorial monsters was very valuable indeed, and Percy was convinced he was that man.

Winston humoured Percy. He didn't really mind what his plans were so long as he backed him in the next half hour. At stake was

Winston's entire career as he had planned it. If Percy and the cabinet didn't back his play against Lynch, Winston knew only too well what would happen to the island and he wanted no part of a slow collapse into eternal debt, he'd let somebody else preside over that process from the penthouse. He would have to start all over again, somewhere else, on a much diminished scale.

Winston knew all the men gathered around Percy's cabinet table. They all represented some sector which had helped put Percy in power. They weren't really interested in the issues at stake. As far as they were concerned this was a fight between Kass and Bernard for Percy's decision, and they wanted no part of it.

A familiar feeling of loneliness swept over Winston. He had not felt it for many years, but now he remembered it as familiar from his childhood. It was the feeling of being misunderstood, of being surrounded by people who weren't interested in imagination, who lived in some cripplingly small time frame, within some frugally defined ideal already shared by everyone else. He was once again surrounded by small town big shots.

What was wrong with these men, thought Winston, what was blocking their view of the big game? What was narrowing their vision so that the *real* thrill and potential of their position eluded them?

In the same way that they were captive to the electorate, they were also captive to their wives, or their children, or their creditors, or their bosses; there wasn't one man around the table who was free to side with him, they were all mortgaged to something or other. Each had some factor in his life holding him down, preventing him from seeing over the block in his vision set up by the neurosis which prescribed his limitations.

The fight with Henry Kass started almost immediately.

"When you tell Henry Lynch that you're going to ram a unilateral decision down his throat you are picking a fight with the biggest people in the United States!" shouted Kass, looking toward the Prime Minister, Percy Sullivan. "Who before has ever got into a fight with those guys and got away with it? Eh? Unless they turned communist ..."

"Who has ever negotiated with all the data?" asked Winston. "Up to now we've negotiated as though we were there to beg for the best deal we could get, nobody before has ever gone to them and said 'we can prove the worth of what we are selling'."

"Who says they'll accept your figures?"

"Hugh Clifford accepts them."

"He accepts the principle that the price of oil affects the mining companies even if they import their own oil?"

"The price of oil affects everything."

"They're responsible for running their business; they're not responsible for running the world."

"Then who is? Who's making the money out of the oil price rise? The oil companies and the Arabs. And what do they do with it? Buy arms. And who do the mining companies supply? The military contractors. And Lynch is in the middle of it."

"When a guy like Lynch sees a guy like you, he sees a guy to be eliminated, he sees a guy who will organise a cartel against him, and after OPEC they are never going to let that happen again."

"What can they do about it?"

"What can they do about it? What *are* they doing about it? What have they done about it in the past? They'll come and drop a bomb on your head, that's what they'll do about it, they'll put a trade embargo around you and leave you to starve to death."

"We're talking about a hundred million dollars a year in mining royalties that you're throwing away in the face of a threat."

"What hundred million dollars? I'm talking about the shut-down of the whole damn industry!"

"You know what's wrong with you, Kass? You're a coward. You'd let a man come right into your yard and rob you."

"If he has a gun and I don't have one, sure."

Several around the table laughed. But Winston had been in England when the British had to pull out of Kenya, he had been in Paris when the French pulled out of Algeria ...

"Those days are done," said Winston, "the Americans learned that in Vietnam. Everybody knows the old deal is done, except for you."

"*And* Lynch, and the biggest people in Washington that he represents, and they are not going to allow cartels!" Kass started to shout again.

"Yes, cartels, if cartels are what's needed to keep raw material prices on level with the cost of consumer goods. That's the *least* we have to negotiate for, otherwise who are we representing?"

"You're a very ambitious man Bernard."

"I don't consider that a defect."

"There are a lot of people walking around barefoot because they once got too big for their boots," said Kass, shifting his gaze to the Prime Minister. "And I warn you, if you get these guys angry you're going to put this island in serious trouble."

Kass was holding Percy's attention to the exclusion of Winston at the other end of the table, and at that moment a note was placed in front of Winston.

Winston opened it. '*Good luck, HC*' was all it said, but it was enough to effect a dramatic change in Winston's mood.

"Percy," he said, holding the note, "can I see you about this for a moment?"

Percy was surprised by the tone of Winston's voice. It was one he hadn't heard since they were youngsters, but it was unmistakable: the only time Winston had ever used that tone of voice with him before, they'd had their only fight. Winston had knocked him cold.

When the two cousins entered the small office beside the cabinet room, Winston turned on Percy in a cold rage, but his emotions were under control to such an extent that the face he presented to Percy was the extension of a shrug.

"This is a note from Hugh Clifford, which, so far as I'm concerned, confirms our deal in writing."

Percy looked at the note, and apparently wasn't impressed.

"Listen Percy, if you don't have the balls to stand up to Kass and Lynch you're going to lose me, you'll be in Kass's hands. You'll be a stooge for Kass and he'll be a stooge for Lynch, and those guys will put this island in a debt trap that you'll never get out of, instead of taking off with an injection of a hundred million a year!"

"You really think Kass is bluffing?"

"Of course he's bluffing! We already have a deal with Clifford, he'll have to come to terms."

"Do Mark and Michele both back your position?"

"To the hilt."

In fact when he had tried to go into details they were both much too caught up in their own plans to pay serious attention, but in a crisis Winston knew he could count on them and Percy couldn't.

Suddenly Percy felt a sense of great relief. Winston was offering to take over, to run the country and set him free for the world at large! Growing up together, Percy had always run third in the pack to Mark and Winston. Percy knew they were each individually smarter than he was, and together ... Besides, who would ever know? Let *them* fight Kass! Whoever won, he would still be Prime Minister. If Winston and Kass were on a collision course, why not get out of the way and let them collide? See who gets knocked out ... and who gets up ...

"OK," said Percy, reaching out with a smile to shake Winston's hand.

The switch took Winston completely by surprise, because with that handshake Percy was asking Winston to assume all moral authority within the family circle for the burden that Percy had been elected to bear but that he found too heavy.

By the time Winston saw the situation through Percy's eyes and realised he'd walked right into a psychological trap, it was too late.

As he walked from the air conditioning of the Prime Minister's office into the blistering heat of the shadeless car park, Winston stripped off his jacket and tie. He threw them onto the back seat of his car and rolled down the windows, but the air inside was too hot to get behind the wheel right away. As he waited for the car to cool down he felt the clamp of tension start to tighten on the back of his neck.

The city streets were filled with throngs of people. Caught in a crowd, Winston watched as an old drunk staggered up to the window of his car. The man leaned in and searched for Winston's eyes. "Hey, rich boy," he said, when he had found them and focused, "without a leader the people perish, remember that!"

As Winston looked at the sea of humanity around him, he felt for the first time in his life that he had taken on a job that could stretch him beyond his limits. He had just taken it upon himself to provide for the numberless urchins he saw running around the streets; his decisions would affect what they would eat, whether or not they would learn to read or get medical care ... to have to worry about that, all the time ... no wonder Percy had offloaded the responsibility. A pain to make him rigid had grown from between Winston's shoulder blades and run up his neck into the back of his skull.

By the time he'd reached home, parked the car, got inside, and found the painkillers in the bathroom cabinet, he felt as if he was about to have what other people had described to him as a migraine, with a hint of some added whirring sound.

Winston took the pills, turned on the stereo, and lay down in the late afternoon light of the living room to listen to music.

Not for the first time in his life Winston took refuge in the gigantic scale of orchestral music, allowing it to sweep away his own emotions in torrents of Mahler or Verdi or Beethoven.

His mind flew out over the view of the city. The rich lived in the hills; the poor were trapped in the shanty towns that filled the flat land between the mountains and the harbour, and for many their dream was so different from the reality of life in the city that they had to choose between killing the dream and risking death to keep it alive.

The city was a time bomb waiting to explode, duplicated in versions smaller and larger across the face of the earth. Everybody knew something had to be done. Nobody did anything that would cause fundamental change, yet without fundamental change anybody who took an overall view of things could see a future looming that Winston didn't want any child of his to have to deal with. And why was nothing done? Because everywhere the world was being run either on a capitalist or a socialist agenda, both disastrous in their Latin American versions.

The capitalist agenda followed the same plan everywhere throughout the region. To the degree that when the rich were feeling greedy they would put up interest rates, take money out of the country, induce inflation, refuse credit at the banks, force all financing into mortgages, induce hyperinflation, and foreclose ... at which time they would bring back the foreign exchange and buy up everything for nothing.

They would then turn around and lease back everything to the people who had been buying it in the first place, but who knew now that they would never be owners.

It always worked and it always ended up causing a revolution, but sometimes the protest could be suppressed for generations, by which time enough money would have been made by all concerned to make the plot irresistible as a replay.

But the socialist plan was even worse because it perpetuated the rule of the paper people. Red tape. The religion of the socialist bureaucrat: red tape and paperwork.

Winston had always dreaded getting buried by the paperwork side of his career. From the first day he went to school he realised that if he wasn't careful he would end up giving his mental energy to people who were willing to sit you down for eight hours a day, from the age of five till you were eighteen, and teach, with deadly seriousness, things that you would neither remember nor use for the rest of your life. After school, people with the same mentality locked themselves up for the rest of their lives, doing the same thing, attending to thousands of little details, none of which mattered in the least or produced anything but more paper. These people would leave home early and return after dark for the next forty years, and they thought the best thing they could do for you was ask you to join their ranks because, after all, the paper people controlled more than half the world.

Their deliberate plan was that no money should move without their instructions, and everybody took it for granted that they could throw you into jail if you did fool around with money without their knowledge and permission.

No, the two established alternative systems were not working. There had to be a better way, and Winston Bernard was convinced that he knew what it was.

He had been handed power on a platter. If he didn't take the chance that he had now, what right did he have to bring a child into a world that he had given up on? If he didn't try, who was going to? And how many chances would *he* get?

His personal happiness as well as his professional conscience was at stake, Winston argued with himself, he had had no choice. He was right to have followed his impulse with Percy, of course he had had to save his plan! It was the only one that could work. By the time the music ended Winston's headache was gone, and he had started to count his victories of the past twenty-four hours. What a pity it was, he thought, that Michele wasn't there to share the moment.

When Winston had awakened that day, Michele was long gone. By the time he had gone to bed the night before, she had been fast asleep. It seemed to him that their life together was more and more being lived apart.

There had been no problem for the first years of their marriage, because she had set her timing to suit him. It wasn't an effort, it was what she was in the mood to do; she wanted to reinforce his life, to make his dreams come true, and whether that involved giving a dinner party or merely understanding in full what it was he was trying to achieve, Winston got addicted to the idea that when he turned to her, she'd be there. But she hadn't adjusted her timing to suit him since she first got involved with the musical ... no, since before coming back to the island, before the election, before the musical ... ever since she'd lost the baby, because he'd been so obsessed with the job he was doing for McNamara. Things hadn't been the same since then and he'd been too busy to do anything about it, but now, now that everything was in place and going according to plan, now was the time to sit still, to bring some balance back into his life. If he really was going to run the country, balance in his personal life took on a whole different dimension. Nobody wanted to have a one dimensional man in charge. He really would install a home computer; he'd start to delegate, build a team that allowed him to withdraw from the day to day pressure, to take a broader view. This was his chance to give Michele what she had always wanted: a house with a big garden, children, more time together; he knew time was getting short.

He fell asleep thinking that he was lucky that Michele had held on waiting as long as she had.

Chapter Five

∞∞∞

Michele's trip was going well. Zack had arrived from New York in a great mood, feeling free as a bird to be flying alone after moving with twenty people for weeks on end.

On the plane to Antigua, Michele outlined the deal.

"I'm going for a million, two hundred and fifty right away to start the album; another two fifty on completion of the album; the other half million divided between backing the new tour and paying off all your bills. We'll give him the option to renew for two more albums if he puts up another half million within six weeks of the release of the first album."

"How im mek im money?" asked Zack.

"Gambler. Horses. Made enough in racing to start buying picture—"

"Wha' kind of pictures?"

"Paintings. You can make a lot of money if you know what's good. Then he started buying buildings and backing bands in the sixties."

"Wha' bands?"

"You never see his name on anything, nobody knows what he's involved with, but I know he had dozens of investments in music back then and he made enough to really do anything he wants."

There were only three businessmen in the international music business who understood both the language of the corporate world and the slang of the island's ghettos, and of them DeMalaga was the only one who could hold herb smoke and percentages in his head at the same time; he was the only one who could scribble up an agreement on the back of a menu and forward up the cash right after the meal, and when he called to say how much he liked the cassette of Zack's music that Michele had sent him, she felt that powerful sense of satisfaction that came to her whenever a talent she was prepared to gamble on sparked a response in someone else whose taste she admired.

Things looked good, but Michele warned Zack that until they actually had the deal they couldn't count on anything. DeMalaga's mood swings were notorious. His mood could switch in seconds as his computer mind calculated the odds during a negotiation, margins of win or lose being reflected immediately in his stance.

Michele understood that she couldn't expect anything factored in for old time sake, because to ask DeMalaga to go soft in a business deal was like asking any player to deliberately play badly in a game that they enjoyed and were particularly good at.

"Him know music?"

"Oh definitely, he doesn't invest in anything he doesn't like."

"An im hear de last tape?"

"Yes, he loves it, that's why I set this up."

My God! Maybe I've really found the money man I can deal with, thought Zack.

Zack didn't have a lawyer. He didn't know any, and he figured that if he tried to negotiate through a lawyer it would put him at a disadvantage, because any lawyer familiar enough with the workings of Babylon to help him would get embarrassed representing Zack when it became apparent that Zack wasn't going to sign anything he didn't understand. The lawyers respected the accepted rules of a game that Zack had never had time to learn. He had, however, had lots of opportunity to observe that it was a game whose rules made losers out of most musicians, and he had long ago determined to sidestep the conventions and insist on a straightforward deal in simple language. They wanted to talk in percentages. He would demand to talk in numbers. They wanted to talk about three per cent of ninety, he wanted to know what that meant for every hundred dollars earned at the record shops. He had seen the embarrassment spread around the table in three different negotiations as the lawyers realised they were either going to have to explain twenty pages of tight legalese to this, no doubt musically talented, slum dweller, or they could just drop the whole thing. Three times they had dropped the whole thing. They had held out a cheque and the "standard agreement" with an impassive expression on their faces, and when Zack didn't sign, the lawyers sighed and looked wounded and gathered up their papers and left, slowly shaking their heads.

Zack had been deeply disappointed each time, but he had always managed to survive and build his business a little bigger each year without giving over control of his work to anybody; he was prepared to wait until he had something they wanted badly enough, interested to see how much money would have to be involved before they would deal with him in his own language, intrigued by the thought that maybe it wasn't a matter of money, perhaps they weren't prepared to bargain in terms he could understand no matter how much money was involved.

Covering too much ground on too little cash had always left Zack on the brink of financial disaster at the end of a tour, and he had always accepted that falling back into the frantic scramble that characterised showbiz in the slums was the price one paid for the exposure of touring. But maybe not this time!

All it had taken was a number-one hit single worldwide, and now he had it. As he drank champagne with his lunch and watched the coral shoals of the Caribbean rising up outside the plane window, Zack felt sure he was landing at last to reap the rewards of the truly gifted.

DeMalaga was at the airport to meet them, driving a Mini-Moke and wearing a pair of swimming trunks. His manner was that of a star in his own right. The strength of his personality lay in its combination of opposites. He was a businessman with the lifestyle of an artist. He was rich but by no means entrapped by formality. He was a gambler but he wasn't reckless. He'd earned his money in the quicksands of show business, but he'd built his fortune on the rock steady foundations of real estate. He was a sport but he was always working. He was physically at ease in the tropics because as a child he roamed his father's cattle properties barefoot with a band of peasant kids before being shipped off to school in England. Max had realised early on that if he could combine the advantages of being rich and white with the cool of being poor and black, he'd have the best of both worlds.

He was a white man in love with black music.

On leaving the airport they drove southeast for about ten minutes, then turned off the main road onto a track that led down to a long deserted stretch of beach.

"I hope you don't mind," said DeMalaga, "but I've just got this boat and I thought you might enjoy coming for a sail on her."

In his business DeMalaga had long realised that the key to success was entertaining the entertainers.

It was a bright afternoon, the sunshine was glinting off the sea, and there, lying at anchor about a hundred yards offshore, was an ocean racing yawl.

DeMalaga picked Zack's bag out of the Moke and started walking towards a dinghy drawn up on the beach.

"She's made of this new stuff that's quarter of an inch thick and five times stronger than steel," he said, "it's incredible what they are doing nowadays."

As they rowed towards the yacht, Zack had an overwhelming sense of something crafted for pure pleasure and excitement.

The rigging towered over him as he came onboard, spotless gleaming slivers of stainless steel, as intricately balanced as a gigantic mobile, the stays aquiver and humming in the wind, even at anchor.

Highly strung ... Zack thought there might be a lyric in the memory.

Boats didn't represent luxury to Max DeMalaga. He had first turned to them when, as a youngster, he'd been threatened by penury with the collapse of the family fortune. At first he'd been stunned, then he'd been angry, and finally his mood had turned to defiance. When the shock wore off, he made a decision that was to be the guiding principle of his life thereafter: he was never going to live an ordinary life of survival, he would keep gambling. But to gamble like a gentleman he would have to be unafraid. To be unafraid of poverty he would have to combine low living costs with a fun lifestyle, and DeMalaga bought his first boat.

It was an old wooden sloop which he raised the money for by selling his car which was in need of repair that he couldn't afford, and with five hundred dollars in cash he sailed the boat to a cay outside the entrance to the harbour, and there he sat as the sun went down and the lights came on in the capital city under the crescent of a brand new moon. By the time it was full, DeMalaga knew, he would have to have achieved something. By the time it was on the wane he would have to have reached his next destination, because obviously he would want moonlight on the open sea. Then and there he set up his plan, the first of hundreds to come, plans that materialised one after the other over the years; the five hundred dollars went into Haitian paintings, the Haitian paintings went into the Virgin Islands and a quick sale for a profit of four thousand. The four thousand dollars largely went on phone calls and studio time on a demo track for a group he believed in ... in and out ... that was DeMalaga's style, and his real pride was that when he gambled on his taste, he won.

"Can I get you anything to drink?" asked DeMalaga, picking up a bottle of chilled white wine.

"No, thanks," said Zack.

"Smoke?" said DeMalaga, holding out a spliff.

"Thanks," said Zack. He felt very relaxed, very pleased to be there. He felt he was in exactly the right place at the right time.

The crew of three was already preparing to set sail without instructions from DeMalaga who sat in the cockpit with Zack and Michele, his hand on the helm, his eyes moving between his guests and the crew.

"I must tell you, your song is the strongest thing to come out of reggae since Bob. I'm really hoping we can put something together."

"Time for an album now."

"Absolutely, an album from you right now would be a monster."

"I'm ready," said Zack.

Ready! How many times had Zack been caught muttering to himself as he struggled not to forget a line before he could find a pen and paper—frantic to avoid interruption, knowing that if he could only get the first line down another might follow, and another after that—and how many times had distraction won over, allowing the lyrics to drift away, gone from his mind like a piece of erased tape!

For years Zack had been trying to get together enough money to record an album, enough to pay not only for the studio, the musicians, production, promotion, but money to set up all the people who depended on him for a living, or who looked to him to help them when they were in trouble. They were the real burden. To be free of them for long enough to fall in love with twelve tunes one after the other; to be able to drift into an open-ended trance in which lines of melody could linger and grow at their own pace, gradually deepening into twenty-four tracks of sound! The luxury of that freedom to concentrate was Zack's fantasy of happiness.

"You should make a fortune on 'Don't Be Afraid'," said DeMalaga.

"I can't wait for dat money to come in," said Zack. "Is pure 'sixty days' and 'ninety days' dem a deal wid, and I want to recard now, before de band cool out from de tour. Once dem cold is a bitch fe warm dem up again."

"You're right," said DeMalaga. "You're dead right ... plus if you wait six months you'll have to start all over again with the deejays. They forget so fast. You have to make the album right now."

"That's why I'm here."

"How much money do you need?"

"A million," said Michele.

DeMalaga moved his attention towards the rigging again. The sails were going up with an enormous flapping in the wind; the three crewmen were darting across the deck, tending the winches, their precision drawing Zack and Michele's attention, as well as that of the skipper.

DeMalaga cut the engine and eased the yawl into a sailing position. The sea was quite choppy as they came out from under the lee of the island and started to pick up the full weight of the open Atlantic Ocean wind. The boat heeled and bucked, and some spray flew in, then Michele and Zack watched as DeMalaga steadied the helm and called out adjustments for the genny and the mizzen stays'l; they noticed his grip ease on the wheel when he had the trim of the sails set and eighty-five feet of mast combined with sixty-eight feet of hull and ten tons of keel balanced as a mere quiver on his fingertips. He turned his attention back to his guests and smiled.

"What sort of album do you have in mind?"

"Strong message."

"What message?"

"Political, fe de youth."

Michele saw DeMalaga's enthusiasm fade.

"Well, you know, what I really love about your music is that it's great for dancing," said DeMalaga.

"Message you can dance to," said Zack, sensing that his description of the flavour of the new album was not exactly to DeMalaga's taste.

"Message music you can dance to is very rare, you can count the number of people who've pulled it off on one hand."

Michele looked across to Zack and could see that he was insulted, that DeMalaga had just told him he doubted his ability to do it ... she saw a wall of reserve start building between the two men and she realised that she must somehow pull it down ... but DeMalaga was intent on making it plain that the risk of a message album could change the whole deal.

"Listen," said DeMalaga, "I'm terrified of preaching. What makes Rasta attractive is that it's a religion that's not boring, but the minute it begins to preach it does get boring, because then it's like every other religion, you know what I mean?"

"Hey! Listen brotherman, when it come to music I doan deal in boring at all, so doan come to me wid dat argument."

DeMalaga shrugged.

"I'm speaking from experience and that's the way I feel; when it comes to music I'm only interested in magic."

For awhile nobody said anything. It seemed to Michele that each man was at the centre of his own world, each as finely balanced as a spinning top, and that, like two spinning tops, for them to mesh the timing would have to be perfect or one of them would be kicked off to a drunken sprawl.

Zack looked back towards the shore to take a measure of how far they had sailed and it seemed to him they were far at sea already, and then when he looked back at DeMalaga and saw that he had again started to concentrate on sailing, Zack realised the moment was crucial. It wasn't a matter of money or music that was the key, the main question that was evolving now was whether Zack and DeMalaga were going to like each other after all.

Something very deep-rooted in DeMalaga's nature was offended by the idea that he should put money into anything that didn't appeal to him emotionally; something very deep-rooted in Zack told him that he wasn't to be controlled by another man's emotions ... and the million dollars started slipping away with the passing waves.

"Do you want to keep sailing or would you prefer that I dropped you back?" asked DeMalaga.

"Drop me back," said Zack. "I'll try make a connection through Miami this evening."

"OK," said DeMalaga, instantly switching his attention to the deck. "Geddes!"

The three crewmen looked back towards the skipper. They were all small-island men, seasoned professional sailors: a Saban, a Haitian, and a Caymanian.

"When I take her round we're going to make a broad reach back to Parham, and I want to fly the spinnaker. Tell me when you're ready!" shouted DeMalaga.

Options. *Thank God for options*, he thought. If he hadn't been sailing he would have wasted the whole afternoon. He spun the wheel to slice the boats bow headlong into the waves and the wind; the ocean racer turned on her deep lead keel, the sails stopped flapping and filled again, and the sheets ran out and held taut; the hull steadied and measured the rhythm of the swells on this new quarter.

"Spinnaker!" shouted DeMalaga, and the billow in the new sail shot the boat forward, racing the crest of a wave, the white foam from the wake cutting a dominant line through the dark blue water.

Michele looked over to Zack. He was looking out to sea, a deep loneliness in his eyes. She knew what he was thinking, he was trying to imagine what he was doing on this fucking boat out in the middle of the sea, his time totally at the mercy of these people. He was trying to imagine why he hadn't made DeMalaga come to him. He was trying to imagine how he would avoid the despair that he knew would overtake him as he waited months for his money, as the band dispersed, as the people around him lost their excitement for the hit because it had brought them nothing yet. She watched as he became aware that he would have to start all over again, or sell out control of his music and his life to someone else.

Michele's heart went out to him. How long, she wondered, had he been struggling, confident that his spirit would win out in the end? How long had it taken him to come to this point only to discover that not only had the struggle not been won, but that it had only really begun if he insisted on dealing only on his terms.

These men are both gamblers, thought Michele. But there are two types of gamblers, the emotional gambler and the mathematical gambler. The emotional gambler has to risk everything, the mathematical gambler spreads his risk so that no matter what game he goes into he can lose and laugh. In this game the two men were playing out before her, the one who had everything was risking nothing, and to stay in the game the one who had nothing had to risk everything, but Michele knew she would always be on the side of the real risk, the real excitement.

"Let's do it this way," said Michele, "why don't you put up the money for the first track and if you like it we go ahead with the whole deal? That way we wouldn't lose any momentum because I'm sure you'll love it."

"How quickly would I get it?"

"In two weeks," said Michele.

"OK," said DeMalaga, "I'll give you the money for the first track this afternoon."

Zack had never met a woman like Michele before because he had only just surfaced on the horizons that they scanned for talent. For women like her, that discovery is their greatest thrill. The recognition of talent is their greatest gift. Michele's deepest instinct was to keep the dreams of a man like Zack alive so that he'd go on making music. It would come naturally to her, if she had it in her power, to give him a reward at this crucial moment, rather than have it turn to bitter disappointment. The thought stirred something in her that had not been touched for too long. Just a flicker, because she'd still not realised that if Zack were to have his dreams come true, the number one dream was having her. She also didn't know, because he gave no clue, that he was terrified.

When "Don't Be Afraid" took off and the women in the audience started to sing it and look at Zack with a bright shine in their eyes, he came into focus sexually for the first time, and he was afraid that they would find out the truth about him. The truth was he knew nothing about sex at all.

When he was a child, he was so weakened by asthma and occasional malnutrition that until he was fourteen he wasn't strong enough to play music seriously. Once he started, however, his strength grew very fast, and when he was eighteen he tried to make love for the first time. But Zack was a poet, an idealist ... the musical, political, and ganja trade top rankings already had any girl in the ghetto who could have been ideal. His nervous system was jangled with inexperience, and afterwards he felt he had put himself to a test that he had failed miserably. He prayed the girl wouldn't tell anybody, and he didn't take that risk again.

As the strength of his music grew, so did the discrepancy between his image and the reality of his sex life. Sometimes on tour he would take women back to his hotel after a concert and crash out with an exhaustion that nobody questioned. But apart from that he simply put all his passion into music and ignored sex altogether, and up to now his lust for musical success had left no emotional vacuum ... up to now.

When they got back to the dock, Michele got off the boat with Zack, drove him to her hotel, booked him into a room. All the weariness of the past few weeks had caught up with him, not so much in his body as in his mind, and he was glad to give himself over to her care, to her timetable, to her plan.

They had dinner on the balcony outside Michele's room. The night was warm, the moon was like a translucent pearl cupped in a crescent of silver, the lawns surrounding the hotel were deserted in the moonlight, and out beyond the lawn the marina was filled with moonbeams bouncing off the curved hulls of thirty large yachts, each one the fulfilment of somebody's postponed dream: they were all silent, their owners somewhere else.

"You mustn't be discouraged just because we didn't get all the money, just assume you'll get it and press on with the music," said Michele.

But, for the first time in years, Zack wasn't thinking about music. Music had carried him as far as he could go without some other recompense. Before he could sing again he needed something new to sing about ... he needed love. He needed the love of this woman, and if she offered it to him as a gift and he was not able to accept it, he didn't know what he would ever find to sing about again.

By the end of the dinner, the touch of her arm, the smile in her eyes, the presence of her mind in his affairs seemed to Zack like old habits he had become dependent on in just a few hours. He felt as though if he had this woman on his side there was nothing he couldn't do and stay cool, but he didn't feel cool now; he was in anguish till he knew whether or not he was making foolish assumptions, his body tingled with a level of anticipation that only concerts had been able to generate in it before; he couldn't wait any longer to find out.

As he kissed her, the force of his emotions rushed through his structure, but not to his ears and hands to be released in volumes of sound enough to reach twenty thousand people—no, that night the force of Zack's emotions burst upon him in a spasm of surprise and shame.

His body went slack and his chemistry revolved full cycle in ten seconds. He drew back, kept one arm around Michele's shoulders, and held on to the balcony railing with the other to steady himself. He looked at Michele, but if she knew what had happened she gave no hint of it. There was a long pause.

"I've never known anybody come off tour like you've just done without their nerves being very frayed ... but you seem to be in good shape."

"Why do you say that?"

"I think you were right to stand up to DeMalaga for one thing."

"I hope so."

"Of course. Don't even think about not having money for the whole album. Concentrate on the single, make it great, he'll love it, we'll go ahead with the album; you don't have to miss a beat."

"You know how long I really wait for dis? You wouldn't know, you couldn't guess, and is you do it fe me."

Michele smiled.

"You did it for yourself. Now you can plan to do anything you want."

And even as she said it, Michele knew that what Zack wanted now, more than anything in the world, was her, that anything else would be meaningless for him unless he had her tonight.

She turned and moved across the space of the balcony in the moonlight, humming his tune, stretching as she walked, her limbs extending like a dancer.

"Don't be afraid ..." she sang in a whisper as she turned towards him.

Zack felt the second charge go through him, starting in his knees and running into his loins, but now there was no sense of urgency as he felt the power slowly coming back; the strength of the force that he felt then was as great as his longing when he lay in bed at night knowing that he stirred the hearts of millions but had not one to hold in his arms; it was as great as a million moments of frustration which, when released as music, could make the airwaves scream ... a force powerful enough so that when the music wasn't there and the spirit wanted its daily exercise in his muscles it worked its way out of him in an ague, and left him shaking with fever. When that force reached Zack that night, and his system was ready to express it, his body and spirit made a connection through Michele Azani Bernard's flesh and blood that caused every memory of delight in her entire ancestral experience to dance with joy till dawn.

Chapter Six

∞∞∞

By four o'clock that morning, fourteen teenaged ghetto gunmen were moving through deserted streets. Two delivery vans, one with a muffler missing, were moving towards them.

IZion and Wire both felt the chill of the early morning breeze that swept down from the mountains to the sea before dawn, cleaning the city of polluted air for a few short hours, and bringing the echo of dogs barking as they do all night in a nervous city where they are trained to mark anything that moves.

IZion and Wire were the same age, had the same ambitions, dressed the same; both wore locks, had smoked the same herbs, meditated on the same God; they were both respected as dangerous fighters, and they would both have moved to kill each other on sight because they lived in different parts of town.

The two delivery vans came to a cross roads and split off in opposite directions; within minutes each was deep in opposing territory. The van with the muffler missing came to a stop, and eight youths emerged from the shadows. They were frisked and told to climb into the back of the vehicle. IZion entered first and sensed that there was already someone there in the darkness.

"Hail," he said in a low voice.

"Who dat?"

"IZion. Weh Star?"

"Mi nuh know. Him suppose to here."

"Him nuh here?"

"Mi nuh see him."

"Him seh him would meet we here," said a youth sitting beside IZion.

"Den tell di driva mi nah go," said IZion, but the door to the back of the delivery van was already shut, and the vehicle had started to move off. It was too late.

Where the other van stopped, six youths, including Wire, were waiting for it. The others were frisked and sent into the back, Wire waited to one side.

"Come here," said one of the two men who had come out of the front of the van.

Wire didn't move. "Wat you want?" he asked.

"Star seh him no wan' no gun inna de transport."

"Star seh? Star seh?" There was rising anger in Wire's voice. "Who di rass is Star fe tek I gun?"

Wire moved to get back in the delivery van, his gun still on him, but the driver blocked his way.

"Tek weh yu hand, nuh touch me!"

Wire's voice was loud in the empty street. The driver was anxious. If they didn't let Wire through he looked like he was going to fight, or call the others out of the van.

"Let him go," said the driver, "we late already."

"Weh Star deh?" demanded Wire as he climbed into the back with the others.

"Inna di adda van," said a voice in the dark.

By the time the two delivery vans came together again and headed east on the road out of town, they had fallen behind schedule, they were eight minutes late. A pre-dawn glow was rising over the end of the highway, littered with garbage and covered with smoke from the city dumps that smouldered with the heat of decaying rubbish day and night.

Five miles from town, both vehicles turned off the highway onto a dirt track that led into a deserted scrubland along the seashore.

As the vehicles came to a stop and both sets of political gunmen merged, there was just enough light to see the shape of soldiers with machine guns coming out of the bushes.

One frightened youth called out, "Star!"

Wire heard the click of a gun bolt, grabbed his .38 revolver, and dived to lie flat on the ground.

Searchlights blinded those behind him as firing broke out over Wire's head. He saw a soldier about fifteen feet away swing the barrel of his machine gun in his direction; Wire flung his arms straight out and, aiming at the thickest part of the looming shadow, he pulled the trigger a split second before the soldier with the machine gun could blast him, and the man doubled over and fell, hit in the stomach.

Wire pulled his knees up under him and in one bound was on top of the man with the machine gun. The man was groaning, and as he felt the weight of Wire's body land on him he screamed with pain and terror, "Lawd Jesus, nuh kill me!"

Wire prayed that the machine-gun safety catch was off because he didn't know how to release it, and when he pulled the trigger and three shots burst off, a hot flush of excitement coursed through his body. For the first time in his life he was up against Babylon on equal terms. Now it wasn't forty shots from them for every one shot from him ... now he too had a machine gun.

Trapped between the line of soldiers and the delivery vans, the other youths from the ghetto were blinded by the searchlight as their bodies were ripped apart by the hundreds of pieces of steel fired into them at close range. In a burst of terror and light and pain, twelve of the other thirteen youths were transformed from human beings to corpses within ten seconds.

As the soldiers fired, so they moved in on their prey, and as Wire crawled outward, the soldiers were lit by the same bright light that lit the slaughter. Wire stood up. He knew that if he opened fire they would spin round on him, but he was going to do it. He backed away as far as he could without risking a miss, and then he pressed the trigger and swung the barrel of the gun in an arc that dropped three of the soldiers just as they had stopped firing and were starting to gloat. They spun to shoot at Wire, but now it was they who were blinded by the lights.

Wire dropped the gun and started to run in such a way that he knew they would never be able to catch up with him, for his mind was absolutely clear and his legs felt sure, and as he tore through the cacti and undergrowth leaving a trail of blood, he felt no pain.

A youth of twenty-two named IZion was the only other ghetto gunman who escaped death that morning.

As the others had emerged from the vehicles, IZion had held back near to the vans, and when he saw Wire dive he had dived too, just before the searchlight snapped on. As he hit the ground some instinct told him to roll back under the van, and it was from there that he saw the bodies falling and the feet of the soldiers advancing.

IZion knew that as soon as the shooting stopped and the men with the machine guns bent down to examine the dead bodies he would be discovered; then the paralysis of his terror was replaced by the spring of action as Wire opened fire and all the soldiers spun around to fire in the other direction, giving IZion the chance to run for his life.

IZion rolled out from under the delivery van and ran till he got out onto the beach. As he plunged into the sea, he heard what sounded like machine-gun fire peppering the water around him, and he didn't surface till he had to gulp air, and then he dived again ...

He had learned to swim as a child in the country and it was now going to save his life. He prayed that he wasn't bleeding because he knew that there were sharks in the harbour. He swam and stopped, swam and stopped, till finally he saw a buoy in the central channel which he climbed aboard, exhausted.

On that fateful morning, as he sat and shivered on the buoy in the harbour, IZion watched a helicopter coming out to start searching the swamps for Wire, and he decided to leave the city.

Growing up in the country as a child, his contact with the city had been by radio. Any night someone listening to the African chants of a Pocomania meeting with one ear could have been picking up WINZ/Miami with the other. As the influence of both foreign and local radio spread with the transistor across the island, so did the message of the radio commercials:

"Don't settle for less than the best," sang out the jingles night and day, *"Get on top! Get it now!"*

Clothes, appliances, motorbikes, cars, houses—banks were on the air inviting the public to come in and borrow the cash to buy them, and the people in the countryside gained the impression that there was a lot of money in the city, but obviously the things that he'd been promised on the radio and that he'd come to town to get were in short supply and well guarded.

He realised that morning that he didn't really want them anyway. What he wanted was to get home to the mountains, because IZion had lost his appetite for the sweets of Babylon.

Although they had been fighting on opposite sides of the political war, the only real difference between IZion and Wire lay in the fact that whereas IZion had been drawn to the city of his own free will, Wire's grandfather had been inspired to come by

63

Marcus Garvey in the 1920s. It was because of Garvey's ambition, and not from his own choice, that Wire found himself in the city. He had grown up there and knew nothing else. His destiny had been chosen for him by his forefathers. They had placed him in the war zone. They had put him in the front line. They had cut him off with no avenue of retreat because they had sold their land in the country long ago.

Wire hit a patch of swamp and had to stop running. Not more than a hundred yards away he could see the outline of the road back to town running through the pattern of mangrove roots and water that separated him from a chance to escape. He studied the strength of the mangrove roots carefully. If they could bear his weight he would walk from one root to the other till he reached the road. He didn't know how deep the water was, and he couldn't swim, but he realised that within minutes the helicopter he had heard thrashing towards him would be able to trap him where he was until the soldiers sweeping the area flushed him out.

Wire went up on the first mangrove root, and it held. He stepped from the first to the second, and it held too. He started moving faster, and slipped. He clung on, knowing that if he fell into the muddy water he would look like a fugitive on the roadside. He had to stay clean. Slowly he hauled himself up and went carefully from root to root till he reached the road.

By this time he could hear the helicopter almost overhead, and he had made up his mind—if the driver of the first vehicle that came by refused to stop, he'd hijack him. He still had his .38 and two bullets. He tried to bring his breathing under control as he heard the sound of a car coming around the bend ... quite slowly a robot taxi appeared, crammed with six riders ... Wire held out his hand early, and whispered praises when he saw that the driver was going to stop and pick him up.

Fifteen minutes later he was back in the middle of the city.

The news that Wire brought back with him sent shock waves of repetition through the streets. Within an hour the leaders of the Rasta youth who had been conscripted into political gangs were roaming the four square miles of ghetto on their motorbikes, crisscrossing it in frenzied bursts of acceleration, interrupted by meetings when they would move around each other in tight circles, shouting rumour and crossing previous boundaries to check out what they had heard.

What they had heard was news of a double-cross so extreme that the political system which had ruled for years in the slums was now breaking apart.

Fear had kept the system in place, but for the youth their worst fears had already materialised. Brothers in arms from both sides had been massacred, they had to find out what was going on and they couldn't do that unless they broke out of their areas, crossed boundaries, made contact.

By the special magic of mass communication that sometimes occurs in slum streets, the Rasta youth suddenly realised that it didn't matter anymore which gang controlled the ghettos because politics was dead with the massacre of youth from both political parties in the same place at the same time.

The island had a two-party democracy, with free elections every five years, but every time there was an election and the government changed, there was a big change in slum clearance plans; thus politics in the slums determined who would be bulldozed out of their shacks to make way for projects to be built and filled with political supporters; politics determined who would have steady work for as long as their party was in power, and who would have to scuffle like criminals till they could win the next election.

Eventually, in the slums, politics came to mean life and death.

There were no guns at all in the first election after independence from Britain, but by the time the second election came along in 1968 there was a gang of five men with pistols who were rumoured to be working for one of the candidates. He won.

During the next five years an atmosphere began to prevail in which, first owners of the Gaiety Cinema and then all the other theatre-owners in the slums put in concrete screens because gunmen in the audience more than once attempted to outdraw the likes of Clint Eastwood and Trinity. By the third election all shanty town candidates had bodyguards and hard-core organisers who carried guns. By 1972 the death toll had risen to nearly three hundred political gunmen killed in the six-month election period. By then the ten main gangs in the slum were all fighting under the leadership of two supreme top rankings: "Red Roy" Truman led one side, and "Biga" Mitchell led the other. Each had five ranking lieutenants who carried machine guns, and political violence mixed with extortion became commonplace. Anyone doing business in the ghetto would have to support the gang in their area with some cash if they didn't want a bomb through their front window.

Mongoose Run, Concrete Jungle, Dunkirk, Vietnam ... the streets that defined zones of allegiance were the first names a stranger who came to town would have to learn after learning the name of the ghetto warlord who controlled the area in which he lived.

Any political top ranking commanded the allegiance of every youth in his area. Up until the mid-seventies they had shared celebrity in the slums with the top-ranking singers and ganja traders, but by the time of the fifth election any singer still trapped in the ghetto might have to sing propaganda; and as to the ganja trade, the political gunmen not only took over from the leading traders in the city—they forced the Rastafarian youth who lived off the trade to either leave town or enlist as troops in the election war of 1976.

Over the course of ten years the city had been zoned into areas of political allegiance to such an extent that if a man wanted to walk from Mongoose Run to East Beirut, he could not simply cross through Vietnam to get there. As a stranger he would be stopped and questioned. If it was discovered that he was a resident of Mongoose Run, it would be assumed that he supported the Mongoose Gang, and he'd be treated like a spy. If any direct link was established between the man and an opposing high command, he would be tortured till he told everything he knew, or he'd be held hostage indefinitely.

The political gunmen were the officers. They alone had automatic weapons. The conscripted youth had everything else. Swapping ammunition was to them at fifteen what swapping marbles had been at ten; street warfare had become the central excitement in their lives, weaponry an obsession.

Guns proliferated in a dozen calibres, homemade shotguns, long-range rifles, revolvers; they were bought off freighters, slipped out of the army camp, stolen in raids, and by 1976 some were coming in from both Cuba and Florida.

"Dem promise we AK47," said one side, "dem tell we dat since we win de election we was going drop yu fe all time."

"Dem promise we M16," said the other side, "dem seh since we lose de election we was planning insurrection."

"Biga and Red Roy conspire together wid de higher Mafia to wipe wi out," said one youth.

"Dem only want to use we fe fight election."

"Dem only want to use we fe fight war."

"Is politics dem deal wid, dem nuh want deal wid Rasta."

"De most dem want from we is herb."

"Not even herb, herb money; dem nuh seek herb wisdom, and we all fe cruise on a religious cause, you nuh see it?"

The crowds, feeding on rumour, were growing bigger and more frenzied, starting to go round in circles, trying to make sense of the betrayal they felt from both sides, trying to make sure they weren't caught in the middle of greater ambitions than theirs, ambitions which could wipe out those who hadn't already been killed off by each other.

"Although dem fight during election, when election done is easier fe dem talk to each other than talk wid we, yuh nuh see it?"

"Dem 'fraid."

"Dem vex when dem realise if we a fight war we want machine gun too."

"Is dat mek dem move fe kill we off."

The youth knew now that when they moved they had to move together ... that not only the division into political parties was past, even the division into rich and poor was outmoded; now the division was between the army and whoever in the ghetto dared to pick up a gun to get what they wanted.

Wire, IZion, and the youth in the slums didn't start out wanting to pull the rich down from their heights; they imagined how sweet their lives must be, and they wanted to join them as they sat by their swimming pools waiting for the maid to call them in to dinner, the lights from their houses and pool terraces twinkling down on the town like semi-precious stars, already half-way to heaven in the land of the living. But now the ambitious poor had been sent a message and the message said that no matter which political party won they would not prosper because those above them were too greedy. When the army killed the youth of both sides those who were still alive got the message that any protection they'd ever had from politics was gone. No longer could political connections spring even a top ranking if the army locked him up, and suddenly the youth of the slum armies rebelled against their high commands.

"Is divide and conquer dem deal wid."

"We ha' fe unite!"

"Weh Zack deh?"

"Him a tour."

"Him back!"

"Zack is the voice I heed," said Wire.

Chapter Seven

From the moment Zack cleared the airport and left Michele, he felt the tension starting to build. Magic. DeMalaga wanted magic. Who was DeMalaga to demand magic? Had he ever created magic? Did he know where it came from? No. Nobody did. Yet he knew exactly what DeMalaga meant ... he knew what he wanted, and what he was prepared to pay money for. A tune with magic was one you fell in love with, it was as simple as that, a song you wanted to hear over and over, a song that you couldn't wait to hear again while you were under its spell. Everybody knew it when they heard it, but nobody on earth could command its presence.

Zack lived and had his musical headquarters in a big old wooden upstairs house that had belonged to a rich merchant in the days when there were large open savannahs surrounding the centre of the capital. The days when the wealthy drove their carriages—from their docks, warehouses, offices, stores, lawyers' chambers, law courts, government buildings, and gentlemen's clubs—to their sprawling residences surrounded by broad lawns, dotted with fruit trees, and afternoon light, and nannies and children at teatime. Drinks would be waiting in the large upstairs verandas ... mahogany louvres, flowering vines ... the old houses were dark and cool even in the heat of the day.

Long-ago abandoned by the merchant's family, who now lived in the hills if they still lived on the island at all, Zack took over the place just in time to prevent the upstairs verandas from crashing down on their columns . The house had been engulfed by urban sprawl, surrounded by used-car lots, bars, and narrow streets—a lower middle-class section of the city verging on slum. There were some cars that slept in the neighbourhood and lots of TV sets, but the drains on the side of the road ran in open concrete gutters, water the colour of thin milk growing bright green moss in the centre of the stream.

Zack managed to keep two of the original four acres around his house. The lawns had turned to dust in those patches where cars and motorbikes swirled in and out of the yard and there was another area which had been worn bare by the bopping of footballs, but Zack spent as much money on the water bill as was necessary to keep his surroundings green. The outbuildings that had been built as servants' quarters, laundries, and kitchens behind the big house were separated by vegetable patches and fenced off against the goats and chickens that roamed the yard. Flowers grew wild in broad areas of shade provided by three majestic mango trees, fifty years old and in their prime.

Zack shifted his position on the bed, watching the patterns made by the late morning sunlight on the high wooden ceiling. He knew that if he signalled to the rest of the house that he was ready to talk people would start moving up and down the stairs, fires would be lit for dinner, the telephone would be taken off the answering machine, and throughout the garden surrounding the house there would be a stirring of at least two dozen people who were waiting to talk to Zack—musicians and singers, their wives, girlfriends and children; cooks, yard-boys and washerwomen, herb sellers and spliff rollers, messengers, secretaries, accountants, road managers, recording engineers, carpenters, electricians, contractors, salesmen of all sorts, gardeners, watchmen ... two journalists had left messages that they wanted to talk ... there was a madman that often came into the yard looking for fruit and demanding to see Zack. They all wanted to talk to Zack before making their plans, but Zack had nothing to tell them. He hadn't got the money from DeMalaga for the album ... and he never would unless the first track had "magic". Suppose the magic didn't come?

A telephone rang. It was the third call to come in since Zack had gone to his room to rest. Time was getting short. Within minutes he was going to have to make a move, make a decision, issue orders, clear his headache, put some life back into his limbs. Only inspiration could put the life back into them. Only an album could capitalise on the hit and bring him the money he could count on. Only an album or another hit single. The first one had taken ten years, what were the chances of another in the next ten minutes?

Only music could save him. But how could he concentrate on music with the constant threat of interruption for money that he didn't have? Just the thought of it would drive music away from him, because music was like a jealous woman where money was concerned, the very hint of worry about one drove away the other, yet how could he stop worrying about money when he had dozens of people breathing down his neck for a plan, ravenous for cash and action, ready to pull him down off his high into a thousand little hassles at dust level? Ever since he was fourteen, he had been hustling, working for his bread daily, always worried about something, always something was there to block the flow of music to his mind.

I must have time to think! The thought screamed in his head, but not loud enough to drown out the roar of the motorbike posse led by Wire as he wheeled through the gate to Zack's headquarters.

Zack looked all around the room at the dark faces in the shadows, wreathed in smoke, their eyes the bright spots in his view, the eyes of the younger brothers and sons of the generation that Zack grew up with in the ghetto.

"You want me tek de whole city onna my shoulders," said Zack, "you want me mix up inna politics, and is dat I running from all mi life ... how many year now I been preaching to you to figet 'bout politcal ism shism bullshit? Fascist, communist ... one claim to fight di adda, but de two a dem is de same ting, de two a dem use de same police and army fe beat you down same way, meanwhile you fighting among yuself."

"We done wid dat Zack I," said Wire, "we learn dat lesson well."

"Tek army fe show you what you should a see fe yuself long ago," said Zack.

"Seen, Zack I," said several of the youth in agreement.

"De whole a dem deal wid I as a petty tyrant when I couldn't defend I'n'I," said Zack.

"If we fight any at all we fight together Zack I," said Wire; "but yu ha' fe show di way fe both sides. A yu ha' fe raise de banner Zack I, yu ha' fe raise di voice."

"My voice raise already," said Zack.

"And we respond," said Wire.

"And now you want more."

"Now we want a day to day communication," said Wire.

"Heh!" Zack laughed, and pulled on the chillum.

These were children he was dealing with, children looking for a father, and he didn't even have one son of his own yet. That was always the way in his life. The crowd came first.

"I struggle for twelve years to mek it in music and I jus' begin to see where I could mek it if I think a nuttin else, and now yu want me to go put down mi music altogether to mix miself inna politics which can bring mi nuttin but trouble and maybe cost mi mi life. Politics never raise I'n'I to I heights," said Zack. "Politics never give I anything but trouble, music give I everything! Music. Jah music!"

Suddenly the room was still, and Zack followed the gaze of the others to where Biga Mitchell was standing in the doorway.

Biga Mitchell, one of the two supreme political top rankings in the ghetto. The other was the ideological fanatic, Biga Mitchell was the thug. Ideology was not his thing. Pure bullyism was at the core of Biga's politics, and since he had carved out his territory as a young man, nobody had survived who had dared to challenge him. For twenty years either you bowed to Biga or you moved to another part of town, and now he hears that half the youth under his command is reporting a crisis not to him but to some little singer guy! This was a man who would set fire to your house, or blow up your car, or threaten to shoot your people, picking them off one by one; Biga thought nothing of riding into Zack's yard with twenty of his henchmen to find out what was going on. Seeing nearly two hundred motorbikes parked around the house barely slowed his momentum, and he didn't break his stride till he had pushed through the crowd on the outside verandas of the house and stood at the doorway in what had been the hallway of the old house.

The room was dark and clouded with smoke from the chillum pipes. The smoke, pierced by shafts of light coming from the louvred shutters, swirled around the dreadlocked heads of the young street fighters from both sides—Red Roy's as well as Biga Mitchell's.

"What you wan'?" asked Zack.

"I wan fe know what Wire doing yah," said Biga; "I wan fe know what Razor doing yah." Biga continued to sweep the room with his eyes, making sure that all who were seen knew they were seen, and marked. "I wan know wah 'appen out de beach dis mawnin, I wan know wah gwaan."

"Politics betray we! We nah mek war fe you again, Biga!" said Wire

"Is a peace revolution," shouted Razor, "dat a wha gwaan."

"A wha?" asked Biga, incredulous.

"Is a peace revolution we a deal wid," said Wire. "Yu day done, Biga."

Biga started to laugh.

"We de yout' nah deal in politics again," shouted Wire. "We unite!"

"Rastafari!"

The shout that went around caused Biga Mitchell to stop laughing, but his obvious contempt sent a chill around the room. When he and Red Roy got together to wipe out this Rasta foolishness he planned on making some cries ring out in the night.

"Is politics you dealing wid wedda yu like it or not," said Biga. "An de beatin yu gwine get in it—you mightn't live."

Biga Mitchell was a man so ignorant that he preferred to risk losing his life than an argument. Zack sensed that if Biga went unchallenged, in that very moment he would already have started to break Wire's movement.

Zack looked at Wire. Would that boy really be able to run a slum war? From Biga's point of view the challenge of a "peace revolution" to the established political order was a piece of naivety deserving death. He would take the time and trouble to destroy Zack if Zack annoyed him too, and unless these youth were serious he would certainly succeed. But the youth Biga was dealing with now was a different breed of youth, and only they knew it.

It was a magical time in the ghettos of the capital city during the seventies for the first generation of black tropical slum youth who could go to a movie and see themselves on the screen, who could switch on the radio and hear people they knew singing of their personal concerns.

"I want mine now, tonight!" shouted Jimmy Cliff from the movie screens, and the packed audiences exploded every time.

"Get up, stand up! Stand up for your rights!" sang the Wailers from a hundred jukeboxes and sound systems across the island, and the message echoed out into the main roads and side streets, and from village squares into the hills around.

"If not here, where? If not now, when?"

There was a strong feeling among the city youth that it was up to them to make it; that if they didn't make it now, nobody poor or black was going to make it again. *"Do you remember days of slavery?"* asked Burning Spear. *"Please remember ... it suit you to remember ..."*

In no other city the size of the capital anywhere in the world were there ten recording studios turning out nearly two thousand tunes a year. Every hour of the day and night there was somebody somewhere cutting a tune, for there were millions in the outside world willing to pay money to share the excitement. Zack had already reaped rewards from the dream; how could he refuse the risk to keep it alive?

Just yesterday Zack had told DeMalaga that he was going to raise his voice without fear, could he now deny these youngsters his help? But what use was his help if their distractions made him musically impotent? He looked into Wire's face and saw the dangerous side to fame. He saw that if he didn't lead the youth their dreams would die.

Zack knew that even if all the youth combined to form a fighting force, they couldn't hope to win against the political gunmen and the army unless the vast majority of the people in the slum supported them. The first law of guerrilla warfare dictated that the people—who had the choice between hiding them and giving them away—should take the risk of siding with the youth. To get them behind the youth, the people had to hear a voice that they could trust. It would make the difference between the start of a social revolution and the mopping up of a bunch of criminals.

Zack drew on his pipe and, as he inhaled, the high tossed the dozen thoughts spinning around in his head, and his mind became a juggler. Then it cleared and he saw how ugly Biga was, and how the youth were looking to him for protection and how clear the division of good and evil had become in his house, and he told Biga Mitchell to get out of his yard.

"Yu facety little bumbo claat yu!" shouted Biga to Zack as he rode out. "The next song yu sing yu gan bawl fe mercy."

As they heard Biga and his posse ride out, Zack felt the eyes of Wire on him, trying to read his thoughts.

"How many guns yu have?" he asked Wire.

"Yu nah fe fight Zack I," said Wire. "Yu haffi sing, but we will fight."

A feeling of enormous relief flooded through Zack. This youth was prepared to die for his notion of justice. The singers had put out the call, and now an army had responded.

"How many guns yu have?" asked Zack again.

"Thirty-two," said Wire.

"Twenty-eight," said another young gang-leader.

"Twelve," said a third.

"All right," said Zack, "remember we nah declare war, we declare peace."

"But we nah give up we gun," said Wire.

"Seen," said Zack, amid the murmured agreement of the whole room.

The meeting ended quickly. Already Wire was taking charge, issuing instructions, setting meetings for later in the day. Within ten minutes Zack's yard was clear as the young gunmen scattered, eager to announce the peace and consolidate before Biga Mitchell and Red Roy could strike back.

By the time the army started searching for Wire he would be underground again, but not before he was seen coming out of Zack's house embracing Razor, known throughout the slums as Wire's fiercest enemy.

As the motorbikes roared away from Zack's in every direction, the strategy spread from the middle, and at the centre of the storm Zack found himself alone again.

Chapter Eight

∞∞∞

General Mark Bernard, 6'2", fifty, Military Chief of Staff and Minister of Security, had been up since 6 a.m. His house was on a ridge in the foothills above the city, and while doing his early morning exercises he saw the sun rise over the mountain peaks, and he watched as the rays of daybreak sunshine ran down into the mist of the valleys that were spread out in front, above, and below him.

When Mark and his brother Winston were boys, they had spent several summers in the country with their father's brother who lived in a big old house on an eight hundred acre cattle ranch. Uncle T had a physical energy that was still an inspiration to Mark forty years later. Even if he stumbled into bed dead drunk at three o'clock in the morning, the old man never missed a dawn. "If you can see a sunrise like that," Uncle T used to proclaim to his nephews, "and still not look forward to the rest of the day, don't plan to spend the day with me."

That morning Mark was particularly expectant for what the day could bring because he hoped to make a decisive start on cracking a problem that had the potential to paralyse the city.

Mark knew, everybody knew, that during the recent election campaign there had been a leakage of arms from the army to the bands of political thugs used by the politicians in the slums, but in three weeks of investigations he had only progressed so far as to find out that there had been a leakage to both parties, and that the ghetto violence had been so widespread that all the slum youths had been drafted into gangs for street warfare. Mark thought that if he could get through to the leadership of the youth, he could show them that they were being manipulated by the politicians; that the army was neutral; that he'd give amnesty if they'd stop fighting. In return he hoped to get hard evidence against the politicians who were responsible for the violence in the slum sections of the city, and he wanted to weed out those in the army who took orders from them. Mark's plan was to set a trap, to promise youth from both political parties a supply of machine guns and to capture them for questioning with an ambush when the gunmen went to pick up the arms. The operation had been planned for early that morning and he looked forward eagerly to knowing what those youngsters could tell him.

When he had finished his exercises at the side of the swimming pool, Mark dived in for a swim. He'd been in the habit of swimming before breakfast since the days when he was training to become Under Sixteen Champion Athlete of the Year, 1947 — the first of many titles he was to win in sports. He had always treated his body with care and that morning, as ever, he had taken time to warm up with breathing and stretching so that by the time he plunged into the pool for a leisurely twenty laps he was "ticking over like a diesel", in the vernacular of his locker room days.

There had been a lot of pressure on Mark to train for and enter the 1952 Olympics, but even as a teenager the prospect of a gold medal didn't outweigh the thrill of a chance to fly jet fighters, and that's what he did instead. He left the island and got his wings in the Canadian Air Force before volunteering to fly with the Americans for the UN in Korea. There he proved himself an outstanding fighter pilot. He shot down five MIGs, and, before being shot down himself, made friends with a group of American pilots, one of whom had risen to represent the Air Force on the Joint Chiefs of Staff at the Pentagon.

Mark climbed out of the water, showered off the chlorine, then dried himself vigorously as he walked to the doors which led directly from the terrace bordering the pool into his bedroom.

When he stepped back into the darkness of the bedroom, he noticed his wife, Vera, was still in bed. Vera was elegant and passionate in the style of well-born Latin American women, and at this point in the day she was either up, in which case she had breakfast with him, or she wanted him to make love to her.

As Mark bent to kiss her good morning she murmured something to him in Spanish and pulled him gently into bed. She did this a couple of times a week because Vera loved Mark's body even more than he did, and she felt that his body kept hers young. As her version of a tone-up exercise, pre-breakfast sex was one of Vera's little luxuries.

Mark had always intended to be a family man. He had waited until he was thirty-five to marry because he wasn't prepared to compromise, he had chosen his wife with great care, and once he had taken Vera from her father's house, it was at the heart of Mark's most personal pride that every time her family had seen her since, she looked happier than the time before.

The General listened to the seven-thirty news while he shaved. He took note of a news item about his friend Hussein of Jordan and the trouble in the Middle East. In Iran it was becoming obvious that the Shah would fall. In Teheran unarmed mobs were defying an army with the most modern weapons money could buy, and Mark had no doubt that the mobs would win. Mark had no use for Pahlavi. His whole life had been one long pretension; he couldn't hold it together, and my God, thought Mark, what an opportunity he's missed! He allowed his family to steal $500 million a year and lost everything.

In Nicaragua the Sandinistas were obviously gearing up to push Somoza the same way, and Mark wondered what his friends in the Pentagon thought about Carter's refusal to intervene; Comandante Cero sounded like a 1978 version of Camilo Cienfuegos to Mark ... warriors worldwide. Mark kept up on what all of them were doing.

The General's uniform had been hung out on a clothes rack the previous evening. The khakis were starched to a particular degree by a batman who had acted as Mark's valet for ten years, and they were brought to the house each day by the driver for a final inspection by an eighty year old nanny who had been working for Mark's mother, Lady Edna, when Mark was born.

At 7:45a.m. Mark kissed Vera goodbye, said he would remember to have coffee sent in to her, and went out to the front veranda where the table had been set for breakfast. The house had been sited long before anybody guessed that industrial smog would one day ruin the sight of the city in the early morning, so the view looked out over the low-lying, dirty-grey cloud that covered the plain below. Mark always felt that the view was the mildest preparation for what he drove into each day when he left home. So, in spite of the smog in the distance, breakfast continued to be served together with the view from the front of the house.

Freshly-cut flowers decorated the breakfast table which was set with embroidered linen, a choice of fruit, fish cooked in a sauce of tomatoes with onion and lime, coffee, and hot toast with marmalade and guava jam. Nanny came to the table as Mark sat down and brought him the morning papers.

"Good morning, Nan."

"Good morning, Mr Mark."

"Miss Vera is asking you to bring her coffee to the bedroom," said Mark, and the old servant took up the cup he had poured for Vera ...

"Children soon come for Christmas," said Nanny, on her return.

"Day after tomorrow," said Mark, genuinely happy that by the end of the week the whole family would be around the table.

Everybody in the household shared a sense of family to some degree. There was some memory, some personal connection that each could rely on. The family had put two of Nanny's children through university. Her father had been nightwatchman for the house when Mark's father lived there and Mark was a child, and every night after making his rounds the old man would come and sit outside the child's bedroom window and tell Bible stories, with the twelve-bore shotgun cradled in his arms, till Mark fell asleep. Even the cat, asleep on the terrace, came from a line of Burmese that the General's mother had been given when she was a young girl, at least seventy-five years before.

The family shared a sense of security that was all the more remarkable because it was taken completely for granted. It was unthinkable that anybody should do harm to someone that Mark loved and get away with it; after all, to even threaten one of his people and survive unpunished was to render impotent the image of an entire army. But his ability to inspire loyalty was based on more than making others feel secure or threatened as the case might be. Mark was capable of inspiring loyalty because he himself was intensely loyal, not only to his family, but to the army, to his ideals as an officer, to those who he knew shared those ideals; yet in all this sense of duty there was also a sense of fun. Rolling around on the floor with a three year old was the insulation that Mark needed against that dreadful pomposity that characterised most successful army officers ... but now both children were away more than half the time; that too was family policy.

Although he missed his children, Mark felt it was essential to send them away to school during their teenage years if they weren't to be hopelessly spoilt. Their mother spoilt them, the servants spoilt them, people in general deferred to them because of Mark's position—it was inevitable so long as they stayed on the island. Over and over again Mark had seen people bring up their children with a taste for privilege and no idea whatsoever about the responsibilities that leadership entailed. Mark was no longer sure that there was an educational process anywhere dealing with that. In England the whole question of leadership was so grotesquely intertwined with class that it had produced a kind of social comic opera, and it seemed to Mark that the Americans had become so obsessed with equal rights that they were apparently embarrassed by the notion that anybody had to be educated for the responsibility of running the country. Far from being trained to deal with crises, the children of successful people in the US were sheltered indefinitely, most of them growing up without even the threat of a beating. Old Uncle T, who had been in the trenches in First World War, always used to say that a boy had to be prepared for three beatings in life. The first should come as a warning from someone who loved him, because the second would come from someone who genuinely wanted to hurt him, and the third might be from somebody who was trying to kill him.

Mark sighed as he turned the page of the newspaper. Little did he realise that the time had come again when he would have to concentrate a hundred per cent on matters that were far outside his immediate family circle altogether.

Breakfast finished, the General went out to find his batman. He was standing beside the spotless chocolate brown Mercedes which flew the flag of Mark's rank. The car had been started and brought to the front door five minutes earlier. The sergeant saluted and opened the back door of the car.

"Good morning, Byles."

"Good morning, sir."

"Anything to report?"

"No sir."

"Good."

Mark settled into the back seat and prepared to read the news in more detail. He knew Byles would switch on the radio when it was time for the local news at 8:00. Mark's life ran like clockwork because for him routine wasn't boring, routine was simply a matter of working out the best time for doing everything that had to be done, and once that was established, routine was necessary to hit each part of the day right, to hit it running, without loss of momentum. Everybody who took part in the process of making Mark's day efficient knew exactly what was required of them and did it precisely as they had done it the day before to keep him humming along.

The editorial of the leading daily was calling for "discipline in society". Discipline. Discipline was what Mark believed in. He looked to see if the writer had made a distinction between discipline and conditioning. He hadn't. They never did, and the difference was crucial. Discipline was personal, conditioning was institutional. Discipline came from within; conditioning was imposed from the outside. If an officer led a thousand disciplined men he was one man transmitting the energy of a thousand. If his troops were merely conditioned, they would be a thousand carrying the energy generated by one man. That was the difference. But there were so many who didn't begin to recognise discipline in any form, who *had* to be conditioned, that the vulgarians always prevailed, and it was hardly worth making the distinction.

As his car carried him downtown, Mark wondered, as he did daily, at the extent to which the city had been allowed to deteriorate. The streets were filthy with garbage everywhere. Three of five traffic lights weren't working properly. One set of lamps had been missing altogether for ten days. Everywhere one looked there were young people lounging around with nowhere to go, not even first thing in the morning. There was no electricity because the government couldn't control fifty-seven workers in an essential service! In the past years wildcat strikes had shut down virtually every essential industry on the island for disastrously long periods of time. Last night a bus conductress had been stabbed in the breast; this morning there were no buses running.

Well, thought Mark, at least the daily paper agrees with me. A front-page editorial was headlined "FIRM LEADERSHIP NOW!" and it continued:

> *...The latest strike of electricity workers is outrageous. It is the fifth stoppage within two months. The impact of the power cuts is cruel beyond endurance for commerce and industry as well as domestic households. Apparently the workers feel they must get what they want whatever the cost to the nation, and this constitutes an industrial blackmail that cannot be tolerated. If the Ministries of Industry and Labour cannot deal with this disgraceful state of affairs, then some higher authority must act. What is the Prime Minister doing about it? Where are the Security Forces? The nation weeps for firm leadership...*

Mark's cousin, Percy Sullivan, had come to power with the promise to provide leadership, but Mark had very little confidence in Percy. In his opinion, Percy was at the mercy of the same conflicting demands that were rendering politicians helpless throughout the tropical world, forcing the military to take the responsibility for government in one place after another.

Everywhere the common denominator for politicians seemed to be practical incompetence, and the fact that they had to make promises to get into power that they couldn't keep when they got there. They were invariably lawyers, or trade unionists, or academics, men who had no experience in actually making things work, and they were pompous into the bargain. They didn't know what they were doing but they couldn't admit it, not even to themselves. Well, when they came begging Mark to save their skins he would teach them a lesson in leadership they wouldn't forget. He'd have the place turned around in six months. It could be done. Lee Kwan Yew had done it in Singapore.

At a busy intersection, the car of a senior cabinet minister pulled alongside the General's Mercedes. Both drivers knew they must report the proximity of the other car to their man as he read his paper. Both drivers knew that when there was no reaction from his boss they should not pursue the matter. Mark found that the morning paper was the perfect shield. He knew that one day he was going to have to move against the man in the car next to his, and he didn't want him to so much as guess what was in his mind. Let him read the morning paper, thought Mark, what's in my mind is on the front page.

The drivers did not exchange glances as they drove off, but they would discuss the significance of the moment in detail when they met for a drink later that evening. The power game was played at many levels, not the least of which was in that network of drivers and helpers who knew what was really going on privately throughout the entire residential and business sections of the city.

As the General's car approached the front gates of the army camp, a Rastafarian broom seller was approaching from the opposite direction, walking along and chanting praises for the brooms he had made from natural straw—no plastic involved. He was happy, he was healthy, he was dressed in spotless white robes, his head was wrapped in a turban, and he wore a broad sash of red, green, and gold. He had smoked a chalice before leaving home that morning and he was spaced out of his head, so he took no notice of Mark's car. As it swung into the gate, the broom seller was stepping across its path. The sergeant driving

Mark blew his horn, and, leaning out of the car, cursed Prince Ebenezer.

The "prince" stopped and focused on the car as though coming out of a trance that had hitherto made him oblivious of whose path he was crossing, but now he saw who it was; now that the flag was waving in his face and the car was threatening to knock him over, he recognised the guy in the back seat as a man he had been observing for thirty years, from the days when he was a youngster and used to park with a Syrian girl out by the beach; Prince Ebenezer knew the General, and he knew the General knew him although they had never spoken.

As he smiled in recognition and started to advance, Mark considered pausing to greet him, but the car moved off again and the moment was past. "Babylon," called out the broom seller to the General, "tek care you nuh run out a gas!" Mark took note of the warning with the same level of interest that he'd shown in a bad horoscope on the back page of the paper. As he drove to his office that morning, the General still had no hint of anything seriously wrong, certainly nothing he didn't feel easily capable of dealing with, for he was a supremely confident officer.

By the age of forty, he had seen lesser contemporaries go from shared staff officer courses and UN testing grounds to take over countries of fifty, eighty million, and get themselves involved in continental politics and survive. They had all had enormously greater scope for their careers than Mark, and he longed for that time in his life when the wealth of his experience would be tested against large-scale opportunities, but in the meantime he knew, and they knew, that with the possible exception of Murtala Mohamed in Nigeria, now dead, there wasn't a black general anywhere in the world who was known to the West and who had a better military mind than Mark Bernard.

As the car flashed through the camp, Mark noted how far away he was from each soldier when the man became aware of his presence. He'd been watching the men in the army for fifteen years, on and off, but unfortunately he'd been off quite a lot, and while he wasn't watching there had been shifts in the officer corps and in the ranks that he wouldn't have made himself, but he'd sort that out now that he had the power to do it.

As Minister of Security he controlled not only the military but the police as well, and in a time of crisis Mark's power would be virtually unlimited. Even in normal times the need of every other institution automatically took second place to the needs of the Security Forces. If more money was spent on security than on education or health, that fact only increased Mark's determination that the money be well spent in the final analysis. When the hooligans got out of hand it would be the best investment the island ever made.

The army camp occupied over a hundred acres of prime real estate in the middle of the city. It housed three thousand men and sixty officers who could be put on instant call at any time. As commander-in-chief Mark had the power to order them to risk their lives. Nobody else on the island had that class of power, and in the crunch it had to be decisive. Mark felt the crunch was coming sooner or later, and he had set in motion a plan to bring the decisive moment closer because he knew the longer one waited, the bigger the mess would be in the end.

Mark believed that if he couldn't make a showcase out of his own little island, everybody could kiss away any hope for orderly development anywhere in the Third World, but if he could turn it around the island would be a springboard to much bigger things. Before he could tackle the country as a whole, however, there was a certain amount of cleaning up to be done in the army, and he looked forward to the meeting he was driving to because he'd made a decisive move early that morning and he wanted to know what had happened.

As soon as he entered his office, it was obvious something was wrong.

"Where are the captives?"

"There were no survivors, sir," said Major Cox, the officer in charge of the ambush.

"What happened?"

"We had to open fire, sir."

"You killed all of them?"

"Two are believed to have escaped, sir."

"Why didn't you have cover on your perimeters?"

"We had men on the perimeter, but once the shooting started—"

"Did we lose any men?"

"Two wounded, sir. One of the men who escaped captured an M-16."

"Are the men seriously wounded?"

"No, sir."

"And you have no captives for questioning?"

"All dead, sir".

"Who started the firing?"

"The gunmen, sir."

"Do you have any captured weapons?"

"No, sir, the men who opened fire were the ones who escaped."

"And they grabbed an M-16 on the way out?" asked Mark, sarcastically.

"Yes, sir."

"Who was the NCO?"

"Morris, sir."

"Was Wilson there?"

"No, sir."

"I asked that Wilson go."

Cox said nothing.

"Send for Morris," said Mark.

Something was wrong with Cox. Mark had always considered him affable, almost jovial, but now he was changed. Already the man was almost unrecognisable. The weakness of his eyes, mouth, and chin combined with the grossness of his neck and stomach to obliterate the once genial features of the chap Mark knew and turned him into an ugly caricature of himself. Was it possible Cox was in league with that group of officers who were trying to politicise the army?

Mark's reaction to political influence among his officers was deep disgust, till now he'd been sure he had them under control. In every corner there were men who owed him favours for decisions he had made over the years on the side of simple justice; virtually every NCO was a man Mark had seen tested in some way at some time, every man had been assessed and sorted by Mark accordingly: cowardly, brave; liars, and those that told the truth; the ones who made promises that were never kept, and the ones who came back when a deadline was approaching.

Sergeant Morris, big, black, fat; arrived, saluted, looked at Mark without looking at Cox, and stood to attention, waiting. Mark didn't know Morris as well as he would have liked because Morris was one of those who'd been making rapid progress while Mark was abroad.

"Why did you go instead of Wilson?"

"Wilson didn't get to camp in time, sir."

"Why not?"

"I don't know, sir."

"Who gave the order to shoot?"

"We returned fire, sir."

Mark looked at Morris and detected no flicker of insincerity. Sergeant Morris was a born actor. On the other hand, when Mark looked at Cox, he looked more terrified than ever. He looked like a man caught in a double-cross. Was it possible Cox was in on a plan to prevent Mark from finding out what was going on in the slums? Perhaps he had never intended to take prisoners, had never intended to help explore the links between the street violence, the politicians, and the army; perhaps there were too many people involved.

Cox wasn't stupid and neither was he a gambler, thought Mark, if he'd calculated the odds between siding with Mark and being killed by the officers who wanted to displace him, and had decided that the odds were overwhelmingly against the General ...

"All right, Morris, you can go. Stay in camp. I might need you again." He waited till Morris had gone before he spoke to Cox. "Report back to me in an hour, till then, stay in camp." Mark kept the tone of his voice casual, but he had to restrain himself from pinning Cox to the wall by his throat and demanding instant information.

In the news about military governments taking over from politicians in the Third World, there was a pattern of counter-coups after the military took over. Mark knew that the commanders who survived were the ones who had stayed put, who never took their eyes off their men, who maintained cast-iron control over all promotions, and Mark knew he hadn't had the patience to wait quietly in the wings over the years. He had travelled too much, and while he'd been enjoying life abroad, his enemies in the army, those whose loyalties were to the politicians, had been seizing control of the key positions in the chain of command. If they had already gone past a certain point, they would be able to demonstrate that such a great weakness as impatience could knock one out of the power game in the very first round.

Discipline. Discipline should have held him on the island during the waiting years, Mark now realised. He had allowed himself to be seduced away by the pleasures of diplomatic life abroad, by increasing recognition through UN service that he was a world-class warrior. Most of all Mark had been unable to resist the pull towards flying jets that the postings abroad brought him. He started testing jets with Hussein for the Jordanian air force, and thereafter became the prime consultant for the Arabs and Latin Americans when they went into the market for the latest jet fighters and had to make a choice between buying in England, France, Israel, or the US. Mark couldn't resist the thrill of streaking across the sky at more than a thousand miles an hour; breakfast in Amman, lunch at Le Bourget in Paris ... meanwhile he had allowed his home base to erode.

Mark felt flickers of cold running through his body, checking the circuits, testing the heart, the stomach, the neck, the scalp—all of them felt the testing surge of fear pass through his nervous system. Mark recognised the feeling. He knew it well. It was combat-level excitement, and when it hit him he realised that he hadn't been in mortal danger for many years, and this time the stakes were higher than ever before. Always before, the greatest fear he'd felt was for his own death, but now his death would be a mere detail in a catalogue of catastrophe if he failed to keep control of the army.

The tremors in his nervous system completed their circuit, sucking sugar out of his bloodstream—before another charge of chemical release came, this time one of adrenalin.

Mark realised how prudent he had been to stay fit. He knew that in the coming months he might have to deal with this kind of pressure daily. As he accepted it, the pressure eased, and Mark felt the strength of anger drive out the weakness of fear. Certainly he could deal with any threat posed by a weasel like Cox.

Cox was just an early warning signal as far as Mark was concerned; he could never really have been a part of Mark's inner circle, somebody crucial in a crunch, like now ... now, finally, the waiting was over. Mark wasn't afraid of excitement; it was the dead time in between that he dreaded, and now that he'd absorbed the initial shock of betrayal he realised that this was what he'd been waiting for, an excuse to move, a signal to start the confrontation that he'd been planning for all along. The first round of the fight had started with an unexpected blow, but after all it was he who was in command; he'd have to be a real idiot to have a plot succeed after he'd found out about it, and he turned his concentration back to dealing with the situation that confronted him.

Clearly the first thing he had to do was alert those he knew to be definitely loyal.

"Please get Sergeant Wilson," said Mark over the intercom that connected his desk with that of his secretary, Dorothy, in the outer office.

"Yes, sir, and there's a call from the newsroom at Sun Radio on line two, I was just going to buzz you about it."

Mark had OK'd a press release about the ambush the day before; now that would have to be rewritten, to say the least.

"Get Marilyn as well and tell the station she'll call them in fifteen minutes."

"Very well," said the secretary.

Mark turned from the intercom and started to jot down a list of names under three headings: "Political", "Neutral", and "Loyal".

Opposition to Mark's command came from a group of political officers who had had virtually no influence when the previous government came to power. But they had gradually assumed more and more influence over the subsequent eight years as a government, which had started out with a big popular base, had gone bankrupt paying for oil and had drifted towards crisis. Just before the elections which Percy won, it was assumed that if democracy was abandoned and a state of emergency imposed, the army high command then in place certainly wouldn't have invited Mark Bernard back to the island in any capacity.

This group of officers had consolidated their strength in one battalion, the Fifth, the one with the armoured vehicles and helicopters, the one with the mobility and firepower; the one battalion that could run rings around the other four. Mark had postponed reorganising the battalion until he had had time to sort out in his own mind where individual loyalties rested after elections, but now he wouldn't have time for subtleties.

"Ah, Wilson," said Mark to the sergeant when he appeared. "Why didn't you go on the mission this morning?'

"I woke up sick dis morning, sah, I jus' heard de news."

Mark could tell that Wilson wasn't frightened to be summoned by him, that in fact he was immensely relieved. Wilson knew that there was a good possibility Mark would be ousted by the officers in the Fifth Battalion if he didn't move against them soon, and, if Bernard went, Wilson would be a goner too. So would at least half the army. Mark hoped like hell Wilson knew which half.

"The patrol that went on the ambush this morning killed twelve men that I wanted for questioning. They killed them in cold blood, they didn't bring me a single captive to interrogate. I believe there's a deliberate plot to prevent me getting information, and I'm going to make a lot of changes today. The first thing to do is secure the armoury of the Fifth Battalion, and you will be in charge of that."

"Very well, sah."

"What's your opinion of Morris?"

"I don't trust him, sah."

"Anything specific?"

"No, sah."

"How widespread is the disloyalty?"

"Not so bad, sah, is only while you were away things get slack."

"All right. What about Clarke?"

"Him OK, sah."

"Benton?"

"For you, sah."

"DeSouza?"

"For you, sah."

"Blake?"

"I wouldn't trust him, sah."

For twenty minutes, Wilson and Mark reviewed the NCO structure for the lists that were lengthening on the General's desk: key disciplinarians, communications technicians, mechanics. The NCOs could give him the pulse of the army as the officers never could.

Immediately after the meeting with Wilson, Mark put in a call to his friend Gen. Ayub Singh, a Sikh contemporary for whom Mark had genuine respect and affection. He was at that time the general in charge of the UN peacekeeping force in the Sinai.

"Hello, Singh," said Mark when he got him on the line, "I hear you badly need a colonel and a major for UN service in the Sinai—"

"Yes," said Singh.

"I have two men who have just come to me and expressed a wish to volunteer immediately. Please send me a telex now and I'll have them on their way tonight or tomorrow at the latest."

"Right ho," said Singh.

"Dorothy, are you there?"

"Yes, sir."

"Give the General's secretary the telex details, please."

"Yes, sir."

"Thank you, General," said General Singh.

"My pleasure, General." Mark pressed the button to call his ADC. "Get me Colonel Ricketts and Major Jones from the Fifth Battalion, keep them waiting in your office till I send for them."

He buzzed his secretary again. "Dorothy, tell me as soon as you have the telex in your hand from General Singh."

"Marilyn is here to see you, sir."

"Good, send her in."

Thank God for Marilyn ...

She had started out as his secretary ten years before and she still organised his office, but she had increasingly taken over the confidential side of life for Mark in many different areas. Vera was a spendthrift, so it was Marilyn who kept an eye on Mark's personal finances. It was she who advised him on all dealings with the press. It was she who kept abreast of all political gossip that could possibly affect him. Her loyalty was such that if he couldn't trust her he couldn't trust anybody, and it would be useless to go on. The mere sight of her coming through the door gave a boost to his spirit. Marilyn was a fighter.

"That little bastard, Cox, slaughtered the gunmen we were going to question about the arms leaks!"

"Oh my God!"

She was horrified not only at the thought of the carnage, but also the effect that the murders would have on any effort Mark might make to deal with the ghetto problem.

"So far as I can make out, he did it because the whole officer corps is so riddled with political influence that he thinks he's better off with them than he is with me."

"He might be implicated in arms leaks himself."

"It's possible ... but right now I'm not too concerned with Cox. What I want you to think about is how we're going to handle the press." Mark stood up and started pacing again. "We've also got to try get back some credibility in the slums. We still have to find out who the real force is behind the youth movement down there and try to reach him. How would you deal with that?"

"It's going to be very difficult after this morning."

"What about our agents down there?"

"None of them have any cover."

"What about that fellow, Star?"

"God knows what will happen to him now," said Marilyn, "*everybody* must be looking for him right now."

"Hmm ... " Mark went back to his chair and sat down. "Sun Radio has apparently heard about the ambush already and they called for a statement. See what you can do about drafting something for me."

"OK."

"Check with me in an hour."

"OK," said Marilyn, and she left.

Mark went back to his lists of those he thought were loyal to him and those he doubted.

The intercom had first buzzed on Michele's desk at nine-thirty that morning when she got in from the airport. It was the editor calling from the newsroom.

"There was an army ambush before dawn this morning," he said, "it has set up a big storm in the west side slums."

He knew few details. Driving to work, a reporter, David Wilmot, was stopped on the outskirts of the city at a roadblock, there was a helicopter flying up and down a strip of swamp by the roadway, and it was obvious there was a manhunt going on. As soon as he reached the station, Wilmot called his contact in the ghetto, a man named Rufus who owned the Soul Shack record store beside the central bus terminal. Rufus was at the centre of an information network which, though informal and of his own devising, was as widespread in scope and as reliable for accuracy as any in the city.

Rufus hadn't moved from one spot for more than twenty-five years, but he did a lot more than sell records. He started out as a message centre for people going to and fro on the buses. When he demonstrated that messages left with him got delivered correctly he became a man that people would trust to hold cash for someone else to pick up. Eventually Rufus became something of a banker to the music business at street level. He inaugurated a hit parade by being the first to pin up a list of the best sellers from his shop. Reporters began to check with him for that and other news. Power brokers in the ghetto, realising that he had access to publication, soon started coming to him to give and get news. No matter who told him what, Rufus always checked it out. Everybody knew this. His reputation for honesty grew to such proportions that anybody who harmed Rufus would automatically be accused of trying to hide the truth, and would be condemned by so many who trusted "the news man" that, whoever else was endangered by what they believed he knew, Rufus himself felt safe.

With the installation of a phone, the pace of his business increased rapidly; if there was a rumour downtown, he could in-stantly check it uptown, if there was a rumour uptown, he could check it downtown, across town, island-wide, internationally ... his reach grew wider, but he didn't move. Never. Night and day he was to be found at the Soul Shack, he didn't mind if you woke him . As his business grew, he made more and more money, but money wasn't the compensation ... more than anything he wanted to know what was going on. He was a news junkie; he would have done it for free. Every time an item of news weaved its way through the surge of humanity and traffic that swirled around his store, every time the phone rang, Rufus got a fix. His compulsion to be at the centre of things had kept him in one spot twenty-four hours a day for twenty-five years, and there was nothing he could think of to do with his money that could tempt him to leave.

"I hear there was an army raid this morning out Six Miles way," said Wilmot.

"Don't say raid, say ambush, say massacre," said Rufus.

"How many killed?"

"I hear twelve but I have to check it out. One, Wire, get weh, I know dat."

"What you say about an exclusive on this one, Rufus?"

"Dis one too big fe dat, is fe yu fe call me first, same twenty-five dollar as usual."

"OK, I'll call you back."

"Cool, my bredda." Rufus hung up the phone.

"You should go on to that story full-time," the news editor said to David Wilmot when they met in Michele's office. "Spend the day in the slums and try to find out what's happening."

"I will see what I can find out from the other end," said Michele, "I'll call camp."

"OK," said the news editor, "we should have something by eleven-thirty for the twelve o'clock news."

When Michele placed the call to Marilyn to see what Mark had to say, she was told that Marilyn was with Mark and her secretary was reluctant to transfer the call into the General's office.

"OK, ask her to call me, please," said Michele

When Marilyn got back to her office, she found the message that Michele had called from the radio station, and Marilyn returned the call right away.

"Marilyn," said Michele, "I'm hearing about an army massacre early this morning, what's happening?"

"There was an ambush and some men were killed. I don't have the full details yet. Certainly it should not be described as a massacre ... "

"I hear they were shot down in cold blood."

"Some soldiers were shot as well. Look, let me get more details and call you back. Till then let's not jump to any conclusions."

"Try to call me in time to catch the midday news or I'm going to have to go with what's on the streets."

"What's on the streets?"

"The army killed young gunmen from both parties, and it's had the effect of sparking a unified protest movement in the ghettos."

Marilyn was shocked at how far and how fast things were moving in the wrong direction. If Mark's plan was to succeed, he needed popular support even more than he needed support from the media. Cox and the others had put him in a very good position to lose both.

"Listen, Michele, maybe you can help me. Mark is very upset about this whole thing. He is trying to reach the ghetto leadership directly. I know you have connections downtown who would know who he should talk to."

"Marilyn," replied Michele incredulously, "the army has just pulled a gigantic double-cross on these people and you want me to disclose the details of their leadership? What is Mark going to do, invite them to tea?"

"I think you should give Mark the benefit of the doubt."

"Well, let me put it this way: I would want to think long and hard before I used any contacts I have to put the leadership of what is now being called the "Peace Movement" in the slums at Mark's mercy after what's happened this morning. If he wants to reach them why can't he make a statement directly to them on radio? Why can't he come out and say exactly what he wants?"

"Because there are lots of other problems that I don't want to discuss on the phone, and I really think you should hold off the story as much as you can."

"I can't. I couldn't if I wanted to and I don't want to. Ronnie Morris's switchboard is glowing, and quite rightly. I think this kind of thing is a damned disgrace and I hope Mark has a very convincing explanation, public explanation, for it. In the meantime I'm going to run it on the midday news that the army ambush this morning killed gunmen from both political parties and it's started a peace movement in the slums."

"I'll get back to you," said Marilyn.

By the time Marilyn got to Mark's office, he was dealing with the transfer of Colonel Ricketts and Major Jones from the Fifth Battalion to the Sinai and she wasn't able to interrupt that meeting, so she returned to her office after leaving a message for Mark to call her as soon as he was free. He didn't call her till it was too late.

If Marilyn had been able to make the connection between Mark and Michele, and if that had led to a meeting between Mark and Zack, and Mark and Wire, perhaps the misunderstanding that eventually led to war would have been cleared up right there, but there were too many natural obstacles in the way of making those simple calls ... there was a conflict of spirits at the level of ancestral instinct, and the vital fifteen minutes that could have occurred anytime between ten and noon on that morning passed without anyone even realising they'd gone by.

Mark rather enjoyed his meeting with the two hard-core subversive officers from the Fifth Battalion.

"Gentlemen, I'm afraid I have a shock for you," he said to them, as they advanced into the room and he held out the telex that he'd received from Singh. "I've just received a telex from Gen. Ayub Singh of the UN command in the Sinai requesting that two officers with your qualifications be seconded to his command immediately. I have promised him that you will be with him as soon as possible. I have arranged for you to leave today via New York and London." Mark could hardly suppress his laughter as the shock spread across their faces. He held out the telex for them to read for themselves:

Urgently request colonel and major for UN duty, Sinai, as discussed. Most grateful for your help in a tight spot.

Singh

"Will we have time to go home?" asked Ricketts.

"No, I'm afraid not."

Now there was no doubt. If they offered a flicker of opposition, they knew that Mark would lock them up. Ricketts and Jones had no choice but to answer the call of the UN; the call of the wild.

Let them taste a little desert for about six months, the bastards. Teach them a lesson, thought Mark.

"He's a great fellow, old Singh. In my opinion he's one of the three best mobile artillery men in the world. He saved my life when we were serving together in Korea. I think you'll learn a lot with him, and certainly I can't let him down, so there we are. Captain Vernon will be with you till you board the plane. Have a good trip, gentlemen, and give my very best regards to General Singh." Mark pressed the buzzer to his secretary's desk. "Dorothy, please tell Captain Vernon that Colonel Ricketts and Major Jones are ready to leave for the airport now."

"Yes, sir."

"And Dorothy, please ask Colonel Thompson and Major Cook to come in."

While Mark was speaking, his ADC appeared at the door and escorted the two officers away. By the time Mark looked up they were gone.

The briefing of Thompson and Cook took less than half an hour. Simply put, they of the third Battalion were to take over the armoured vehicles and the entire operation of the Fifth Battalion because the colonel and the major of the Fifth had been seconded into UN service, and Mark wanted a policy of revolving battalions because he wanted to upgrade two more of them to armoured vehicles very soon.

A memorandum summarising what he said was put out by Marilyn. Nobody asked any questions. Everybody did precisely what they were told to do. The army was back in firm hands.

By mid-morning euphoria about the Peace Movement was sweeping through the slums like a wind of shouts and whispers. Graffiti four feet high sprouted instantly ...

PEACE YES! POLITRICKS NO!

RASTA REJECT TRIBALISM!

ONE LOVE!

Quite suddenly, it seemed to everybody that the news was overdue, that they had lived under unreasonable restraint for far too long. Crowds formed and grew bigger. A party atmosphere seemed to take hold and the youngsters swept across the city on their motorbikes, spreading the news, meeting with agreement, forming another whirlpool of discussion before speeding off again.

Mark and Marilyn listened to the midday news as reported on Sun Radio.

"In a pre-dawn ambush this morning, twelve gunmen from both political parties were killed by the army. Two members of the Defence Force were also wounded. Sun News has not been able to contact a military spokesman for confirmation. The massacre has sparked a peace movement in the ghetto areas of the city where our roving reporter recorded these interviews."

There followed five street interviews in which the view was

loudly proclaimed that the ghetto youth were going to lay down arms against each other and take them up against "Babylon".

"Jesus Christ!" said Mark, shocked at how the public was already beginning to perceive him. "At the very least I have to make it plain that I don't approve of the killings."

"DeCartret will exploit it to the hilt if you don't," said Marilyn.

"I don't care about DeCartret," said Mark.

DeCartret was the man who had ended up as prime minister in the previous government when, towards the end, radicals had threatened to take control.

"He can put together a story that has credibility for the foreign press," said Marilyn. "He can paint you as a right-wing general who encourages the use of death squads. It's a stereotype they'll buy if you don't establish your own position."

Mark said nothing.

"There's a lot of pressure building from the media. You have to respond."

"Alright."

"In that case I'll set a press conference for late this afternoon. We'll catch the evening news but have as much time as possible beforehand."

"Good, and get a note to Percy drafted so we get him before he calls us."

"I'll have it in half an hour," said Marilyn.

Mark felt badly unprepared for the public side of the situation. He was enraged at the prospect of having to defend himself to the press on the charge of slaughter, and the anger now started to overflow. He buzzed Dorothy.

"Get me Colonel Brown," he said.

Brown was the senior colonel in the army, next to Mark, and he was the man who should have briefed Mark on everything he knew when Mark came back to take over. Brown had given him no warning at all, though he must have known what was going on.

Brown was quite blustery and officious when he first came into the office, and for a while Mark let him build a mood of pompous indignation about the fact that "... all sorts of changes are being made, I gather, and it seems I am not being kept very closely in touch."

"It seems like *I'm* the one who's not being kept very closely in touch," said Mark.

"What do you mean?"

"You let me walk into a situation—without warning—that makes me look like a fucking butcher."

"What are you talking about?" At first he'd been merely offended by Mark's manner; now he was becoming alarmed. Mark made no attempt to conceal the anger in his voice.

"I'm talking about the fact that I sent out a patrol this morning to bring in some gunmen for interrogation, and they slaughtered every one of them."

"What's that got to do with me?" asked Brown.

"Weren't you in command up until three months ago? Didn't you see all the intelligence reports? Didn't you approve all the promotions? Wasn't it you who allowed the army to become so riddled with politics that—"

"Ha!" said Brown. "Look who's talking."

Mark got up from his chair behind his desk.

"What do you mean?"

"Look who's talking about political influence," said Brown, certain he was on firm ground in arguing this point. "Considering that your cousin happens to be prime minister, I think it's a bit hypocritical ..."

Mark started moving slowly around the desk towards Brown. "What did you say?"

Brown became hesitant to repeat what he had just said.

"You think I am where I am and you are where you are because of Percy? You dare to use a word like hypocrite to me?"

Without warning, Mark's open palm slapped Brown's face. It was a gesture of contempt, designed not so much to inflict hurt as degradation.

"I'm sorry, I shouldn't have said that."

"Sorry?" Mark paused for effect. "You're sorry already and I haven't started on you yet? Suppose I lock you up in a dungeon and come and beat you every day till you realise that in any army run by me you don't play politics. I don't compromise my duties, not for communism, fascism, religion, race, creed, colour, family, money, pussy—none of those things can force me into hypocrisy where my duty to the army is concerned."

"I'm sorry," Brown said again.

Mark walked away from him still fixing him with his eyes as he circled his chair. "You think you are up to my job, Brown? You really think you can do it as well as me? You think because we held the same rank in a period of peacetime that you're as good a soldier as I am? Have you ever risked your life anywhere, anytime, for anybody? You've never in your life even heard a shot fired in anger. You're not a soldier; you're a joke, except that you can get people killed ..." Mark completed the circle back to his chair but didn't sit down. "You belong as second in command. Believe me, you won't want to make the decisions that will have to be made very soon. You'll be glad you're not in command because you won't have the guts to do what will have to be done."

"What are you going to do," asked Brown, "declare a state of emergency?"

"Maybe," said Mark, "if it's necessary." Mark was obviously serious, and under a state of emergency he could do anything he wanted to Brown.

"And what do you want of me?" asked Brown.

"I want every detail of any political accommodation that's been made in the entire time I've been away," said Mark, sitting down and taking up his pen.

Chapter Nine

⌒⌒⌒⌒

Zack was still sitting in the empty room after Wire's exit when the first line of the song came to him:

> *Babylon beware! Jah children hear!*
> *I'm warning of worldwide-genocide.*

He got up and scribbled it down, then called for some breakfast. The melody for the song had come to him before he went on tour. The musical ideas were so insistent that he had recorded ten or twelve tracks in the rush before leaving — in spite of the fact that he could get no words then. He already *had* the magic in the music, and now the lyrics were falling into place!

Midway through his meal, more lines came to Zack:

> *Teargas, napalm, AK47,*
> *what for us is hell, for them is heaven.*
> *If we don't see it now,*
> *we never will,*
> *those we're trained to obey*
> *have been trained to kill.*

He jotted down the lyrics, finished breakfast, and called Michele at the radio station. He was put on hold, but rang off when an entire verse came to him. Zack again wrote out the lyrics and then lay down and closed his eyes to pass the twenty minutes till the bass player for the band arrived.

The phone rang. It was Michele returning his call.

"I got the song," said Zack, "I going recard dis afternoon."

"Fantastic!"

"It been coming to me all morning."

"That's wonderful. Does Eddie know about the studio booking?"

"Yes, we recard de backing tracks before we went on tour, him doing da session himself."

"I wish I could come."

"Yu have fe come, come round eleven tonight, I get to da voice track by den, should—"

"I don't know. I'll try."

"OK. Big news inna di ghetto dis morning."

"Yes. What did you hear?"

"I don't hear, I know, army shoot down youth from both sides in an ambush and di youth decide fe renounce politics and are a peace movement."

"Who's their leader?"

"Well, dem come to me fe dat," said Zack. Michele gasped. "Some popular youth get hit so one who escaped has decided to lead everyone from both sides."

Speaking to him again for the first time since Antigua, the thrill of his voice, of his presence, of his risks, came as a shock to her ... she realised she'd pushed him out of her mind because the effect of it all had been so powerful.

"What you're doing sounds dangerous."

"Everything in life dangerous, sis."

"But you're not a street fighter, you're a singer."

"Is a peace movement dem ask mi fe lead, not a war; I don't say man mightn't bring war to we, but—"

"It has to be explained to the public."

"The song is going to do that." His voice was calm, but she could tell he was very excited. *Of course, DeMalaga! Everything!*

"I'll see you later," said Michele, "be careful in the meantime. Stick to the music."

"OK. I hear seh some a di dead youth dem very young, thirteen, fourteen all dem age deh."

"I'll check it out."

"Love," said Zack, and hung up.

Michele made a note to send to the news room telling them to check the ages at the morgue, then she turned back to the meeting going on at her desk.

There were now five people sitting around the table waiting to see her, three of them for a union meeting; the lawyers for the radio station hadn't arrived yet, so Michele dealt with the other two. They had brought her a demo tape of the new station ID spots she'd ordered. She listened to them and approved two out of the five for production. When the lawyers for the union negotiation arrived Michele let them handle it. They had handled it the year before, and the year before that. Michele didn't care about the outcome of the meeting from a managerial point of view. On the one hand, she wanted the people around her to earn as much as possible, on the other hand, increases in salary cut into production budgets ... It was six of one and half a dozen of the other as far as she was concerned, and she mentally dozed till Marilyn returned her call. Nothing that Marilyn had said so far lessened Michele's suspicions of an army outrage, but she had the impression that it had taken Mark by surprise as well. His office was on the defensive. It seemed strange for Michele to think of Mark as being on the defensive in any situation, and yet there was no question that as this power game was starting, he seemed to be winded in the first round.

Michele's confidence grew. All her life she had been turned on by a sense of power in men, and now she saw the men she had tested herself against in the past testing themselves against each other ... Percy, Mark, Winston, and now Zack? She didn't know who would win because, frankly, she felt she was in a stronger position than any of them. They were all stars in their own world, but she knew she had the power to project them better than they could possibly project themselves.

Michele switched on the radio again. 'Hot Line' was on, the phone-in show from eleven till noon, starring Ronnie Morris: radio lawyer, technical investigator, spur to the civil service. At the height of his previous power he had been able to call government ministers, businessmen, and trade union leaders to account on the air before a live audience of hundreds of thousands who were listening keenly. The power of the programme grew so great that the public came to regard Ronnie Morris as a kind of dial-up ombudsman.

As things grew worse for the previous government, there was increasing interference with his programme; those in authority refused to take his calls, and when he was eventually barred from the airwaves because he wouldn't slant his thinking towards the government it was seen as a move that, more than any other single act, caused those in power to lose credibility.

Michele had reunited Ronnie Morris with his listeners just the day before. Yesterday he had solved a crisis involving an old people's home where inmates had been bitten by rats—he arranged for volunteers to deposit a dozen hungry cats on the premises. Today all the calls, without exception, were about the army massacre and the Peace Movement. There was a single-mindedness about the volume of calls, an excitement in the voice-pitch of the callers, which left no doubt that Ronnie Morris had returned just in time to tap a volcano of feeling on the subject.

It was apparent to Michele that the Peace Movement euphoria was feeding on a long-suppressed yearning for unity in the slums; all it needed was a focus. If Zack's new tune caught the mood in the streets, his could be the voice that would give the wildfire of emotion a centre, a rallying point that the ordinary citizen could respond to.

Zack *could* do it, thought Michele, her excitement growing. Peace in the ghettos! Who could possibly have predicted the spontaneous cooperation on every side? What politician speaking piously of the possibility as some unattainable ideal over the years could now believe that in half a day everything had been turned around? The biggest negative factor in the whole society had suddenly sparked something so positive that, quite possibly, nobody in power would recognise it as a gift at all.

Michele thought of Zack and how he had become caught up in a political whirlpool that could either make him unique as a singer in the world, or cause him to end up dead so fast for stepping into ghetto politics without protection. Only enormous talent could save him, she realised. He was so young and so great in spirit, he was so passionate; he had needed her so badly ... she didn't regret giving him that night of lovemaking in Antigua. She remembered how she seemed to drown in his passion as it overflowed from the bed, like a tide that rose against the walls, until the whole hotel room was awash with it; how she'd felt her body leap like a dolphin in the surf of passion, able to twist, and turn, and dance in the liquid weightlessness of love.

If he sang well enough to reach the people and make enough of them love him and support the cause he'd taken on, he might live. But if he failed to be that good, he might die, and at that moment Michele loved him for the faith in his talent that had impelled him to take the risk.

She instinctively began to think of ways to help him. A concert, perhaps. A peace concert might be able to express something that was growing rapidly past mere explanation as a news event. Peace in the ghetto! If handled right, they could pull it off! The foreign press would understand in a flash what was going on in a concert setting. If the radio station built stars out of the young gang leaders who had declared for peace, they would become alternative heroes, there would be a legitimacy to their meetings and new arrangements when, as spokesmen for their areas, they declared for peace.

If Michele was able to dramatise the situation so that everybody understood what was going on, what was at stake, what was possible, there was a chance that the whole thing wouldn't just dissolve into chaos; wouldn't survive merely as a mad euphoric dream, something remembered only in a song.

The afternoon went by rapidly as Michele pursued the concert idea. She also spoke with her brother, Eddie, about the progress on Zack's song, and she spoke with the deejay of the late night music show, enlisting his enthusiastic support for the premiere of the song on his programme. She arranged some promo spots. She noted that the announcers were promoting the Peace Movement with no prompting at all.

At 4:30p.m. Michele left her office and started driving out of town. She dropped off a young reporter/photographer who was on his way to the morgue, and bought an evening paper at the traffic lights while he got out of the car. On the front page was a picture of Wire and Razor embracing and proclaiming Zack the spokesman for the Peace Movement. There was also a large photograph of Zack.

Little did she think that when Marilyn saw the same photograph and statement, she would immediately call for a profile on the singer, and Michele continued on her way towards a recording session with one of her most unlikely radio stars: a Rastafarian preacher named Burru, who lived on the beach about ten miles out along the coast in the opposite direction from the spot where the ambush had taken place.

By five-thirty that evening Michele was walking barefoot in the warm surf on a deserted beach. She was glad to be alone in the vast empty landscape of scrubland, dotted with cacti, that stretched back from the coast in lines of low hills. Nobody lived in all that space except a handful of fishermen and wild-hog hunters.

Michele had first come to the beach as a child on her uncle's boat, and when she returned to the island and found out that a road was being built across the swamps that separated the beach from the nearest village, hers was one of the first cars to push past the end of the half-finished road and explore the sand tracks that led to the cluster of fishermen's shacks by the sea.

It was a quiet evening after a hot day and the sunset filled the whole sky with wisps and slashes and shoals of pale pink cloud across the infinity of fading blue.

During the time she was working on Percy's political campaign, Michele got into the habit of retreating from the pressure in town by going out to the beach to swim, sunbathe, and relax completely, and, sometimes, think about what she was going to do next. Certainly she wasn't interested in politics as a full-time preoccupation. Her main interest in working with Percy was as an exercise in mass communications first, and politics second; and while her job during the campaign meant communicating a message to the poor, she had become increasingly interested in what *they* had to say. As she took that perspective on things during her trips to Burru's Beach, Michele came more and more to focus on the people who lived out there. She started listening to the stories that the fishermen told each other as they clustered around their domino boards, chatting, laughing, and sometimes taking off into flights of expression—mostly inspired by the Bible—that made Michele instinctively reach for a tape recorder. Soon she started recording with Burru whenever he went out to the beach.

Michele took a pathway leading behind some sand dunes where she found a small shack made of driftwood and thatch. Beside it was an almond tree with a hammock slung under a low branch, and scattered around the yard were some fish pots, fishnets, dogs, puppies, and ten goats. A radio was playing in the hut.

"Hail, Burru!" called out Michele.

"Hail, Sister," replied Burru, as he came out of the shack to greet her.

He was a small man, and he moved with the natural grace and strength of one accustomed to the wilderness. He was only about twenty-five, but his eyes had the look of an inspired preacher.

His forefathers had been brought to the island when the planters were importing indentured labour from India to work in the cane fields, work that the black people would no longer do once they were freed from slavery. Coming from a caste so low, his ancestral memory contained no flicker of luxury in a thousand years, and for all that time those of his forefathers who refused to bow to other men had been forced to live apart to avoid actual abuse. Obviously many had chosen to do so, because to Burru solitude had come as a familiar blessing, at one with his spirit like an old friend, available once again to save it from bullyism.

He wasn't bored living in the wilderness; as the years went by he fished the reefs along the coastline and raised goats. He roamed the swamps, listened to the radio, read the Bible, and meditated. Occasionally he would walk the ten miles into town to a movie, but he felt no other pull to the city. He had been provided for in abundance where he was. He, who had nothing, had everything he wanted. Those who had everything apparently wanted more ...

"For unto everyone that hath shall be given, and he shall have abundance: but from him that hath not shall be taken away even that which he hath."

As Burru sat and watched the tent of dirty air grow thicker over the city with each passing season, he pondered what he read in the Bible, and a very specific notion of evil and judgement began to form in his mind.

One day he heard the noise of bulldozers. Three days later, when they were still working, he went to see what was going on. He saw that the government intended to build a road across the swamp, and as he watched over the next few weeks, he realised that the road was heading in his direction. It would hit the coast exactly where he had his camp, and it seemed to Burru that fate had decided to show him something, so he decided to stay where he was and see what happened.

Burru took the portable tape recorder from Michele and went into the hut to set it up for her while she went and lay in the hammock, where she watched the patterns in the sand cast by the late afternoon sun, and turned her mind to the programme she'd come to record.

Even before hundreds of thousands of people loved him as a radio star, Michele had felt Burru a powerful presence, and her judgment had been proven correct as his sermons started sweeping the airwaves like the gathering in of an entire spirit on the island when he was on the air.

As darkness fell, five men and two women gathered in Burru's house, lit by a kerosene lamp which hung from the middle of the roof. They were talking and laughing, telling stories. They were the poorest people Michele had ever known, but she had never felt sorry for them. She had always suspected that people as poor as this had some secret sustenance, and had been intrigued to find that this was true. Burru and his friends had become her instructors in the consciousness of poverty; when she was with them she relaxed completely into their point of view. Now she was waiting for another gap to be filled, another bridge to be made in her understanding of the poorest of the poor.

"Burru," called out Jack, a man who roamed the bush with five dogs hunting wild-hog for a living. "You hear how lion eat a boy inna zoo Wednesday?"

"Is the second time de boy enter into dat den," said Burru. "The first time de lion look at him and didn't trouble him. De boy grateful and amazed dat de lion jus' look at him, and love him, and recognise him like another lion, for the boy did wear dreadlocks and him did look dread, and the spirit of Jah inna him dat time." Michele was recording. "The boy did nuh understand that is Jah-Jah give him the presence to dress back a lion," continued Burru, "and you can imagine that by the next day many man start to praise him. The more man praise him. The more the boy feel is fe him personal power keep de lion at bay—before a few days pass the boy seh de lion fear him!"

"Him start to feel famous," said Jahman, an old Rastafarian. "When women tell him how beautiful he is 'im feel like if is not fe him power do de deed him nuh want it again."

"Him go inna de den de second time fe prove is fe him power," said Jack.

"Lion eat him rass," said Jahman.

"Ah," said Burru, "right deh so, him lose him mind, lose him life, lose everything."

"Once yu are serving a spirit yu have de power of dat spirit," said Jahman, "but when yu serve yuself you have only de power of a man, Jah."

"Praises! Give thanks!" said the poorest of the poor.

"Burru," said Michele, reaching for the record button on her recorder, "do you know that the army slaughtered some children this morning?"

Burru replied that it was a sign of the times, that Babylon was crashing, that multitudes were soon going to have to flee the city. Many who had nowhere to go were going to have to flee the city and trust their faith in God if they were to survive. How were

116

they to know that by the very words she was recording, Burru was going bring on himself a test the scope of which neither he nor she could possibly have foreseen?

Michele checked the battery level on the recorder and switched it off. With minimal editing she had another programme. She thought of how miraculous it was that she could connect the stories from Burru's beach with a radio audience across the island because of the power stored in three small batteries. If she knew more about that, she'd know a lot more than she did now about everything—but now she had to come down; she had to go back into the city, to God only knew what development. Things were moving so fast, it seemed like every hour brought excitement. In the next hour she'd have heard Zack's song; she'd have heard Mark's press conference statement; she'd find out what happened to Winston's plan in cabinet. She would pull it all together, she would coordinate the conflicts and explain the joint policy and smooth the way for the plan to move forward, that was her job and nobody could do it better.

Chapter Ten

೧೦೦೦

At a quarter to six that evening, fifteen minutes before the press conference was to begin, Marilyn got a call from her contact at the national airline. She had checked Zack's recent travel records and found out that he had been in Antigua after finishing the "Don't Be Afraid" tour.

Assuming he had been there for business, she checked on the passenger lists from the airline to find out who he was travelling with in the hope that she'd know his lawyer or get a lead on his business connections, and Michele's name had turned up. By itself that wasn't much to go on, but the thought of both of them on the same plane sparked Marilyn's imagination. Marilyn had her secretary call the island's airline and check the stewardess roster for the flight. Since Marilyn had been a stewardess herself for several years, she knew two of the five girls on the flight and she placed a call to the senior stewardess who confirmed that Zack and Michele had indeed travelled together.

"Quite together," she said.

"What do you mean?" asked Marilyn.

"Chemistry," said the stewardess, "but maybe it was just my imagination."

Marilyn immediately called for, and got, an Interpol status on her request for Antiguan immigration records. Within a few hours they would be able to check out all the hotel registers and get back to her. It was very wild speculation, she realised, and certainly she had no intention of getting Mark excited until she had more to go on, but the major hotel computers were geared to respond rapidly to calls from Interpol, and Marilyn decided to play her hunch and see what happened.

When the press arrived, Mark sensed a high level of anticipation as the reporters came in, said hello, and settled down in his office. The big circulation centrist daily was for him, he knew that. The afternoon tabloid was pretty much neutral. The man from DeCartret's magazine obviously would be hostile, and Mark had no idea what to expect of the reporters from the two radio stations, one of which was controlled by Michele.

At 6 p.m. Mark held up his hands and the room fell silent.

"Welcome," said Mark, "Marilyn tells me that there are some questions you want to ask."

"General Bernard," said the journalist from the daily, a man whose column had been read by the end of breakfast by every prime minister and colonial governor for twenty-five years. "We understand that there was an army ambush this morning in which several men were killed. We expected a statement."

"There was an ambush this morning," said Mark. "Twelve gunmen were killed and two members of the security forces were injured. I postponed a statement pending investigations."

"The ambush is being described as a massacre," said David Wilmot, the reporter from Sun Radio. "Why were the youths from the ghetto slaughtered, apparently in cold blood?"

"I deeply regret the killing," said Mark, "and I want you to know that I've started an inquiry into the whole matter. If there isn't considerable justification for what happened I will take severe disciplinary action against those responsible."

"You'll pardon my scepticism, General," said David Wilmot, "but army inquiries into army conduct don't usually result in much."

Mark wasn't accustomed to dealing with insolence, but he knew that he had to stay cool.

"When the findings of the inquiry I've initiated are published, you can judge for yourself," said the General.

"General, would you care to comment on the Peace Movement that is now sweeping the slums?" asked the reporter from the afternoon paper.

"What peace movement?" asked Mark.

"The word is that because the army killed youth from both political parties, the ghetto gunmen have declared peace among themselves in order to fight the army."

"If there's a genuine peace movement in the slums there won't be any fighting," said Mark.

"Do you mean that you are prepared to stay out of the slum areas and leave the gangs there to their own devices?" asked the journalist from the daily.

"If by some miracle the "Peace Movement" suddenly brings peace, that's fine with me," said Mark.

"Suppose the peace movement among the gangs of gunmen is in fact a consolidation movement for a united front against the army?" asked the reporter from Sun Radio.

"I'm not going to leave the ghetto areas at the mercy of gunmen," said Mark, "if the Peace Movement is genuinely for peace, they will have to give up their arms. If they don't, united or not united, I'm going to wipe them out."

"To wipe out a united force of gunmen, many of whom are widely supported—"

"The gunmen are not widely supported; the people don't want to be at the mercy of a bunch of criminals."

"Those you dismiss as criminals are regarded as freedom fighters in other circles, General," said DeCartret's reporter. "The people look to them for leadership."

"It's time the people were able to look to the government for leadership. And I intend to see to it that they'll be able do so. I'll not tolerate guns outside the hands of the law. The guns have to

120

come in. The gunmen have to be controlled, or captured, or annihilated. The system that has protected them and tolerated them all these years is no more. That is the basis on which I agreed to serve this new government, and I intend to carry out my promise to rid this country of the crime that has crippled it for years. We all know that both political parties have increasingly depended on gangs in the slums. Ten years ago, when guns were first introduced into the situation, I warned that it would get out of hand, but my warning was ignored and I was still too junior in the army to make my influence felt. Five years later, when I had risen to a position of influence, I started a vigorous campaign to get rid of the gunmen. If I had succeeded then, we wouldn't be having this trouble now, but again I was prevented by the government of the day from doing the job I had set out to do. Today conditions are even worse than I warned of at that time. Then, decent people couldn't walk the streets of the city without fear at night, but now they can't avoid the threat of violence any time of the day or night. I took on the appointment as Minister of Security in this new government because I was guaranteed by the Prime Minister that I would not be thwarted in fulfilling the promise made to the people to clean up crime, and this time I don't intend to stop with the job half finished."

"A lot of innocent people will be killed in the cross-fire if you persist," argued the reporter from the radio station. "You're talking about a state of war in the ghetto."

"War?" Mark looked at the youngster and shook his head. Why had Michele sent a kid to interview him? Because she had no respect for authority, she had no concept of responsibility, real responsibility, the type where you actually paid for your mistakes up to and including life and death. If one was to take the responsibility for life and death one had to be prepared to die oneself, and now Mark spoke with the authority of a man who was prepared to risk his life at any time. That was the difference between him and Brown. That was the difference between him and Percy, but how could he explain that without being mistaken for a megalomaniac?

Sitting in the glare of the television lights he took his time to think.

"I sincerely hope it won't come to war," he said. "Many times around the world, I have seen a situation in which the politicians have failed; the courts, the civil service, the manufacturers, the banks, all the people who are supposed to keep things going have collapsed, leaving the society at the mercy of killers, men who will loot and rape and burn. At that point it is the duty of the army to take over, to stop it. I pray it may never come to that, but if this tendency of lawlessness goes on being indulged it will come to that one day. If things get that bad, the army, under my command, will step in to prevent the looting and killing and arson. There will be no choice but to declare a State of Emergency."

Mark looked around the room and he could see that some people in it took what he said as a promise and some took it as a threat, but everybody took it seriously.

"When we achieved independence, this island led the entire tropical world in racial harmony, in sports, scholastically ... in almost every field we set standards envied by other countries. Today I see the sons of some of those high hopes lost in confusion, ready to give up the standards they've inherited to a lethargy, a laziness, a general lack of discipline and self-respect that I would not have believed possible. I'm ambitious for this island. All we need is discipline to be respected by the world again, to run with the winners, to set standards; but to do that we have to turn everything around. Crime, drugs, marijuana ... until these things are brought under control they will sap the youth of this island dry."

"Are you anti-Rastafarian too, General?" asked the young reporter.

"Rastafarians live in a dream world because they smoke marijuana," said Mark, "and in a dream world people love one another and I think that's a marvellous idea; I wish it were true, but the world as I know it is quite different. The world I have observed is one in which either you can protect yourself, or you end up as a servant of someone else's interests. Either we are going to pull this island together and make it work, or we are going to slide back into subservience; we'll slide right back to the situation we were supposed to have left behind forever when we achieved independence ten years ago ..."

Mark spoke with such conviction that he carried the press conference, but as the young reporter who had been the most aggressive in his questions was leaving, he thrust an envelope into Mark's hands and said, "I think you should look at these, General, because the whole country is going to see them tomorrow."

Mark took the envelope, went into his office, looked at the photographs, and suffered the deepest shock of the entire day. Some of the so-called youth were children!

He immediately thought of his favourite son. How, as a little boy, his son had lived to get his hands on his father's guns; how he had been fascinated by the helicopters, jeeps, and armoured vehicles Mark had taken him for rides in; how he would beg, for days on end, to use a walkie-talkie or touch a machine gun. Both his grand-father and his great-grand-father on his mother's side were generals; quite apart from Mark's influence, the army was in that little boy's blood and Mark knew, without doubt, that if his son had been thirteen years old in the ghetto he would have been among those who went out to pick up the automatic weapons that Mark had used as bait to tempt the young Rasta fighters towards him.

When Mark imagined his young son's face mutilated with machine-gun bullets, he got up from his desk and barely made it to the basin in the bathroom before he vomited up most of his lunch. Then he went back to his desk and brought his mind under control to confront crisis calmly. Mark realised that when the pictures were published in the papers and shown on TV the next day, he was going to need Michele.

He had fallen in love with Michele when he was nearly thirty and she was barely twenty. Even then there had been something dangerous about her for him, something beyond his control, a freedom of spirit and action that Mark would never have allowed at the centre of his life; and in spite of the fact that she had married his brother, Mark had distanced himself from her over the years ... had tried ... but now, after all this time, here she was again, centrally located, apparently unavoidable.

Mark didn't want power as a tyrant. He knew he couldn't declare a military state of emergency without the broad support of the people. He had to be a popular leader to achieve his ambition, and while Marilyn was good to a certain level, it was Michele who would know how to make his intentions understood. Perhaps now was the time to come to terms with her after all. She could interpret his image to the foreign press in such a way that he'd escape the stereotype of the military ogre which was threatening him now. Perhaps the time had come to take her totally into his confidence, thought Mark, to tell her everything, to let her in on the overall plan. Then, surely, she would understand his position. If she chose to do so, she could project his image in ways that he never imagined, his image good or bad.

Mark called her at the station and was told that she was out but would be coming back to the office before going home, so he left a message asking her to call him and pressed the intercom for Marilyn.

When Michele got back to the office, the first thing she saw was the message to call Mark and she responded immediately. But

Mark's secretary took Michele's call and said the General would call her back.

As Michele waited to talk to Mark, she started to go through the litter of paper that had accumulated on her desk while she was out, and she opened a large brown envelope containing the photographs of the slain children. As she leafed through them, her initial gasp of horror turned to anger.

Michele realised that for all her travels and for all she had seen, she had never before seen the work of the devil. She had never before felt the need to hate something, but now she wanted to know who was responsible for the slaughter of those children, she wanted to hate them, and she wanted them to hate her. She knew that the rage she felt was stripping away the protection she had enjoyed all her life because she had always been a truly pacifist person, but ever since taking the step from the outside world back into the life of the island, she had felt the stakes escalating like mercury in a barometer which measured fever in the national mood, and it was now obvious that some of the players in the power game were frighteningly casual about the risk of death, or the value of life for that matter. Those who killed children were the ones who put up the ante because if they came out on top, life wouldn't be worth living ... But who were they? The army had done the deed, but Mark wasn't responsible — she was certain of that.

Did that mean that Mark was in danger of losing control of the army? That DeCartret would try to pull a coup d'état while all his military people were still in place? Could he get away with that? If DeCartret could sell the foreign press on the idea that Percy and Mark were right-wingers running a government with a death-squad mentality, a lot of people in New York and London and Paris would be able to say: "Oh yes, the Central American syndrome." They would then vulgarise the whole thing, explain it in clichés readily accepted by left-wing media everywhere. If he got enough support from the foreign press, DeCartret could get away with a coup d'état. Everybody would forgive him for toppling a murderer of children.

If Mark got stuck with that image, he'd be in very serious trouble, thought Michele. She realised the time had come to re-establish proper contact with Mark, professionally, for the good of the country. Before leaving the office for the beach, Michele had stalled on returning three overseas calls from press contacts who wanted her take on the massacre story. She'd stalled because she didn't want to misrepresent what was going on, but she'd have to call them back tonight ... after the press conference, after she'd heard what Mark had to say.

But Michele never got through to Mark. Marilyn got to him first, and when she went into Mark's office it was with the evidence that Michele had slept with Zack in Antigua.

"They booked into adjoining rooms and the maid—and household records—confirm only one bed was used," said Marilyn.

"Get Winston on the phone for me," said Mark, "warn him that it's personal if he's in a meeting." While Marilyn set about finding his brother, Mark, momentarily, let his mind go blank; it had taken the third unexpected serious blow in one day, each one more serious than the one before.

Dealing with the first problem, he had been in control of all the actors. This time he was dealing with factors he could not control single-handedly. Michele! Who the hell could control Michele? Winston would have to help him persuade Percy to get rid of her, it had to be as simple as that, or it was too difficult for Mark to contemplate fully right at that moment.

"Winston says he'll call you right back," said Marilyn, "he's in a meeting. He seems very tied up."

"Did you speak to him yourself?"

"No. His secretary took the note into the meeting and brought one back to the phone."

"OK. Call back and say it's important we meet tonight at my house. Make sure he realises that we have to meet tonight."

As Marilyn left the room, Mark lay back in his chair again and turned on the radio to catch the seven o' clock news, but it wasn't quite seven yet and the announcer was doing a promo for the music programme later in the evening.

"The voice of the people will be singing out with a brand-new tune, brothers and sisters," said the deejay; "listen for it: the new monster from the old master, exclusive to this station till the whole world turns on. Listen out for Zack's new message to the masses. It's called "Genocide", people, from the man who tells it like it is."

Chapter Eleven

⁓⁓⁓

Winston swung his Jaguar past the two armed sentries at Mark's front gate, parked, and walked cheerfully into his brother's house. Having finally made the decision to take over from Percy, his mind was filled with fragments of the plan; they were coming to him as rapidly as he could assimilate them, and he was excited but relaxed. He felt easily able to plan for excitement and stay cool at the same time.

He got his first hint of trouble when Vera, having fixed Winston his drink, left the patio by the pool where the men were sitting and called the children after her.

Mark came straight to the point.

"How come I have to find out from my security people, without warning, that Michele is sleeping with some reggae singer?" he asked. "Didn't you know?"

"No," Winston replied.

"I warned you against Michele years ago. You were crazy to marry her in the first place."

Winston sat—stunned. Mark leaned forward to examine his brother more closely, and was shocked at the impact the news had on him.

Mark thought back to the days when he had been in love with Michele, and he admitted to himself, for the first time in twenty years, that he'd never since had a woman as exciting as she was in his life again. But that was exactly it ... she was too exciting, living with Michele was like living with a volcano.

"God knows how you have stuck it this long," said Mark.

"Michele was dangerous when she was a girl and she's grown a damn sight worse in the meantime."

Winston was slowly coming out of his daze. He'd got up and was slowly moving towards the front door.

"If you're serious, you've got to get her out of your life," said Mark, trying to hold his brother's attention, "you've got to get rid of her, Winston."

"And you mind your own damn business," said Winston.

"It's very much my business. Look, Winston, I don't understand you. You're at the peak of your career, ready to take off, and you saddle yourself with a woman you can't trust: your wife! Nobody in your position can survive that kind of distraction. If things get critical, and I think they're going to, I tell you frankly I wouldn't be prepared to trust your judgement with Michele around your neck. You wouldn't be able to trust yourself. You wouldn't be reliable." Mark put out his hand and gripped his brother's shoulder lightly in an attempt to delay his leaving. "If you only have one woman in your life, she has to be faithful," said Mark "if you can't trust your wife, you either have to have other women or do without them altogether. You have the worst of all worlds right now."

Michele had already once completely crashed him in the middle of a flight of fancy: when they first got married she had inspired him to his best work ever, and then at the height of his involvement with the plan in the Western Pacific she had brought him down, had brought him so low that for a while he had considered giving up his ambitions altogether. Now, this, again ...

These were the decades when women would take revenge in twenty years for all they had suffered throughout the ages. They had suffered because men were terrified of the power women had to strip them of their pride and strength of paternity in a single stroke; it was to protect themselves against the dreadful possibility that men had lost their sense of justice, but now, for all they had done in an effort to protect themselves, men of Winston's generation were defenceless in the throes of the women's revolution, and the greater their fear and the greater their attempts to protect themselves, the greater was the punishment they suffered as respectable women committed the previously unbearable sin, quite casually, in front of their very eyes.

Winston knew that he and Michele had achieved every fantasy they'd set out to fulfil—yesterday he'd finally decided on the child! Still, it wasn't enough. It wasn't enough in these times for a woman to have everything a woman could get, they wanted to live like men, and in the sixties and seventies they did, at last, succeed ... they'd heard rumours and they had suspicions, but when they found themselves living the real thing! When they'd *finally* plumbed the depths of egomania and cynicism that men took for granted in other men but were appalled to find in women ...

As Winston drove, he felt a surge of rage replace the shock that had so far held him down ... the excuse for rage was political betrayal; the real pain came from sexual jealousy, an instinct as outdated in men as the urge to domesticity had become in women. Perhaps even in the times before jealousy seemed laughable some men never really felt it, but then perhaps some men never really cared.

Michele had run the gamut of sexual culture, from the restrictions of the Middle East to the liberation of the sixties and seventies in New York and Europe, and she'd always felt she could depend on one common denominator: she had always felt that she'd had it in her power to seduce any man she'd ever loved, up to now. But now it seemed that the men she was dealing with were moving beyond sexual temptation, she sensed that they were in the grip of a lust of a stronger kind;

they wanted something that excited them more than the promise of possessing her.

Now as she watched Winston coming towards her, she didn't know what would happen next.

"Mark was right about you," said Winston, "he was always right about you; you're a deceitful, dangerous bitch!"

Michele was terrified. She had no idea how he had found out, or exactly what he'd found out, but it was obvious she couldn't deny it. She knew that if she lied to him he might become violent. In ten seconds her marriage was being torn apart!

She'd not considered the possibility of Winston's discovering Zack, but now as he was walking towards her his eyes were wild with pain, and for the first time she had no idea what he would do next.

She sensed that she mightn't seem frail to him, not if she wanted, needed, and could absorb the strength of another man's body ... she knew his mood was dangerous.

As Winston approached Michele, she suddenly took on the aspect of a stranger to him ... she was no longer his woman, she who had been in bed with another man the night before, giving over his innermost privacy, handing the key to his soul into the power of someone he never even knew ... now she herself was a stranger.

He walked past her without looking into her eyes, went outside onto the veranda, leaned against the railing, and looked out at the fireflies pulsing in the darkest shadows of the garden, waiting for some semblance of sanity to return before he said anything.

She followed him and stood silently, a short distance apart, waiting for the mood to change ... waiting to find out what he knew, how he knew ...

"Michele," said Winston quite calmly, "you really mean to say that at a time when we have the entire island to think about, when every opportunity we ever dreamed of is there for us to seize ..."

"Us? Who's us? And I'm not talking about the economy, or

two million people, or a hundred million dollars, I'm just talking about us; you and me."

"We're there, we're in the middle of everything that's happening, don't you see what we can do together?"

"You're not talking about us, Winston, you're talking about your plan. You know why I made love with that boy in Antigua? Because he's on top of the world right now, all his dreams are coming true, but I know that I excite him more than anything else does ... he needs me, he needs me like you did when we first met, when you were terrified that you were going to turn into a computer. Then you really did love me, you really did need me more than your plan, and for a while that really saved you, but once you were reassured that you really were a human being after all, you went and plugged right in again."

Winston felt as if his whole life was going to move forwards or backwards from this moment, that either he had to start all over again or go forward without love.

"You're too troublesome, Michele, you want me to sacrifice my concentration, my pride, my sanity, because you feel like the pressure of running an entire country isn't enough of an excuse for taking any attention off *you*; what *you* need, what *you* have to have *right now*."

"I can't wait! Life is nothing to me if I'm not in love ... songs mean nothing! Food has no taste! It doesn't matter if something is beautiful or ugly or mediocre. You live on your brain, but I live on my feelings, my emotions. I *have* to have love, and I feel sorry for anyone who doesn't, and I don't *want* to change!"

"Well ... neither do I, and I decline to sacrifice my life on the altar of your greedy pussy."

Ever since the first moment he saw her, Winston had thought about Michele at some time in every waking hour of his life; he'd never looked at another woman; he'd been prepared to give her the last cent in his bank account ... he'd been "in love", and what was so great about that? What was so wonderful about being captive to somebody who could betray you? What was so wonderful about being susceptible to a pain that was more terrifying than anything he'd ever suffered physically? What was so great about being in love? She needed it. He didn't need that bullshit in his life, he suddenly thought, and he moved inside the house to start packing his travelling bag.

Michele began to weep.

"For God's sake don't cry over me," said Winston.

"I have to cry for people like you because you have no feelings. I cry for you because you'll end up like all the others—eaten away with your obsession till there's nothing left to love, ending up alone ..."

"I don't mind being alone. In fact, it's a very attractive prospect to me right now." He was zipping up his bags, moving as though he couldn't wait to get away. "You want to tell me I don't have feelings? Well I do have feelings I assure you, and my strongest feeling now is to do without love till I find a woman I can trust."

Winston was at the front door. There was something about the briskness with which he had dispatched their marriage that made Michele dry her eyes.

"You know one thing you're right about?" she said, "I should stop crying. Because if people like me don't stop crying, people like you will never weep."

Three minutes after Winston had driven out, Michele was in her car on the way to the recording studio.

Fifteen minutes after Winston had first entered it, the house stood empty.

Chapter Twelve

By a quarter past eleven that night , Zack was ready to put the voice track on his song. He watched as Eddie cued the tape, and waited for the intro. The opening chords came to him even sweeter than the memory; the organ gentle and strong, the horns on top reinforcing the melody, the percussion underneath setting the bass line for the first turn of the tune.

As the music played on, Zack remembered five days of work, fourteen hours each day; seventy hours of repetition, of detail in phrases eighteen tracks deep—now it was all coming back to him in three minutes, consolidated stereo.

He thought of all the tests he'd had to pass to reach this time and place. How, even as a child, he had felt that he would one day be a singer to sing of justice, to stir it in people's hearts, to make that connection for the spirit he believed in. He remembered his struggles at every stage. He thought of the practise to play at least three instruments well enough to get work as a musician, of how long it had taken to get the first money for instruments and amplifiers. He remembered the waiting it had taken to get into the recording studios with his own band, and how he had passed that test and won. He thought of the number of times he had tried to get his tunes to the deejays in the ranking sound systems and of how he had gradually converted them to his music. Once he had passed that test he had to try again at the radio stations. Then the struggle to get the money so the stamper plant would press enough 45s while the tune was still on the radio.

There was another crucial time when he had had to distribute his own records, pay for the transport, pass around the shops, collect the cash—always he'd got through to face another hurdle.

He'd had to start touring, he'd had to get his music to singers who were already in the charts, and, when he had achieved that, he had been forced to pass a paper test with forms to be filled out so he could borrow money to buy his headquarters, and by that time he was being tested daily, and he knew he would lose the race with his ambitions if he couldn't get a hit worldwide, and he had passed that test as well.

He had passed a test for talent. He had passed a test for courage. He had passed a test for love. He knew from past experience that each time he triumphed he had been rewarded with a greater and greater inspiration ... he thought of how, in that very hour, family and friends who had been separated for years by the tribal zoning of the political system were now coming together again, free to visit each other and catch up on the news. As a result of Zack's meeting with Wire that morning, mothers and daughters, fathers and sons, previous lovers, all were hearing news that they could cross boundaries and reach each other, with increasing excitement. The power of Zack's music had triggered all that, and the greatest he had to offer was yet to come.

As the tape ran on, Zack marvelled again at the power in music. By the time the song had been on the air for two hours, the twenty key ears in town would have picked it up, and by the time the song had been played on the air twenty times, hundreds would have committed the tune to memory, and the Rasta youth would know that he was in touch with them, connecting them to everybody.

Why him?

Zack was convinced that the yearning for justice was in everyone and that en masse it was like a vast latent lake of gasoline that the lit match of a single lyric could ignite: unleashing gigantic energy, enough to consume any force that dared to face its rage, enough to have fuelled a thousand revolutions in the past.

Zack had travelled a long way to the centre of things, and now he was very nearly there. All he had to do was put his voice into the music ... Zack began to sing.

Babylon beware
Jah children hear,
I'm warning of
worldwide genocide!

Teargas, napalm, AK47
what for us is hell
for them is heaven,
and if we don't see it now
we never will:
those we're trained to obey
have been trained to kill.

Between the bully and the rebel
there's the hatred of the devil.

Drill!
Shoot to kill!
Paranoia in you wire
goin' bring down
sniper fire.

For two thousand years
we've been warned,
three hundred years
we've been scorned.
If we don't know it

now we never will:
those we've trained to obey
have been taught to kill.

Some call them pigs,
Some call them hogs...

Zion know dem as de emperor's dogs,
mek dem eat crumbs from his table!

Zack shouted the last line to end the song on a note of defiance.

His eyes were shining, he was sure he had a hit, and as he raised his eyes he saw Michele in the control room beside her brother, Eddie, laughing and clapping her hands, saying, "Give me a dub of that one!" As she waved and blew a kiss to Zack, he truly felt that he had won the ultimate reward.

Eddie Azani, Michele's brother and the owner of the island's best recording studio, had cancelled a poker game to engineer the recording himself he liked the tune so much, but he didn't feel comfortable with the ending. He didn't like politics any more than DeMalaga.

"The emperor's dogs can put a rocket up your backside from fifty miles away if you fool around with the emperor, my friend," was Eddie's comment.

"Time for dem to heed a new voice now," said Zack.

"Maybe they'll heed your voice and put a rocket up your backside," said Eddie; "maybe they'd rather do that than kiss it; maybe you'd better pay me the five thousand dollars you owe me before that happens." The words were apparently said in jest, but Zack knew Eddie was trying to issue a serious warning. "As for me," continued Eddie, "if I cannot be emperor, I prefer to be the emperor's dog because if I am the emperor's dog, I eat the emperor's food, I sleep beside the emperor's bed, I bite any man

in the empire who is not the emperor himself and get away with
it ..."

By midnight the recording studio was silent. Michele was
anaesthetizing the pain of the break-up of her marriage with the
happiness that she had brought Zack, and Eddie Azani was
prowling the floor of his gambling casino.

It was a small, intimate club with red velvet wallpaper and
genuine crystal chandeliers over the gaming tables. The
atmosphere was as far removed from a Las Vegas casino as is
choice gorgonzola from processed cheese. The heaviest gamblers
on the island met there every night. They were mostly Chinese
or Lebanese merchants who made their real money somewhere
else, but had to have enough of it at risk at all times to sustain the
gambler's obsession with handling cash. They earned it all day
and risked it all night. For years on end many had stopped
handling it only long enough to eat and sleep.

When Eddie Azani was ten years old he'd seen his uncle die a
broken man, wiped out by poker losses to many of these same
players. They had no mercy for pretension. If you wanted to
spend time in their company and you were not smart enough, it
would cost you several thousand dollars for an evening. They
dealt in skill, cash, and luck. Luck came third. Many think
gamblers deal primarily in risk but in this class of gambling they
did the opposite: they dealt in covering against it, calculating
and spreading it, in taking as little risk as possible till they felt
lucky. Only then did luck enter the play, and no amount of
money or skill or calculation could demand her presence. That's
where cash and magic met, and the only humility in the lives of
those who played regularly at Azani's casino was the fact that
they were forced to believe in magic, they were forced to submit
to the timing of Lady Luck and occasionally beg her for mercy ...

but begging for mercy was not frequent among them because they knew that the gift of luck would not be forthcoming if they depended on it for survival. For survival they counted on calculating the odds as they had done from time immemorial, generation after generation, accumulating the instincts of the oldest trading spirits of humanity.

For a thousand years Eddie's family had been penetrating deep into Africa. For two hundred years they had done business in the Caribbean, always at street level. When the British colonials surrounded themselves with lawns and sprinklers, and earned a few thousand pounds a year—the Lebanese traders lived above their shops in the heart of a hundred tropical cities, surrounded by dust, handling millions.

They could read a twitch in national mood that would go unnoticed by anyone else who had money. What those who dealt in credit would take weeks or months to learn was immediately apparent to those who dealt in cash, and they always moved in time to shift their money to a brother or cousin, placed in strategic positions across the Caribbean, in Mexico, in Miami, and all the way back to Beirut.

Eddie not only presumed to gamble with the heaviest from this set of businessmen, but for twelve years, from the age of thirty-two, he had been their host, the man who determined their credit at his tables, a prodigy in his chosen profession. He had been happy with his status for many years, but lately he had sensed that there were bigger games in the offing than any being played in the casino.

Eddie could sense a time coming when society at large would be thrown into a gambler's world, a world in which only luck could avert disaster, a world in which the old order would crumble and a new one would prevail. During the transition there would be chaos, and Eddie knew that the composition of the new ruling class would have a lot to do with who stayed cool in the crisis.

The crumble had been a long time coming, all the way back to the colonial era.

As the British lost their grip, and as the island's formal economy became more and more dependent on foreign aid, as senior civil servants and politicians became increasingly aware of the bureaucratic comforts which were forthcoming when government played the credit game, Azani and those like him found that they were surrounded by formal institutions which were dealing in debt to such an extent that they had virtually no cash at all, and they were planning to squeeze the uncontrolled cash flow of street level business to get some.

In that clash of interests, Eddie was prepared to gamble heavily that they would create a situation they couldn't control and that he, Eddie, would make money out of it. He believed that whatever happened, no matter who did what, somewhere along the line everybody was going to need what he had, and he'd come out ahead.

At 2 a.m. Eddie closed the casino and walked across the patio towards the stairs that led up to his apartment. He was short, broad, and heavy, but he walked fast and was light on his feet, and the sense of alertness that he gave off swept his surroundings like radar. The entire compound housing the casino and the recording studio was walled around, and on top of the ten-foot-high walls was a line of broken bottles. Eddie owned three guns, employed five guards, and was himself skilled in martial arts; although he had long ago decided to live dangerously, he took all possible precaution against unnecessary risk.

"Ha, Lola, Lola," said Eddie as his Alsatian rushed down the steps to meet him, wagging her tail and circling around his legs as he walked up the broad veranda where he would spend the best part of his working day.

Occasionally, when he was in need of a sudden infusion of cash, Eddie would put his main energies into gambling, but the casino wasn't his main source of income any more. His main business was as a banker and his opening hours were from one till three o'clock in the morning.

In the seventies, Eddie lent money at twenty per cent whether you kept it for a year or a day because he lent money to people — mostly in the ganja trade—who were dealing in large amounts of cash for a very short time. If the deal went through in a day, they were glad to pay the twenty per cent because they had made a lot of money. If they'd lost on the deal, it would take them a long time to recover the money they'd borrowed, much less the interest, and Eddie wouldn't deal with anything piecemeal. Two transactions—one out, the other in—plus twenty per cent; that was the only way to stay out of a lot of bookkeeping, and for people who could deal with bookkeeping there were always the banks. "The bankers believe in credit and contracts," Eddie would say, "and I believe in cash and trust. I don't say which is better, but I know I prefer to do business my way."

When he reached his seat, he put down a bag containing ten thousand dollars in cash beside it, took several deep breaths of the cool night air, shouted out "Leroy!" to the houseboy who would bring him something to eat, then sat down, picked up the phone beside the big chair, and called the night watchman to find out who was waiting to see him.

"Ha, Action!" said Eddie.

"Burden is here to see you, Mister Eddie," said Action, the old man who kept watch at the entrance to Eddie's compound and who guarded the stairs heading directly up to his boss's veranda. From sunset to sunrise every night of his life, that was where he was to be found, the keeper of the gate.

"No Burden, I don't want to see Burden."

"I've told him you won't see him, but he just keeps begging."

"Who else is there?"

"Jackson, and Williams."

"Send Jackson up. Does Williams have all the money?"

"So him seh, sah."

"Count it," said Eddie, and he hung up.

Food arrived: lamb, chapatti, hummus, salad, fried plantain, rice and peas, avocado pear, candied carrots, and gravy mixed with fried chicken. There was a stack of plates beside the food, and when Jackson arrived Eddie motioned him to pull up a chair and serve himself.

"Leroy, bring two cold beers," Eddie called to the kitchen. The boy emerged almost immediately with two bottles and he put them on the table without glasses. Jackson declined the invitation to eat, but he took a drink from the beer bottle and then produced a small packet of ganja wrapped in brown paper.

"Ranking sensi," said Jackson.

"Leroy!" called out Eddie. The boy put his head around the corner. "Roll two spliff out a dis and bring dem come," said Eddie, holding up the parcel for him to take. "And don't spit on the paper neither, use water."

"Yes sah," said the boy, disappearing into the kitchen once more.

Jackson was a tall, thin, serious, black man who was in the trucking business. He had done business with Eddie in the past. He wanted to go to Miami to buy some spare parts and he wanted to buy some American dollars. Eddie had them in his bag of cash at the standard black-market rate of twenty-five per cent over the official rate posted by the Central Bank, and matching the rate paid in the concourse at Miami airport.

Eddie sold Jackson two thousand US dollars, they chatted for five minutes, and then Jackson left. Lola escorted him to the top of the stairs and waited for Williams to appear. He was slightly nervous, Lola growled as he came up the stairs, but she allowed him to pass her and walk on towards Eddie.

Williams was a small man, thin, dark brown, with large black slightly thyroid eyes. There was some East Indian in him. Eddie motioned for him to take a seat, but did not offer him food or drink.

"Sorry I tek so long to see you," said Williams, "I wanted to pay back—" Eddie held up his hand for him to stop the further explanation. "Three times I come with something—" Again Eddie held up his hand.

"Once," said Eddie; "once in, once out. Simple. If I have to see you three times to get my money I not only have to do three times more work for it, but I have to do three sets of accounting. It doesn't suit me. I've told you already. You have all my money now?"

"Yes."

"Did Action count it?"

"Yes, here it is." He leaned across and handed Eddie three thousand dollars in island currency. Eddie picked up a large address book, looked under 'W', looked for Williams's receipt, hand-written on the back of a leaf of paper from a small memo pad, and when he found it he tore it up.

There was a pause long enough to be awkward for Williams.

"I wouldn't mind do some more business with you," said Williams at the moment when he had to either say something or leave.

"Why?"

"Well, I want to buy some—"

Again Eddie held up his hand to stop the man talking.

"Why you want to do business with me in particular?"

"Well with you—"

"No collateral, ha? Is that attractive?"

"Yes, but—"

"When you don't pay me I don't come look for you; you like that too?"

"Yes, I really appreciate that."

"You owe the bank money, they come and take your car, they come take the furniture in your house, they send you notes every month, isn't it so? A different colour note every month? Ha?"

"It's simpler to deal with you," agreed Williams.

"But you want to make my life complicated. You want me to do a lot of arithmetic to find out how much money you owe me. You want me to be simple, but you want me to do more work than you. If you do business with the bank you can go and see them every month, every week, they love that kind of stuff."

"I never really know before how you operate. Now I know".

"How much money you want?"

"Five hundred dollar."

"Nah. Too small. If I lend five hundred dollar is just personal business, you know."

"OK," said Williams, rising, "thank you anyhow."

"Thank you," said Eddie, "say hello to Benz fe me."

Benz was the man who had introduced Williams to Eddie in the first place. Benz was the local heavy in Williams's area. The fact that Eddie wouldn't deal with Benz while he thought Williams might default on the loan had caused Benz much anguish. Benz's anguish, Eddie guessed, was capable of causing Williams much pain; and when Eddie saw Williams's face light up at the greeting to Benz, Eddie knew he'd been covered all along.

When Williams passed the gate on the way out past Action, Eddie buzzed again.

"Mr Eddie, what about Burden?" asked the gateman.

"Anybody else there?" asked Eddie.

"Jose pass by, but him seh him will come back tomorrow ... but Burden, Mister Eddie, him a burden to me; him won't leave."

"All right, send him up."

The moment Lola smelled Burden coming up the stairs she went wild with barking. She could pick up the scent of anybody who didn't like Eddie even if they were passing on the street outside. She could signal the amount of tension in a visitor on a scale of ten. She was Eddie's instant Dunn & Bradstreet.

Eddie called the dog back just enough to prevent her from actually biting the man, but she blocked his way, snarling and barking, backing only a few steps at a time down the twenty yards of veranda that the man had to cover to reach Eddie's chair and the bag of cash that sat on the floor beside it. When eventually he was within a few feet, Eddie called off the dog altogether and she sat to one side grumbling and watching Burden.

"Ha, Burden! How come I find it so easy to remember your name? And old Action too, he tell me the same thing. He say every time he sees you he sees trouble; he remember your name right away." The man said nothing. He eyed the dog warily. "My dog will not bite you. She just want to make sure I know she don't like you. What you want?"

"I want another chance," said Burden, "please, Mister Eddie."

Burden was young, black, dressed in the kind of clothes that should be worn occasionally for going out at night, but that Burden had been wearing night and day for a long time.

"No," said Eddie.

"Please, sah, I'm begging you," said Burden, not realising that the more he begged, the more pathetic he became, and the less chance he had for re-employment.

"How long did you work for me?" asked Eddie.

"Six months, Mister Eddie, and only in the last week—"

"Six months!" shouted Eddie. "Six months you waste my time. Six months you waste the time of the man who replace you, that's one year already of time you waste."

"Mister Eddie ... please, Mister Eddie,"

"You see me? I'm a first-eleven guy. If I bet, I bet to win. If I have a team, I want the best players on my team, I want a winning team, I want to play in a winning league; you cannot play on my team, you are not good enough."

"All we is human being. All we can change," said Burden.

"No. No, it cannot be changed. You are a liar because you're lazy, and you're lazy because you're always tired, and you're always tired because you never get excited about anything, and you never get excited because you have no imagination, and you have no imagination because nothing good ever happened to you, or your father, or your grandfather ... it will never change."

The boy could tell that Eddie would not now change his mind, and he had started to weep. Eddie took out twenty dollars and gave it to him.

"Look, you go now and don't trouble Action again, and try to get a job with the government; government have the right job for a guy like you."

As the boy walked away, Lola merely growled, she did not get up.

One hour and four more transactions later, Eddie rose, stretched, and looked out towards the city surrounding him and thought again that his life was going to change; everybody thought that now the socialists were out of power the capitalists would make everything hum again, but Eddie could see no real difference between them. They were both tied up in red tape. Left to them, half the business on the island would wither and die waiting. They both desperately needed the Azanis to keep things going at street level ... they always had.

The phone buzzer went again. This time, Eddie knew, the gateman would be calling about a woman. "Pussy is like cash," Eddie would say, " you must have more than you can use to use it well." Eddie seldom paid cash for sex, which is not to say a lot of hookers didn't come to see him, they did—Eddie knew a lot of hookers and had helped them in the past—but they came to see him when they wanted to spend some time with him, when they remembered the times they had spent in the past and were in the mood for an evening with Eddie the way they might be in the mood for any other entertainment from time to time.

Once or twice in a month, if nobody turned up to see him, Eddie might cruise the clubs to see who was around, and if that didn't turn up someone who wanted to have sex for free then he might pay someone to come to the club, but he couldn't remember the last time he'd had to do that ... he had too many friends.

For thirty years, ever since he first met Winston and DeMalaga as three boys exploring the waterfront together, Eddie had added another girl to his life every two or three weeks, and now there were always at least a dozen women around town whom he was glad to hear from when they called him from time to time. He could not imagine living any other way; his way of life satisfied a sexual instinct in him that was as old as the harem.

At the end of the veranda, two figures stirred in the shadows.

"Who's there?" asked Eddie.

"Agnes," answered the woman's voice.

"Ahh ..." said Eddie, delighted. "You came."

The woman stepped into the light. She was about thirty-five, well dressed, good-looking, her skin shiny with blackness. Both her smile and her eyes were friendly. She was a big woman, getting buxom, but her body exuded cheerfulness.

"Have you eaten?" asked Eddie.

"Yes, long ago."

"Were you given something to drink by Action?"

"Yes, thank you."

"Smoke?"

"I brought you some roots."

"Ahh ... you are so kind. How's business?"

Agnes was a hairdresser. Eight years before, Eddie had lent her a hundred and fifty dollars to start the business. She had long since repaid the loan.

"Business is fine," she said.

The other figure, now coming forward hesitantly into the light, was that of a much younger girl.

147

"This is Marie," said Agnes, "I wanted the two of you to meet."

Marie was sixteen. She had come up to the city only the week before. She came from a part of the island that had been settled with poor whites several generations before. They had intermarried somewhat, but Marie had the woolly red hair and freckled brown skin together with pale blue eyes that still characterised many from the region. Since coming to town the girl had got herself into trouble with the relations she was supposed to stay with because the man of the house wanted to rape her. Ten years before, Agnes had been in almost exactly the same predicament when she met Eddie. For two or three years he had seen her regularly twice a week, always at three o'clock in the morning when he closed the casino and wanted to relax and smoke, and listen to music, and make love before going to sleep.

"Make love?" Sometimes. He had made love often with the hairdresser when she was a girl because she loved him as the only man who had not tried to press her, or possess her, or use her in any way except for pleasure. And he always guaranteed something in return—often orgasm, certainly food and drink and ganja. At worst he always paid money in some form or the other.

"Will you stay with us?" Eddie asked Agnes.

"I can stay for a few hours," she said, as she took the girl by the hand and headed for the bedroom.

Eddie let them go ahead. Agnes knew where everything was. She would show the girl, would punch some tunes on the jukebox in the corner of Eddie's bedroom … he stretched again and looked out into the night sky, and thought back on the day… it had been a good day, he had particularly enjoyed recording with Zack.

Suddenly Eddie laughed. He remembered how Zack had come into the control room from the studio after recording the vocal. His face was shining, he felt he had a hit, and Eddie was able to agree with him, but while Eddie was able to congratulate him musically, politically he felt Zack was making a big mistake. Eddie remembered what he had said to Zack about preferring to be the emperor's dog, and he chuckled to himself as he moved towards the bedroom. He could hear the celebration parties for the Peace Movement still echoing across the city. More naivety, more megalomania, thought Eddie.

The centre had gone and the place was up for grabs. All those who would only bow to a strong prime minister would stop bowing to anyone when they perceived that Percy had no strength, that he was only a pretty face, only a figurehead, that he was only where he was because he had won over the public by projecting an illusion; by being a good enough actor to make them believe it. The illusion would soon be gone, and then those who could only be controlled by a strong leader would all start looking for the crash, and they would all think that when it came they had what it took to take over.

Mark believed in the power of discipline.

Winston believed in the power of intelligence.

Michele believed in the power of freedom.

Zack believed in the power of the people's need for justice.

Many who believed in the power of their particular spirit were prepared to risk their lives to prove that theirs was the strongest in the crunch, that the people's yearning for what they believed in and represented would give them the ultimate power in the power game, the power that would come to them if a belief in the supremacy of their spirit spread among the masses.

Personal relationships aside, it didn't matter to Eddie who won. He was confident that whoever won this round they would need what he believed in, what he had, what he had spent all his life accumulating.

Eddie Azani believed in the power of cash.

Part Two

Elimination Rounds

Chapter Thirteen

When Winston left the home that he'd shared with Michele, he instinctively headed for the penthouse of the hotel beside the Central Bank building on the waterfront, and the first thing that he did there was call the bell captain and head of room service.

The bell captain, a dignified black man with a shock of white hair, and known universally as "Missa D", was acquainted with the Bernards from the time when Winston was a boy.

The hotel in those days was no air-conditioned tower: it was a place of broad lawns with peacocks, royal palms, and a sea-breeze that swept up through pavilions where lunch was served by waiters in starched white jackets while a military band, dressed as Egyptian Zouves, played show tunes in the distance. The part Winston remembered best was down by the seaside where the harbour chop slapped up against the wall of a huge salt water swimming pool with a thousand memories of fun. Beside the swimming pool was a bar on a wharf that buzzed with launches bringing passengers from the banana boats of the Great White Fleet, and behind the bar was Missa D, shaking rum punches, and making lime squashes that little boys would remember as a standard long after they were grown.

Missa D had been fond of Mark and Winston from those times, aware, as they were not, that they came from a handful of brown families prominent enough to enjoy themselves on the premises of the United Fruit Company in the 1950s.

Missa D could tell right away that Winston had suffered a serious rupture in his routine, and he took an educated guess that he knew what the trouble was. The old man had seen it all before: that look of loss as men who'd been cuckolded over the years first sought frantic refuge in a good hotel ... successful men whose first great success had been the winning of their wives, and who, with that first fantasy fulfilled, later became addicted to making other dreams come true, fantasies that tended to be further and further away from the original focal point ... the demands of winning always starved time, the first fantasy would shrink ... It was a recurring theme.

Winston explained that he would be using a great deal of room service, and asked detailed questions about the menus and the various chefs. By the time the meeting was over, he had also met the chief maid for his floor. The hotel manager was put on a special retainer to bring food and drink from the outside world at any time of the night or day.

There were at least ten restaurants scattered around the business district to which he could send out for excellent Caribbean food, as well as Chinese, Lebanese, and Indian. Even if he had to live without some of the comforts of matrimony, eating well was not going to be one of the things he'd be giving up, Winston promised himself.

Momentum. Momentum was the key to staying sane. If he could just keep going fast enough, he wouldn't have to think about Michele, there would be no chinks in his armour where thoughts of her would creep in to loosen jealousy like poison in his mind, nausea in his chemistry; no — momentum was key, and Winston didn't slow down for three weeks after he moved into his new abode, and when he did finally pause it was to fall into a deep sleep for a long weekend of three days.

Once reassured that Missa D's team would take care of his immediate needs, Winston's attention turned to the design of his new home.

First of all, everything in the room would be cleared out; then he would design the use of the space as a work machine into which he could plug himself whenever he wanted. He had always intended to set up such a room but the opportunity had never arisen, either because he had always worked in offices designed by somebody else, or because Michele had never had any incentive to extend Winston's working life into their home. Now, at last, there was no reason for not setting up the working conditions he had dreamed of since the days when he was working on his first PhD.

Twenty-three years before, he had argued that the nucleus of a thought originates when the connection is made between two facts; that while no thought can come out of a single fact, connecting any two facts will produce a thought of some kind. His premise was based upon the assumption that so long as facts were being spontaneously attracted to the nucleus of a thought, the thought should be allowed to keep growing, and that, as the stream of facts adhered to the thought, it would take shape based on the information received instead of being programmed to fit some preconception. Winston envisioned setting up dozens of programmes that would assemble facts and grow with little more than guidance from him. His own mental capacity need not then limit the range of his ideas because the system would be transmitting intelligence instead of generating it, and while the mental energy of one mind is finite, the quantum of intelligence it can transmit is infinite, and that idea was the key to the design that Winston was now evolving for this large room with the huge view.

In the middle of it there would be a round desk, but Winston would not be sitting around the outside of it, the desk would encircle him. He would cover it by swinging from section to section in a swivel chair. When his desk was set up the way he was planning, he would be able to call up ideas at random on the one hand, and, on the other, punch buttons to summon figures. In this way he would be able to instantly confirm or refute any current questions blocking the integration of his ideas into the thoughts they were related to.

Starting with a notepad, Winston would swivel effortlessly from phones, to fax, to copying machine, to rolodexes; to a computer which could retrieve information not only from any government file but also from any information service anywhere selling data useful to him. Beside the computer were more pads for notes, a typewriter, a radio with shortwave as well as AM/FM for getting market reports worldwide, a TV with satellite dish controls which enabled Winston to see whatever was on the satellites in those days before scrambling. There was a cassette player/recorder, a VCR, and a magazine rack. Finally, there was a small exit gap, before coming back full circle to the notepad.

No space was reserved for formal paperwork in Winston's set-up. Formal papers were brought for discussion by lawyers or bureaucrats from the bank who would be met by Winston, either in an area with armchairs and low tables at some distance from his workspace, or around the boardroom table in the bank across the street.

Those who brought formal documents took them away again. They merely passed through Winston's system, they didn't stay to clog it up.

Outside on the terrace he'd have the trampoline transferred from the address he'd left behind; the trampoline would relax him. He had to stay relaxed, Winston was aware of that.

Relaxation plus precision—he needed both. Without relaxation he'd turn into a data junkie, without precision he'd fumble at speed. The utmost relaxation would be in jotting down random thoughts as they occurred, the utmost precision would come out of the computer with its instant information. Relaxation allowed the acceptance of any line of thinking, allowing the information to take the true shape dictated by the facts ... that was the discipline of his method, and the abhorrence of it from those who wanted to force the facts to fit.

As important as the relaxation of the swivel chair, was the precision of the computer. That's where the speed came from, and with the speed momentum, and with momentum revelation—the rush in the brain that men like Winston crave as their favourite thrill.

Totally relaxed as to the wanderings of his mind, incredibly precise in his ability to test his imagination against reality, Winston planned to rise to that egoless state of concentration familiar to Zack when playing music, or to Burru when he was preaching, to Eddie when he was playing cards, Michele when she was making love, or Mark when he was in the middle of a fight; that same state of mind attained by anyone when they are doing the thing at which they are naturally gifted.

When the room was finished, he would be able to stay in a state of advanced concentration for days on end—to let thoughts emerge like Polaroids from calculation to calculation till a picture of reality formed out of previously meaningless figures. And as fantasy was tested against reality, and as the dimensions of that reality grew, Winston's calculations would develop so fast that the changes themselves would form into discernable patterns, lifting his perspective higher and higher.

Chapter Fourteen

Wire woke up at about two o' clock, three nights after Zack's song was released on Sun Radio.

It was pitch-black, but he could see the glow of fire out in the yard.

"Ashanti," he said in a low voice.

"Deh yah, King Man," murmured Wire's guard.

"Mek some tea," said Wire.

He got out of bed and went outside, crossing to the far corner of the yard and gazing up into the sky as he peed into the dust. For the first time since the ambush he had time to remember his two closest friends who had been killed in the blinding light. He felt lonely, in need of counsel.

"You hear Zack tune on radio?" asked Wire.

"Three time it play since night," said one of the men by the fire.

"We hear your name in deh: 'Wire sniper fire'," said another.

All day long the radio had been at Wire's side, a constant inspiration to him as it broadcast news of the spreading peace and acknowledged that he was the man behind it. The deejays had promoted him from a kid on the run into a household name, and he noticed that others approached him differently as his fame grew. They became increasingly reticent about interrupting him at any time, and they jumped when he called, in a manner that Mark Bernard took for granted but that Wire had never before experienced. He had started the week as an unranked ragamuffin street fighter, and he had ended it as the commander in chief of a force in national affairs. He didn't feel much different ... his surroundings were no more luxurious.

His headquarters were in a yard, deep in the slums, with three approaches and three guards. The guards watched for the enemy and Wire watched them, and he could tell by their attitudes, even when they were silent and standing still, that they were conscious of working personally for the boss. What had started out as a nightmare of oblivion had turned into a dream of fame beyond his wildest imaginings.

Zack and Michele had helped him a whole lot with the radio connection, it was like magic how the deejays had attracted help for the Peace Movement by making him famous, but Wire knew that all the fame in the world wouldn't help him if Red Roy and Biga Mitchell got together to wipe him out, and pressure was building for a decision from him in any case. Most of the Rasta youth that were flocking to Wire couldn't go back to the zones they'd fled, they were looking for somewhere new to go, and so was Wire. The sections of the slum that were won over by the Peace Movement could give cover for a time, but Wire was looking for a new base of operations entirely ... the question was where?

Until he found his new base his people would either have to hide or concentrate on promoting the Peace Movement further, ostentatiously crossing former boundaries, preaching peace and preparing for war only if it was brought to them, waiting for the time when they had a place of their own to defend.

As he fixed his trousers and turned towards the fire on the other side of the yard, Wire decided he wouldn't fight to control the slums; he would set up his new base somewhere else, letting the old turf wither and die. When politicians lost the youth they would not only lose street fighters with guns and ammunition, they would also lose the cash out of the ganja trade, which was the source of all disposable funds in the ghetto areas they controlled—apart from the pay bills and kickbacks from the construction projects in slum clearance. Ganja money was the condensed milk in the coffee, the cheese in the bun, the coin for the juke box; Biga and Red Roy wouldn't be able to fill the void left by the cash-ebb when the Rasta youth left their camps, and they'd have to call for more money from those who depended on them to stay in power, or they would gradually crash.

Wire crossed to the fire to drink his tea.

"I want two a yu fe come wid me," he said to his guards, "de other two go ahead fe Bertie, an tell him I am coming. One a yu come back an tell me if everything irie. Yu will find me by Rufus."

Rufus was key.

His was the communications centre.

"Lay low," went out the word.

All that next day both Biga and Red Roy also lay low, assessing their positions, trying to decide if they should unite to wipe out the mutiny of the youth, trying to decide if the threat posed by Wire and the Peace Movement was greater to them than the threat they posed to each other. One would decide one way, the other another way, but all during the daylight hours they remained undecided, both skirting a meeting.

Eventually, around nightfall, Biga sent a message to Red Roy. He had decided that they should get together and make a plan.

Biga felt it wasn't too late to save the situation. Their personal strongholds were still intact; the Peace Movement had not spread to every zone, there were still many who had heard what was happening elsewhere but who didn't dare to institute change in their immediate vicinity—yet for them the wild infectious fervour for peace was coming closer all the time as, into the fourth night, the crowds chanting for change kept growing. Biga's message to Red Roy was that if they didn't move fast, they'd soon find out that Wire's forces were stronger than both of theirs combined. They had to plan and act together now, later they could get back to fighting; but if they were rendered impotent by Wire they would have nothing to fight each other for.

Biga made it plain that he saw the meeting as a last chance for cooperation.

Red Roy saw in Biga's invitation an opportunity of a different kind. He wasn't as much worried by the Peace Movement as was Biga. He agreed that for a while the political system would be discredited, for a while everybody would have to cool it under the threat of Mark Bernard's guns; but suppose Mark Bernard's guns could be used to the political advantage of Red Roy? Suppose the army could be induced to wipe out Biga Mitchell for him? Then when, sooner or later, the politicians took over from the military again in the ghettos, when the people realised that a Peace Movement wouldn't put food in their bellies and Wire had been discredited, then Red Roy would emerge as the only surviving slum warlord; he'd have the exclusive franchise on violence in the whole area. Accordingly, Red Roy sent a message to Biga Mitchell agreeing to meet with him early the next day.

Biga didn't trust Red Roy and he took the precaution of alerting ten of his best fighters to meet him at the rendezvous. The meeting was set for seven-thirty the next morning when the streets would be full with crowds going to work, and road blocks would be easier to slip through or around. Biga planned that, just before Red Roy and his men were due to arrive, he would set up his ten bodyguards to be prepared for anything that his rival might do. He didn't guess that when the next day dawned, it wouldn't be Red Roy and his men he'd have to deal with.

On the evening before Biga and Red Roy were due to meet, a shoemaker named Herman was carrying his young son Rupert home through the celebrations in the streets.

In that short time, when the people of the slums thought that because peace had been declared by the previously warring factions, the bloodshed would cease; before they realised that what they had thought of as trouble before was just a preliminary skirmish; in those few evenings of innocence, there was a mood of happiness in the streets which, in the words of Bob Marley coming from a kerbside jukebox, was like a *"natural mystic flowing through the air"*.

Although he wanted to celebrate the Peace Movement, Herman didn't tarry on his way home because he wanted to catch Burru's broadcast. Herman was a big Burru fan. From the first time he'd heard Burru on the radio, Herman felt that the wild man in the bush had a message for him, and he hadn't missed a programme since.

His woman had deserted him some time before, and he lived with the child in a tenement yard where ten other families shared three water taps and one toilet. In his little room he had a bed big enough for both the child and himself to sleep in comfortably, a two-burner stove, a Bible, and a radio. Materially he was prepared to live with even less if it meant that he could avoid violence, and he was overjoyed to think that the Peace Movement meant an end to random death on a scale that justified fear even in the innocent.

As luck would have it, Biga Mitchell had a girlfriend in the tenement yard where Herman and his son lived. Biga did not visit the girl frequently so nobody would think of looking for him there, and thus he chose it not only as the place where he would spend the night, but also as the rendezvous for his meeting with Red Roy first thing the following day.

A small Bell helicopter flown by Mark, lifted off from the car park by the Central Bank and rose above the cluster of modern high-rise buildings to swirl in a big arc across the sky above the city.

Mark had often asked Winston to accompany him on his early morning flights and Winston had always been reluctant to take the time off to go, but now in the air he couldn't imagine why he had refused so many invitations, and he could easily see why helicopter travel was so addictive to rulers almost everywhere.

As the helicopter flew low across the city, Winston was amazed at the detail with which he could see what was going on underneath him; every backyard, every gully, every detail was revealed. As they rose higher to see the whole city laid out below, Winston had a panoramic sense of the problems that faced him as a planner. To the north and east the city was hemmed in by the mountain range. To the west expansion was blocked by cane fields that stretched for thousands of acres to a big sugar central whose smoking chimneys could be seen from the helicopter fifteen miles away. The city's southern limit was set by the harbour. To the southwest, however, there was a vast tract of scrubland which without water was semi-desert, but with water piped into this area had started to sprout subdivisions of pre-fabricated houses that already numbered five thousand units.

The helicopter crossed the harbour flying parallel to the causeway which had been constructed by the same people who had financed the high-rise buildings in the waterfront development. For the areas in which the subdivisions were spreading, the same group had dredged landfill, put in the roads, constructed the houses, found the mortgage financing, established the insurance companies, and negotiated with the labour unions and public utilities. They built supermarket plazas, and either manufactured or imported everything that filled them: cars, clothes, processed food, kitchen appliances, TV sets, and stereo systems; everything that suburban dwellers everywhere in the world required was provided by the Kass Group of Companies.

Five brothers, the eldest of whom was Henry Kass, were starting out in life with very little when they recognised a pattern of development in Puerto Rico that seemed possible to duplicate throughout the Caribbean.

Henry was the politician. Another brother ran the accounting and financial side. A third was an engineer. Yet another brother was in charge of merchandising, which was excellent because the brothers were so highly motivated themselves that energy rubbed off on everything they handled.

The brothers had all been to college in the States in the fifties and sixties, and their success had been the fulfilment of an American dream that was being emulated by people like them everywhere. Hard work and attention to detail had put them where they were: at the centre of the plan that formed the basis for all major urban development on the island, no matter which government was in power. And because of their continuity they had become the group that overseas businessmen felt they could rely on no matter what was going on politically.

Winston had liked the brothers, up to the point where they had divergent ambitions. They were even related to him by marriage through Michele's brother, Eddie, but on the mining issue Henry Kass had realised that Winston posed a serious threat to his control of the planning process, and Winston knew that he had to take very seriously the threat posed by Henry Kass as an enemy.

The Kass's were powerful because they represented the position of major investors worldwide. The formula for the type of development they had become experts in was the standard one accepted by all North American and European banks, insurance companies, and other financial institutions. Not only could their ideas raise financing relatively easily; any other kind of development was difficult if not impossible to finance at all. Every financial institution lending money to developing countries already had so much invested in similar systems that it was unthinkable to them that anybody would seriously challenge their concept of development, but, as he flew along, Winston was trying to add up the cost of the crash he saw coming to the owners of the thousands of little concrete boxes laid out below.

In the age of the pocket calculator, the lower middle class had mortgaged itself with a fine precision for the next twenty years to pay for a life-style that already they could no longer afford because the price of oil was making all plans drawn up before 1973 increasingly impractical. But who would be the first to admit that the system they had all invested in wouldn't work? Because if it didn't work there was no alternative plan for living where these people found themselves ...

Refrigerators that could run only on electricity had to be filled with frozen food from supermarkets that could only be reached by air. The promise had been that in the suburbs these would be basics, not luxuries, but now there was little choice between having everything and having nothing but grief, because while the Kass's had the seventies formula for success down cold, it *was* a formula that they followed, there was no original thinking anywhere to be found.

The helicopter circled closer to look at things of interest to Winston. He was calculating problems with sewage, garbage, roads breaking up, playgrounds without grass, pedestrians having to walk miles in dust past growing traffic jams ... From the helicopter Winston could see how far away the next bus was, but those waiting could only guess.

Winston motioned to Mark and the helicopter passed on over the houses already built, out over the dust bowls where they were currently building, and beyond that towards the land around

Burru's beach which was already encircled by half finished roads.

As the helicopter passed over and out beyond the fishermen's shacks, Winston saw something by the end of the water pipe that had come in with the roads which made him sit up as though he had seen a vision: there was a patch of green vegetable garden in the unlimited expanse of brown. With water, people could support themselves on this land! There was lots of water in the mountains. If it was brought to the plain, the city could be absorbed into a green belt of small farmers, each family self-supporting and selling food back into the city. It was viable, it was practical, and it was the alternative to an endless urban sprawl stretching out forever in poverty and dust.

Winston was just asking Mark to circle for a closer look when news came over the radio that sniper fire had broken out in the slums.

Mark immediately swung the helicopter up and towards the city, calling instructions into Headquarters as he travelled full speed towards the trouble spot.

Biga Mitchell and ten of his gunmen had been trapped by the army in the tenement yard where Herman lived with his child. Instead of going into the meeting with Biga, Red Roy had called the army and told his contact there where to find his enemy. Instead of cooperation, Red Roy had decided on extermination, and the rendezvous that Biga found himself trapped into was with three armoured cars and at least a hundred soldiers who had surrounded the entire block of the building he was in.

By the time Mark and Winston were hovering over Herman's yard, two large helicopter gunships were approaching fast from the direction of the army camp.

Suddenly a sniper appeared in a window-frame and took aim at the helicopter before a volley of shots from the soldiers on the ground drove him back into the room where he was hiding.

Winston was scared. He had never planned on being killed in a situation as arbitrary and ridiculous as this, but he looked over at Mark and took some comfort from the fact that his chances of survival were very much improved for being beside his brother in the fight.

It was as though Mark was genuinely delighted to find others who would join him in a round of the sport that he really loved best of all, and getting hit was not his preoccupation; he was fully absorbed in planning a strike that would demonstrate the precision and overwhelming fire power he could employ against the rebels. Watching him, Winston realised that it was moments like these that Mark lived for.

"Alpha One to Bravo One, over," called Mark into his helmet intercom.

"Reading you, Alpha One, over!" replied the major who was in command of the troops on the ground.

"Test your loudspeakers," said Mark.

"Roger," said Bravo One, "over and out."

The loudspeaker could be heard above the noise of the helicopter: "One, two, three, testing..."

Mark circled the block to check the army positions.

"Alpha One to Bravo One," the General called again.

"Reading you, Alpha One."

"Announce the evacuation of the building. As the people come out each one must be searched. Be prepared for a rebel effort to hold them as hostages. Prepare to give covering fire. Confirm that informers are in place to identify rebels. Over."

"Informers affirmative."

"Make the announcement," said Mark, "over and out."

As the major called out the message for evacuation over the loudspeaker, Mark positioned the helicopter gunships and warned them to be alert for sniper fire from the room on the top floor of the building that overlooked the open courtyard.

"Confirm identification of the room as the one with the zinc patch on the western slope of roof," said Mark.

"Affirmative," replied both helicopter captains.

As they heard the announcement that they had to leave the building, the tenants were torn between the terror of staying and the fear of losing all their possessions if they went; and their confusion was increased dramatically when the army officer switched off his loud speaker and Biga Mitchell screamed out *his* message that the people inside the building should stay where they were.

"Dem a go kill we!" screamed a woman in hysterics. "Dem a go use we fe shield!"

"If you leave the building they will burn it down," shouted Biga Mitchell.

"Dem a go burn we alive!" screamed the woman, her voice rising above the others that cried out in fear.

Suddenly a man burst out across the courtyard, dodging as he went. A shot splintered a wooden cart that he had dodged behind, and as the man flung himself forward, his arm was torn open by a wooden splinter five inches long.

"The bastards!" said Mark, and as he spoke Winston heard the guns from the helicopters pour bullets into the windows and along the balcony of the room where the rebels were hiding.

A fire had started on the ground floor and smoke was pouring out of a window into the street. The entire building was made of wood. It could go up in flames within ten minutes. If the tenants were not cleared out now, the rebel gunmen would escape with the stampede of the innocents.

"Bravo One, come in, over."

"Reading you, Alpha One, over."

"Tell them this is their last chance to get out of the building alive."

"Roger, over."

"Put Barnes on the blower."

"Roger."

"Barnes, calling Alpha One," said Barnes from the ground.

"Do you have any grenades?" asked Mark.

"Affirmative," replied Barnes.

"Do you see that open lot on the northern side of the target building?" asked Mark.

"Affirmative," replied Barnes, "over and out."

Winston felt the machine dance in the air as Mark demanded response from it like a rider from a horse. The plastic bubble swung away from the building, and within eighty seconds was hovering over the vacant lot, its landing grid a few inches away from the ground. Barnes appeared out of the swirling dust kicked up by the rotor blades and handed a grenade to Mark who took it, thanked him, and lifted the helicopter off the ground again.

As the helicopter rose, Winston saw that the fire was spreading fast, with flames now flicking out through the smoke.

A fire engine came around the corner. Already the firemen were jumping down to connect the canvas hose that was rolling out from the top of the truck.

"Bravo One," called out Mark, "come in!"

"Bravo One, reading you, over."

"Stop the firemen from going into the building."

"Roger," said Alpha One, "over and out."

Mark's decision meant that the building and everything inside it would burn, but Mark felt he had no choice. If the firemen went in, the gunmen would escape in the general confusion, but if the innocents were to get out before the entire building went up in flames, the snipers would have to be killed immediately.

Mark had foreseen this moment when he called for the grenades. Now he called on the helicopter gunships to rip the zinc patch off the roof above the room where Biga Mitchell and the snipers were huddled by a window looking inwards to the middle of the yard, allowing them to shoot at any tenants who tried to make a break for it out into the street.

Within seconds the bullets from the helicopter machine guns had peeled off the zinc patch from the roof to leave a gaping hole.

Winston held his breath as Mark eased them towards the hole in the roof. He didn't hurry his movements as he pulled the pin from the grenade with his teeth and lobbed the small black bomb from the palm of his hand into the vicinity of Biga Mitchell's ankles with the grace and control of an athlete.

In the instant before the room was shattered by the explosion, it seemed to Biga as if his whole life had come and gone as one extended reflex action ... he felt that if he had had time to make even one idea work out right, everything else would have fallen into place, but Biga had been on the run ever since he could remember; always the rivalry with Red Roy had sapped his strength for anything better, always the fact that Red Roy would kill him if he could had dominated his thoughts night and day since he was fifteen years old; that is all that he ever had to remember, and the only time he forgot—it cost him his life.

"Alpha One to Bravo One," called Mark, "come in."

"Nice one, sir," shouted Bravo One.

Mark was delighted with the reaction but ignored it.

"Alpha One to Bravo One," he repeated.

"I am reading you, sir."

"Send in the fire engines now," said Mark.

"Roger, over and out," said Bravo One.

Mark knew that it was now too late to save the building, but in a sense that was a good thing. It would demonstrate to the entire city the folly of harbouring gunmen.

From the helicopter, Winston and Mark watched as one last gunman, trapped between the flames and the soldiers, tried to shoot his way out. He didn't make it. He lay crippled on the ground in the centre of the courtyard as the soldiers closed in to kick him in the testicles and shoot him in the head.

Winston felt nauseous, not only with revulsion and the aftermath of fear, but also with shock at the realisation that, until ten minutes before, he had not known his brother's true ferocity.

"Alpha One to Bravo One," called Mark.

"Reading you, Alpha One."

"Leave ten men at each check-point to finish the search and get everybody else back to camp. I'll see you at eleven hundred in my office. Well done! Over."

"Thank you, sir!" said the officer.

"Over and out," said Mark.

Mark looked exhilarated. The two helicopter gunships were already specks on the horizon as they headed back to camp.

"How about some breakfast?" Mark asked Winston.

"No, thanks," said Winston, "just drop me back at the office. I have a lot of work to do."

Chapter Fifteen

⁓⁓⁓⁓

By the time the firemen started to fight the blaze, they were no longer merely trying to save the one building where Herman lived, they were making an attempt to limit the spread of the fire from engulfing the entire block.

Hundreds of refugees from all the buildings threatened by the fire had started to pile the possessions they'd been able to save in the surrounding streets. The scramble to hold onto what they could was frantic, but those not caught up in the frenzy seemed stunned, moving in a daze.

Herman held his son and looked about. Something was different about him. He felt higher than he had ever been in his life. He had seen evil like a sign that he had been waiting for, and now he was going to leave it behind him. He was joyous to be on his way. He was ready to take the plunge of faith that would put his life and that of his son in the hands of God, not men. The only possessions he had bothered to snatch from the fire were his Bible and his radio/tape-player.

Herman had recorded Burru's sermons since the first broadcast.

"...an wat is Babylon?" Burru had once asked over the airwaves, "Babylon is man who mek rule like dem a God. Dem waan tell yu wha fe eat, wha fe smoke, wha fe drink, 'ow fe tink ... an a who gi dem dat autarity?"

Burru's voice had come to Herman like the greatest comfort he had ever had in life, after the love he felt for his son. Burru said that if you lived *ital*, God would provide—and Burru was

172

only twenty miles away. Herman would walk to him and beg him to show him how a man could live by following that plan.

He loaded his tape-player with a recording of Burru's voice, turned the volume up as loud as he could, and started to move away from the destruction he was determined to leave behind.

The joy in Herman's progress attracted followers. Many put their belongings on anything that could move and started pushing, and by the time he reached the outskirts of the city Herman was being followed by a line of at least a hundred refugees.

On the causeway across the harbour they stretched out over the length of a quarter-mile. There was almost a carnival atmosphere among them, an irrational gaiety; some sections of the crowd were singing, some were praying ... all were buying patties and snow cones from the Honda hustlers who rode up and down the line selling food in exchange for money and goods off the pushcarts.

Michele, to her horror, discovered that the crowd was headed to Burru's beach when a reporter, who had passed the line of refugees on his way in from the suburbs, got to the TV station and relayed the news to her.

Michele realised right away that she would have to help Burru. She called Eddie, told him he had to come with her immediately, and left for the casino to pick him up. As they drove out to the beach, Michele explained the position. She felt responsible. Had it not been for her these people would not even have known of Burru's existence; now they would expect him to work miracles.

Michele was the only one whom Eddie would have even

considered helping with such a problem, but there was a reason why Eddie would do anything for Michele.

When he was five years old and Michele was just an infant, they had been orphaned. An aunt and uncle in Beirut had taken them in ... Eddie was seven when, one day, he and his little cousins dared to touch his uncle's gun. They had always known its hiding place under the bed, but this was the first chance they had ever had to see it because it had been taken out for cleaning when Eddie's uncle had been called away for several hours. For the first time, the little boys saw the gleaming dark blue-black steel of the revolver barrel, glistening with the thin layer of scented oil which combined with the thick leather of the holster to give off a smell which was subtle but precise in Eddie's memory forever after.

Seeing bullets on the table and thinking that the gun was empty, the children had started clicking the trigger in a game of 'beg-you-don't-kill-me'. With each click they thought that the gun was safer, but in fact just as his little cousin was begging Eddie to spare his life, the forgotten bullet reached the barrel, and Eddie blew the child's brains out all over the family living room.

In an instant Eddie became a devil in the eyes of those who had previously loved him. He was never again to see his aunt without tears in her eyes, and he himself cried for three days. But when he saw that not all the sorrow in the soul of a seven-year-old boy could kindle a flicker of affection—he stopped crying, and he never cried again.

While he waited to be put on the ship to the Caribbean, Eddie spent long hours alone sitting besides the crib of his baby sister. She was the only one who loved him still, who would laugh and joke with him; hers was the only warmth in a world gone cold and hard beyond belief, and Eddie's gratitude and love for her had been constant ever since.

Even for Michele, however, he didn't see how he was going to help these people. Where would it end if he made himself responsible for them? By God, he'd have a town of hungry mouths to feed!

Eddie had planned to leave Burru's Beach as soon as possible after sparing Michele the pain of announcing the disaster, but he lingered and he got caught ... the children got him. When he saw the incomprehension of calamity in their eyes, Eddie was carried back to his own childhood for the first time in his adult life. As emotion crept up and engulfed him, he knew he would either have to help those he now pitied, or weep for the misfortunes in his own life that their suffering reminded him of. Eddie left the crowd and walked alone out on to a cliff of limestone rock surrounded by surf.

When he was Rupert's age, sitting beside his sister's crib, waiting for the ship that would take him to exile in the Caribbean, there had been one other saving grace for the little boy besides Michele. Five times daily the call had come to him over the rooftops: "... God is great ... God is merciful ... God forgives ..." called out the voice of the messenger of God ... "God forgives ..." the child was grateful for the message, and at that tender age he gave himself over to meditation when he heard it, and, certain that he was loved, Eddie felt so strongly he could count on his luck that his audacity in gambling made him a millionaire while still in his twenties.

As he looked out to sea, Eddie's mind cleared. He knew that the refugees from the city could only be saved by the greatest good fortune on the next roll of dice in a game that was growing into something bigger than any game ever played in the casino. This time Eddie would be gambling with more than money; he would be gambling with life and death, but he sensed that he had no choice. He sensed that the time had come when he alone could not keep winning, that he would have to share the wealth if his blessings were to continue; yet he also realised that if he pulled off even a small percentage of this coming game it would be greater than the sum of all his winnings to date. This was going to be the type of gamble where he might even have to close the casino and mortgage the luck he called in on a hundred games of chance, for one big bet.

Once Eddie had decided that he could trust Burru, the situation wasn't difficult to deal with.

For a hundred dollars a week, the man at the end of the water main would let them have as much water as they wanted. There was no metering system in yet anyway. Burru said he would supervise clearing the land and planting. The cost of planting was no big thing, a hundred machetes and files, sixty hoes, twenty forks and pick-axes, a couple thousand dollars for tools—Eddie could get up to thirty per cent discount. There was lots of wood and stone around the area for use as building materials. Zinc and concrete for each hut would come to about two hundred dollars each. Twenty thousand dollars would cover building thirty huts. It would cost another twenty dollars a week per person for food and kerosene until the first crops started to come in in six months' time, that was another sixty thousand—Eddie calculated it would cost him up to a hundred thousand dollars to set up the community, but the potential earnings from the investment were enormous.

He'd be able to recoup his money from selling food in the city if the worst came to the worst, and if he handled the situation right, he could make money on every piece of cloth and item of hardware sold to the squatters for years to come.

If Burru's beach developed into a township, Eddie saw where he could make millions if he maintained control. The people there would not only be growing food, they would also be handling ganja, and Eddie would make sure it wasn't sold on the local market for a few dollars an ounce, he would sell it in Florida for real money.

It was a big gamble, but Eddie was a big gambler. Eddie figured that if he couldn't find a way to make a profit out of an entire town founded by his own money, he deserved to lose a hundred thousand.

By that evening, eight truckloads of supplies arrived: lamps, kerosene, cooking oil, rice, flour, and dried fish.

Michele, Burru, and Eddie, looked on as the people set themselves up for the night; some fetching water, some tacking up the first of the zinc sheets for cover, some making up cooking fires.

As darkness fell and Eddie watched dozens of little bonfires spread across the plain, he told Burru the scene reminded him of Bedouin camps on the edge of a desert in the Holy Land. He'd seen them as a child.

"Ten years ago when I flee Babylon, I flee alone," said Burru. "Now Babylon so bad is a multitude has to flee."

"Dreader and dreader, Bredda," said Herman, clutching his son Rupert to him, delighted to be out of town, delighted to be reasoning with Burru and Jahman and all those he'd been listening to and come to know on the radio.

Herman could not understand now what had taken him so long to leave the city.

"A man can live with nature the way a man live with woman," said Burru, "if a woman feel that a man love her, and understand her, and treat her with respect, she will give him everything for nothing. Even if he is an Eskimo living in snow, or an Arab living in the desert—Mother Nature would give him what him need to be comfortable, much less we living in this island. But if a woman feel man nuh love her, she charge him for everything him get, if him can get it at all. Now, man in de city, him ha' fe pay fe everything him get, if him even want to breathe clean air him ha fe pay for it; him paying more and more and getting less and less, till him feel now that if nature is a woman he is living with a whore. So him turn vile, and him decide to turn around and rape nature fe get what him want ... so ah dat him a do ... but Mother Nature going turn round and give him one rass claat lick fe teach him to behave himself." Burru had risen from his seat, his eyes blazing. "De Bible seh 'In one hour! In one hour, so great riches will come to naught!'. De Bible seh 'Alas, alas, great Babylon, in one hour thy judgement come, and the merchants of the world shall weep and mourn over her for no more buying of their merchandise anymore'."

"Atom boom," called out Jahman.

"Judgement!" shouted Jack.

"Look how God good," said Burru, "in Babylon if you borrow a dollar from a man, you ha' fe give him back one dollar and ten cents or one dollar and twenty cents as the case may be; God give you one seed that value less than one cent, and if you plant it and care fe it, it will give you back ten dollar, and a hundred seed."

"Zion!" called out Herman.

"God can afford to be that generous," said Eddie, "but as for me, I want my money back." He looked around at these people. It had taken so little to give them the first chance they'd ever had to gain something of their own. With water, their chances weren't bad. With herbs ...?

"I'll tell you one thing," said Eddie, "you'll never see a better gift from Jah than a good crop of sensi in the next six months."

Chapter Sixteen

∞∞∞

In the ghettos things were calm. With Biga gone, and Wire quiet, the entire slum section of the city was up for grabs, but Red Roy knew he couldn't grab it yet. He knew that Mark Bernard was watching for any flicker of trouble, and he had already seen him in action against Biga ...

In his penthouse, Winston had attained his fantasy of uninterr-upted concentration to an unexpected degree. For weeks he had been able to alternate sleep with work as he examined the feasibility of one plan after another: in agriculture, in tourism, in international banking ... but most of all, Winston spent his time pressing the tax legislation through parliament. Kass had put every possible delaying tactic in the way, but finally after a last push on Percy, the new mining tax was law.

Winston had got the final confirmation that afternoon, and he'd decided that there was cause for a celebration.

He switched off all the computers and stopped the flow of notes, and decided to head out into the town and enjoy himself; then he realised that although he wanted to call somebody, there was nobody he really wanted to call.

Since leaving Michele, he had made no new liaison, no one he could talk to, no one he could rest with. Suddenly a wave of loneliness swept over him.

Winston walked out onto the terrace and around the trampoline, but he wasn't in a light enough mood to use it; he returned to the penthouse and put on some music, but that didn't change his mood either ... Michele ... he mustn't let this mood infect his mind with thoughts of her!

The hotel had been built beside the Central Bank in an attempt to revive not only the business life of the waterfront, but also to turn the immediate surroundings into a fashionable high-rise residential area. The idea had not caught on. The hotel was still in the middle of a slum that had only become progressively uglier and more violent. So, as office equipment spent the night in air conditioned luxury, and malnourished, mosquito bitten children slept in the surrounding collapsing ramshackle, and the perception of those who lived elsewhere was that crossing the five miles of ill-lit ghetto that lay between them and the hotel after dark was an invitation to hijack and robbery—the result was that the hotel was virtually empty when the sun went down.

Winston didn't mind the area at all, quite the contrary, the waterfront section of the city had always provided excitement, especially after dark.

On the way to the seafront hotel as a child, his chauffeur-driven Buick had more than once prowled down streets that were filled with signs for bars, and, on the steps leading up to them, Winston had been mesmerized to see painted women, in outrageous clothes, with not the slightest shame for what they were. Between the ages of ten and sixteen, Winston daydreamed of nothing more often than his first visit to those streets when he could get to know those girls *much* better.

As it happened, he was part of a trio that shared the adventure—the other two teenage intrepids being Eddie Azani and Max DeMalaga.

Always in a hurry, bored by formalities, none of them was inclined to beg respectable rich girls for a hint of what they knew they could experience in the flesh. While Mark and Percy were heading off to teenage parties to dance, Winston and Eddie were always off in the other direction, a route that had no stop signs or prescribed conventions. While Mark had played football, Winston had travelled the waterfront, looking at the girls who only came out when the American fleet was in: half-Chinese girls, half-Indian girls, black girls from the country; there were even some girls who were rumoured to work in the banks when the ships were not in town; sometimes there were Latin dancers from Santo Domingo; women old and young, fat and slim, shy and brazen ... the boys made contact when ships were in port and followed up later. Winston didn't learn to pet to Presley, he learned to fuck to rhythm and blues; and because neither he, nor Eddie, nor DeMalaga wanted to pay all the time, they made a serious study of what gave most pleasure to women in bed. Afterwards they compared notes, and scored when they gave so much pleasure that all they were charged for was drinks and the room.

DeMalaga gave up hookers when he fell in love with Michele ten years before she and Winston ever met, but Eddie had never really given them up at all, and in those first few weeks of desperate disorientation after he had left Michele, Winston took great comfort in the thought that one phone call to Eddie would have a sexy girl en route faster than an order for Chinese takeout. Still, Winston had not returned to his sexual origins although they had pleasant memories for him. When he met Michele, it seemed to Winston as though he had been playing scales sexually and now here was the real music ... eyes not thighs became the focal point, and he'd never shifted back.

Winston never dreamed he'd ever find himself in such a situation again, for years he'd thought of no woman other than Michele, but this was where she'd put him; now for his sexual survival he'd have to revert to a time when sex was part of that vast impersonal yearning so universal that the touch of flesh from a stranger was as close as one could get to personal feelings of any kind; a need so desperate that since time immemorial, millions had gratefully suspended reality long enough to accept the pathetic illusion ... *Distraction! Disruption! Confusion! Chaos! Madness! Michele!*

He went and had a shower and dressed to go out without having any idea where he would go, and then he remembered an invitation to a diplomatic party that he'd seen in the mail the day before. Every week there were invitations to three or four diplomatic parties, but he had not gone to one since his return to the island. When he was with Michele he'd never bothered, he was bored by the cocktail circuit, but now, suddenly, any party seemed like a gift from the Goddess of Social Affairs, whoever she was in mythology.

As Winston walked out of the hotel and across the car park, he thought of how, when he was growing up, the business section of the city had been filled with men of independent means, men who took hundreds of individual decisions in dozens of different offices scattered around town. Now those offices were filled with accountants and lawyers, and they worked for people who took decisions only in a committee. In those five monolithic buildings that lined the waterfront there were barely five men with the means for making independent decisions; so decisions were taken very slowly and everybody outside those sealed-off towers just had to wait.

Because Winston was still Governor of the Central Bank and controller of all foreign exchange in the formal economy, he was the man whose decisions most of them were waiting for.

As the car rose from the residential foothills, and the presence of the city was reduced to a carpet of lights on the plain in the distance, the idea of the cocktail circuit as a sexual cornucopia grew in appeal for Winston. Many of those reticent teenaged middle-class virgins of his youth now promised the ardour and experience of idle middle-aged women who were still in excellent shape.

The embassy was a huge house set in a large expanse of landscaped lawns. Across the lawns, lantern-lit pathways led towards the buffet and bar set up beside the pool.

Winston felt a strong sense of interest greet his entrance to the party. Lending money was the chief work of the ambassadors from the rich nations, and as governor of the Central Bank, Winston was the man who officially did the borrowing and knew better than everybody else where the economy that he supposedly controlled fitted into the aid game.

In the past five years, lending had become the cornerstone of foreign policy for the industrial nations, linked with a corporate and political plan that made Winston think twice about much of the money offered by these various proconsuls. Theirs was a dangerous game to play, both from the point of view of the recipients and the lenders: aid was a high stakes business.

Zaire had already gone bankrupt, so had Peru. The Americans had narrowly averted financial disaster in Chile, but with a scenario that wouldn't play well again. Times were tense. Nobody wanted to see money go down the drain in the Caribbean, but the ambassadors knew that if they didn't implement loan programmes, their careers would suffer because the unions and workers in the US and Europe were raising hell with their politicians about unemployment, and in the seventies there were still enough workers as opposed to robots to make themselves heard.

To keep production growing for as long as possible while they themselves switched to next generation technology, the industrial-ised countries lent money to those who would buy obsolete equipment in the tropics. By the time the northern manufacturers had their new equipment in place, the tropical competitors would have their investment in machines that couldn't compete.

It was a double blow. First lose your cash, then lose your recovery.

Winston was greeted by his host, then spoke briefly with the American ambassador, the Cuban ambassador, the Russian, the German, the French. But he had not come to the party to talk business, and as he walked around the floodlit pool, he gradually made his way towards a blonde woman in her forties who he had noticed was looking at him. It was only when he was ten feet away from her and heard her voice that he realised he not only knew her, but that he had once known her very well.

She was an Aussie, a journalist, the old girlfriend of an ex-friend of Winston's from university days.

"Jill?" asked Winston.

"You didn't recognise me, did you?" she said.

"Well, my God, it's been twenty years. How's Hans?"

"He's in Chile. I haven't seen him in ages."

"What's he doing in Chile?"

"Chile is Hans's dream come true, he can serialise and computerise night and day and they'll still buy more controls."

"Hans was always thorough."

"He's more than thorough: he's obsessed; he's addicted to knowing everybody's business. The political thing is just an excuse. Any excuse would do."

It was an old argument. Both of them remembered the quarrel when Winston broke with his friend over the eventual purpose of the computer systems they were programming. Winston felt that the system should be used to spread information from the few to the many, Hans felt that inevitably a central computer system would be used for control of the many by the few.

At university it had been an academic argument, but when they started to build their careers they went in opposite directions.

"What brings you to the island?" asked Winston.

"Doing a story," said the journalist. "I was going to call you tomorrow. I hear that you've got Percy under control and that you're the real power in the land."

"Oh really!" said Winston. "Is there any evidence for this theory?"

"The mining tax," said Jill.

"It was overdue." said Winston.

He was glad to see her, and he felt that he'd have a better time with her alone than at the party, because although the assembled company claimed to represent every ideology in the political spectrum, in fact the attitudes of all those assembled was exactly the same; whatever they claimed to represent politically the central concern of their lives was staked in middle-class concerns—but Winston wasn't interested in air conditioning and imported food, he was interested in seeing the island build on what was there, he was interested in seeing something new, and all these people were experts in the existing system.

"Have you had dinner?" Winston asked Jill.

"No," she said.

"Let's go," said Winston.

Over dinner they discussed the 'state of the world', but more and more he wanted to forget that; tonight he wanted to float in a sea of the senses ...

"All those people there tonight ..." Jill was more drunk than Winston had realised; she didn't lower her voice significantly as she leaned in to continue "... third eleven, darling, none of *them* have the guts to try something new. You were always first eleven when I knew you, definitely ..."

She looked at him with the momentary penetration of a drunken stare.

"If you came back to a place as small as this you must have a plan to take over, if you haven't already done so." She searched his face for a flicker of conspiracy, but Winston had decided to back off. "The whole world seems to have gone third eleven, somehow," she said. "I've done nothing but travel for the last ten years looking for even one place where they've got it right ... nothing fancy, just the basics. I've found no one I can believe in. No one I can conceivably write up as a hero. In the whole world, not one! They're all eaten up by megalomania within five years ... all the ones in power that I know are so mesmerized by their own dicks they can't get it together to answer the phone."

Winston thought of Percy and laughed.

He drove her back to the hotel where she was also staying and she accepted his invitation to come up for a nightcap. Winston hoped that the switch from mind to body would come with the last drink, but she never did overcome her professional fascination with his political opportunities, and as the moment of decision approached Winston realised he wasn't really in the mood for making love.

"Can't *anybody see* that it's more fun to get it right?" said Jill. "What could be more exciting than running an entire country and getting it right? Is fucking everything up just to steal a couple million dollars more fun than that?" She put her hand out and touched the side of Winston's neck. "You're not into stealing money ... you could get it right."

It should have been a turn on to have her tell him how great he was, but tonight he wasn't seeking affirmation of his importance, tonight he was seeking an escape, a celebration, he wanted a woman who didn't care what else was going on in the world because she was a world in herself, a world of pleasure, of perfume, of movement silken in its ease; rhythms that took him deeper and deeper into sublime relaxation ... tonight he wanted Michele.

When he had seen his old friend Jill to her door, Winston walked several laps of the terrace before going to sleep. As he circled the penthouse to the north, he thought about the rich in the suburbs; as he looked out to the west, he thought about the poor. Now that he had the mining tax, he would put into effect the plan that would make the island a better place for both. He, Winston, would do it. But tonight he didn't want to be a hero in macro-management, tonight he wanted the other side of his soul.

Chapter Seventeen

⚬⚬⚬

When day broke on the first morning after the crowd came to Burru's beach, Herman and his son Rupert got up from where they were sleeping and went off to relieve themselves. In spite of the fact that thirty or forty others were doing the same thing at the same time there was no feeling of intrusion on privacy; there were thousands of scrub bushes to squat behind, and it was an easy matter to cover shit with sand so there was no danger of anybody else sticking their toe into it.

In the city this part of the day provided an experience in crowd living at its worst. The wait was always urgent, particularly for Rupert; the stench was always horrible, and the act was always rushed. By the time that Herman and Rupert came back out of the bush, relieved and ready for breakfast, they knew that in at least one respect this new way of life was an improvement on what they had left behind.

On that first day, the crowd at Burru's beach cleared land and used the trees that were stout enough as uprights for the framing of shelters that were springing up all through the bush. Once the uprights were in place, everybody cast about for the smaller tree trunks and larger branches that would form cross-beams and framework for the roofing; as this wood was cut and hauled, the bush melted away to reveal landscapes. Views started to form. What was previously a flat wall of bush and cacti had started to open up like a vast stage on which something new could be seen every ten minutes.

By nightfall there were twenty sets of uprights on a piece of land the size of ten football fields. Now most of the huts had cross-beams already nailed into place, framing outlines for the zinc roofing that would be put in place the next day.

On the second day, some of the people went on with building; some with clearing bush.

Already small businesses were starting to form as some took in washing and others cooked food to sell. The sound of music was everywhere. The bush had not been thinned out so drastically that there was no shade to sit under between bouts of work. Men didn't labour under the sun in lines like convicts in a chain gang; each man worked on the land around his shelter, and each man worked at his own pace.

Burru never stopped circling round and round. He did not speak to groups, but instead dealt with single individuals. He didn't give general advice, but solved specific problems. Years before he had had to deal with the hindrances that he saw others coping with all around him now, and with the knowledge that he could get cash from Eddie to solve problems that could be solved no other way, Burru got high on the speed with which plans were making progress.

Many men who had planned to work before eleven and after three so that they wouldn't labour in the heat of the sun found that eleven came and went and they didn't stop working. They enjoyed the sweat because when you had sweated for hundreds of years and got nothing for it—to sweat clearing land that you intended to keep for yourself was a pleasure. It was exercise for the brain as well, and many tried to guess how much they would have had already if they had laboured for themselves from long ago.

When cleared, the land looked flat and hot and ugly like a piece of grassless, overplayed playground in the city. Dust started to swirl around and at the end of the first week a depression settled over the camp; then the pick-axes and forks began to break the crust of the ground, and as the digging spread so did the water that trickled down trenches, shallowing out with each turn till the stream disappeared into the thirsty earth, the moisture making the colour of the soil richer, deeper.

Six days after the first seeds were sown, the first sprouts popped up and the weeding started. Herman learned from Burru what was to be weeded out and what was food, and he in turn taught his son. Herman and Rupert spent hours together, the child chatting away as they cleared the weeds.

One day, Rupert tried to count the yellow flowers on the pumpkin vine that Herman had shown him was a sign of pumpkins to come, and soon he reached a number beyond which he couldn't count.

"Is how much pumpkin a go sell, dadda?" the child asked Herman.

"A good-size pumpkin sell for four dollars in town."

"All dese-ya pumpkin going grow?"

"If Jah Jah willing," answered Herman, "if insect nuh tek dem or other disaster."

"Jah will mek dem grow," said Rupert, confidently.

"I count seventy flower on de vine dis mawning," said Herman. "Dat mean I coudda earn two 'undred and eighty dolla outta pumpkin alone, an it keep bearing. We coudda reap four hundred dolla outta dis one pumpkin vine alone before we 'ave to plant again."

For days Herman had been trying to do calculations for the vision of wealth that he saw growing around him, and Rupert could tell that his father was excited.

"In four weeks we will see calaloo," said Herman, "in six weeks, red peas; little after, tomato, cabbage, lettuce ..."

"Is plenty money dat, dadda," said the child, now infected by his father's excitement.

"Yu nuh hear 'bout money yet, Prince Boy," said Herman. "How much herbs seed we plant?"

"We plant all over."

"How much will grow?"

"A hundred," said Rupert, and Herman laughed.

"Say twenty grow," said Herman, "every leaf worth money. Anytime you want a hundred dollar you just go and pick it off."

They had a right to believe in miracles.

Just a few weeks before, Herman had carried Rupert in his arms out of a raging furnace of death. Man and child had taken a plunge of faith together that their forefathers had planned for generations. In the same moment both Herman and Rupert realised that their lives could change forever, and with that realisation came an emotion not stirred in their ancestral memory for over a hundred years.

Now Herman knew what it was to promise his child a future, and Rupert knew what it was to feel as a child does when he is so close to the success of his father that he looks into the future and sees no limits to what he feels he can do with his own life.

Every evening after working in the fields and before they started to cook the evening meal, Herman and Rupert would go along with many others to swim in the water-hole which had been formed where the water gushed out of the end of the main pipe that had been put in, along with the road, for servicing the planned development. Long before reaching the swimming hole, one could hear shrieks of children enjoying themselves; the water was deliciously cool after the dust and heat of the day. As their children learned to dive and swim, parents stopped regarding them as a source of anxiety as they had been in the city. A feeling for the fun of family life took hold under the cascade of water and seemed to spread with the kids as the current carried them away down the irrigation canal.

It was at the swimming hole that Herman met Eunice and fell in love. She was twenty; a decent, hard-working, quiet girl; good-natured, with beautiful, cool, smooth black skin, shining with muscle as she romped in the water.

"Hello," said Herman, when he realised that he had to talk to this girl.

"Good evening," said Eunice.

"Can I ask you a question, please?"

"I suppose so."

"Are you in love?"

Eunice was surprised. "No," she said.

"What," said Herman, "no boyfriend?"

"No."

"No baby father?"

"No."

"No husband?"

"No."

"Ah," said Herman, "so that's my chance."

"Why you asked me those questions?" asked Eunice.

"Because I know a nice girl like you: once she's involved with a guy, you don't stand no chance with her again. Honest woman, nuh true?"

Eunice said nothing, but she smiled and dived under the water. When she came up, Herman was still there.

"So, can I ask your name, please?"

"Eunice."

"And how do you spell that, please?"

"E-U-N-I-C-E," said Eunice, wondering what he was going to come up with next.

"Acardin to de spelling," said Herman, "I wouldn't pronounce your name dat way deh. I would say: *you nice*, eh?" Herman cocked his head to one side and smiled, and this time when she smiled back, a shot of pure happiness went through him ... swimming there in the canal at the end of a hardworking day, with the sun going down and a full moon rising ...

As the bitterness Herman felt about Rupert's mother eased and he started to think about women with love again, the shy smile that Eunice shared with him gradually moved to the centre of Herman's plan in life.

Soon Herman's prospects were bright enough for him to propose marriage with a sense of honour. Apart from the fact that he was reaching the point where he could not only feed his family but also sell food, his shoemaking business had never flagged. He had retrieved his tools and a small machine from his workplace in the city, and his business had grown rapidly. He was well-known at Burru's beach—he *had* led the original march to it—and his workplace was so popular that he added a store, brought in two apprentices, set up a small sound system for background music, and expanded into making goatskin bags and other fashion accessories. Soon, he started to invest in goats. He was building his wealth slowly; as he did so he felt like more and more of a star in the drama of his own life, and as that happened, Eunice gradually fell love with him, her love growing slowly to match the intensity of Herman's feelings for her.

On the night of their wedding, Michele and Eddie went out to the beach for the celebration. There was food and drinks for two hundred. There was constant music from the dance-sized speakers that Rufus had sent out from Soul Shack. Everybody was dressed up in a blaze of fashion. Michele had brought her camera, and she spent a good deal of the evening taking photographs of Herman and Eunice and Rupert: on the motorbike riding into the yard from the church, Eunice sitting side-saddle, Rupert with his feet over the handlebars; Herman and Eunice in a formal pose, Eunice visibly pregnant ... dozens of portraits were flashed off by Michele that evening, and everybody wore a smile.

As Burru's Beach grew, so did the traffic on the road from the city. On weekends motorcars crowded out to the new-found beach, and quite soon stalls sprang up serving fried fish and bammy and beer as yet another business attached itself to the growing overall action.

One Sunday the traffic to the beach brought with it an elderly senior civil servant from the Ministry of Public Works. He observed, to his amazement, that there were a lot of people out there using a lot of water, and he wondered where it came from. When he got back to the office on Monday morning, he was scandalized to find that the water was coming from the regular water supply for the city, which was already so low in the reservoirs that the city was enduring severe water rationing.

For the past five months water restrictions had been in force throughout the city. It was strictly forbidden to sprinkle lawns, wash motor cars, or keep flowers alive. Even before the prolonged drought, water restrictions had become an annual occurrence. The problem wasn't water; there was lots of it in the mountains. The problem wasn't money; water schemes were a favourite investment for Aid Institutions. The problem was that the investment required for the water schemes was constantly thwarted by conflicting advice from those who had a vested interest in supplying projects to the handful of mega-contractors competing for airports, dams, harbours, and everything else involving big money for infrastructure worldwide.

First the British had a plan. Then the American consultants found a flaw in it. Then the Americans were asked to submit their feasibility study, which the British in turn picked to pieces. While this was going on, the businessmen, who were developing the waterfront and the suburbs, brought in their own advisers who suggested that both the American and British plans were flawed—they offered an Israeli alternative.

Each plan took five years to research. The World Bank, faced with such conflicting alternatives, finally decided to send their own experts into the fray. Twenty years had gone by since the need for an expanded water supply to the city became obvious, and urgent, but still nothing had been done. Every time the government changed, so did the directorate of the Water Commission. The only thing they had in common was the fact that none of the political appointees had the technical expertise to make a decision one way or the other.

In the meantime the city was parched, and farmers across the island continued to plant and then watch as their crops shrivelled and died for want of water instead of thriving, as they should have done, on an island where water was abundant.

With water, the small farmer should at least have been able to feed and clothe his family, have a house, a bike, and a TV set, and send his kids to school. Without water, he might as well have been living in a previous century.

The bureaucrats in charge of water had not only failed to supply it when and where it was needed, they were arrogant as well, and while they were high up on Winston Bernard's hit list for reform, he was unable to do much about the department until he had the cash from the mining tax to force the changes through—until then their word was law.

These were the people who, in their collective wisdom, decided that they could no longer supply water to the community at Burru's Beach.

Next morning, by the time the first child with a big bucket on his head arrived at the canal, he found only mud where water had been.

Burru knew some wells in the area that provided enough water for cooking, but the wells were brackish from the drought.

There were no political strings that anybody could pull to save the people at Burru's Beach, because they formed no voting bloc in any constituency. Michele tried to reach Percy about them, but he was leaving for a trip abroad and wouldn't be back in time to save the situation.

Finally, one evening, Eddie drove out to tell the people there that he could not afford to truck water out to them any longer, and that they must be prepared to move if rain didn't come to save them.

The impact of the disappointment for the crowd that had gathered to hear the news was such that many started to wail as they wept. Within days the only promise of comfort they had ever known would turn to dust. For some, being without hope was so familiar a state of misery, that in an instant the promise that had sustained them since they had marched away from the fire was as distant as a dream.

After Eddie left them and darkness had fallen, Michele sat with Burru and Herman, and looked out to sea. There was a moon, and in the distance there was lightning. Rain had been hovering on the horizon for nearly two weeks. Nobody had noticed except Burru because until the morning when the water was cut off, nobody much cared if it rained or not, but Burru had watched the signs out of habit. He had no luck in the casino to mortgage as Eddie did, but he had his own kind of private deal with the Almighty. He felt that when he listened, God always sent him a message, and if he watched, God would always show him definite signs early enough to prepare for the verdict— whatever it might be.

As he sat silently looking out to sea, watching the flashes of lightning, there was something calm and fatalistic in Herman's mood as well. It was as though he was interested to know, once and for all, what fate had in store for him and those he loved.

Throughout the community, work had ceased. Some decided to wait for the rain that Burru had said was coming, but many had started to move; carrying everything that Eddie had bought for them as they went.

Although he felt that rain was coming, in the past Burru had seen it go by, day after day, five miles out to sea. He had even seen rain fall in the mountains and advance down to the city and stop two miles short of the parched land on which he stood, but he had also seen the rain come straight in from the sea, and after a long drought like this one he knew that steady rainfall could settle in and stay for days and weeks on end.

Eight days after the water cut-off, three days after the last water truck had made its delivery, Burru watched as a line of dark-grey rain approached from ten miles out to sea. It was laced with forked lightning which started at thirty thousand feet and crackled to the horizon, illuminating what seemed like a solid wall of water. The thunder rumbled out of it like the voice of God in a bad mood, warning that this time what he gave should not be wasted.

What is man that he has grown to ignore thunder? thought Burru.

"Tell them, Jah!" exclaimed Herman every time a clap of thunder echoed across the sky.

For the two hundred squatters whose happiness hung in the balance that night, the rolling of thunder and the flashing of lightning that slowly engulfed them came with the intensity of an enormous natural orgasm.

The first drops of rain were huge, but few and far between. Burru had seen relief come so close and still skirt the coast. Then came a sustained flurry of wind, and the first real squall. Flashes of lightning confirmed for eyes to see what ears could hear as the thunder moved nearer. One last tremendous thunderclap exploded directly overhead, and then the rain began to fall in torrents.

Eunice ran to find whatever she could to catch water. Rupert ran out into the rain to play. Suddenly both of them looked to see Herman, arms outstretched, spinning around and around in the

197

rain. He was striking poses and shouting "Nice one, snap me again, Jah!" every time the lightning set off a flashbulb in his mind.

The rain lasted for three months. By the time it ended, the reservoirs of the Water Commission were overflowing, restrictions were lifted, the right man was bribed by Eddie Azani to open the valve again, and water flowed unregulated to the next dry season.

Burru's Beach grew even faster than Eddie had anticipated. The food sent to the city had been sold at a time of rapidly rising prices, and the money earned had been spent immediately for buying more of everything: building materials, kitchenware, furniture, cloth ... all were supplied by merchants who paid Eddie an overall commission and gave him a volume discount as well.

It was the first shipment of ganja, however, which really provided a surge of cash big enough to expand his plans beyond anything previously imagined.

In the seventies, the ganja trade at the Caribbean end was largely an amateur enterprise in the sense that those engaged in it were not experienced in crime, crime was not their career. They were smuggling something they were convinced brought nothing but good vibes to their customers in the US, and the business was suffused not with menace, but rather with a gentleman's agreement type friendliness that lasted right up until the professional criminals took over.

In the late seventies, Eddie Azani was able to make three shipments a week via small twin-engine planes.

There were no Super Constellations turning back and forth across the tip of Florida, their huge umbrella-like antennas spread out above them, scanning for hundreds of miles anything that moved ... no, in those days if a pilot was prepared to fly a small plane for four hours into the Caribbean night to land on whatever landing strip the locals had been able to get together in the bush, to risk arrest by the local police, or risk someone spilling gasoline all over his plane just when someone else was lighting a match—if some ex-Vietnam danger junkie was prepared to risk all that, he had nothing to worry about on the US end.

When he got back to the States, he simply joined the small-plane traffic across the coast into one of the big cities, and then headed for the isolated landing strip of his choice. In those days nobody cared. Everybody was still minding their own business.

Barry Sedgwick was smuggling weed from the Caribbean into the US for several reasons. One, he didn't want to work a regular job as a pilot because they tested you for drugs all the time; two, the money was great; three, he loved the islands. He wanted to live there. He liked the people, especially the ones in the mountains like IZion and Ashanti: hacking strips out of pasture, blocking off stretches of highway for the crucial half-hour in the wee hours of moonlight in the middle of nowhere. He admired them for what they did and they admired him for his skill and daring.

Eddie Azani had found him through the grapevine, starting at the Miami end, where the best contact that Eddie had in the smugglers' community confirmed that the most reliable pilot he knew was Barry Sedgwick.

The pilot told Eddie Azani that he was already committed to IZion and Ashanti. They sold him good herb at a fair price and they were friends. But yes, he did agree that mountain strips were dangerous, that inevitably, sooner or later, there would be a crash.

Eddie Azani went into the mountains and found IZion. He made a deal with him. He, Eddie, would arrange flights, landings, gas, transport, payment for the herb to the farmers; all that IZion and Ashanti and their posse would have to do was concentrate on quality, and Eddie would do the rest. IZion agreed, it was a good deal for him. So here was Barry Sedgwick easing the Cessna twin over the central mountain range of the island, heading for the first landing in the Burru's Beach area, peering forward to see lights on the landing strip.

Eddie stood at the side of the new road that ran in a straight line through the swamp that separated Burru's Beach from the nearest town, watching the movement of his nine men around the two parked trucks—one carrying ganja the other carrying gasoline.

When he heard the drone of the small plane approaching, Eddie called out "light up". Burru lit his kerosene-soaked torch and called out "light up" to Herman, who lit his torch and called "light up" to the man next down the line. "Light up! Light up!" the cry ran down the runway, till the burning lamps stretched for several hundred yards. The glow from them lit the excited faces of Eddie Azani's smuggling team as Barry brought the Cessna in out of the darkness and dropped it smoothly onto the surface of the new road.

"Ay Ashanti, how yu deh brother?" said Sedgwick, simultaneously grasping the big Dread's shoulders with his two hands in greeting. "Hi IZion, Hi Eddie ..."

"What can we get for you?" asked Eddie. "You want a spliff, a drink, something to eat? You want a girl?"

"No thanks," said the pilot, "I'll just get a nap for fifteen minutes."

"You want some coffee when you wake?" asked Eddie.

"Yeah that's good," said the pilot as he stretched out on the back seat of Eddie's car, confident that IZion and Ashanti knew how to load the plane.

Fifteen minutes later the Cessna had been loaded with several hundred brick-sized packets of compressed ganja, all plastic-wrapped and taped. The plane had been refuelled and the lamp lighters were standing by to light up the strip once more.

Eddie woke Sedgwick and gave him the cup of coffee.

"All ready to go," said Eddie.

The pilot handed him an envelope of sixty thousand US dollars in one hundred dollar bills. Eddie did not look inside the envelope or count the money; he merely put it in his pocket. Then he and IZion, watched by all those present, walked with Barry Sedgwick to the plane.

The crew had been well trained, and the operation was over so fast that there was a sense of anticlimax when the plane's engines started up and it turned, light from the relit torches flashing off its surfaces, to roar away and be swallowed up in darkness again. As the sound of the plane's engine died in the distance, it was as though everybody left on the ground had had the same dream. But the dream had come true, and a sudden roar of laughter and celebration swept up and down the road; figures dancing jigs of joy, slapping hands, and bending over double with laughter as tension built up over days and weeks was released in an explosion of happiness.

Eddie looked on and laughed. "Alright," he said, "come ... money time now."

That first herbs shipment out of Burru's Beach was an inaugural flight of such impeccable precision and profitability that it triggered an explosion of commerce great enough to turn Burru's beach into what eventually became known as Rasta City. The planes that took out the ganja started bringing in a wide selection of spare parts for motorbikes, cars, and trucks. Even at this early stage, when there were still parts to be had from the authorised dealers, Eddie could sell at competitive prices. By avoiding the twenty-eight stages of documentation in the passage of the goods through formal channels, he was clearing a hundred and seventy per cent profit.

Within two months, Rasta City became the central cog in a maze of wheels that ran around the island supplying spare parts for cash. Not only did the smugglers have the parts to sell that Eddie had imported on the ganja planes, they also bought out the stocks of the authorised dealers so that later on, when they were selling spare parts to owners of vehicles that had been sitting idle for months on end because they lacked one or two pieces, profit margins of three hundred per cent were considered moderate.

In Rasta City the buzz of motorbikes passed to and fro around the clock. Every shipment of herb that went out involved checking crops, negotiating with growers, making and receiving advanced payments, arranging transportation, bribing police, preparing landing strips, stockpiling gas for refuelling the planes, and getting accurate messages to the pilots.

Dozens of people were involved in these operations, hundreds of arrangements had to be confirmed, hundreds of thousands of dollars had to change hands; the goods coming in had to be stored, sold, and delivered. While the executives in the formal economy were in a panic at the delays in starting up their plans that were "in the pipeline", a nation of barefoot illiterates was running the multimillion-dollar organisation originally put together by Eddie Azani.

Thousands who had never seen more than twenty dollars in their hands at any one time were now earning two or three hundred a week on a regular basis. By the time the trade had been in full swing for six weeks, Herman, Rupert, and Eunice not only had a motorbike and a stereo, but they had added a kerosene refrigerator and two more rooms to their house. At

Burru's Beach alone there were over a thousand families now living better than they had ever thought possible, but so far as the manufacturers, builders, importers, bankers, insurance companies, and unions were concerned, development had not started yet.

Chapter Eighteen

Each evening Winston checked the price of oil on the spot market. It was rising. It wouldn't stop rising for years, not until everybody without oil was not only broke, but had gone into debt borrowing back the cash they had paid for oil the year before. Winston got up and stretched; he walked out onto the terrace, and over to the trampoline he'd had brought in and set up. He'd never used it, though, because ever since it had arrived he had been grounded by tension in his fight with the mining companies over the mining tax.

The battle had never ceased. First of all Kass, with Lynch in the background, had brought every imaginable pressure to bear on individual members of the Houses of Parliament to prevent passage of the law. Eventually Percy had had to use valuable IOUs to push through the law and make good on his pledge to Winston, but when the law was finally passed, the mining companies had simply started the second round fight. They instituted a round of appeals, and they threatened to go to the federal insurance fund to claim loss from investing abroad. Thus involving the US Government, they tried to link their loss to aid money coming from Washington, and they announced that pending judgement of the various appeal courts to which they had referred the dispute, they would withhold the mining tax.

Winston, furious, had counter attacked. He threatened to prevent them shipping ore from their mines, and he threatened that if they did not abide by the law of the land he would nationalise their operations. They knew he was serious. They knew he could do it. He could do it because Hugh Clifford could come in and take over, and he could do that because he could sell the ore through Switzerland on the world market at a price that allowed everybody to get their share and stay profitable. Winston had done his homework and now his study of the industry paid off because now, and for the foreseeable future, the free market price that Winston had predicted was going to hold not in the US, but in Geneva.

The phone rang. It was Hugh Clifford. He was in Caracas. He was flying to Montreal that evening and wanted to stop in and see Winston en route.

"Of course I'll come to the airport," said Winston, "what time?"

Winston drove out to the airport at dusk, parked at the edge of the apron for private planes, and chatted with the immigration officer who would deal with Clifford's pilot while Winston spoke with the old man. When he arrived, Hugh Clifford got out of the plane to stretch his legs, and he and Winston walked out of earshot—two solitary figures silhouetted against the evening sky.

"I thought we should talk, and not on the phone, because some very serious opposition is starting to form against you," said the old man.

"Lynch and Kass want round three," said Winston.

"They've got Percy," said Hugh Clifford.

"Percy? Are you sure?"

"They're threatening him with an Allende-style response because you threatened nationalisation."

"When did Percy agree?"

"Lynch got through to him about three days ago."

Winston stopped walking and looked out past Clifford's Lear jet to the fins of three 727s in the distance that bore the emblem of the national airline; they were probably drinking gas at a thousand dollars a minute.

"Even if I go and they keep mining, how is Percy going to pay the oil bill without the tax money?" asked Winston.

"They've offered him an IMF agreement."

An IMF agreement! For the government to accept it was like an open admission of defeat; not just defeat by the mining companies, but by the entire international banking system. It was like failing an exam at school, and the punishment was close supervision by the schoolmasters.

They would arrive and start to issue guidelines. They who had had six days' experience in thinking about the island's economy, would start to instruct the local bureaucracy. Winston's assistant, Alistair McFadden, was a perfect number-two man precisely because he had no imagination, he would do exactly as he was told by whoever was in charge. There would be devaluation after devaluation, foreign exchange would become like gold, the black market would spiral; it would be a crime to get caught with foreign currency, but the local money would be worth less every week, every day... like Santo Domingo, Venezuela, Jamaica...

"Percy knows perfectly well that everywhere that's been tried it's caused riots."

"Percy assumes Mark will handle the riots," said Clifford.

"Hah! They don't know Mark. He's not going to do Percy's dirty work for him. He'll declare a state of emergency and take over."

Clifford smiled. "In that case I assume we'll have you back in your old job again."

"Unless Mark wants to spend all the money on the army," said Winston, "yes, I think that's a safe assumption."

"OK," said Hugh Clifford, "let's leave it like this ..."

If Winston was fired, Clifford agreed to keep on mining and shipping, and apparently paying the same rates as the other mining companies, while in fact putting aside the amount he had negotiated with Bernard in a holding account. Winston would tax the other companies retroactively when he got back into power, and if he ever made it and the tax was never imposed, Clifford would simply keep the money he had put on deposit.

"It'll work out," said the old man as he got back on board his plane again. "Remember, Gulf has never stopped pumping in Cabinda."

Back in his office, Winston did nothing. He knew that as long as he did nothing, Percy certainly wouldn't force a confrontation, and so long as he did nothing to oppose what was going on, nobody else would trouble him. He would sit and wait and watch the scenario unfold.

Chapter Nineteen

∽∽∽

DeMalaga paused, but not for long. He was attuned to talent, to sensing when people were desperate to do something because they had something inspiring them, and when they were merely desperate. When he listened to the tracks that Zack had recorded for the album, he could sense that Zack was ready to do something big, and that he was capable of riding the huge wave of energy that could come to him now. DeMalaga could sense Zack's appeal to the young crowds that were there in the seventies: his message was spiritual but not boring; religious but not restrictive. So Max DeMalaga committed the eight hundred thousand dollars for finishing the album and starting the tour almost as soon as he'd heard the dub of "Genocide" that Michele had sent him.

When she heard the news, Michele put down the phone and looked at Zack.

"You've got the deal!" she said. "Lock, stock, and barrel; tour money, press lined up, album release simultaneous with the tour—you've got everything we asked for!"

She jumped up to embrace him, to go to the refrigerator for the champagne, but Zack somehow didn't share her euphoria. She was ecstatic because the plan had succeeded, the fantasy had turned into reality, but now, Zack realized, she would look for the next discovery; now he was going to be lost in a swirl of travel and loneliness for her with only music to save him, to absorb the feelings of emptiness he'd suffer that could not be eased by bigger limousines, hotel suites, and concert crowds.

"Here's to the music," said Michele, raising her glass to him. "Amen," said Zack.

In the slums of the capital, the economic crunch was growing truly desperate. Neither Red Roy's regime, nor the Peace Movement inspired by Wire was bringing in any money, on the contrary, since no politician could claim credit for the Peace Movement it had been left to die. Even the money for slum-clearance projects was stalled. The Minister of Housing in Percy's cabinet had lost his muscle in the slums when Red Roy wiped out Biga Mitchell, and he wasn't spending housing money just for housing; it was the cash pipeline to his street fighters, and now that they were in disarray he had turned it off. But while the Minister of Housing had no power in the slums, Red Roy had no contact in the cabinet. In the resultant confusion everything came to a standstill.

It hit home for many just how much the action had moved out of town when, one day, those who came to look for Rufus at the Soul Shack outside the bus terminal could not find him there; Rufus, his shop, his telephone, his hit-parade list, his message box, the drawer in which he kept his money: all were gone to Rasta City.

With nothing left to poach in his domain, Red Roy began eyeing the import/export trade going on through Rasta City like a hungry fox watching an apparently endless parade of plump chickens, and he staged some raids. He didn't venture into the area around Burru's Beach itself, but business was spreading island-wide. The goods and ganja had to be transported on some long and lonely roads. Substantial amounts of cash were being carried from place to place by motorbike messenger.

When three trucks had been hijacked, Eddie called Zack.

"I think you are in trouble, my friend, your peace movement brought peace, but it has not brought jobs, and now the youth that looked to you for leadership is beginning to look to you for money."

Zack said nothing, Eddie was right. The Peace Movement had inspired "Genocide", and "Genocide" was building into a big hit worldwide. The time had come for Zack to tour, not get himself bogged down in slum problems. The acclaim of the slum youth had projected Zack's image as a rebel hero to the foreign press, and that had helped him greatly but ...

"When people claim you as their leader it is an expensive embrace," said Eddie. "I warned you about politics and you wouldn't listen. Now you have to feed the gunmen that the politicians were feeding before, and they are getting restless. Earning money for a band is bad enough, but earning money for an army? You are not that class of businessman, my friend; you are that class of musician, but for that class of business you need to be a businessman like me."

"I want fe get back to the music business," said Zack. "I wan fe go on tour."

"You go on tour, you do what you want. It's perfect: you are the figurehead, but I take care of business. Everybody wears your badge; everything is done in your name, but you are not there. You are free to go because I will keep Wire and his soldiers busy. He will thank you for the money because you will bring him to me. You will still be a hero but I will pay for it."

"What will Wire have to do?" asked Zack.

"Every time I make a shipment, Wire's people will protect my trader till the goods get to the customer and the money gets back to me," said Eddie.

Thus, Zack went on tour and at last Wire found his own territory out of town. He ran his side of the operation with military precision, yet no one would ever have known it by watching the youth who were under his command. They wore no uniform. They practised no drill. Only those closest to them were aware that they slipped away from time to time for a day or two, carrying their guns with them.

In the first ten missions that Wire's men went out on to protect Eddie's traders, they were attacked three times. Twice they lost the goods they were supposed to be protecting, but the third time they beat off the raiders and captured one of them. The captive was brought to Wire and a ring of gunmen who sat in a circle around the edges of a room that had no furniture in it except for a small bed where Wire sat, his back propped against the wall, his legs stretched out on the bare mattress.

The captive was terrified. Any one of the fifteen men in the room would have killed him without a qualm, and he knew that nobody took prisoners in ghetto warfare: there was nowhere to keep them. When a man was captured he was usually killed. If he was released, it was often after a beating that rendered him unable to fight again.

Wire knew the man who was awaiting his judgement. All the gunmen knew each other, and this captive had always been one of Red Roy's main men.

"I never know you was a tief," said Wire sarcastically. "I thought you was a revolutionary."

"I is not a tief."

"So why you attack I cargo?" asked Wire.

A wave of antagonism swept around the room.

"Fucking tief!" muttered Wire's lieutenants.

"Man like dis fe dead," said one.

"Every man ha' fe live, Wire," said the captive, "you mus' agree, every man ha' fe live."

Wire looked around the room, lengthening the pause for dramatic effect.

"Not every man ha' fe live," he said. "Some man ha' fe dead. Is dat we a deal wid right now."

A wave of laughter ran around the room. Everybody enjoyed a trial except, of course, the sinner.

"You were always a fucking tief," said one of Wire's gunmen, "from the first days I know you outside East Central School when you did want to bully down bwoy fe dem lunch patty, and later you start bruk shop ..."

"I remember Red Roy and him boys den," said another street fighter. "When, as boys, weself we go down and dive penny from cruise ship, and when we dive all day done and we tired coming home, dis same pussy-face boy and him frien', another one name Alvin, and Red Roy, de three o'dem come down pon me an' tek weh me money because why? Dem couldn't swim ..."

"Dem could never do more dan tief."

"Up to now ..."

"Man like dis fe lock weh in government prison, because if we ha' fe deal wid dem dem ha' fe dead."

The atmosphere in the room had changed from amused curiosity to a mounting rage. The prisoner realised he would have to speak convincingly in his own defence before the lust for revenge spread further.

"Ever since de peace we nuh get no money," shouted Red Roy's man. "Is only lately yu yuself get a break, but yu tek everyt'ing fe yuself, yu nuh leave nuttin fe we; I myself would like fe join yu but yu nuh treat we like bredda ... you treat we fuck up, and yu lef we fe starve. And I never know it was fe you t'ings neither; is only tonight I am finding out. I never know. Red Roy never tell we."

"It nuh matter who it belong to, is not yours; yu still a fucking tief, dat is why I nuh wan yu in none o' my movement none at all, because any man I move wid ha' fe look out fe me. I can't look to see if 'im is really goin' to do me harm when I lookin' to 'im fe protection."

"I hear is Red Roy dat gi away Biga," said a gunman.

"Dem man deh fe dead," murmured the chorus again.

"Have mercy," said Red Roy's man. "I wan work fe yu, Wire. All a we want work fe you."

"No way you can work fe me," said Wire, "you too tief."

Wire had risen from the bed and was advancing toward the man, conveying to him the anger that he was in turn to communicate to his boss. Wire slapped the man across the face with the back of his hand, and then whipped his hand back across the man's face in the other direction as he spoke.

"I goin' let you go because I want you tek a message to Red Roy fe me. Tell him to dress back or I will kill his rass!" Wire kicked the chair the man was sitting on so hard that the captive spilled out of it to lie sprawled on the floor.

"Tell Red Roy fe mi dat he will have to change his ways or he is going to dead. Tell him dis is serious times we livin' in now. Tell dat rass, Red Roy, dat him haffi stop think 'bout how him alone a go tief and start think 'bout how him can mek something fe de people benefit if him want power."

Red Roy's man was crawling his way around the room. He knew that his only hope of escaping serious punishment was in looking as pathetic as possible, allowing Wire's gunmen to kick him casually as their leader delivered his sermon.

Wire paused. The man stopped crawling. He didn't lift his head. He didn't move. He didn't twitch. He didn't dare guess what was going to happen to him next. The wretch knew he would get away with his life, but he felt sure he would have to bear some mutilation back to Red Roy as a token of Wire's wrath. Seeing him cower like a dog, waiting for the next blow to fall, Wire smiled silently and looked around the room. His amusement at the man's terror when Wire had nothing but a smile on his face struck the others in the room as hilariously funny, and as the laughter spread around him, the captured man slowly raised his head.

Wire walked to the door and opened it wide.

"Yu understan de message I gi' you?" he asked.

"Yes," said Red Roy's man.

"Get up," said Wire. "Turn 'round!"

The man turned around to face the door.

"Bend down," said Wire.

When the man bent double, Wire placed his foot on the man's rump and got ready to push. The room stirred with laughter again, and then Wire sent him flying through the open doorway to crash in the passageway outside, before scrambling to his feet, and running for his life.

"Mek *sure* yu tell Red Roy everyting I seh," Wire shouted after him.

Thus ended the peace. Soon there was a running battle between the two factions of gunmen led by Red Roy and Wire. Wire was in firm control of the Rasta City area, but Red Roy had no competition in the city, and he was able to rally many of Biga's gunmen who had not followed Wire and had nowhere else to go.

Eventually the fighting spread and intensified to the point where Eddie Azani became uncomfortable. Rasta City was now a far cry from a few huts and a band of refugees from ghetto violence. The town's founders had not only survived: they had been the base for something that had grown beyond anybody's calculations, and Eddie knew that if he wasn't careful his people would end up spending more time fighting than smuggling, and that wasn't his plan at all.

Eddie was just deciding whether to come out of the ganja trade altogether, when one of his men was captured by Red Roy.

Burden, the boy that Eddie had fired long before, was the weak link in Eddie's chain. He'd never found a job; had nothing better to do than to watch the comings and goings from Azani's corner, and he became particularly fascinated by the progress of his successor. Within a month the new boy was riding a Honda 50 and moving around town like he was Azani's key messenger. Burden became obsessed to know this new guy's secret and he took to following his movements.

After three months Burden noticed that his replacement began travelling with a bag and going away for quite long stretches of time—like he was on a new, regular, important, mission. Burden decided to track the new boy, and set out to do so by following him as far as possible each day. Day by day he followed as far as he could; went the next day to the point where he'd lost his trail, and picked up the next leg. After four days, Burden found himself out in Rasta City making a note of the gate that Eddie's courier eventually turned into, carrying his usual large parcel. Later that same afternoon, Burden took note of the fact that lots of Dreads known to be associated with Wire's high command were in the area when he passed through. Burden knew of the war between Wire and Red Roy. What would it be worth to Red Roy to know that Eddie Azani was sending bundles of cash to Wire?

The next day Eddie's cash courier disappeared.

For months Red Roy had been trying to find out who was really running the ganja trade, but in spite of the fact that the trade employed more people than anything else going on among the poor, there were no clues to follow in tracking down the control centre—until now.

"How much money you give Wire?" asked Red Roy.

"I don't know; de package always seal," gasped the man, before another lash from the three-foot piece of doubled up electrical wire tore into his flesh.

Red Roy had been beating him steadily for forty-five minutes: a lash here, a lash there; punctuating the questions.

"You seh Zack nuh give you no cash?" asked Red Roy.

"Mi nuh work fe Zack," said the messenger.

Red Roy felt a surge of ego as he realised that although everything was done in his name, Zack wasn't big enough to live as a superstar and run a smuggling empire at the same time. Not even Zack could match Red Roy when it came to slum triumph in his generation.

"Who you work for den?"

Red Roy had asked that question first, and the messenger had refused to answer then, but that was an age of pain ago. Now, as Eddie's trusted courier watched Red Roy twirling the length of wire in preparation to rip into his flesh again, he decided that his employer would not want him to suffer more pain; Eddie was prepared to look after himself—and the youngster admitted everything. So Red Roy came to know: although Zack was the figurehead, Eddie was the real Don.

"Eddie Azani!" shouted Red Roy. "You mean Zack bow to a white capitalist pig like Eddie Azani?"

Again a feeling of well-being flashed through Red Roy. He was justified! Everything he had ever done! Every racist vulgarity was reconfirmed; every ideological cliché renewed as basic truth.

"Those fuckers!" said Red Roy. "Dem still control black man down to de last penny in de last back street in de far'est slum."

His disgust mixed with a thrill of vindication; his voice had a half-laugh in it as he spoke. He had always known that he wasn't too tough, that you couldn't be tough enough to fight those who had the cash and intended to hold on to it till the end of time. All the rage, all the killing, all that he had done had been necessary if Red Roy was to fulfil his destiny.

"Zack is a stooge!" said Red Roy.

The crowd around Red Roy enlarged on his indignation.

"You mean you never gib Zack no cash at all?"

"No," said the prisoner.

"Zack have money fe go play music and grine white gal dem in foreign," said one of Red Roy's men, "is only dat im have use fah."

"All like Zack fe cut out," said another man.

"Azani is de main one," said Red Roy.

Chapter Twenty

∞∞∞

Eddie patted his dog, Lola, on the head and talked to her as she drifted off to sleep. She was quite old and was about to have her last litter of puppies. Eddie had always chosen her husbands with care, and every litter had been snapped up before Eddie could ever keep a puppy for himself. Lola was probably the most famous dog anywhere in the city, and everybody wanted her offspring in their home, but this time Eddie promised himself he was going to keep and raise the whole bunch, pick the best for himself, and then others could beg him for the rest.

It was two o'clock in the morning and time for bed. He stretched, scratched his belly, and then stepped through the doorway leading from the veranda to his bedroom, with a big smile on his face. In one corner of the room there was a pinball machine and in another was a jukebox with a stack of magazines and comic books on top of it. The room could be darkened with dimmers on five different circuits, and Eddie changed the mood frequently with the lights.

The bed was huge, large enough to hold Eddie and three women at a time without crowding. Women came and went around the clock: sleeping, reading, playing music, experimenting with make-up, rolling joints, getting food from the casino kitchen, recording their sexual antics on the video camera that Michele had once given Eddie for recording auditions by singing acts. Many of the girls had been professional rumba dancers, and they shrieked with laughter as they watched each other in the playback of their erotic performances on screen.

At the bottom of the bed was a large brass tray holding a telephone, a pile of herb, and a litter of accumulated cosmetics ... the smell of sex mingled with perfume and ganja smoke to fill the atmosphere of the room with a smog of sensuality and the sweet smell of excess.

Sitting on top of over five million dollars in cash stashed under the bed, Eddie didn't plan to go anywhere until the time was right to leave with the money, and he intended to be both comfortable and amused till then.

Eddie slept for two hours, and when he awoke the room was dark except for beams of light that bounced off a spinning mobile above the bed and circled the room like swirling stars. Without turning on a light, he picked up the intercom and buzzed the night watchman at the front gate.

"Any messages?"

"No, Mr Eddie."

"Anybody there?"

"Yes, Mr Eddie; Phantom sah."

"What time is it?"

"Four o'clock, Mr Eddie."

"Tell him to come back in an hour."

Eddie put down the phone, stretched, and checked out his vital organ. He thought of it as his best friend, the friend he'd played with since he was an infant, but that over the years had developed a personality and a set of moods all its own. Time and again when there was disagreement between them, Eddie had been proved wrong, so he long ago learned to follow where he was led by that ever youthful independent part of his being.

Slowly he started moving. His bed was like a pond filled with shallows and beaches of flesh. He would feel here, stroke there, and test the mood with his lips till he met response. He recognised the breathing of Juanita, a woman he had first encountered when he was fifteen and she was a young maid in his uncle's house. But Eddie had rekindled, many times, the excitement of those early expeditions into the blackened claustrophobia of the tiny rooms in the servants' quarters, and he passed on. The second woman was a Swiss traveller, based in New York, who had been given Eddie's number by someone else in one of a thousand of · those networks which have no names and certainly no organisation, but which manage to let those addicted to sex around the world know about each other just the same.

The Swiss girl had visited Eddie three times in two years, and he brushed lightly against her in passing, but she merely turned over and started sleeping on her other side. He continued his progress towards a body which was not asleep, but which was waiting tensely in the dark, and the closer he approached, the tighter the body of the young girl clamped itself shut.

"You've been here before," said Eddie as a beam of light, reflected from the mobile, passed across the girl's face.

"Yes."

"You came with Agnes."

"Yes."

"You are from the country, and your uncle was fooling around with you, right?"

"Yes." She was so tense she could hardly talk, but she did have a nice soft voice.

Eddie paused, looking at her as the light passed across her face again. Seeing just a glimpse of her every few seconds, the girl's face took on a completely different look every time he saw it. Without knowing her features well to begin with, he could imagine he was looking at a child, or an old woman, as easily as the girl of eighteen he vaguely remembered meeting. Only her eyes remained the same each time the light passed, and her eyes were frightened. If she was frightened, why had she returned?

"I didn't think you would come back," he said, deliberately trying to put the girl at ease by talking in a teasing tone.

"Why not?"

"Because I thought maybe you didn't like me ... or you just like to watch?"

She *had* watched in fascination as Eddie and Agnes made love that first night. She had always slept in small rooms crowded with family, and she had never seen unbridled passion. The girl was amazed at how Agnes seemed able to absorb any amount of weight and pressure from Eddie. She had been fascinated by the way in which Agnes used it to set free in herself the explosion of an orgasm that had put her in a smiling mood for nearly two days afterwards. Ever since that night, the images of their lovemaking had filled the young girl's imagination as she lay awake. Then they had started to enter into her dreams, until finally she was drawn back to the big bed with the spinning lights.

She had not answered Eddie's question.

"That Agnes," said Eddie, smiling, "she love to fuck, but she been doing it much longer than you, nuh true?"

"Yes."

"You ever love making love?"

"No ... I don't think so."

"Ahh ..." said Eddie as he reached around to get a spliff and light it. He turned on the radio, found music, took three draws of the spliff and then offered it to the girl.

"No, thanks," she said.

"You don't smoke?"

"It get me jumpy sometimes, and sometimes I feel cold when I smoke it."

"Are you feeling jumpy now?"

"I feel cold."

"Come," said Eddie, "I will give you a massage ..."

For ten minutes Eddie eased the tension out of the girl's neck and shoulders. He started high up in the nape of her neck and worked down, feeling for knots of muscle and easing them out into the surrounding flesh. He was a good masseur because he loved women's bodies; it had always thrilled him to play with their chemistry. He explored the contours and textures of her back in detail, and by the time he reached her buttocks he could sense excitement replacing relaxation as relaxation had replaced tension.

He passed by the crucial central square inch without pausing except to slip off her panties, and he continued slowly down her body to work on the upper thighs and calf muscles of each leg.

When he reached her ankles, he rolled her over, feeling for the stiffening of resistance in her body, but he felt none. He could tell this young girl was not in his bed for money, she was there because he and Agnes had turned her on to fucking, and Eddie felt a thrill run through him, and a strong message of support reached his brain from his best buddy.

This time when he offered her a smoke, she didn't refuse. He placed an ashtray nearby so she wouldn't have to worry about hot ash, and then he went to work on her feet. By the time she had inhaled deeply five times, he was halfway into the second joint on the third toe of her left foot, and she had started to feel weightless, to float away on the tingle in her toes. She had never before felt the hands of a man play lovingly with her body; she had never felt the energy flow from his fingertips transmitting excitement as he allowed himself to become intoxicated with lust, at first in measured proportions ...

By the time she had finished the spliff, Eddie was expelling the last nervous impulses from her system by kneading them out of her insteps, and she became acutely aware that the place not yet dealt with was starting to crave attention.

Supporting all his weight on his arms and knees, Eddie shifted the length of his body above hers, brushing her belly with his chest, stiffening her nipples with his lips. He could sense his best friend straining to take it further—as sensitive to nuances of moisture and suction as any finger, probing and pulling back; alternately playing around in the easy grip of her acceptance, and then pressing gently forward to take possession of a further half an inch.

"They never met before," Eddie murmured to the girl, "they need time to get acquainted. She must be careful, she could catch love fever from that boy."

"What you mean 'love fever'?" asked the girl.

"When you catch love fever you have to make love every day or you sweat and think about nothing else, you want to make love all the time; if you don't know when you're going to get it again, you feel like you go crazy."

To Eddie's buddy it felt as though this girl's tight young pussy was composed of six sets of lips, each one of which was salivating separately to suck him ever more deeply into the ultimate embrace.

"You crazy already," she said affectionately, and at last she took him fully into her body.

Eddie moved to the music for a while, and then he slowly pulled out, almost to his full length, testing tension; when he slid back into her again, he travelled in two seconds the distance it had taken five minutes to penetrate before.

The girl moaned, and Eddie felt her body buck under him. *Love fever injection. Love fever infection.* Up to now Eddie's rhythms had been gentle, but as she accepted him fully and was asking for more, he lifted the controls on his own yearning. For the length of two records on the jukebox they moved together as easily as they would have done on a dance floor, his body telling hers with the precision of music and the relaxation of dance that although they had just met, his spirit had mingled with hers for a thousand years.

His mind drifted off to memories of women in general—mood memories—of shyness and seduction, of laughter and kindness; and of caring and crying, of heartbreak and hurt feelings. Pain and passion ... the experience of each mood was always the same, it was the woman who changed. Two different women in the same mood were more alike than the same woman in two different moods; so it was the mood that Eddie recognised, not the woman: that's why he tended to make love in the dark and deal with bodies as pure spirit.

The spirit that had this girl writhing in his arms was one with which he craved communion. Since the time when he had lost his mother, since the day he had shot his cousin, since early childhood, Eddie was forced to turn to strangers for love, and the communion of need for it had saved his sanity over and over again.

Love fever. Once infected never cured. Those who caught it passed it on, more addictive than heroin. The young girl from the country had fallen into the arms of a man who had to have a fix for his habit every day, and her limbs had succumbed completely to the rhythms of his need, setting up swells within her that moved around and around, across and back again, in and out, in a figure of eight ... until the muscles of her grip on gristle grew tighter and tighter, plunged deeper and deeper; till a ball of warmth grew in her womb, and spread like a flash up into her belly, and down into her legs, making every massaged muscle in her body buzz with pleasure shock.

As the tremors passed through her structure, the girl felt Eddie's arms around her, letting her know, as she poured her passion into his safekeeping, that he would catch her essence and keep it till she returned to herself.

Long ago he'd learned that the only way to fuck three times a day was not to come, and the only way not to come was to fuck three times day; it was a delicate balance to maintain, and so he was accustomed to taking women's pleasure as his own; he seldom expended his own energies in orgasm.

After a while, he drew away from her slowly, and she lay stretched out and still, her body limp with exhaustion.

"Can you sleep?" he asked.

"Yes," she replied.

"Can I get you anything?"

"A glass of water."

He got her a glass of water and a towel; then he moved all the pillows around again for sleeping, and covered her with a sheet.

Lying there with the reflected beams of light passing across her face, Eddie still had no idea what she really looked like. He wondered if he would ever see her again; if they would become friends. Perhaps she would take what she now knew and give it to a boyfriend ... perhaps she would think that what he'd given her could come only from him and from his best friend. Whatever happened he was grateful ...

After a few moments, Eddie crossed to the phone and called the night watchman at the front gate again.

"What time is it?" he asked.

"Five minutes to five, Mr Eddie."

"Is Phantom there?"

"Him never reach back, Mr Eddie."

"Nobody there?"

"No, sir," said Action.

It was unusual that there was nobody waiting to see him. Everything seemed to have shut down ...

"Send Phantom when he comes," said Eddie, and hung up.

He got out of bed, put on a dressing gown, and stepped out into the cool night air on the veranda. He was just crossing to where his dog lay to see if she had had the puppies yet, when she jumped up and started barking.

Red Roy's car pulled up outside Azani's casino and he jumped out, followed by three bodyguards. The guard at Eddie's gate could hardly make out Red Roy's features when roused from his snooze because Red Roy wore a hat pulled down over his face, but old Action immediately sensed danger in the man's presence.

"Is Azani here?" asked Red Roy.

"Who wants him?" asked the gateman.

"Tell him, Red Roy."

The gateman pressed the alarm button on the floor; it buzzed in Eddie's apartment upstairs and in a back room where three guards were resting. The buzzer was not heard at the gate. Azani's guards were armed, and the whole compound was surrounded by a wall ten feet high with jagged glass implanted all along the top of it. If Red Roy and his men had wanted to force their way into Eddie's property they would have had to shoot their way in, and they would have had to send for reinforcements.

"A Red Roy says he's here to see you, Mister Eddie," said Action into the intercom.

"Really?" said Eddie in surprise. "How many men does he have with him?"

"Three," said the gateman, in Arabic. Eddie had taught him to count to ten in Arabic for just such an occasion. He also knew how to say yes and no.

"Are they armed?"

"Yes," Action said in Arabic.

Eddie paused. He was interested to know how Red Roy had reached him.

"Tell him to come up alone," said Eddie. "Tell Baba and Chin to cover the other three. Bogart is to circle."

Eddie put down the phone, swung a revolver in a shoulder holster over his neck, buttoned it, and covered it with his dressing gown. Then he sat down to watch Red Roy approach. Eddie did not plan to walk the length of the veranda to meet his uninvited guest. He would leave the first greetings to his dog.

When Red Roy got to the top of the stairs, the Alsatian went mad with rage. She sensed the hostility in Red Roy like pepper in her nostrils. Had Eddie not called her back she would actually have attacked and bitten Red Roy, but Eddie's voice kept the dog on an invisible leash, backing away as he advanced, keeping the distance between them within the bounds of a spring for his throat.

Red Roy did not slow his pace as he walked towards Azani, who was already sitting down in one of the several chairs clustered at the end of the veranda.

"Have a seat," said Eddie, pointing to a chair opposite him. Red Roy sat down and put one leg over the arm of the chair. "What can I do for you?" asked Eddie over the snarling of the dog.

"Call yu dog," said Red Roy.

"Quiet!" called Eddie sharply, and the dog spun around and looked at him. "Come here and sit down and shut up!" The dog did as she was told. "What can I do for you?" Eddie repeated.

"I tink we have some business to discuss," said Red Roy.

"Really ... what kind of business?"

"I understan' yu control da ganja business."

"I run a gambling casino: you can only do business with me if you want to gamble."

"I nuh wan fe gamble; I wan fe mek certain."

"Certain of what?"

"Certain dat no ganja trading go on inna slums, or inna Liberation City, dat is not accountable to de People's Movement."

"Liberation City?"

"Dem used to call it Rasta City, but is Liberation City now."

Eddie laughed out loud. "What is your proposal?" he asked, curious to know what Red Roy's idea of a deal was.

"We wan everything to go jus' as before," said Red Roy. "De only difference is, yu nuh pay us, we pay yu."

"Why would I have anything to do with you at all?"

"Because if you wan fe go on doing business yu have no choice."

Up to now Eddie had been treating this man lightly because of his naivety in business, but now he knew Red Roy's real business was revolution.

"Man, go and fuck yourself," said Eddie.

Red Roy was a killer because he was a fanatic, and Eddie hated fanatics; he hated their mindless cruelty.

"Get out!" said Azani, and the dog started growling.

Eddie's sudden hatred for Red Roy was so strong that it took on a quality of physical compulsion. In the same way that often a sense of lust overwhelmed him with the desire to touch a woman gently, now he was having an equally powerful reaction to the man who had invaded his living quarters with a vibe of such ingrained bitterness that Eddie wanted to punch him in the middle of his face just for the look in his eyes.

Red Roy had risen, livid with rage. He had come to get money, and Azani was prepared to lose everything rather than give him any.

"Yu gi' me money yu fucking Syrian, or I run yu and every last member of your tiefing fucking tribe out a dis island."

"You bring race to me as an excuse to take my money, you bastard?" said Eddie, rising from his chair.

Red Roy was backing away down the veranda, his anger so high he didn't flinch from the snapping of the Alsatian.

"Yu a pig, Azani. Yu can only live by tiefing people who can nuh protect demself."

"What are you worried about me and my money for?" asked Eddie. "You have the whole fucking country. Make your own money if you can, but you can't. You know why you're so worried

228

about getting your hands on my money? Because you know you can't make it yourself. You don't know how. You will never know. You can drive me out of this island, but you can never acquire my spirit. Oh no! My family has been trading since the beginning of time—they were in the first caravans. Anywhere they have gone ever since, trade and money followed. Anywhere they left, trade died. You give any man on this island the choice between working for you and working for me, and we will see who will choose whom. You will be left with the dregs, the killers, the people you have right now ... and after you have slaughtered five or six or ten thousand ..."

Eddie felt the adrenalin burning in his blood as he watched the other man backing away.

"You want my money, my house, you want to kill my family; or maybe they would be lucky—maybe you would let them get in a little boat and you would push them out to sea to drown trying to escape your hatred? Ha! All in the name of race, and you're not even a black man!"

Red Roy had reached the top of the stairs, but the dog had him cornered and didn't want to let him go; then Eddie saw Red Roy's hand flash for his gun. As the dog yelped and fell back, hit in the leg, Eddie felt as if he was coming out of himself with rage. He leapt at Red Roy, smashing him against the railing of the veranda with a karate blow to his stomach. As Red Roy crumpled, Eddie hit him again, screaming curses as he kicked him down the stairs, restraining the impulse to kill him only because he didn't want to kill him as much as he wanted to get to Miami; so Eddie was satisfied with feeling Red Roy's nose smashed in; seeing his face covered with blood, and his body convulsed with pain.

Finally, when Red Roy lay sprawled and motionless at the bottom of the stairs Eddie called out, "Baba! Chin!". The two guards came forward while Action and Bogart watched Red Roy's men outside.

"Put him outside in the road," said Eddie to the two men. "No, wait! Hold his head so he can see me." Eddie pushed his face right up to Red's glazed eyes and caught a flicker of understanding. "I am letting you live because one day I want the pleasure of beating you again, you race-mongering bastard."

Then Eddie Azani spat in Red Roy's face and walked away.

By six-thirty that same morning Eddie was driving his LTD high in the mountains about forty miles east of the city. It had been raining and the roadway was splashed every few turns by streams still gushing out of the dense green tropical forest. The light in long valleys leading up to the heights of the mountain ranges had a misty quality which would soon be pierced with yellow rays from the early morning sun.

Eddie turned off the paved road at a small hand painted sign that proclaimed "Abyssinian Consciousness Assembly". He drove down a steep slope to the valley floor which was cultivated right to the edge of a riverbed filled with huge smooth boulders and water that fell in small waterfalls to fill large, slowly swirling pools all along the river.

Eddie slowed and stopped beside a bunch of children who were walking along the roadside. Suddenly confronted by this white man they were inclined to run, but they were trapped between the road and the river.

"Weh Naya Joe?" asked Eddie.

None of the children answered. They had seen Naya Joe talking with white men before, but the white men were always dressed up to look like Jesus.

"Is alright, me and Naya good frien' from long time," said Eddie.

"Him aan yah, sah," said a little girl in a bright purple dress who couldn't contain herself because she was sure that if she told the man she knew where to find Naya he would have to give her a ride inside the magic chariot; it would float her down the road, gently rocking on its springs, filled with disco sounds, and a sense of fun.

"Beg yu a liff, please sah?" she said.

"All right, jump in an tek me to Naya."

Eddie had met Naya when he had his first job after school, selling cloth for his uncle. The thrill of the job was in the use of the station wagon, and the young country girls that it could attract; for nearly a year Eddie had cruised the island from one end to the other, selling cloth to every tailor and dressmaker he could find along the way.

Of all the young tailors, Joe was the most successful; he became Eddie's best customer. There were six women and four other men in the establishment, but Joe was the star: the man who could slash with chalk and cut fabric for style. Even in those days Naya Joe was religious, but he would always have a few drinks with Eddie after concluding business. Even back then he had talked of owning land, and during the years when Eddie didn't see him, he heard rumours that Joe had realised his ambition beyond his wildest dreams. His Abyssinian Consciousness Assembly was the first group of cultivators to plant ganja along with food, to behave like grassroots farmers instead of fugitives, and to form a single farm of five acres. Naya Joe's operation had expanded, over twelve years, to control more than a thousand acres in four parishes, and to employ over six hundred men and women.

Joe had never been pretentious, but Eddie was still surprised at how little he had changed in manner over twenty years. A small black man, naturally good-humoured and courteous; he got up from fixing a tractor when he recognised Eddie.

"What happen, Naya?" called out Eddie, as he climbed from the car.

"Praises!" shouted Naya Joe in surprise.

He rose to embrace Eddie, who looked around him with an air of admiration.

"I come fe look fe yu on yu ranch," said Eddie; "I hear 'bout it but I never know is so beautiful."

"A jus Jah blessings," said Naya Joe.

"Him luv yu fe true," said Eddie.

"I feel so," said Naya Joe, and smiled broadly.

The two men who had been working on the tractor were waiting on the boss.

"We can start again later," he said, turning to them. "Beg yu, put up de tool where I show yu dis marnin."

"Ites, Naya," they said, and moved off.

Joe picked up a newspaper from the furrow that was attached to the back of the tractor, and he spread it for Eddie to sit down on. He himself squatted in his jeans and t-shirt, and pulled out a brown paper bag with ganja and rolling paper in it. Now Eddie remembered that as a youngster Joe's eyes were exactly the same as they were now.

"I'm not afraid to work, so why should I lie?" Joe had once said to Eddie years before, and now looking at him again, Eddie remembered that candour had always been the hallmark of his character.

Groups of men and women passed on their way out to the fields, walking slowly, talking and laughing ... they didn't call out to Naya Joe. They could see he was in a meeting.

"I hear yu ship out nearly two thousand weight a herb last Christmas season," said Eddie.

"Two thousand, three hundred."

"Yu not easy," Eddie laughed and leaned forward to slap the palm of Joe's hand, "yu turn millionaire on me now."

"Money run like water," said Naya Joe, shaking his head "It run in and it run out same way."

Eddie nodded his head in sympathy. He'd heard rumours that all wasn't well in Naya's dominion, and that was largely why he had come.

In the late sixties, before ganja became such a big business, a group of young white Americans who were into reggae music and dope opened a chapter of Abyssinian Consciousness in Miami, and they found themselves sitting in the midst of a growth market for which they had the most reliable source of good product.

Naya made very good money from the smuggling operation they set up, but the Miami end made four or five times more. They made so much money in Miami that the leader of the white group, Brother Soul, became convinced that he was a man of destiny—the link between white America and the spirit of black Africa in the New World. He grew his hair down to the middle of his back and started wearing white robes, and he hit upon an idea that would indeed give him an historic role to play: he decided to sue the US Government for the right to use ganja as a religious sacrament in the Abyssinian Consciousness Assembly, in the same way that Indian tribes are allowed to use peyote for their religious ceremonies.

Before getting involved in the "alternative economy", Brother Soul had been a bright young lawyer, and he was able to prove that in Abyssinia, herbs and religious meditation had gone hand in hand for thousands of years. To forbid his joining Abyssinian Consciousness was racial prejudice. To forbid his right to smoke ganja was to interfere with the practice of his religion.

All this was not being taken too seriously by the narcotics bureaucracy which depended for its living on the fact that ganja was illegal. But then, in the very first round of the court proceedings, Brother Soul was able to call a witness who convinced everyone in court that he'd been cured of cancer with a course of ganja treatment. And when the press showed signs of interest, suddenly the officials realised that the situation was getting out of hand.

If ganja was legalised, the people who were smuggling it did not stand to suffer loss on the scale of those employed by government. It was they who would have to go without the supplementary income from bribes, and who would lose the boats, planes, and helicopters that they had been given to play with in the war against crime. But the loss from legislation would spread far beyond the interests of any one group. The owners of the illegal landing strips and jetties would suffer, as would the people who rented planes and sold black-market gasoline, the craftsmen who customized yachts, the technicians who manned the radar and computer systems ... a huge industry had grown up around the illegality of grass, and the people at the centre of it decided to strike back at Brother Soul before his megalomania stirred dangerous energy. A call was made on Brother Soul in his Miami mansion, and he was told he'd have to drop his crusade to prove that ganja was harmless, or drop out of the ganja trade. Brother Soul didn't think twice. If he stayed in the trade he'd be just another dealer. If he won his case he'd make history. He told his visitors there was no deal and it seemed for a while that Brother Soul was a man of destiny after all.

"I hear yu 'ave a good crop to sell right now," said Eddie.

"I 'ave five tonnes ready fe shipment," said Naya Joe, wondering why Eddie had come to see him, wondering if he had come to help him in his hour of need.

"I hear yu having trouble wid de shipment dis time."

"Where yu hear a ting like dat?"

"I hear it from Miami about t'ree weeks ago, seh yu people court case going too well and the narcotic Babylon dem get vex and tell Brother Soul fe drap de case, but de brother refuse ... is true?"

"Him seh him a go drap de tradin' and fight fe him rights in court," said Naya Joe. "Him come down fe tell me late las' week. Him feel seh him a go win."

"But yu nuh win," said Eddie.

"Mi ha' fe prepare fe meet it because Brother Soul 'ave a mission, yu no sight? Yeah man," said Naya Joe, "him a go prove point."

"But yu no ship no herb."

"Nah," said Naya Joe. "I rig fe come out a de export. Too much money, too much Mafia on every side."

"But since I have de cash an you have de herb, we can do a deal still," said Eddie.

"Most natural," said Naya Joe.

"I nuh pay yu in America. I pay yu here."

"Is here I need it."

Eddie's heart jumped. He had at least six plans lined up for getting his money out of the island using ganja as the medium of change, but this plan with Naya Joe was the best—the only one big enough to forget about planes and yachts and dodging authority. This would be a mainstream shipment, handled the way shipments were handled for the biggest smugglers, the ones with attachés in Latin-American embassies and the United Nations, the ones who travelled on official passports, who represented authority: the authority of massive cash.

When Eddie came down out of the mountains, he went to the house of a cousin in the furniture business. Every week his cousin shipped a huge container filled with furniture to Miami. The containers travelled on custom-built ships and were off-loaded onto special trailers which were towed by trucks to any warehouse they were destined for. Once a container was filled at a warehouse in one country it would stay sealed till it arrived at its destination in another.

The cousin was nervous: "Suppose you don't make the right connection and they open my container and find ganja?"

"You think I could be sitting in Miami for ten days with two million dollars in cash and not find out who the man to bribe is? I would deserve to lose the shipment," said Eddie.

"Those people don't just give out information just like that," said the cousin.

"The system don't work on password," said Eddie. "The system work on cash. All I need to find out is who is the key man in the terminal you use, and how much him get. Rass, that's no big thing. Think of how much I am risking, compared with what you are worried about."

"You're the gambler, not me."

Eddie could see that he would have to insure his cousin if he was to do business with him.

"If the container is opened, I will give you the casino," said Eddie. "I will give you the title to hold before I leave, plus I will give you two hundred thousand dollars if the shipment goes through, plus I will set it up so that there is evidence the container was hijacked and the furniture dumped after it was loaded and left your warehouse; so don't be an asshole. You never dream you'd ever be able to do business with me and clear a quarter of a million without doing any work. You haven't got that in the bank after working fifteen years, and if you *don't* do it I will tell Sylvia what she missed and she will break your fucking neck."

Two days later the container was loaded as usual with furniture at the furniture factory, but the truck to pull the container back to the wharf did not arrive before nightfall. When it did arrive, the watchman let it in and within fifteen minutes the truck was hauling the trailer out onto the road. It didn't drive to the docks, but instead drove far into the countryside. At two o'clock in the morning Eddie watched as the furniture was dumped into a gully and replaced with ganja, pressed and wrapped in bales secured with metal bands.

It took an hour and forty-five minutes to fill the bulk container, and when it was done and sealed, Eddie tipped the loaders a total of two thousand dollars, picked up his three lookout men—all of them armed with submachine guns—and followed the truck and trailer to the main road. Half a mile along, Eddie brought the truck to a stop on the roadside where the truck driver rested till daylight, feigning engine trouble.

At ten-thirty the next morning Eddie's container was hauled into the container port and put in line with two hundred others awaiting shipment out of the island. Just down the wharf were another five hundred awaiting trans-shipment from at least ten other terminals in the Caribbean area alone. All looked identical—each with only a small serial number to identify it from ten thousand others—but this one, loaded with five tons of marijuana, would be worth 50 million dollars when it got to the other side of the fence in Florida. All Eddie had to make sure of was that, of all the hundreds of trailers being shifted around, the one supposedly with his cousin's furniture inside would not be one of those spot-checked, and he felt confident that that could be assured for a fraction of fifty million dollars.

In spite of his worst intentions, Red Roy had elevated Eddie to a level at which very big smugglers take very small risks.

Chapter Twenty-One

꧁꧂

Two days later, just as he was finishing his breakfast, Winston got a call from Sidney at the IMF in Washington.

"Winston, is this line private?"

"Sure." Winston had been expecting this call.

Sidney Jones had been senior to Winston when he was at the World Bank, and he hadn't changed his tone of voice to reflect their new status.

Sidney Jones was accustomed to talking to people like that. All the people he dealt with were so desperate for money they were happy to pay someone to take the tone and relay the terms to them in cabinet. How was Sidney Jones to guess that Winston wanted to borrow as little money as possible from him or anybody else?

"I've just been going over the figures for the last month. There's been a collapse down there. What's going on?"

"You can see for yourself from the figures, Sidney."

"Why didn't you warn me?"

"I warned you three months ago—"

"Good God!" said Sidney Jones. "Tax inflow's down sixty per cent in the domestic sector, price average index up twenty-eight per cent, wage claim estimates on current negotiations: eighty per cent! Foreign reserve account loss of sixty million! I was away in Geneva at the NIEO conference; I get back and the first thing I see is this!"

"Well, what did you expect?"

Sidney Jones pretended that he hadn't heard.

"I'm sending Oscar Delgado down," said Jones, "I certainly hope you two can come up with something for the next budget."

The very next day Oscar Delgado and his colleague, an Indian economist, arrived on the island from Washington. Nobody took any note of their arrival. It was not in the newspapers as they had declined to be interviewed by a reporter from the radio station. They made no statement of any kind about what they were doing, but what they were doing was taking control of the economy.

The men in the IMF only earned the salaries of well-paid civil servants, but when it came to playing around with huge sums of money the bureaucrats in the international lending agencies had more scope for their imagination than anybody except their colleagues in oil. These were the fellows who decided, for example, that if Italy needed a break, they would revalue the lira so some Fiats could be sold in France or England; since the end of the Second World War they had been accustomed to juggling national currencies all over the world to the satisfaction of those who controlled credit internationally, and Oscar Delgado was one of their top men for Latin America and the Caribbean.

Oscar Delgado had a Hungarian mother and a Chilean father. They met when his father was appointed First Secretary to the Chilean embassy in Budapest, and Oscar was conceived among the splendours of Central Europe in the giddy twenties ... producing a congenital weakness for eating. He was addicted to good food, and had the air of a man who had lived extremely well for many years on expense accounts.

For two days Oscar and his colleague poured over figures in an air-conditioned conference room that had no windows. Winston knew the figures they were analyzing, and he knew how they would interpret them. Five years before, he had been doing their job; he watched them working now, with detached amusement, sorry for the burden of ignorance and boredom that they had to bear—the boredom of having to add up other people's figures, and the almost total ignorance of the real conditions which were producing those figures ... the real factors and personalities; the key moods, motivations, and love affairs ...

After three days of seclusion, Oscar told Winston he was finished working, and Winston told Oscar that it was time for a good dinner. Winston had chosen a restaurant high up in the hills, and they enjoyed their meal together, gossiping about their business.

The lending institutions were filled with technocrats from the tropics who had come to know the ropes when they were borrowing money for their various governments; they played along as borrowers when their people were in power, and lived very comfortably as international banking bureaucrats when they weren't. But Delgado knew that Winston Bernard wasn't down at that level of manoeuvre, and they spoke with unusual candour.

Delgado admitted that the banks were swimming, drowning, in cash. The Arabs and the oil companies didn't know what to do with it, it was coming into them so fast, and the banks they deposited it in were as anxious as they were to lend it to whoever would borrow.

"When they started the ball rolling in 1973, they didn't see where it would end up," said Delgado. "They couldn't see anything but twenty billion dollars in arms sales. They decided that if the only way the Arabs could pay for it was by putting up the price of oil, that was OK, the money was coming straight back. But the Arabs figured there'd have to be some cash in the deal for them too, and suddenly everything was out of control. Now they don't know what to do with the cash."

"They have no trouble lending it," said Winston, "people like us have to borrow it to buy oil whether we like it or not."

"Yes, lending the money isn't the problem," said Oscar, "the problem is getting it repaid."

Winston smiled as he took a piece of paper out of his pocket and handed it across the table to Delgado. Delgado in turn handed Winston a piece of paper and each man read what the other had written; each had jotted down their estimates for the percentage of devaluation that Washington would set as a condition for more money to keep traffic on the island's roads. Winston's piece of paper said twenty-five per cent and Oscar's said twenty-eight per cent.

"You still remember the formula," said Oscar.

The formula for deepening impoverishment.

They settled on a twenty-five per cent devaluation immediately, with a further devaluation in three months if inflation hadn't dropped to ten per cent. They both knew that that was impossible, that another devaluation was inevitable, that the bankers represented by Delgado might not get their money back, that squeezing tighter wouldn't help; but to admit that was to admit that the whole system was out of control ... and who, among those in control of the system, was going to be the first officially to admit that?

Chapter Twenty-Two

The scenario Winston had predicted continued to unfold. With the death of first the informal and now the formal economy, no money moved unless it was in the direction of buying US dollars.

Businessmen, in order to buy from abroad, had to submit an application to the Central Bank. The staff at the banks couldn't handle the extra work and in any case didn't have the foreign exchange to sell. Foreign suppliers, sensing trouble, started to restrict credit. Men who had been successful in business for thirty years could either wait for a meeting with a bank clerk at which they would have to explain themselves like schoolboys, or deal on the black market, which itself was starved for cash since Eddie Azani's exit.

After devaluation a whole series of price rises were announced. Gas went up, of course, and so did beer and soft drinks, food, bus fares, all building materials ... but while the cost of everything else was rising, wages were frozen.

"The IMF, the lending agency for the western imperialist banking system, is in a deal to take over this country and run it like a colony of the United States," shouted Maurice DeCartret to a political mass rally.

He called for a general strike in all essential services to protest the price hikes, and he was overwhelmingly endorsed by the crowd.

Next day there was no electricity, no public transport, no service station open to sell gas, and no telephone service. Some areas were without water.

The workers of all other unions followed the lead of the DeCartret unions and the second day after the devaluation a general strike was in effect right across the island.

"What the hell is Percy thinking of?" asked Mark. "Is he really going to sit back and let this chaos spread?"

"Percy's not worried," said Winston, "he's still prime minister. He figures you and DeCartret cancel each other out. If you try to oust Percy with a state of emergency, DeCartret will cripple you with strikes, and if DeCartret goes on crippling him with strikes Percy can threaten to let you loose on him. He stays in the middle and threatens you with each other; meanwhile both of you need him if you're to stay legitimate."

"A legitimate government runs the country," said Mark, "and if he isn't prepared to do it, I'll brush him aside, the gutless son of a bitch."

"It will put you in a lot of trouble for international credit," said Winston; "if you were literally to push him aside you'd have to go for re-negotiated loan agreements as a new government."

"How long would that take?"

"It would take at least three months to clear up the confusion," said Winston.

"Percy is finished no matter what happens," said Mark.

"Finished for making policy, but as prime minister he could go on forever. That's what DeCartret is promising him if he goes with the left ... one-party state ... lifetime job. Not bad from Percy's point of view."

"You can't be serious."

"I'm perfectly serious. Percy would rather be seen as a populist than as a military stooge; even in America it would be better for his image."

"He can stay on with me too as long as he doesn't try to make policy," said Mark.

"That's all he wants to hear," said Winston.

"Well, I'll tell him," said Mark, "I'll tell him that at the same time I tell him that if essential services aren't restored within forty-eight hours, I'm going to declare a state of emergency."

"Well for once in his life it looks like Percy's going to have to make a choice," said Winston.

"He no longer has a choice if he wants to stay in office."

That afternoon, there was an editorial, printed in red, on the front page of *Liberation!* the evening paper that supported DeCartret's unions and political party:

"... all over the world the pattern is the same. In Zaire, and Peru, and Jamaica the masses are rioting because the bankers have decreed they should do without soap, without rice, without cooking oil, or spare parts for motor cars, or essential medicines. Faceless, nameless capitalists set policy without debate and enforce it through local stooges like the Bernard brothers, but everywhere protest is stirring ... in Africa, in Latin America, in the Caribbean ... at this very moment when the fascist dictator, Somoza, is getting ready to flee his country and rape the national treasury, this very same IMF is giving him millions to put in his personal bank account while our people are being asked to go without the necessities of life. For too long there has been an assumption that everything can rise with inflation except the wages of the working class. We say strike!"

Mark set aside the paper and started stroking his cat as he sat by the pool having a drink before dinner. The cat, purring contentedly in his lap, had never had a really unpleasant experience in its life. Anybody, anything within Mark's control was secure … always had been, up to now. Now if he didn't discipline the hooligans, they would reduce the island to a state where it was indecent to feed an animal because people were starving. Somalia, Cambodia, Uganda—starvation was the first thing he heard about every morning on the BBC. It was entirely possible for it to happen on the island.

"Every day's delay is going to mean a bigger mess to clean up in the end," said Mark to Vera. "All I've been waiting for is a good excuse, and DeCartret's going to give it to me on a platter."

Thirty thousand workers came to the second Anti IMF Strike rally, but Red Roy made sure it wasn't a purely union affair. He added two thousand political supporters from the slums he controlled, just to make sure DeCartret, and the politicians, and the guys who ran the unions, understood that they alone would not reap power from this state of unrest. Red Roy made his presence felt as his people, many heavily armed, swarmed through the crowd, heating it up, claiming allegiance with the workers, proclaiming solidarity in the name of their joint party and joint leader: Maurice DeCartret.

When Red Roy's thugs had raised the heat in the mass meeting to the point where police and army units moved in, all hell broke loose. Twenty-seven were wounded in the cross-fire between Red Roy's men and the army. Four died on the afternoon of May 20th between five o'clock and five-thirty.

By six o' clock Mark Bernard had given the go-ahead for the coup d'etat. Eighty-three military personnel, including five officers, were arrested. The radio station was surrounded by soldiers and all programmes were interrupted for an announcement that General Bernard would address the nation that evening.

An hour later Percy was in Mark's office in a last-minute attempt to resolve the crisis.

"It's still not too late, Percy," said Mark, "I'd much prefer to have a state of emergency with you as prime minister than a military government."

"Ok," said Percy.

When Percy was gone, Mark sent for Maurice DeCartret, who had been held and conducted to military HQ. He was intensely angry as he came into the room.

"Who gave you the authority to order me into your presence?" shouted DeCartret. "Do you realise where this is going to put you in the eyes of the international press?"

"You're an irresponsible son of a bitch," said Mark, "you have deliberately caused a riot directly responsible for the death of four people ..."

"You wait till I'm through with you," said DeCartret, lawyer and legislative expert, "in parliament, at the UN ..."

"Shut up DeCartret," said Mark, "I've declared a state of emergency and you're under house arrest. I'm putting you into indefinite detention."

Winston watched on television as his brother spoke to the nation that night.

"...I feel a personal responsibility to the citizens of this island," said Mark, "because I am Minister of Security. When unruly, undisciplined elements in the society seek to intimidate the government and allow chaos to reign and violence to control the streets, when they threaten every form of normal everyday activity—then I say to them I am not intimidated. The nation is not intimidated. Tonight you have electricity. Later tonight when you pick up the phone, it will be working. Tomorrow you will be able to send your children to school, and take a bus to work, or buy gas for your car. We're back to normal ladies and gentlemen!" Mark smiled broadly and nodded to the camera. "Good night to you all. Sleep well!"

Winston rushed to the elevator and down to his car. Some impulse warned him that he'd have to reach Mark very early or he'd be too late. Perhaps he was already too late.

When he got to the radio station, he found an armoured car blocking the front gate, and beyond the entrance way there were dozens of soldiers who looked like they were preparing to repulse an attack on the station. They were all carrying weapons and wearing metal hats, strung around with field telephones and ammunition, and they all seemed insulated with that anonymous, impersonal stupidity that belongs to men in battle dress.

There was a machine gun by the front steps of the main entrance to the building, and searchlights were set up in the middle of the car park.

"Is General Bernard still here?" asked Winston.

"He's left," said the officer in charge who recognised Winston.

"Do you know where he went?"

"I think he went to camp, sir."

"Thank you," said Winston, and he switched on the radio again as he drove towards the army camp. An announcer was reading the new regulations: "*Nothing will be published or broadcast without reference to clause fifteen of the Emergency Regulations Act. No one will leave their homes between midnight and seven o'clock in the morning ... the authorities have right of entry to any premises without a search warrant ... the authorities have the right to detain any suspicious person for questioning without bringing a specific charge against them for up to three months... There will be no assembly of more than ten persons for any reason other than a religious service in an established church without written permission from the authorities ...*"

When one was free from it, the very idea of military rule seemed so absurd, so far-fetched. It seemed so unlikely that adult citizens would react en masse, like school children, as generals read out the list of rules. But when one actually came up against the military mentality, within minutes it seemed as though it was the continuing reality—that freedom was the fantasy, a brief interlude here and there in history ... playtimes, at the end of which the whistle always blew. His elder brother's image on the television screen, his voice, his sense of authority: it took Winston back to his childhood, to the moment at boarding school when he was brought into the prefects' common room and told that he was going to be beaten "for attitude". Mark had said to him: "We don't like your attitude."

Winston was ten and Mark was thirteen, and Mark was going to beat Winston to help him prove that he wasn't a sissy. Mark had warned him when they were home for the previous holidays: "You might think it's alright to read books, but if you don't play football, sooner or later, you gwine get a bussass."

Winston hadn't mended his ways, and now Mark was hearing whispered rumours that Winston wasn't tough enough to play football, that he was soft. "Bend over," Mark had said, pointing to the railing of the stairway with his cane, and then pointing it at Winston.

The first stroke seemed to cut straight through the thin material of Winston's pyjama pants and into the flesh of his backside; he was so surprised at the intensity of the pain that he didn't quite believe it. He was just catching his breath when the next stroke cut him. He was about to turn around and cry out and ruin the whole exercise, when the third stroke slashed across his buttocks and he heard Mark say, "stand up".

Mark and Winston had never discussed that moment since, except once when still teenagers; Mark had said, "You lucky, when I went thru that I got six." But Winston vividly remembered the look on Mark's face. He wasn't the least bit sorry; just relieved that Winston had passed the test. Mark had beaten him to prove that Winston wasn't a coward and to ease his entry into the inner circle. But Winston's only reaction had been to stay as far as possible outside it for the rest of his life.

They had been right to beat him for attitude, those authoritarians, they knew instinctively what his attitude towards them was, that of all the attitudes against them his was the worst because he had been offered membership in their ranks, and he had spurned it.

'Sir', the officer at the gate of the radio station had called Winston. Winston could still join Mark's team, but he still didn't want to, not even as second in command, not even as the brother of the Commander-in-Chief.

When Winston got to Mark's headquarters, he could tell at a glance that this was to be the centre of things for some time to come. Trucks, searchlights, constant motion: this was where the action was. As he parked the car, he saw the helicopter taking off; a huge searchlight looked down from the front of it, powerful enough to see into any little nook and cranny of the city that Mark cared to examine from on high.

Again Winston was too late to catch his brother. He got into his car once more, and, following the flight path of the searchlight in the distance, he realised he'd be able to meet Mark at home.

Maybe that was better, thought Winston, as he drove once more in pursuit of Mark. Maybe in the privacy of his home, Winston would be able to warn Mark not to get carried away with the momentum of the power that was suddenly his, to resist the temptation of a clean sweep, to warn him of the dangers of sweeping away things which were too complicated, too subtle, for the military mind in the middle of a crisis ...

There was no traffic on the streets. There were few people on the pavements. Winston checked his watch against the warning of the midnight curfew. It was ten-thirty. Mark would probably have to give him a pass to get back to his hotel!

When Winston reached his brother's front gate, he was stopped. Before, the guards had sat to one side of the gate, but now they were blocking the roadway, and a sergeant poked a flashlight into Winston's face when he stopped the car.

"I'm the General's brother." said Winston.

"The General's brother is here," said the sergeant, speaking into a walkie-talkie.

There was a pause.

"Tell the visitor to identify himself by name," came the voice over the sergeant's receiver.

"Say, Winston." He thought of telling them that the General only had one brother, but realised that kind of intimacy, even in Mark's home, was now no longer appropriate. They were, after all, protecting the only man on the island who really mattered to them that night.

Mark was delighted that Winston had come to see him, but when Winston saw Mark, he realised immediately that he was already too late.

"Come in!" said Mark, crossing the patio to meet him and taking him by the arm to two seats out by the pool. "It's great to see you."

Mark was starting to feel isolated. He was already in need of someone to talk to who he knew would not be fazed by the responsibilities he had taken on his head, by the power he needed to discharge them; Winston was someone he could talk to frankly. "What did you think of the speech?" asked Mark as they sat down.

"I didn't realise you had such flair for PR. 'Sleep well' was an unexpected touch."

"God! I can almost feel the relief, can't you?"

"Yes," said Winston, "the people are sick and tired of all that nonsense Percy and DeCartret were carrying on with."

"I had no choice, you know that, no choice at all."

"Yes, I know that."

"I've seen this moment coming for a long time." He hadn't realised how much he wanted to talk to Winston, to unwind, to be able to explain to even one person what had brought him to this point in his life. "I don't want to sound melodramatic, but have you ever felt a sense of destiny?"

"You mean like a responsibility to do something?"

"Yes. Like you're the only one who can do it."

"Yes ... I've known that feeling."

"Sometimes it comes to me very strongly," said Mark; "sometimes it comes to me like a force that just carries my body along. I first felt it when I was running at school; it was a feeling that I couldn't lose, but I didn't think too much about it. Perhaps I even thought that everybody felt it. It wasn't till later, in Korea, that I realised it was something special."

"Like voices, you mean?"

"No ... it's more like a presence."

He broke off speaking and Winston realised that Mark was telling him something he'd never confided in anyone, not even Vera.

"What happened in Korea?" asked Winston.

"We were on a carrier, at sea. It was very cold and very rough. It was my first combat mission, and I was scared shitless—not of the flying, but of the takeoff and landing. A jet fighter landing on a carrier in those conditions, at that speed..." Mark shook his head and looked away. "I thought, for the first time in my life, that I was going to die. There probably aren't more than five hundred pilots in the world who could fly jets off a carrier in those conditions, but they control the world. It was more important to me to be one of them than anything else, and yet I thought I wasn't going to have the nerve to climb into the cockpit. I hadn't known before that a man could go right to the edge of his ambition and turn back at the last moment because of fear; then this feeling, this presence, that used to take me over when I was running at school, came back, and I realised that *that* was what I was afraid of, *that* was what would kill me ..."

Mark looked to Winston for his understanding. "It's as though there is a spirit that has carried the family forward for hundreds of years, in our father, our uncles, both grandfathers, and back far beyond that. They had always struggled, they had always gone further than their contemporaries, but they had always been pushed back. Generation after generation getting it from both sides, black and white, always struggling, always ahead of everybody in their class, but never making it to the top. Well that night I realised that if you got to the crucial moment and turned back, all those old guys would get together and their rage would snuff you out in a minute ... that they'd just snuff you out and start looking for the next one who could carry their spirit."

Mark did not speak like a man demented. He seemed quite calm. Obviously, he was no longer terrified by the demands of his ancestral spirit. He had long ago decided to obey it.

The two brothers sipped on their drinks, and looked out over the lights of the city to the crescent of a quarter moon in a sky that promised rain.

"I wonder what the old people would have made of all this," said Winston of his parents.

"I know exactly what they would have made of it," said Mark, "I overheard them once, in a quarrel."

"A quarrel!" Winston was surprised. He'd never imagined that his mother had ever succeeded in getting his father into an argument.

"Oh yes," said Mark, "they'd been out to a cocktail party, and some white woman had insulted Mother, and Dad apparently had failed to step in—"

"What do you mean insulted?" Winston interrupted.

"She'd slighted her in some way, been patronising."

"Oh ..."

"It wasn't what the woman said that upset her so much as it was Dad's reaction. Apparently Mother had bridled at the woman's remark, and Dad's reaction was to get her away from the confrontation rather than back her up."

"I see," said Winston.

It had been a recurring theme in his parents' life. His mother was passionate. His father was cool.

"Anyway, as you know, he didn't usually stand up to her, but this night he decided to tell her the facts of life from his point of view, and it was the only time I ever saw him lose his temper."

"Really? You mean he would have hit her?"

"Definitely, he held her down till she'd heard what he had to say."

The thought of his father using physical violence against his mother astonished Winston. He'd never imagined such a thing.

"What *did* he have to say?" Winston asked.

"I'll never forget it: 'Listen' he said, 'do you think the games the British play are played on the tennis court? Their games are played with guns, bombs, and serious money; and they may tell you how ravishingly beautiful you are in London, but so long as you are a black woman married to a black man in one of their colonies, you're nothing but a pawn. And until *we* have guns, and bombs, and serious money of our own, they will remind you of it any time they feel like it.'"

"Ha!" said Winston. "That must have been long before the title."

"The title meant nothing to her."

"What did she say?"

"She was a bit tipsy, you realise," Mark said, grinning at the memory. "She said, 'well, go and get some planes, and some guns, and some bombs, and some serious money; and go and take away something the white man really treasures, and bring it to me. Then we'll talk about being lovers again.'"

Mark had risen and was walking slowly up and down, arching out his arms in a slow-motion athlete's stretch.

"I see," said Winston quietly ... so Mark had decided as a child that he would make good on his father's promise.

Then Mark came right out and said it: "I mean, what the hell is Fidel Castro's army doing turning back the South Africans in Angola? That should have been done by a black general. Are we going to leave that job to a Latin American? Do you know how many troops it took to overrun Amin? Four thousand! Four thousand half-trained troops are winning black wars in Africa, and they have to deal with the Boers!"

"And you feel that you are the man who can lead the black African army?" asked Winston, excited by Mark's vision in spite of himself.

"Yes," said Mark, staring out over the city —the streets quiet, the lights back on. "Yes, I do."

Now Winston saw his brother's plans in perspective. For Mark, the state of emergency was a small preliminary detail, necessary if he was to put his home base in order, and the least he would expect of Winston was that he would find the money to pay for it all. For a moment Winston wished that he was able to believe in his brother's dream, to finance it for him. Mark was right, if anybody could fulfil the destiny that Mark had outlined it was Mark Bernard. If Black Africa went to war with a leader like Mark, the Africans could win. It was worth any price to reap that satisfaction for people like Mark, but while Mark was his mother's son, Winston was his father's. He felt he had a better plan for winning because he thought warfare was out of date—as impractical as suicide. Winston thought Mark was magnificent, but that he was old-fashioned—Mark wasn't proposing to change the game, he just wanted to put together a winning team.

"What would you do if somebody didn't agree with your plan?" asked Winston.

Mark seemed surprised by the question. He didn't connect it with his brother directly; he merely thought that Winston was asking for information.

"You mean in a state of emergency?"

"In war."

"Oh. In war if you don't obey you lose your life," he said, as though stating the obvious. Then he leaned forward. "Listen Winston, I know the torch passed to you for a while, but it's gone past what you can control. It's passed to me now, and you have to trust me, and you have to back me up."

Back at his base, Winston looked out over the city. He was feeling very weary. He too needed someone to talk to, but those who spoke his language were not to be found on the island. To talk to his brand of revolutionary he would have to go to the only place where a revolution had ever succeeded, the only country where the people really were, ultimately, in control; the only place where Mao Tse Tung's dream of constant political turmoil was a reality, the only place where the power game was a popular sport invented to displace the old fashioned games of theocracy, royalty, and dictatorship. With their genius for revolution these people had invented a game that everybody could play—the name of the game was 'Business', the biggest game of all. The next morning the first thing Winston Bernard did, was book himself on a flight to New York City.

Chapter Twenty-Three

From the moment Winston entered a cab at JFK and the meter started ticking, he knew he would be in a race against time till he left town again.

Driving in over Triborough Bridge, looking at the towers twinkling in the distance, Winston thought how Manhattan had always had the excitement for him of a gigantic Christmas tree, every window a leaf alight, and he realised how much he loved it—the speed. From Wall Street to Harlem, everybody was addicted to excitement, everybody was caught up in some game or other, all playing at maximum velocity.

In Manhattan, speed was key. A phone call not returned within the first few available minutes was an insult, because speed was so important that status was assessed by who could keep who waiting ... who could raise whose pulse with anticipation and keep them hanging on, which men could treat other men the way those men treated their women.

Winston thought about the number of times he'd stepped into this ring with the heavyweights.

He had started off as a technician, able to compute and interpret statistics fast enough to give the winning edge to someone else's power play; later on, he went in as a player, but with money controlled by other people. Now, for the first time, he was planning to play with money that he controlled himself—the assets of an entire national economy ... if everything went according to plan ... a billion dollars ... if he could prevent everybody else from wasting it.

As the cab raced south down East River Drive, name after name popped into Winston's head of men who were accustomed to dealing in bigger stakes than one Caribbean island. The cab turned west across town and the New York street buzz came in through the car window. Madison Avenue, Park, Fifth, in every tower in mid-town there was a king of the block whose rating of Winston Bernard's concerns wouldn't place them higher in the order of things than what he himself was doing.

That's what Winston loved *most* of all about New York. When he was there the scope of his imagination never seemed outrageous, his ambitions seemed reasonable, he didn't feel like a megalomaniac, or even outstandingly bright; not with people like Kissinger around the corner, Felix Rohatyn down the block, Charlie Bluhdorn and Diego Zorzano across the park. In Manhattan to set up a billion-dollar plan, Winston felt he had just graduated from the status of a young man with promise, to the level of a serious player, and when he climbed out of the cab on to the Fifth Avenue pavement in front of the Sherry-Netherland, he felt a surge of happiness as the loneliness and sense of isolation that had gripped his mood for months suddenly disappeared.

When he got up to his suite, he immediately called Hugh Clifford's apartment, and they fixed a meeting for eleven-thirty the next morning.

He picked up the phone and dialled again. This time the call at the other end was answered immediately.

"Lucy!"

"Winston! Have you eaten?"

"No, I saved dinner to have it with you."

"Good, there's a little sushi place on Fifty-third between Seventh and Eighth."

"I'll meet you there in twenty minutes," said Winston.

He showered and changed in five minutes, and then took fifteen to stroll past the floodlit fountains outside the Plaza, and along Central Park South with its limousines and old-fashioned horse buggies and models walking their dogs; then he turned south past Carnegie Hall, and on down Seventh Avenue towards Broadway and the theatre district, till he came to the restaurant.

It was small and crowded, but as he entered and slipped off his shoes, he saw Lucy calling to him from a cubicle at the back of the room. Her face lit up with joy at seeing Winston, and when he saw her, he saw a bit of his mother, and a bit of Ada, and a bit of Michele; it was as if he'd made contact with all the women he'd loved in life after a long period of starvation for any love at all.

Ada had married Percy and inspired him to politics, and Michele had married Winston, but Lucy Anderson had decided to make it on her own from the very start.

She didn't have much money, and making money was the first item on her agenda. She wanted to make it quickly without overwhelming effort, however, because once she'd made enough she wanted to use it for other things. The passion for independence that Edna Bernard had instilled in her sons and the girls she treated like daughters was as strong in Lucy Anderson as it was in any of the others.

Lucy was outstanding academically. When she came down from Cambridge she was able to get a job as one of the personal assistants to Sir George, the chairman of a merchant bank in London which did a lot of business in Latin America and the Caribbean. Sir George was an old friend of Sir Arthur's. The job was very good experience for Lucy: it enabled her to learn who was important in the world of international trading, but it did not give her the chance to meet them socially, nor to speculate with any knowledge she might have had regarding their business. God forbid Sir George's secretary should be found dabbling in inside information! So she resigned and got a job as an airline stewardess.

For three months she flew the Atlantic every day, first class. When she wasn't working serving passengers, she was sitting and being served. She had some money to spend on entertaining during the flights when she wasn't working, and within a very short time, she had met and made friends with those men and women who crossed the Atlantic once or twice a week on a regular basis and who were able to tell her all that she needed to know to attempt making money on the stock market herself.

Everywhere she went in the business world, Lucy saw signs that an electronics revolution was coming but that few in Wall Street knew much about it. Lucy called Winston. Winston gave her the best, most up-to-date information about the computer industry and she bought into stock like Apple when it was still just the seed of an idea.

In ten years Lucy Anderson made a personal fortune of ten million dollars; nothing in terms of financial power, but enough money to enable her to pursue her ambitions of political influence at a personal level.

As a political exercise, she studied the futures market for industrial raw materials and discovered that, with the exception of oil, the terms of trade for the tropical exporting nations were bad and getting worse.

She and Winston discussed the current situation in terms of specific markets, not as something they had to commiserate about. They brought each other up to date on numerous negotiations worldwide. Winston told her of his dealings with Hugh Clifford and the mining companies; she approved of all the decisions he'd taken and Winston felt much reassured. He realised that in all the years he'd known her, he'd never been bored by Lucy, and he decided that the quality he loved, the quality that had attracted his mother to her and all her protégées, was a combination of intelligence mixed with excitement.

"What happened with Michele?" she asked.

Winston hadn't thought about it, he realised. He'd so shut off any connection with her that she was like a huge phantom presence in him, waiting to be dealt with, finessed for a time, but eventually ...

"At the exact moment I needed her most, at the exact moment we had been waiting for, I found out she was having an affair..."

"Really?" said Lucy, she was surprised. "Why on earth would she do that?"

"She said she couldn't wait any longer, that she wasn't seeing enough of me. We had postponed the baby too long ... I don't know, I just know that I couldn't forgive her ... and from that moment on nothing's worked," said Winston, "Percy, Mark, myself: we've all gone off in separate directions, there's nobody to explain us to each other, there's nobody to explain us to the public; the whole family has split apart, the whole plan ..."

Lucy leaned across the table and touched Winston's hand. "Michele loves you, I know that. But maybe she just *couldn't* wait, I understand that too ... sometimes ten minutes on somebody else's timing is like an eternity, that's why I never married, never wanted to get married, and will remain unmarried till the day I die; I can only live on my own time, I know that."

"Yes," said Winston, "that I understand."

"I think being wanted is like a drug to Michele, I think unless she feels that somebody would die to fuck her, she doesn't feel she's up to par."

Winston laughed.

"And the way I know that," continued Lucy, looking a Winston and raising one eyebrow, "is that I sometimes feel that way myself."

Winston felt her warmth spread through him like the flush from the sake they'd been sipping. He looked into her eyes, and hummed the snatch of an old tune: *I don't want to set the world on fire*, went the lyric that Edna used to sing, *I just want to start a flame in your heart.*

Lucy laughed softly, and then she sighed.

"You know," she said, speaking with the lilt of an English restoration comedy character in a play that Edna had once produced and that both Lucy and Winston had acted in as teenagers, "I do so fear the effect of gentlemen who can excite lust in a lady's heart and then leave her feeling dizzy."

"Me too," said Winston, attempting to cover his naked need for her with flippancy, "and it is for that reason that I'm reluctant to unleash passions that would have me acting like a beast ..."

There was a long pause.

"It is fortunate, is it not," said Lucy, "that ladies of a certain age know it as a passing phase."

By the time they got back to Lucy's gigantic bed in her enormous apartment, Winston was in an expansive mood, and as they made love, his mind eased in one dimension after another until he was in a state of complete relaxation. The new woman, independent, and taking that for granted, free to do what she wanted: Michele's generation. But this was the flip side, this time he wasn't the husband, this time he was the lover, and now he was in the right place to enjoy the woman's revolution.

Before this revolution, had any man, anywhere, ever, had the gift of a woman like Lucy? In all of history had any man ever been offered pleasure without risk; understanding without having to make a commitment? Had anybody ever had the luxury of making love with a mature woman and not had to put up with the shadow of jealous rage in another man?

As the measure of Winston's wellbeing grew, Lucy, too, felt gifted in that she could give over and not be captured, she could take in with no obligation to give back, and she could feel wanted without being possessed. Thus they spent five hours in an embrace of something altogether new in the world of love, something that would not have been possible without the Industrial Revolution ... and the scientific revolution, the social revolution, and the technological revolution; that night Winston felt like a revolutionary, celebrating the breakdown of every barrier between a man and a woman in a bed. It had taken revolutions to put them there for that night of lovemaking in Manhattan, but it was triggered by an impulse older than revolutions, one which would still be alive when the revolutions were dead and forgotten: the impulse that puts a lonely, passionate man in the arms and legs of a passionate, loving woman ... and, by dawn, the sexual wound in Winston was healed to the point where he was no longer consumed with his own pain.

Next morning Winston walked down Park Avenue till he got to the Waldorf-Astoria, where he bought a bouquet of flowers for Molly Clifford, before walking around to the entrance of the Waldorf Towers and taking the elevator to the Clifford's suite—near the one owned by the Windsors, next to the one Cole Porter lived in, a few floors from General MacArthur's last home ... Even on a sunny day the whole building felt as if it was permeated with the ghosts of great dreams.

Hugh and Molly Clifford greeted Winston warmly and introduced him to Marc Gold, a trader based in Geneva who dealt in precious metals, oil, ore, any transaction that produced a buyer and a seller on a large scale, with Marc Gold in between. He was tall, dapper, with dark hair and very dark eyes. His mouth, one could tell, was shaped by speaking several different languages perfectly, that is to say: his lips and his entire lower face was flexible enough to accommodate five different cultures without detection in any one of them. The English he spoke was with a mid-Atlantic accent, impossible to place.

In Switzerland, Marc Gold did nothing illegal as he traded worldwide, but in the US he had annoyed the authorities. He had failed to pay taxes on overseas earnings, he had failed to report the details of his business to their satisfaction, and he was in the process of closing down his New York office altogether.

In Switzerland, he was operating within the boundaries of a tradition in free trade and banking that started when the Protestants told the Medici they weren't prepared to do business with mafia, even when clothed in the most respectable of trappings, even when sitting on the throne of France ...

The fact that Marc Gold was operating out of a base for his kind of business that had been established hundreds of years before, gave him a certain peace of mind as he joined forces with Hugh Clifford to fight Henry Lynch and what he represented in the 1970s: central mafia, doing what central mafia always did, taxing everyone else to pay for arms with which to maintain control. For century after century the essentials had remained the same, but these guys wanted $300 thousand million a year. A thousand million each working day was the size of their appetite for cash. It was too much. They were too greedy. There was no end in sight, and although Marc Gold knew that his deal with Hugh Clifford and Winston Bernard would annoy his adversaries in Washington even more than he already had, he felt the deal was too good to miss. Never before had anyone fought the mining companies and won. If Winston won, and Marc Gold sold the ore in the open market, Marc Gold would make some of the profits that would otherwise have disappeared into Lynch's address on the monopoly board.

"I'm afraid I have bad news," said Winston, "I'm not going to be working with Mark after all. I'm not going to be in office to implement the plan."

"What went wrong?" asked Hugh Clifford.

"I fell out with Percy and I'm not going along with Mark for the same reason: they both want to waste money. Mark is probably worse than Percy, he wants to borrow as much money as he can possibly get, to spend on the army."

"Doesn't he need it?" asked Marc Gold. "Isn't there rioting down there?"

"It's what's causing the riots that has to be dealt with, and Mark's never going to get around to that."

"Why not?" asked Marc Gold, who, Winston realised, was very curious to know why one brother would fail to support another.

"Because he has a standard disciplinary view of life," said Winston, mindful of the need to keep quiet about Mark's real plans. "Mark doesn't want to stop at riots, he wants to drill the entire nation, and he wants to root out drugs. He feels no compunction at all about sweeping the entire countryside, locking people up by the thousands, destroying millions of dollars worth of crops at the very level where it's needed most—and that's solid foreign exchange. Where does it end? He's going to want national service, he's going to want to control not only what people smoke, but how they think, how they dress, how they wear their hair! You know what I'm talking about, we've seen it a dozen times, it's a military plan!"

"And what is your plan?" asked Marc Gold.

"To leave people alone. To leave them alone and supply them with what they need. Water to grow food; freedom to trade freely, move freely, speak freely; to do what they want to do. And you know what that is? They want to make money. But they want to make money for themselves, not to buy army boots and hats, and helicopters, for God's sake."

Marc Gold shrugged, as much as to say: *I still don't like the way you're leaving your brother in the lurch*, but he said nothing.

"I want to put money into agriculture, education, solar energy, transportation, environmental protection, recycling, health services, tourist development, offshore banking and a dozen other things!" said Winston. "But I don't feel like being party to a plan that will install a military government, wipe out all hope of real development, and eventually load the island with a debt that will mortgage us for years."

He turned to look at Hugh Clifford, trying to assess if he too was judging him harshly for his failure to help Mark.

Hugh Clifford smiled.

Marc Gold said nothing more. The deal was between Hugh Clifford and Bernard. He was merely the intermediary.

"Is Mark aware of our arrangement?" asked Hugh Clifford.

"He's aware of it in general terms. He knows it's not official."

"So if he comes to me for the money ..."

"He knows he can't demand it," said Winston, "but he will come to you for money before he does anything else."

"OK," said Hugh Clifford, and he looked to Marc Gold, who nodded.

"I'll make it plain to him that the deal with me depends on you," said Hugh Clifford.

"Thank you," said Winston.

"He'll have to implement your plan to get the money."

"That's right," said Winston.

Both men nodded agreement.

Hugh Clifford smiled. He felt that his confidence in Winston was going to pay off in the end. He knew the personalities involved, Winston's scenario was the one he wanted to see succeed. The meeting was brought to a close, and he prepared to move on to consideration of the people he planned to meet for lunch.

Back on Park Avenue, Winston walked slowly. Now that he had done what he'd willed himself to do, now that there was no turning back, it wasn't Hugh Clifford's approval that lingered from the meeting, it was the look of distrust on Marc Gold's face.

Chapter Twenty-Four

Mark simply could not bring himself to believe that Winston had disappeared.

Over and over he looked at the handwritten note that Winston had scrawled and left.

> *Don't approve military approach.*
> *Sorry,*
> *Winston*

That was it, that was all. No discussion, no warning, nothing.

It was beyond Mark's comprehension that his brother could be so irresponsible as to leave him in the lurch during a national emergency involving the fate of the entire island. Responsibility was the first insistence in the training they received from both their mother and their father; it had been ingrained in them from the nursery to the dinner table, in dozens of family anecdotes …

It was incomprehensible that Winston could have backed out of a challenge that the family had been waiting for for three generations, a culmination of events that had taken decades to mature to the moment when the fate of the island was in the hands of the Bernards, hands that had not grasped power, but had waited patiently until it was clear there were no alternatives among those who competed for leadership on the island, and now there were none among them who had the capabilities of Winston and Mark working together as a team.

But without Winston, the very centre of Mark's power base kept slipping away from under him. Without Winston, the centre would not hold.

Mark wanted to know what the situation was in the government's finances, how much money was owed, what loans were being negotiated, what payments were due, how much food and oil were left on the island, where new supplies would come from and on what terms. With Winston to handle all the technical aspects of government, Mark would have had instant analysis at his fingertips, but without him ...

For an entire day and night after Winston disappeared, Mark considered who he should call on for help, and eventually he decided on Alistair McFadden.

McFadden was Winston's number two at the Central Bank. Mark had known him in a distant way at school, but they hadn't been close because McFadden had always been an academic on the one hand and Mark a sports star on the other.

From school McFadden had gone Winston's route to Oxford, and from there to a great shock when he took up his first professorship at a university in the US.

For the first time ever in his life, Alistair McFadden then knew what it was to be regarded as a black man, and he was appalled. He fled back to Europe immediately and back to the Caribbean eventually.

Alistair McFadden didn't think of himself as a black man with white genes, on the contrary, he identified completely with his white parentage and regarded the black component as merely a seasoning, like good black pepper on a breakfast egg. The North American angle on colour did not link up with his point of view in any way. No, Alistair McFadden was Oxbridge to his fingertips in style, and a fine style it was in the series of splendid backgrounds he thereafter always managed to place himself against. Always there had been large conference rooms, first class hotels, and chauffeur driven limousines, because there were more institutions that needed Alistair McFadden than there were men with his attributes to go around.

Over the years, however, the lack of competition had produced a somewhat disconcerting problem for McFadden: he had the greatest difficulty in staying awake. He would enter conference halls and seminars and assemblies with a great show of interest, take his seat in slowly spinning motions as he said numerous hellos on the way, then he'd sit down, and the droning would begin ... papers ... speakers ... all in the same tone, hour after hour, morning after morning, noon after noon, night after night, year in year out ... occasionally a muffled laugh, never a guffaw; occasionally a heated exchange, never a real flash of anger ... of course he couldn't stay awake, and over the years he had evolved ways of sitting so that he could close his eyes as though paying close attention, when in fact he was fast asleep. A secretary, or woman friend, invariably accompanied him for the main purpose of jogging him awake if absolutely necessary.

Because he slept so much during working hours, Alistair McFadden was very good fun when away from official duties and, in fact, in his off hours, had poured enough energy into playing bridge to become a regular fixture at international tournaments; an amusing dinner guest at just the kind of dinner parties that Winston and Michele went to three times a week when they were first getting reacquainted with the city.

Before long McFadden had accepted Winston's offer to be his deputy at the Central Bank.

He was perfect for Winston. He could entertain while Winston worked, he was not going to oppose Winston in anything, he was not the least political—which was perhaps the greatest secret of all to his success—and, above all, he could be depended upon to carry through orders without a flicker of his own imagination.

Mark drove down to McFadden's office to see him, and to look around Winston's office for any clues there might be, but all he found in Winston's office was a series of huge filing cabinets filled with very silent but immaculately filed files.

"Winston didn't really operate out of this office," said McFadden, "he left the day to day running of the bank to me."

"You mean you didn't see him?"

"Oh, indeed, he'd wave from the terrace across the way there."

McFadden pointed to the penthouse of the hotel opposite. He didn't seem to think there was anything strange in the fact that Winston didn't come into the office.

"He had a terminal over there," said McFadden, reading Mark's mind, "he knew everything that was going on."

Mark turned back to look at him. Was he protecting Winston? Probably. Was he trustworthy? Definitely. Would he lie? No. Would he tell the truth? As much as it suited him.

"How much oil do we have?" asked Mark.

"Let me see," said McFadden, who went to his computer and punched some keys.

"About three months' supply at normal levels of consumption," he said, "but at the moment we have no arrangements in place for getting more. It will have to be paid for, shipped, refined; all that will take nearly three months, so somebody has to do something right away."

"Do we have any money from tourism?"

"Income from the tourist sector has dropped to zero since the state of emergency," said McFadden.

"What about mining income?"

"That's our only hope," said McFadden, "but the agreement is in dispute and until it's cleared ..."

"Winston told me about some deal he was working on that would enable us to tell the IMF to go and screw themselves," said Mark.

"Really?" said McFadden, reacting with obvious surprise. "Did he give you any details?"

"No, but it was just after the mining negotiations with Hugh Clifford. Were you in on those negotiations?" asked Mark.

Winston had predicted this conversation and had told McFadden what to say.

"Not really, I know that if Winston had the deal we wouldn't have any trouble with paying for oil."

He was beginning to feel sorry for Mark. "Frankly, I think your best option would be to find out what the situation with Clifford is," said McFadden.

Mark got up from his seat and looked over at Winston's empty terrace. "Thanks Alistair," he said, "you've been a great help."

That night Mark lay awake thinking. All kinds of invisible forces seemed to have turned against him. He realised that if aid was not forthcoming, he would have created more suffering with the state of emergency than the people would have had to endure without it. He was stunned by the problems raised by Winston's disappearance, had he really let things slip to that degree?

Whatever else, he promised himself, he wouldn't become pretentious, he wouldn't pretend to be in control if he didn't have the expertise, he wouldn't pretend to have power if in fact he didn't have the basic requirements for carrying on his duties. On the other hand, he *had* taken control of the island, he had given reassurances to the population. He could not just turn around and quit now.

Mark got up and went out onto the terrace so that he could pace up and down without waking Vera. Torn by two conflicting ways of looking at the situation, Mark realised that he was facing the most crucial decision of his life.

One chance was that Hugh Clifford would know where Winston was and carry through on the deal he'd made. But that wasn't Mark's real hope for help. The man he would have to depend on now was Frank Wood, his friend from Korea, who was now one of the Joint Chiefs of Staff; he was the man Mark was going to go to, he was the one who he would have to depend on in the crunch ... and why not? They'd risked their lives together; look at how Singh had responded! Not a question, just support without a moment's hesitation, surely Frank Wood could easily put an emergency team in place. Of course he'd do that, thought Mark, they did it all the time. But Mark would have to go to Washington to see him. He knew that leaving the island now, even for a few hours, involved huge risk, but he'd have to do it; he'd have to do it at night and get back the next day, before anybody really knew that he was gone. He would go the following night: three hours flight to Florida, another two to get to Frank, two hours, at most, for a meeting, he'd come back on a jet, four hours ... the whole operation could be completed overnight. Mark made the decision. After all, what better friend would the Americans have in the Caribbean, ever, if they helped him now?

The next day Mark informed only his two key officers in charge of the Fifth Battalion of his movements, then called Hugh Clifford and General Wood, spoke to neither, but left messages for both to say he'd called, and that he was on his way to see them.

Both calls were picked up by the monitoring system at Fort Meade, both were fed into the computers which would electronically scan the files on the caller and the person called. Every single international call made anywhere in the world went through the scanners of the National Security Agency, and Mark's did not go through undetected.

Some instinct made Mark decide to take Vera along on the trip. Both boys were in America at school, and if things got tough, he wanted her to be with them, and off the island.

Vera knew somehow that she mightn't be back home for a long time. She'd left home as a child three times in similar circumstances because her father, General Urrutia, had been involved in politics throughout his career.

She packed quietly and she packed light. She left several thousand dollars in cash with the old maid who would be in charge of the place while they were away. Then Vera looked around at her home, her garden, her animals, her paintings, her bed, her children's beds ... the innumerable items collected in a lifetime of travel and family love.

Mark watched as she bowed to say a prayer in Spanish, the words of supplication rushing through her heart, easing pain as traditional as childbirth for the women of her family. The strength the prayer gave her was traditional strength, Mark could depend on it, and when she was ready to go, he kissed her tenderly and put his arm around her as they walked slowly and quietly to the car.

They landed at the Homestead air force base in Florida about four hours later, then Mark and Vera flew on through the night to Washington, this time on board a US Army Lear jet, requisitioned by Frank Wood once Mark got through to him by phone.

While the plane was being readied to fly, Mark placed a call to Hugh Clifford.

"Hello," said the old man, answering his bedside phone.

"Mr Clifford, this is Mark Bernard. I'm sorry to bother you at this hour, but it's an emergency."

"That's OK, Mark, I'm glad to hear from you. Where are you calling from?"

"Homestead."

"In Florida?"

"Yes."

"Ah." A guarded tone crept into Clifford's voice.

"I was wondering if you had heard from my brother."

"Yes, I've been in touch with Winston."

"Really!" said Mark, astonished and angry at the same time. "May I ask you what happened at the meeting?"

"Not on the phone, I'm afraid," said Hugh Clifford, who had switched on the speaker-phone so Molly could listen to both ends of the conversation. "But I'd be happy to set up a meeting."

"With Winston?"

"I think all three of us should meet."

That little bastard, Winston! He's using Clifford to force his way back into control.

"You know, Mr Clifford, I'm deeply offended that Winston should deal with me in this way." Mark was trembling with rage.

"Well I think he has his reasons, Mark"

"No reason is good enough, for me loyalty comes first."

Clifford was silent for a moment. "When I was a youngster," he said, "an old man on Wall Street once said to me: 'loyalty is what people call on when they can no longer call on common sense', and I tend to think that's usually true."

"Well, I don't agree," said Mark, and put down the phone.

Within seconds of the completion of Mark Bernard's calls, the computers were clicking again.

Certain names and numbers were programmed for close scrutiny. Both Hugh Clifford and Frank Wood's names were on that list. So were Winston's and Mark's. Both had merited a listing when in turn they took control of the island's affairs away from their mutual cousin Percy Sullivan, who was also listed, because although first Winston and then Mark had taken over the responsibility for running the place, he was, throughout it all, still technically Prime

Minister, the one who appointed the ambassador to the United Nations, the one on *their* records as head of government.

The master list of those who should be listened to with an especially keen ear was broken down into sections of interest. First Mark's call went through to the Latin American section, then the Caribbean, and when those interested in the island's affairs were listed, twelve names came up. With those twelve were listed three names who were to be kept informed at all times if there was any major movement by Mark Bernard. One of those three was a career bureaucrat whose career had been built with the patronage of Henry Lynch.

It was essential to Henry Lynch that in any conversation with another person, he should be able to present them with a piece of information that they did not know, did not previously have, could not have, for they hadn't a network for collecting information comparable to his own.

Information in-depth and as it happened, was the key to Henry Lynch's power, and information on anybody named Bernard and concerning the Caribbean would reach a phone at Henry Lynch's side; even if it was his bedside at two o'clock in the morning.

Henry Lynch wasn't obsessed with the Bernards because of the amount of money involved in the mining operation on the island, he was obsessed with the Bernards because he knew that they represented a new breed; if they won, they would encourage a dozen like them ... a hundred, scattered throughout the hitherto acquiescent tropical world where a few controlled the many, and those few were perfectly prepared to sell out for a price. Sell was probably not quite it: rent was a better description of the relationship between Lynch and the people he liked to deal with south of the tropic of Cancer.

Mark didn't suspect the breadth, the depth of the network around him. Winston could have warned him, Winston knew those guys, was one of them whose game in life was matching lists to make a net into which all information was gathered — more far-reaching than anything since the net of the ancient Inquisition, and, in its Latin American and Caribbean incarnations, at least as brutal.

Vera had called the children from Homestead, had said she was coming to see them the following day, and she was now asleep in the cabin of the little plane as it raced through the night at six hundred miles an hour.

As they approached Washington, Mark sat looking out of the window at the lights on the ground, stretching away as far as the eye could see from thirty thousand feet; an endless number of lights all burning all night, when ninety-five per cent of people were in bed asleep, craving darkness. Meanwhile, he was having to mortgage the independence of the island for oil. This new world that Mark now found himself in, the world that Winston understood ...

Winston ... hasn't the guts to face me...wanted to blackmail me through Clifford ... Winston, click. Throw the switch, cut him off. But, my God, to have done what he did! Click again, and this time Mark really didn't want to think about him anymore.

Now Mark was down to just one option, his friend General Wood. The comrade in arms. The member of the Joint Chiefs of Staff. He was one of the five most powerful men in the US military ... that must mean something, that must mean that he could initiate action, get to the President, explain the obvious: which was that Mark was on their side, that he was worth supporting.

Yet as they got closer to Washington DC, Mark felt more and more fearful for his mission. This was the town that had forced Douglas McArthur to bow, the town where the military bowed to politicians, politicians often bowed to their sponsors, and those sponsors were often the richest men in the USA. And the reason they were so rich was often because they were military contractors ... and so the wheel went around and around.

How much clout did the professional military actually have? Even at the very top? Surely enough clout to get his story across. So the trip was justified, thought Mark, trying to put himself in a positive mood before landing.

General Wood met the plane, as promised, and had a car standing by to take Vera to a hotel.

"Mark can meet you there when he's through with me," the American general said to Vera.

"I think I'll be heading straight back," said Mark, "so I'll say goodbye now."

Frank Wood said nothing.

Mark saw Vera to the car, told her he'd call her as soon as he was back on the island, and returned to his friend, expecting to start their meeting on the spot. Instead, as he came back into the room, Wood was already heading out towards his car.

"Frank, I'm anxious to get back as soon as possible, can't we meet here?"

"The plane can't go back for four hours; we might as well go back to my place."

"Four hours!"

"There's a problem with flight crew because of short notice, Mark, we'll do the best we can."

In the half hour that it took General Wood to drive to his house, Mark filled him in on the situation. He explained why he'd had to declare a state of emergency, why he urgently needed financial aid; explained that he had come to personally assure him that if he did not get that aid, an alternative government in Maurice

DeCartret's corner was ready to enter the stage from the left.

General Wood listened but said little.

When they reached the general's house in an upper middle class suburb, Frank Wood led Mark into the kitchen, where he started to make coffee. Mark was now getting impatient. He didn't know that between his calls to Wood and Clifford from the Homestead air force base, the calls and their contents had reached Henry Lynch who had considered the information, devised a strategy, and put his plan into effect. Word went out that no help should be given to Mark Bernard. The reason? Human Rights. Lynch knew that human rights was an issue with which he could tie up foreign aid indefinitely. He knew where he could substantiate death squad activity in Mark's army. The word had gone out and reached Frank Wood before Mark ever landed in Washington.

Wood wasn't told that the word had come from Henry Lynch. It came to him through the liaison man that the Pentagon had with the State Department, but Wood suspected Henry Lynch's hand. He recognised a pattern of alliances that was in place no matter who held office in Washington. The continuity that Henry Kass provided on the island, ensuring that a deal made would go through regardless of politics, was also to be had in the American system, on a scale so vast that trapping Mark Bernard in one tiny corner of the net was frighteningly easy for an ex-chairman of the Forty Committee.

The merits of those at the centre of political power in the US had varied from time to time, sometimes the melting pot produced evolutions and civil wars, and sometimes the pendulum swung from explosions of freedom to spasms of repression and back again, but in the seventies, and for some time thereafter, the mood in Washington was strictly business; business was the driving wheel that interlocked politics and foreign policy in

Washington DC, and Henry Lynch was in a position to push either brake or accelerator, seated in the middle of the whole mechanism.

Mark knew little of this. He wasn't aware of the threat that Winston posed to Lynch, neither Winston nor Percy had ever discussed it with him. He would have found it hard to believe that the men in charge of the greatest fighting machine in history could have given over to others to the point where they merely carried out orders and had no real power at all, except when ordering a lot of youngsters to risk their lives. This wasn't something Mark would have anticipated in a warrior of Frank Wood's class. No general Mark had ever known anywhere was without the power to make himself heard, so only slowly did he grasp what a profound change had occurred in the American general since the days when he and Mark had been friends in Korea—friends and rivals, because both had been gifted fighter pilots, and rivalry in that league at that age was very hot. But now Frank Wood seemed tamed. When Mark compared his reaction to the reaction he'd had from Singh! Mark knew there was a difference in scale, but still ... Mark had expected help in a tight spot, not this evasive bullshit that he had sensed right from the beginning of his meeting with Wood.

"Look Frank, I want a clear, straight answer. Will you help me or not?"

"How do you want me to help you?"

"Get me to the President if necessary, if that's what it's going to take."

"The President won't be sympathetic to any situation with a human rights problem."

"Human rights? What human rights problem?"

"Someone has smeared you on the human rights issue Mark, you have a bad image."

"I don't give a fuck about image. I'm talking about the fate of my country, and I need help immediately or the communists are going to take it over, and it will be your fault."

"No. It's your fault Mark. You've got this lousy image. The only thing anybody in this country knows about you has to do with death squads for chrissake!"

"Well you know that's not true."

"Yes, I know that's not true, but how the hell do you expect me to help you when you have such a lousy image?"

They were going around in circles.

Wood had been given a scenario to play out and he was sticking to it, but he was embarrassed in the eyes of his fellow general—*I know what he's thinking, he's thinking they've cut off my balls.*

"You have no idea what they can do against you to hold up aid on a suspicion of death squad activity," said Wood, "I've seen the files, there's evidence ..."

"What evidence?"

"Death squad activity in an army under your command, that means congressional committees, hearings ..."

He stopped talking, so intense was the look of disdain on the face of his former friend.

"Do you know what I've come to realise?" Frank continued. "That for the thrill of flying fighters as a kid, I gave up my life to a career in which flying jets was the best part. I can't help you win a political battle in this town, Mark. As far as politics is concerned, I want to finish out my time and retire to develop a dangerous game of golf."

"OK, Frank. I guess I'd better get home."

"You mean you want to leave now? Tonight?"

"Of course, I'll have to get back before anybody realises that I've gone."

"The Lear jet crew has gone off duty."

"Lend me a fighter, get one of your youngsters to drop me

back to my plane at Homestead and I'll be back on the island a few hours after daybreak."

General Frank Wood shook his head, "I'm sorry Mark, that won't be possible."

He leaned forward and took a fax out of the envelope that had been shoved under the door when they had first arrived at the house. Mark had taken no notice of it then because Frank Wood had merely glanced at it before starting the meeting, but now he was holding it out for Mark to read:

> *State of emergency ended by me tonight. I have appointed*
> *Brown to replace you as Chief of Staff. Would like you to*
> *remain in Washington as military attaché.*
> *Best regards, as ever,*
> *Percy*

On getting news of Mark in America, Henry Lynch had immediately called his contact on the island, and Kass had woken up Percy with the news.

It had not been hard to persuade Percy to rid himself of his Bernard cousins. Percy was sick to death of being elbowed aside and abandoned by them. It was relatively easy for Kass to persuade him that Lynch would provide the safest way out of the hopeless mess that first Winston and now Mark had placed him in.

In less than two hours, Kass had talked Percy into making the move that would ace Mark off the court and out of the game before he ever touched down in Washington.

Now that the final blow had fallen, Mark sat silent, but with the play of a small smile around his mouth.

"What are you going to do, Mark?" asked Wood.

"I'm going to wait. I'm going to wait till they come begging for mercy, till they get down on their knees and beg me to come back and save them, but first I want to see the hooligans eat that little weakling raw!"

Chapter Twenty-Five

✺

The scenario unfolded as if Mark had written it himself, but with a speed that even he would not have predicted.

Once Percy took over again, he had to restore order. To do that he called DeCartret and offered a coalition cabinet if he would call off the strikes and demonstrations. DeCartret couldn't do that without Red Roy's cooperation. He had long since lost control of the strike at street level where it was Red Roy's thugs who prevented people from going to work, from "breaking solidarity". DeCartret could tell the workers to go back to work, but if Red Roy's people didn't let them through, how would they get there?

Normally, the army would have been called in to deal with the situation, but with Mark gone and his people vulnerable, with Brown scared out of his wits and unable to make any decision, with DeCartret's officer corps away—still exiled by Mark and not yet recalled—the strongest faction in camp was led by Sgt. Edsel "Idi" Morris, Red Roy's contact in the army.

Sergeant Morris, the perpetrator of the ambush from which IZion and Wire had escaped, the man who's intelligence had exterminated Biga Mitchell, who remained so far in the background that when the officers who would had ousted Mark were themselves sent into exile, Sergeant Morris did not see fit to reveal to anybody that he was the next in line of command for that particular faction of the army.

Even Maurice DeCartret, trade union leader and head of the political party to whom the rebel officers owed allegiance, was not aware of Morris' true position. Only Red Roy, the political top ranking to whom Morris passed arms and ammunition for control of the slums, knew that he was the only man to talk to of certain things within the camp, and what Red Roy wanted to talk to Idi Morris about now was that if they got together to control the guns and the ammunition and those willing to fight for booty in *both* the army *and* the slums, they could threaten the Government itself.

In the meantime, both Percy Sullivan and Maurice DeCartret were striving to restore normality as quickly as possible, and made speeches on radio and TV to that effect.

Red Roy joined Idi Morris to listen to Percy's broadcast appealing for national unity, in a bar that was owned by Idi Morris's long-time girlfriend, a woman named Joyce.

Joyce's Joint served as the headquarters for the spy system that Idi and Red Roy had.

"Dem waan go back to narmal," said Joyce.

"Narmal fe who?" said Red Roy

"Narmal fe dem," said Idi Morris.

"I have fe shed blood fe cantrol di street, mi nuh really feel mi should jus give over de power jus like dat, you know?" said Red Roy to Idi. "And what will appen to yu when DeCartret and de colonel get together, will yu still be de sergeant den bredda?"

Red Roy looked at Idi Morris with an injured, angry expression on his face, not directed at Idi Morris himself, but at the wickedness of all elites and their various cliques.

"Right now yu cantrol de politics, and mi cantrol de army, right?" said Idi, "But when tings get back to narmal, don't DeCartret cantrol de party, an Guvament cantrol de army?" Idi looked to Red Roy to see if he appreciated the scope of his thinking, and Red Roy looked as if he wanted to hear more. "Dis mawnin I search out Bernard's men, to put dem under manners, and I couldn't find one," Sergeant Morris continued, "so is me actually in cantrol right now, because Brown and dem can do nuttin if mi decide fe move."

"Den what yu waitin fah?" asked Red Roy.

"Dem gwine send fe Thompson and Richards," said Morris, knowing full well that if the exiled colonels returned, they would put *him* under manners. "What mi waitin fah? Mi nuh wait fe nuttin."

When Idi left the meeting with Red Roy, he went to military headquarters, drawn by some force of decision that was going to make him survey the scope of the weight he was about to take on his shoulders, but as he drew near he stopped off in the car park, where, sitting in a corner under the shade of a tree, was Mark's dark brown Mercedes, the flag of his rank furled on the little chrome flagpole which rose from the middle of the left fender, the car gleaming with the polish of constant care.

Idi Morris realised that it was now or never. Either he was going to get behind the wheel of Mark Bernard's car and drive it through the camp in the next five minutes, or he'd be a sergeant forever. He walked up and looked into the windows. The keys were in the ignition. Of course. Who could dream that anybody would trouble the General's car parked in the middle of his dominion?

Idi imagined the shock of the sight as he sped through the camp; in five minutes he would have made himself understood as he could in no other way.

He walked to the heavy door, opened it, sat down in the leather seat, and closed the door with a clunk.

Once behind the wheel, he couldn't imagine himself anywhere else. He turned the ignition, he heard the big engine catch fire and he gunned the car out of the car park—one hand on the wheel—scattering gravel as he swung out into the road.

He saw three men he trusted, and stopped.

"I tek over," said Idi.

"OK, General," said the men from his gang. They climbed into the big Benz and Idi headed towards the front gate.

"Where yu say yu going in de General car?" said the sentry.

Two of Idi's men climbed out of the back of the car.

"See de General here," said one, pointing to Idi Morris.

"See de General's authority here," said the other, pushing the muzzle of his gun into the sentry's stomach.

"Give mi yu gun," said Idi's man to the sentry.

The sentry complied. Idi Morris controlled entrance to the army camp.

Maurice DeCartret's office was that of a successful lawyer. He was a gentleman socialist. When he got into politics, he had no intention of getting involved with the likes of Red Roy. It had made him profoundly uncomfortable when Red Roy wrested control of the general strike from the management suite of the union offices to check points on all roads, leading to struck transport installations, factories, offices, and so on.

Once he'd joined the government of Percy Sullivan's coalition cabinet, the first thing he did was send for the exiled officers of the Fifth Battalion. They were due to arrive at any time. That was all he knew when he was told that Red Roy was on his way into his private office to see him. Red Roy, on the other hand, knew that Idi Morris, his ally, was already taking over the army.

Red Roy's whole stance when he entered DeCartret's office was belligerent. Still smarting from the beating he'd had at Eddie Azani's hands, there was in Red Roy an intense unsatisfied lust for continued control, and he had experienced the adrenalin rush of the successful warlord for long enough to act recklessly rather than give up.

"Who tell yu fe call fe de end a de strike an nuh cansult wid me?" asked Red Roy of Maurice DeCartret.

"Listen to me," said DeCartret, rising out of his chair, "Me and the Prime Minister decided—"

"Yu an Percy Sullivan can talk all yu wan, but right now is me cantrol de street, an mi friend cantrol de army, so wha yu gwine do 'bout dat?"

"What are *you* going to do," asked Maurice DeCartret half in jest, "take over the Government?"

"Maybe."

"Who would deal with you? The Russians won't deal with you, nor will the Cubans. They don't know you. They only know me. They will only deal with me."

"Dem can deal wid yu, but you 'av fe deal wid me."

"And suppose I refuse?"

"Refuse? Eh bredda, yu love to talk 'bout revolution all de time an yu don't know a rass claat revolutionary when yu talkin to one?"

DeCartret realised that it was only with restraint that the hooligan hadn't hit him. If he couldn't call on the army, he was at Red Roy's mercy.

"You won't get away with this."

"Why not?"

"Because, as I said, nobody will deal with you! You just won't get through."

"Ha," Red Roy's snort dismissed DeCartret. "So tell me bredda, how de guy Doe get through in Liberia? Amin, an all dem guy deh? How yu tink Duvalier live? Yu tink mi fool, but mi study."

DeCartret too had studied the history of revolution in the tropics, and when he confirmed that Idi Morris had indeed seized control of the army, he knew that the island was slipping into anarchy and he knew that he'd better get the hell out of there.

He was not alone in that decision. Overnight, lines formed around the US Embassy and those of Britain and Canada; those who could afford it left servants in line to keep their place while they went off to have breakfast at the high rise hotel nearby. The hotel was soon so short of food that it refused to serve anyone other than its guests, who were already lined up waiting for buses to go to the airport, with frightened looks on their faces.

Percy left by yacht. He'd had it as a standby for months, and he felt like he was living a scene out of a movie as he made his way by canoe to the Marina, got on board, and splashed the forty foot Hatteras out to sea in the direction of the Cayman Islands. The fact that he hadn't had time to get ice on board to chill the beer en-route was his primary concern.

Chapter Twenty-Six

~~~~~

Percy called Michele as his yacht was pulling out and offered to take her with him, but she refused to leave the island, just as earlier she had refused when Eddie called to say he was leaving. They'd had a terrific fight on the phone, and she expressed the same disgust to Percy when he told her he was getting out. Michele was disgusted with the exodus first of her brother Eddie, then of Winston and Mark, and now Percy. She was the only one left, and she decided to stand her ground. She had a weapon with which to fight chaos that none of the other players had, and she was excited by the prospect that she could use it to win. She had radio: she had the attention of the entire island riveted to the station for news. Idi controlled the camp and Red Roy terrorised the slums, but Michele's reach was island-wide. The familiar voices of the news readers and the phone-in hosts was the one remaining link with normality for a population dazed by rumour and the speed of real events.

Weeks before, Michele had started to put into place her plan for showing both Red Roy's thugs and the army that they were vastly outnumbered by the decent citizens who would not tolerate the tyranny of hooligans. The airwaves were alive with calls for peace and a mood of determined resistance to violence. Michele could call on the churches for support, and on other institutions large and small whose efforts to preserve decency were broadcast and coordinated by Sun Radio. Although businesses were closed, Michele kept the commercials going, because they somehow reassured people that life was still going on as usual.

Idi Morris didn't want to interfere with the radio, it was keeping people cool, and by the time he realised that the peace concert that Michele was planning was not going to put out a message in his favour, it had received so much support that if he stopped it, he would have immediately branded himself a villain of the first order. Up to now people were still confused as to Idi and Red Roy's real characters, and if the public's first impression was that they were against the concert—which Michele had started promoting as the "healing of the nation"—then it would be much harder for Red Roy and Morris to win the support of those they were not able to terrorise in person.

By the time Percy fled, the concert was a mere forty-eight hours away; there was foreign press and TV coming in to cover it. Michele had secured the full support of everybody she really needed for the event, except Zack. He was on tour and every time she called him about the concert she'd had to persuade him to come home to do it.

Why?

Surely he could see what she was trying to do; surely he knew how important it was for them to succeed, to use the power of radio to pull the entire island into an event that would be overwhelming to whoever sought to impose chaos and tyranny on a free people! To produce a crowd that would roar "No!" and sing "Yes!" so loud and clear that the likes of Red Roy would simply hear and know and understand—of course it could work! Already, people were arriving in the city from the country in buses and market trucks; others coming in from the States and even Europe ... what was Zack afraid of? Couldn't he feel the vibe? The enormous force that he could carry behind him if he headlined the concert?

Michele remembered one night they had spent together, months before...

Zack had been restless in bed, sitting up and hugging his knees, rocking to and fro, the words tumbling from him: "I can't solve fe dem problem, I can't find dem food, I can't find dem work—dem haffi look after demself. I nuh serve man, I have fe serve I spirit. Yu lying in bed, or yu flying in plane, and all of a sudden melody come inna yu head, words come inna yu brain—weh it come from? When it leave yu weh it gaan? Dat deh spirit nuh mix up in violence none at all ..." Zack's eyes had glistened as he looked away.

Michele saw his torment then. She saw how terribly he would suffer if he lost the love of his muse, much more than he could possibly suffer if he lost the love of any woman, herself included. He knew what it was to be deserted by his talent when he had nothing else to sustain him, what it was to wait, to wonder if that joyous release would ever come to him again, lifting and carrying him forward like a surfer on a wave of reassurance and inspiration, and Michele knew of the many times he had felt he would be unable to live without it. The gift of music had turned Zack from a weakling child into a superstar, but, thought Michele, just like a woman his inspiration might desert him for sticking too close, if he stuck too close to music, he might miss something to sing about.

"Play dem I music," said Zack, "dem nah have fe look, dem fe lissen now."

But Michele was so sure she was right that, in spite of Zack's reluctance to do a concert, she pushed ahead. She was determined that the reality behind Rasta rhetoric should not turn coward towards Red Roy. The cause of the Rasta youth and the Peace Movement had created so much hope, so much strength, it mustn't be allowed to dissipate now, as though it had been nothing more than the celebration party for the birth of a song! Is that all it had meant to Zack? Really? Was he that shallow? Didn't he realise that even in terms of his career the concert would put him in a class of his own? If he turned back the tide of violence in an entire city threatened by a flood of it, he would become a legend much bigger than two hit songs alone could ever make him. And it was to be broadcast on television! Worldwide! She could guarantee that. But Zack, he wasn't really into it.

All day long she wrestled with the problem. Several times she thought to call Zack and she didn't, each time feeling that they were drifting farther apart.

When she got home she had a long hot bath, had dinner in her bathrobe, and started thinking of Winston. Without him to turn to for advice, she had no idea if a solution to her problem would elude her all night long as it had done the night before. Suddenly she felt a pang of loneliness for him that made her burst into tears. She shook as the blocked emotion, with nowhere else to go, turned back in on her and forced her to sob out the tensions of the day in short bursts of anguish.

When she felt better, she put a stack of her favourite tapes beside the tape player. In times of stress she had often seen Winston relax with music, and that night she decided to imitate his method.

Slowly the conviction came to her that she should go ahead with the concert in support of the Peace Movement, whether or not Zack wanted to sing in it. He had started something, and if he didn't want to finish what he had started, maybe somebody else would; maybe another singer would catch the moment and make it his; would use his voice to turn away the threat posed by Red Roy, to state that the spirit for peace preached by Burru and Wire was dominant, would prevail. Zack himself had been among the first to put out the call; now it was more important than ever that it be his voice that put out the call again, but if he failed her and failed himself, she at least would have to make the effort.

"I am a musician, not a politician," he had said, but music wasn't enough. Its effect was too diffused. Red Roy's men could kick out the plugs to any jukebox playing any tune they didn't like, and it would be all over; but a concert would give focus, a concert would demonstrate strength, would give hope.

Michele remembered that when she called Toots he said that he would sing for peace without a moment's hesitation. She called Burning Spear, he said he would sing for peace. She called Third World, they too confirmed on the spot. On the night they responded, Michele wrote the radio commercials for the concert. Next morning at breakfast time she caught the new mayor of the city before he left home. He confirmed that she could use the park.

By noon the next day, Michele put out the first commercials for the concert. She made no mention of Zack. She made no mention of any singer. She merely stated that the Peace Concert would take place the next week in the middle of the park, in the middle of the town.

The response was immediate and overwhelming, Ronnie Morris had his switchboard lit up with support for the Peace Concert.

All week long the deejays plugged the "Monster Concert for Peace", and announced that "everyone was going to be there".

Michele lived on the telephone, arranging for scaffolding for the stage from Rasta City, getting the mobile sound equipment from Eddie's abandoned studio, arranging for generators and lights from a local film company.

Max DeMalaga called to confirm that a video crew was on its way from New York and that he was already getting calls about cable and broadcast rights.

By the time Michele had made the phone calls necessary to prevent customs confiscating the cameras and the recorders at the airport, Max DeMalaga called to say he was coming in the next afternoon with two of the Stones and maybe Stevie Wonder. *Rolling Stone* was sending Michael Thomas. Peter Simon was coming to take photographs. Steven Davis was coming from

Boston, so was a man Max DeMalaga knew who worked for *Paris-Match*.

He had also spoken to *Time* and *Newsweek*.

"Zack couldn't have a better boost for his tour," said DeMalaga.

"I know," said Michele.

But where was Zack?

How long would she be able to dodge the issue of his non-appearance?

Michele slept at the station the night before the concert on a cot up in her office. She did not hear from Zack. Nobody had heard from Zack. Around two in the morning she went to the park to see how progress on the construction of the stage and the camera rostrums was going, and she drank a beer and ate patties with the builders until she was assured by them that they wouldn't go home until the job was finished. She recorded some interview material to put on the air so Zack would know to check for her at the station, then she went back to her office and crashed. She did not hear from Zack the next morning, nobody did. He had disappeared. Nevertheless, support on the streets was such that as the time for the concert drew nearer, Red Roy felt his grip slipping. Wire's men were back in town. Messages that Red Roy sent out to his people were failing to come back. His key lieutenants seemed uneasy: ready to lie low, unwilling to venture out on the streets with the swagger and sense of possession that they'd exhibited ever since Wire's exodus to Rasta City.

By mid-morning on the day of the concert, after he listened to the Ronnie Morris programme and heard nothing but rejoicing for the revival of the Peace Movement and support for the concert, Red Roy himself went underground.

"Zack is de baas! Red Roy nah rule!" shouted a lady caller on the air.

"Di cancert is crucial!" stated another caller, and in a city where phrases could catch a spark and spread like verbal napalm, the whole town was aflame with agreement.

"Di cancert is crucial!"

Nobody had felt so good since the last time there was dancing in the streets to a message from Zack.

By three o'clock the crowds started to move towards the park. David Wilmot was on the spot with a mobile broadcast van, and as the crowd grew, so he put out the news to draw still more.

The park was dusty around the stands, but fifty yards away there was a large tree, and it was there that the centre of the crowd started to form in the shade. By the time fifty had gathered, the first snow-cone man arrived. Shortly after, the t-shirt salesmen arrived and set up stalls to sell posters featuring Zack; Zack buttons, hats, shirts, belts, buckles, even flags were on sale, silk-screened on the spot under the shade of the tree.

By the time the stores closed and the office workers left work for the day, it seemed as if at least half of the rush-hour pedestrians were headed for the park, and by six o'clock the crowd had swelled to eight or ten thousand.

Max DeMalaga had brought so many people with him that he'd had to cancel the Lear jet and hire a plane with more seats. They were met at the airport, and called from the hotel to say they were settled in. He'd put together the package, and now with the best will in the world, the time had come to talk business. So far he had fronted everything, and he had done so purely on Michele's word that Zack was going to star in the show, but Michele couldn't return his calls until she'd found Zack.

She had expected him to arrive with DeMalaga, but he hadn't seen Zack, only some of his musicians who said Zack had gone ahead.

Michele checked with Zack's musicians for the sixth time, and still none of them had heard from him. If he could only feel the power of the crowd, thought Michele, if he had a hint of the passion for his presence that was building on the field, he wouldn't hesitate.

By seven o'clock when it started to get dark, the lights on the stage in the middle of the park became the focal point for the entire city; the crowd around the stage stretched far beyond the reach of the lights, so that as the reflection from the lights got dimmer, the people packed together did not thin out, but seemed to continue as a tightly moving mass for as far out into the darkness as one cared to imagine.

The first group was already on stage, and the sounds of the band plugging in and testing their amplifiers buzzed through the crowd. The cameramen of the TV crew from New York had their eyes bent down to their view-finders and their red lights on. As darkness closed in, Michele realised that if she didn't get out now, she wouldn't be able to push through the crowd, so she left the press rostrum and worked her way through the clusters of people pressing forward towards the lights, till she found her car, then she drove slowly out of the park and towards the radio studio. She no longer had any desire to stay at the centre of the action, because as the excitement grew so did the disappointment about Zack. She had done all she could do.

When she got to the studio, she walked slowly from her car to her office, dreading the moment when she would find no message, and indeed there was no message from him as she sorted through the dozen slips of paper with other messages that meant nothing if he didn't appear.

Michele looked over at the pile of clothes and towels that her maid Mildred had sent down to her that morning, and she noticed then a note on top of them asking Michele to call home. Michele hadn't had time to do that all day, but now it seemed like the only call she could make.

"Hi, Mildred," said Michele, when the maid picked up the phone.

"Miss Michele! You never get my message?"

"Yes but—"

"Zack was here since three waiting for you."

"Is he still there?" gasped Michele.

"Yes, he—"

"Is he listening to the radio?"

"No. Him nuh do nutten all day but doze."

"Turn on the radio and take it and put it in front of him, and tell him that I'm coming to pick him up right away."

Michele rushed outside and, picking up her walkie-talkie, called the man from the radio station who was standing beside David Wilmot on the press rostrum.

"Tell David I've found Zack; say I'm bringing him now."

Then she jumped into her car and her tyres screamed as she sped out of the car park.

The headlights picked up Zack as Michele swung into the drive of her house, and he jumped in as she was changing gear to back out again.

There was no need for words between them. They both knew that his strength alone wasn't enough to put him in front of the people. They both knew that he had been waiting for the conviction to come to him that would give him strength. He had often had to wait for it before, sometimes till minutes before a concert was to begin ... on nights when his inspiration didn't come, when his muse had flown and he was alone, he paid the penalty of hard labour for alienating her affections ... he'd have to take the emotional weight of thousands of people on his shoulders and try to lift them with the memory of notes and words ... he would stagger for an hour and then collapse; if his inspiration didn't return the next night, he wouldn't be able to do a big show, and if on tour the muse didn't turn up for three nights running, he would be ill. He knew that had he been pretentious enough to go on stage that night without the force of his musical spirit behind him, he would have been utterly annihilated by the weight of the moment. But all that was behind him now ... now he had heard the call, now he had plugged into the voltage of the crowd, now the threats of death could no longer cripple him.

The car seemed to fly through the streets, traffic parted to let it through as though some mystical siren preceded it. As they drew nearer to the grounds, police sirens did actually take up the cry, on every side there seemed to be flashing lights, the crowd parting in a wave as the growing cavalcade of cars hurtled towards the blinding white light of the stage.

Zack jumped out of the car and ran up the steps to his band and his guitar and the mic at centre stage. The beat of the music behind him and the roar of the crowd in front, like two solid wedges of sound that seemed to lift him off his feet. Zack thought of Wire as he shot his arm into the air. And jumped. Shouting his greeting as he rose.

Watching him, Michele felt an exhilaration such as she had never known. She felt utterly vindicated. The effect of the concert had surpassed her wildest dreams. She had used radio to its full advantage, and she felt she had fulfilled an ambition much greater than having a hit on Broadway. She looked at Zack and her heart filled with love for him. He was so brave, he was so strong, he had done what none of them had dared to do, not Elvis, nor Lennon, nor Dylan, nor Jagger, none of them with the power to do so had ever stood up at a crucial moment and entered into the political arena the way Zack was doing now.

"Genocide!" The crowd screamed.

> *If you don't know it now,*
> *you never will:*
> *Those you're told to obey*
> *have been told to kill...*

The crowd roared the titles for one after another of Zack's hits:

"No Way!"

"One Love!"

"Peace Power!"

"Deliverance!"

They spun, and laughed, and clapped their hands; the whole mass of people rippled in a frenzy of motion: keyed to the beat, tied to the stage, to Zack in the spotlight, changing gear, moving to another song, taking them somewhere else, spreading a hush, letting the chords from the keyboards predominate and float out past the sea of faces upturned towards the stage, lit by the reflection of the lights that had been set up for filming. He would reach beyond the faces he could see. He would reach beyond the massive crowd that he could not see but that he knew stretched to the edge of the park and beyond, clogging the roads approaching. He would reach beyond all those on the island who were listening to the radio; he would reach beyond the island to the world, satellite broadcast, video cassettes, and a presence forever. And now as he sang, his thoughts turned to Michele ...

> *Don't be afraid,*
> *love casteth out fear,*
> *Don't be afraid,*
> *tho' the crisis is near ...*

The crowd had started to sing along, swaying as they sang, putting up a sound like a hymn in church. Zack had the sensation that he was floating out of his body. It had happened to him when he was on stage before, but always when it happened he had stayed close, he had felt he was hovering behind his neck, around his shoulders ... but this time he rose much higher than he ever had before, and when he looked down he saw his body crumpled on the stage.

The rifle had a silencer as well as telescopic sights, and nobody heard the shot. Everybody assumed that Zack had collapsed, and they kept singing as they pressed forward to find out what had happened, expecting to see someone bend over and pick him up as though he were sick or had had a fit; but everybody on the stage suddenly scattered, ducking under the amplifiers, tearing off and throwing down instruments in a frantic scramble away from where Zack was lying on the stage.

The stunned audience saw only one figure rushing towards Zack, and when she flung herself down on his body, Michele did not behave like someone holding a sick man in her arms, for she grasped his head to her breast as she let out a scream of anguish.

There was something Euripidean about the moment ... the stage, the lights, the crowd; the drama of Michele's grief was pure theatre for the cameras from Manhattan, but the nightmare of the reality tore apart her vocal cords with such brutal force as to render her virtually speechless for months. That, and the fact that she had nothing more to say.

Chapter Twenty-Seven

Holiday Inn, Peterbilt, Mack, Ford, Corvette, Burger King, Church of Christ, the same names, and signs, and rushes of metal on the highway, repeated over and over. Peterbilt, Mack ... one after another the trucks roared down the highway at sixty miles an hour, stretched out on length after length of tarmac that disappeared into the distance through pine scrub, or farmland, or urban sprawl ... each stretch lasting forever before even the slightest turn.

Winston barely touched the wheel as the big car floated along with automatic transmission, power steering, and stereo radio, setting Winston free from any effort whatsoever besides deciding where to stop for lunch ... Burger King, Whataburger, McDonalds ... often he couldn't bring himself to make that simple decision because of being preoccupied with his mood which was changing from "drift" to a terrible sense of guilt.

He'd always known in his heart of hearts that Mark would not bow to his plan, would not go along with the scenario that he had worked out with Hugh Clifford and Marc Gold, would not recognise a winning plan when he saw one. So it was his own fault. But ever since the look in Marc Gold's eyes, ever since leaving Manhattan and not knowing which way to turn—because east was too short, north was too cold, west was too flat and empty, and south was through Washington—he'd decided to wander in a south-westerly direction; motion was his only hope against coming to a complete standstill in his life.

The deeper Winston got into the Heartland USA, the more he felt a sense of loss for what he'd abandoned, and as he penetrated deeper into redneck country, as truck after truck carrying gigantic loads worth the money of transportation added up in his mind to an overwhelming weight of a world in which black men were peripheral, Winston increasingly felt that he should have held on at any cost to the power he had thrown away.

Each area he passed was controlled and run by a culture so different from Winston's that his travelling took on the drifting quality of a dream, and the nightmare quality of betrayal.

The first thing he did each night on getting into a motel room was switch on the news, and he'd caught the show in which Mark had made a misguided attempt to change his image in the US.

Mark had not been able to get booked on *Nightline* or any of the serious talk shows; they were entirely taken up with the hostage crisis in Iran, and the takeover of Nicaragua by the Sandinistas. But the booking agency threatened to give up on him if he didn't take what he could get, so Mark ended up on the *Phil King Show*, in front of a live audience.

As soon as Mark walked onto the set, he realised he was making a mistake. Phil King introduced him as the "deposed strong man" of his island. "He's come here seeking support from us," said King, "and I'm sure the General will make a very convincing case for why we should give it to him, by clearing up some rather unsettling rumours, as soon as we come back."

During the commercial break, Phil King spoke rapidly with one of his people and came back seconds before the commercials were over to focus on the notes for Mark's story.

"General," he said, when the red light came on, "what is it exactly that you propose we should do down on your island in the Caribbean?"

"We need aid very urgently. I have reason to believe that unless we get it, the island might go communist."

"But even if it does, the average American might well ask, 'what's that got to do with us?'."

"I don't know what it's got to do with the average American, but I do know what it has got to do with the vital interest of your military and your government, and I do know that if the communists take over in my country, there will be a civil war and terrible suffering, and I sincerely want to prevent that."

"Many say that violence has increased since the rightist government that brought you to power was elected," said a lady who had beckoned from the audience and to whom Phil King had given his roving microphone, "you are a right-winger aren't you?"

"I'm not really thinking in terms of right-wing and left-wing—"

"It's well known you're right-wing," said another woman; "there's lots of murder and violence and suffering in Chile."

Mark looked to Phil King for help, but King wasn't looking at Mark, he was selecting another woman in the audience to attack him.

"General," said the next angry woman, as she rose to speak into the microphone as if to address the nation, "we've seen the Shah fall, we've seen Somoza fall, what can you say to convince us that you're any different?"

"Both of them were brutal dictators who had to resort to force and repression to stay in power," said Mark.

Suddenly another woman jumped up in the audience shouting, "He had dictatorial powers!" and pointing her finger at Mark.

"Wasn't there rioting in the streets of your capital city, General?" asked the talk show host.

"Those were anti-IMF riots orchestrated by—" again Mark was cut off by a shrieking, angry woman. "What about the slaughtered children?" she shouted.

"What about the murder of Zack Clay?" asked a young man.

"Isn't it true that he had the people on his side? Isn't that why he was murdered?" the young man continued

"I had nothing to do with that," replied Mark.

"You were in charge," shouted a woman.

"You're just another right-wing dictator who wants American taxpayers to save your skin," shouted another, and now Mark was shouting with anger too.

"And you're just an ignorant hysterical woman who doesn't know what she's talking about."

"Hey, just a minute—" said Phil King.

"This is no way to discuss the fate of my country," shouted Mark Bernard.

"We make the rules here, not you!" shouted a woman out of the crowd.

"You have absolutely no idea what you're talking about woman, and if you're not prepared to listen ... why don't you go home and cook a nice dinner for your husband!"

"He's a chauvinist too!" She was triumphant.

"I'm leaving," said Mark, standing up to walk off the set, "if this is really what things have come to ..."

Winston switched off the TV. He felt sick. This is what he'd brought his brother to! And Zack, dead! That meant Michele ... Michele what? He didn't know, he'd have to find out, he'd have to stop his aimless driving around, he'd have to come to terms with Mark and Michele and put a plan back into action. But how?

By eleven o'clock that night, Winston was sitting, drunk, in the corner of a bar in North Carolina. He looked around the bar and realised that everybody else in there was drunk too, and sitting to one side, alone, was a man of about thirty, staring into space, his mouth trembling silently, tears running down his face.

The others ignored him, but not in an unfriendly way, and Winston sat looking at the image of shocked, endless grief for ten minutes before he asked one of the other guys what had happened to his friend.

"That's my brother," said one drunk, and in answer to Winston's question added a single word, "Vietnam."

"Oh," said Winston.

"Yeah, that's what happened to him," said the brother, taking a joint out of his pocket.

"Hey," said the bartender, "don't smoke that thing in here man, you ain't that drunk and neither am I."

"Kiss my arse," said the redneck, weaving towards the door and beckoning to Winston to join him outside. "Can't smoke pot, can't drive sixty miles an hour, they lock you up for that, they want to "protect" you. Yeah, they want to protect you alright, right up to the moment when they tell you to pick up a gun and crawl through barb wire and mud towards a guy who has a machine gun aimed at your arse. So when I get that arse safe back home, they can kiss it man, it's an object of respect."

Winston's drunken companion looked around the car park, then lit up his joint, inhaled deeply, and peered at Winston. "It's what's known as the military mentality, man—are you acquainted with the military mentality?"

Suddenly Winston started to laugh.

"Yes," he said, "I am acquainted with the military mentality."

Mark and the military mentality!

"The military mentality can kiss my arse," said the drunken redneck, and Winston laughed again.

Fuck Mark! Thought Winston suddenly. For days he'd been driving aimlessly through an alien landscape, crippled with guilt over what he'd done to Mark, but he'd been right! Why was he so worried about Marc Gold: Hugh Clifford was on his side! *He* understood the vision, he could see that Winston was thinking way beyond the others, that he had a plan that could really work ... Not only that, Michele was free again ...

The drunken ex-soldier with the crippled brother offered him a toke, but Winston shook his head. He wanted to keep his thinking clear, he wanted to hold on to the thought that had set him free, he wanted to get back to the island as quickly as possible, he wanted to reach Michele ...

Winston went back into the bar, paid his tab, and headed out to the car park, feeling grateful for the urge to move, walking with a sense of purpose towards the car, pausing only to say goodbye.

"Thanks, man," said Winston to the redneck ex-soldier; drunk, getting high, and with not the faintest notion of what he was being thanked for by this black guy.

"That's OK man," he said, "I like nigras."

When he walked out of the arrivals section on the lower level at Miami Airport and looked around, Winston didn't see Eddie, but almost immediately a man in a dark blue suit and tie came up, doffed his chauffeur's cap, and said, "This way, Excellency."

The chauffeur took Winston's bag and led him across two lanes of traffic to a gigantic Mercedes 600 limousine which was parked in the line of cars waiting to pick up arriving passengers. White curtains were drawn across the back windows. The chauffeur opened the back door, and as Winston stepped into the limousine he broke into laughter. There was Eddie, reclining, telephone in hand, dressed from head to toe in the white and flowing robes of an Arab Sheikh.

Behind his dark glasses, Eddie was hardly recognisable, but as the car door closed behind Winston, Eddie started laughing too.

"I was born in Beirut," said Eddie, "I am immensely rich. Who would dare to ask me questions?"

The huge car cruised majestically out of the airport and sailed down the highway towards Miami Beach.

"You must come and see the house I bought this morning," said Eddie, "it is a palace, my brother, fit for a prince."

Eddie was bubbling with enthusiasm. He couldn't contain his appreciation for the lifestyle of an Arab multi-millionaire in the US. He showed Winston that he could place a call anywhere in the world from his car; he spoke of the likes of Garth Pharoan and Adnan Khashoggi as though they were his blood cousins; he listed the purchases of banks and real estate by Saudis and Kuwaitis as though they were all in the family.

"I have fulfilled my greatest ambition," said Eddie finally, "I am now so rich that I can afford to be honest."

They were half way across the causeway connecting Miami with Miami Beach, when the limo slowed and then turned off the highway and across a bridge which led to one of the residential islands that dot Biscayne Bay, each house looking out to the water across lawns running down to jetties and expensive yachts.

The driver slowed again for inspection by the private guard who controlled the only entrance to the quay, but Eddie the Arab Sheikh was already well-known to the locals, and the guard waved them through with a smile and a salute.

The house was a huge Spanish Colonial mansion built in the thirties, and already it was being filled with things that would remind Eddie of home. A jukebox was being lifted from a moving van and up the front steps en-route to the master bedroom as the Mercedes pulled up in to the driveway.

The driver opened the door for Eddie to gather his robes and proceed regally into the house, but as soon as they passed through the area where the workers were moving things around, Azani started to strip off his jalabiyah to reveal underpants and a lurid t-shirt that proclaimed, "I went to Ganja University".

"Leroy!" he shouted, and Leroy's brother—who lived with his aunty in America and whose name was actually something else—appeared. "Bring me a bottle of champagne." Then, to Winston: "So, how long can you stay?"

"I want to go back tonight."

"Why?"

"Michele, for one thing."

"Try to get her to come here."

"Have you spoken to her?"

"Can't get through. I know she's left the city. My people there can't find her. They say she left when Zack was shot. She cuss my rass before I left, called me a rat, said I was leaving a sinking ship, and see, she went and got Zack to expose himself and he gets shot. At least that's how she sees it."

"I'll find her. Can you get one of your smugglers to fly me in?"

"Sure, I'll give you a good one."

"Thanks, Eddie."

The champagne arrived, Winston looked out across the lawn to the swimming pool and the yacht, on which reclined a young girl sunbathing topless.

"Find her and bring her back here," said Eddie, raising his glass. "I'll pay for the plane to wait two days for you."

"When I find her and bring her back, I want to make a plan again; get back Percy, get back Mark, put the pieces back together."

"You'll need a lot of money."

"Yes ... I'm going to need a half million dollars in cash tonight."

"OK."

"I'm taking it back to the island with me."

"Who's it for?"

"McFadden."

"McFadden! McFadden at the Central Bank? You have me paying taxes now?"

"He needs the cash to keep things going till we get back to town. We don't know how long that's going to take."

Eddie wasn't listening to Winston, he was laughing so hard ... by the time the taxman had got to Eddie, he was the only taxpayer left! The more he thought about it, the more Eddie laughed. Doubled over with mirth, he stumbled out across the lawn, tearing off his underpants and t-shirt as he went, till, still shrieking with laughter, he splashed stark naked into the pale blue water of the swimming pool.

Chapter Twenty-Eight

Flying down to the island that night, Winston tried to sleep but couldn't. Time and again he went over the details of his instructions to McFadden. Over and over he anticipated his meeting with Michele. The moonbeams from a clear sky sparkled on the surface of the sea twelve thousand feet below, glinted off the spinning propellers, and along the edges of the wing, till eventually the dark mass of the island loomed up ahead and he gathered up his nerve for the landing on the small strip hidden away in the central range.

When they landed, Winston was relieved to see an old taxi driver with an even more decrepit vehicle, who had somehow been notified by Eddie, waiting to drive him into town.

The old man chatted all the way into the city. He had no use for communists, no use for Rasta, no use at all for the youth of today. He enthusiastically repeated a rumour he heard that General Mark was going to return to the island, get rid of Idi, and draft all his followers into a local Légion étrangère.

"Since dem want fe, fight dem fe fight," said the old man, "di General shoulda sell dem fe money an send dem go fight abraad."

By the time they entered the city it was nearly midnight. The streets were virtually empty and the driver blithely ran two red lights as he chatted away.

Idi wouldn't be looking for Winston, but if he found him, he might detain him for an interrogation. He would certainly be interested to know why he was travelling with half a million dollars in cash, he would certainly take the money, and Winston didn't want the taxi pulled over by an army patrol for no good reason.

"Hey daddy," he said, leaning forward to interrupt, "why you drive through the red light like that, man? Yuh nuh 'fraid fe police?"

"We can't bow to false idols inna these times," replied the old man, as he ignored the message of a third red light on an empty crossroads.

His remark was the last thing to make Winston laugh for a very long time.

They drove to the street on which McFadden lived. Winston walked to the gate, and left the half million dollars in cash for him in his mail box, together with detailed instructions as to exactly what functions were to be kept alive until Winston contacted him again.

"Birthday present for mi niece," Winston said to the old man by way of explanation, and they drove on to the hotel.

When they reached it, Winston didn't go inside. He had previously gassed his Jaguar, and it was waiting in the far corner of the large car park. Winston paid the taxi man before he reached the hotel, so all he had to do was slip out of the cab and into his car, start it, and drive out. He felt sure that nobody had seen his face.

Still praying that he wouldn't be stopped and encouraged by the fact that Idi's army seemed to be asleep along with everybody else, Winston drove faster as he headed out of town again, this time thinking only of Michele.

Ever since hearing of Zack's death, reaching her had become an obsession.

He was certain that he knew where she was. Years before, when they had first returned to the island, she'd spotted a little place by the seaside that she had fallen in love with and bought with some of the money from the musical. She'd told nobody about it; it was to be her secret, a place where she could write in peace, uninterrupted by the inevitable crowd who would descend on any beach house as pretty as the one she'd found.

Dewdrops in the moonlight covered the mountains the car streaked through like a black bolt of steel; rapids on the riverbeds glistened as the road followed the course of the water tumbling down from the heights; and on the flat strip of coastal plain beyond the mountains, where straight roads cut through thousands of acres of sugar cane, the speedometer crept above a hundred miles an hour. In the fields the fluff of the flowering cane arrows glowed white with the reflection of moonbeams and bowed to a wind which rippled cross the plain, making a soft sound, like a million sighing ghosts.

By the time Winston turned down the final quarter mile of rough road and track that led to Michele's cottage, the moon was already gone, and the glare of the beam from the car hit the little wooden house like a searchlight.

He switched off the headlights and sat still behind the wheel. Nothing happened in the darkness except for the flight of peenie wallies and the chirping of crickets. In the near distance he could hear the slapping of waves against a shoreline of limestone rock.

Winston didn't want to turn on the headlights again and he certainly wouldn't blow the horn, because sitting there in Michele's yard, he suddenly felt like an intruder.

A huge weariness overcame him. He reached down and adjusted the big leather bucket seat backwards, then he stretched out as comfortably as the cramped space would allow, and fell asleep.

He slept till daybreak and when he awoke it was from the first rays of the sun to reach the car window through the trees that surrounded the house.

There was no sign of life in the house, or around the yard. The windows were open, but nothing moved. There was no sound except for the sea.

Winston walked past the empty house and into the middle of the empty yard, softly calling, "Michele, Michele."

No answer.

He'd thought of seeing her come around the corner, of hearing her voice answer, "Yes!", of hearing her whisper, "Winston, thank God you've come!"

It would be like a dream come true when she materialised.

"Michele," he called softly again.

Then he saw her, out towards the seashore where the trees gave way to a broad shelf of honeycomb rock.

She was sitting watching the dawn, her back towards the house, and she didn't hear him approach. He walked slowly, and in order not to startle her he didn't come up from directly behind, but made a circle so that she'd see him out of the corner of her eye when he was some distance off. Still she didn't move.

When Winston finally called to Michele and she turned to him, he was appalled at the change in her. Her forehead was drawn with pain, her eyes distant with grief. In his rush to find her, Winston had forgotten about Zack's murder ... he'd only remembered his death.

"It's my fault he's dead," she said, "I was so sure I was right, and I was wrong."

She said it simply, and when said, it seemed she had nothing more to say.

Winston recognised the signs of shock. He himself had lived through a jolt like it when he discovered Michele had betrayed him with Zack. But there was a sign of more than shock in her face—there was guilt, and Winston knew that too; he had experienced it not only for Mark, but also at the time when

Michele lost the baby ... But then she had saved him with forgiveness, and now she had no one to forgive her.

Looking at Michele, seeing the tremors of shock around her mouth, Winston knew that he couldn't close the distance to the only woman he truly loved; that he couldn't comfort her. He realised he could only be a burden to her now, because if she were to love him again it would only increase the guilt she felt towards Zack's spirit, and it was forgiveness from that quarter that she desperately needed to have more than anything else.

Winston was stunned. He had never really come to terms with the loss of Michele; at the time of their separation, he had finessed his feelings, and instead of facing the loss of her then, he'd poured his energy into work and into planning. Now there was no more planning to do unless she came back to him, there was nothing to distract him from the loss of her, and the enormity of that loss was finally coming home. He'd never before been in her presence without the feeling that he could persuade her to love him; even after Antigua he could have got her back again ... but now she was really gone, her emotions totally lost in grief for another man.

"Michele. Come with me, let's get out of here and get things straight again ..."

Michele didn't seem to hear him.

"Don't shut me out Michele!" Suddenly he was shouting. "Can't you see what his death really means? That it was a mistake! That *we* belong together!"

But Michele still didn't move. She just sat there in the grey drizzle, looking out over the dark grey rocks and the paler grey sea and the even paler grey of the far sky.

"You stupid idiot," said Winston, and he turned away.

He went back to his car trembling with rage. Even in death this boy was blocking him from his wife!

The excitement that had built up in him at the thought of seeing Michele had not evaporated, it had turned to despair.

Now was the time Winston should have been able to look after Michele, to take charge, to give her rest, and security, and peace of mind; but in the situation where he had suddenly and unexpectedly found himself, he felt utterly inexperienced.

In his entire life, he had never grown a plant, or fixed a pipe, or hammered a nail, or cooked a meal ... in his childhood, the kitchen of his home had been controlled by three fat ladies who were always glad to give him food, and by the time he left university he could earn enough money to eat in restaurants. Now he faced a situation in which he might end up having to grow food if he was going to get anything to eat at all.

Once again Winston found himself in the car, driving slowly, because he had not made up his mind where to go.

For a fleeting moment, he considered Eddie's offer to take the waiting plane and return to Miami, but he immediately discarded the idea. He felt leaving the island now would be an utterly immoral thing to do. He had set in motion a chain of events, now he couldn't simply step out of the way. He'd have to face the consequences of his actions and he'd have to do it alone.

I was so sure I was right, and I was wrong, Michele had said ...

He had felt equally sure that he was right when he put his plan into action. Was it conceivable that he too was wrong? Certainly he felt he was a long way now from any starting point that could possibly relate to the position in which he found himself ... he'd started with the computer, he'd based his plan on logic, but how much weight did logic have in the bush?

I was so sure I was right, and I was wrong. The words rang in Winston's brain like a warning bell ... Michele's mistake had killed one man, but if Winston's plan misfired, the country might be plunged into a civil war causing the death of thousands.

In order to give himself some time to think, he stopped at an open market-place in the first large country town that he came to. It was Friday and the town square was packed with traders settled in for the weekend, sheltered from the sun and the night dew by crocus bags stretched out above their two or three square yards of captured ground; calculating the results of their sales without calculators; setting up for the next rounds of frantic trading, right up to the time when whatever they'd brought to the market was gone.

Every market woman selling her food over the next twenty-four hours was preparing to engage in a trading session for commodity futures that would have exercised Lucy Anderson's mind: juggling the condition of their produce against the competition, juggling factors of spoilage against the capacity of the customers to pay, estimating to what extent they were prepared to hold back purchasing until the last moment when the hagglers would either have to sell low or dump. Their tradition for barter and business went back centuries and thousands of miles, to the "market mammies" of West Africa.

The quantum of mental energy in that market-place related to a girl on a computer-controlled supermarket checkout counter the way five hundred labourers with picks and shovels relate to a bulldozer, thought Winston, and he wondered how flabby the brain as well as the body of the average industrial society electronic peasant would eventually become.

The sturdy strength and independence of the crowd around Winston gave his spirit a lift. They would survive no matter what happened in the next few months, and Winston suddenly realised that it was what *they* had to teach him that he needed to learn next.

On impulse he started buying everything he saw: candles, lamps, kerosene, two machetes, files, a hoe, a pickaxe, plastic buckets, lighters, two cartons of matches, toilet paper, soap, towels, crates of beer, pots and pans, three knives and spoons, blankets, sheets of linoleum, a dozen tins of Milo, and three dozen tins of canned fish.

Realising he was ravenously hungry, he ate roast corn and jerk pork from the open braziers by the roadside, and when he was full, he got back into the car and started driving again.

Winston thought about his father and mother and realised that there was nothing they'd taught him that could help him now. But his uncle, Uncle T, his father's brother, the one who lived on the cattle property where Mark and Winston stayed for their summer holidays when they were boys, Uncle T loomed larger and larger in Winston's mind as he drove along.

The old man had died fifteen years before, and his children, none of whom were interested in cows, had sold the property so they could go and live in a Toronto suburb.

The property was divided into two parts: a flat section by the seacoast which was turned into a golf course, and the part on the hills looking out to sea which, subdivided, was ideal for tourist villas. But the plan was made in the sixties when mortgage money cost eight per cent, and as the business euphoria of the sixties gave way to the gradually deepening depression of the seventies, the scheme for tourist development was abandoned and the property was left to go to ruin.

When they first came back to the island, Winston and Michele had gone to look for the old great house where Uncle T had lived and they had hardly been able to find it. The entire place had degenerated into a huge abandoned tangle of bush, the old house sadly deserted, the windows and doors and bathroom fittings torn out by vandals, the shingles on the roof rotting, to leave holes through which the rain poured onto floors that in the old days had shone with an accumulation of polishing which had gone on daily for nearly two hundred years. Winston had been so depressed by the destruction of the place where so many of his happiest boyhood memories were set that he hadn't stayed long and he never went back.

Now, however, Winston found himself being drawn to his uncle's place like a magnet. It was on the other side of the island, but the more he thought about it the more he realised that it was the only place for him to hide, it was the only place he knew, it had a river and, he had more claim to it than anybody else right now, and something akin to a sense of possession for what Uncle T had left behind and which nobody else seemed to want, made Winston aim his car in that direction. Once again the Jaguar stretched out on a cross-country run.

By the time he turned off the main road onto the rutted and half-paved parochial road leading to the property, the countryside was deserted. Once or twice the condition of the road was so bad that Winston wondered if he'd get through with the car, and many times the bush and low-lying limbs of trees clogged the sides of the road to such an extent that he wondered if he had missed his way. Finally, to his great relief, he saw the two stone columns of the great-house gates, twelve or fifteen feet tall, looming up ahead. Twice he had to get out of the car to clear branches from the driveway to the house, and both times he replaced the obstacles in hope that nobody would notice that a car had passed that way.

When he reached the house, he parked and got out to look around. The wide verandas threw deep shadows cast by the dying late afternoon sun, and Winston heard the scurrying of rats. As darkness fell, he took the flashlight and turned away from the house towards the old garage out by the stables which had originally been built in the days when three or four traps and carriages were housed here.

The skeleton of Uncle T's old green Plymouth was still inside, the wheels, seats, steering wheel, all gone. Anything anybody wanted had obviously been taken years before.

The hinges creaked when Winston opened the doors to the garage, but they didn't break off, and within a few minutes, the Jaguar was parked alongside the old wrecked car and the doors of the garage were closed again.

Winston walked around in the moonlight and he tried to think ...Michele ... he had lost Michele ... Mark ... he had betrayed Mark ... survival ... he didn't know where to begin, except that he knew it had to be where he found himself now, and having finally decided that, he got into the car and slept.

When Winston woke up the next morning, it was raining. The sun had not yet risen, and he had to go outside before he saw the glow of dawn.

The first thing he had to do was disassociate himself from the car. If he was linked with the Jaguar in any way, he would be immediately suspect. He was grateful for the friendships he'd had with the peasant children during his holidays as a child, because they'd taught him to speak like them, and that, together with the fact that there had always been something of the natural actor in Winston, made him feel confident that he could be a credible refugee from the city if somebody did happen to question what he was doing in the area. If he had time to settle in and practise the role before he was discovered, he knew he could pass for a poor man, but if he was once associated with the car, the link to Mark would eventually cause his capture.

Hurriedly, Winston took out of the car all that he thought he would need in the immediate future and transferred it to the upstairs of the old house. He wanted to be able to see the approaches to his hiding place even at the expense of having to avoid water from leaks through the roof.

All morning and into the afternoon it rained steadily, and Winston did not move from where he sat on the floor. The only thing about country life that he remembered learning as a child was how to sharpen a machete, and this he did a little bit at a time, sitting on the floor, listening to the rain and the rasp of the file till the machete was razor-sharp.

Excitement is the drug of the powerful; the speed of events is their addiction. They take elaborate precautions to protect themselves from boredom, and to their way of thinking, maturity lies in having so many options that no matter what situation they find themselves in they will know from experience of a way not to slow down.

Winston's mind was used to revving at speeds that needed computers to absorb the mental energy he generated, but now his mind was blank. To have come so far, and to have ended up alone, without love ... what then was all the effort for? What else but love could constitute any real reward, any real reason for doing anything? Was there any car, or house, or jewel worth the risk of turning himself into a human computer terminal? Worth the effort of going to the opposite extreme out here in the bush?

Night fell, and he sat there still, dozing, thinking, unable to move, unable to find a reason for moving, unable to summon the energy to start something he knew nothing about and could see no end to. Unable to start all over again when the last overwhelming effort had resulted in nothing more than this: being alone, without love.

Throughout the night, his mind moved in cycles of anguish. *Michele*. Always Michele ... it always came back to her. There were times when, in order to seek relief, he tried to find some compassion for her suffering, but always the overwhelming rage would return, always he would remind himself that her suffering was for another man, a man whom she'd betrayed him for, and in spite of the need for rest from what his mind was doing to his soul, he would be plunged back into another sequence of memories and imaginings that dragged him into the depths of despair and lust for vengeance—causing him to gloat over her suffering and to weep over his own.

The following day, Winston realised that without the chemistry of excitement, he was too tired to move. As soon as he opened his eyes he wanted to close them again. His limbs felt weak; the very blood in his veins felt light, as though without the missing ingredient, his blood was not carrying the energy to his body that would enable it to shake off its lethargy and start functioning.

He, who had timed his life in margins of minutes to get through all he had to do, suddenly felt he would never know what to do next ever again; he who had more people to serve him than he could count, was now totally dependent on his own energy; the expert turned ignoramus; the man on whom everyone had waited was now himself waiting, and he didn't even know what he was waiting for.

Egomania and idleness—wicked combination.

Winston cleared his throat and tried to regulate his breathing. For the first time since he was a child of twelve, he felt the stirrings of asthma in his chest. He felt the struggle for breath begin the almost forgotten signs of the dreaded punishment to come if asthma wasn't cast out early, brought under control through relaxation—only that could save him, relaxation or work.

Picking up the machete, he made his way down the stairs of the old house and out into what had formerly been the garden.

He had to find something to do, something that would take his mind away from himself, something that would absorb the energy that had turned into anxiety because he could find no positive way to use it, some way to channel the rampage of emotion through his rational mind. But where to start? If he didn't clear the block in his chest, he would soon be helpless, the terrible wheezing effort to draw breath wouldn't bring enough air to his lungs to sustain him ... then he remembered the spliff in the car. He had never smoked ganja to relieve asthma because he had never had asthma in his adult life, but he had seen it bring relief to others, and now, bent double and gasping for breath, he made his way to the garage.

He'd rolled the spliff and left it in the ashtray of the car on the night when he went to the embassy party, so long ago. He'd planned then that if he met somebody to take away from the party he'd have a smoke to offer her as they drove off, but he hadn't used it then and it was still intact. He shoved in the car lighter, lit up, inhaled, stepped out of the car, turned around, inhaled another mouthful of smoke, and stepped from the garage back into the yard; into an altered world.

The first thought Winston had was that psychosomatic asthma was, after all, pure ego. If he allowed it to cripple him he would be just as pathetic, just as compromised, as the men he had sneered at round Percy's cabinet table. He, who had considered himself personally invulnerable that afternoon, would now be struck down by a weakness in his own nervous system which rendered him just as useless as any of them.

Then, as the ganja entered his blood stream and as the blood hit his brain, the relaxation he was seeking began to swing his mood around a hundred and eighty degrees.

Levels of love set standards of freedom, thought Winston, *standards of freedom set limitations on ego* ... and a limitation on ego was the only thing that would set him free to breathe again.

If he was to live, he had to forgive Michele, he would have to accept her power over his mind and heart, he would have to accept her power as the only one that could bring him to humility and not cripple him for life, because she had humbled him with love.

She would make him learn that in humility is strength, that if he was not too proud he would always be free to act, and if he could force action through his body and his brain, the flow of energy would clear the block, and he would be able to go on.

Already his breathing had eased. Slowly he walked away from the garage past the old house and down towards the river, conscious that the clamp on his chest could return at any time if he failed to follow through on the test that Michele had brought to him, one which he had not previously realised he'd have to pass just to survive, much less graduate to, the next round of the power game ...

Until people like me stop crying, people like you will never weep, she'd said it so long ago, when he was leaving home, when she was begging him to stay; and when Winston remembered that out there in the bush, in the rain, he sat down on the stump of a tree, and, as his breathing eased, he began to weep.

Chapter Twenty-Nine

∞∞∞

Back in the city, now more than ever back in control, Red Roy rode through the slums like a warlord, recruiting, and drilling his motorbike battalion to wipe out Wire. A list was forming in his mind of all the people still alive who had earned his hatred. He was in the mood to kill and he wanted to get it over with all at one time. Now was the time for the three policemen who had tortured him; now was the time for the man who had killed his brother, for the man who had beaten his mother, for the man who had seduced his woman, for the doctor who had left him to die because he couldn't be bothered to save his life. That was seven. There were others, the list stretching back to his childhood.

Red Roy had the training and instincts of an international terrorist. He was the illegitimate son of a half-white man and a black woman, and although his hair was thick like a black man's hair, the ginger colour reflected some errant Irishman, perhaps the genetic benefactor of Red Roy's terrible temper and the anger that fed it constantly. His only heroes were terrorist killers; his blood raced at the thought of how a handful of men could paralyse a city, cripple a government, threaten even those who had had everything locked up for so long that they felt nothing could threaten them, the people who figured it was OK to drop bombs on the poor but who deplored a bomb in a cafe because it killed rich people and their children. His thrill came from being able to make those who had always felt safe tremble, from seeing the innocent scream. In Red Roy's world, innocence was a sin. Belfast, Beirut, Munich, Red Brigade, Arafat, Carlos: these were the locations and the stars in the world of Red Roy's imagination, and his aim was to stamp his name on that map. Yet in his own back yard, there was a goldmine over which he had not been able to gain control for a long, frustrating, impoverished time, and now he was going to put that in order, he was going to wipe out Wire and take over Rasta City and the ganja trade. He had the men, he had the arms, all he needed was the cash flow from the ganja trade; then even Idi Morris would have to acknowledge him as the toughest guy in town. Never again would anybody mistake him for a petty criminal beebopper.

The news of the impending attack reached Wire at midday. That same night, the cast of Burru's radio show made their way to the station to broadcast an appeal for help from all the Rasta youth who had fled the city for the countryside beyond Burru's Beach, many of them to plant herb for the export trade.

In the studio, Burru, Jahman, Herman, and two others from Burru's Beach were preparing to broadcast live. In spite of the fact they comprised the cast for what was undoubtedly the most popular show on radio, none of this show's stars wore shoes. Burru, as usual, had on nothing but a pair of bath trunks, and a shark's tooth on a piece of cord tied around his neck.

"We used to call it Burru's Beach," said Burru, but lately we call it 'Rasta City'."

"We have been warn of a clash at dawn," said Herman.

"Beebop seh him can mash it down," said Jahman.

"Beebop is a baldhead," said Herman.

Burru, Jahman, Herman and the others were huddled around the mic, their hands rocking back and forth in meditation, their eyes closed, treating words as notes and conversation as skat ...

each taking their turn ... their words becoming song ...

> *Baldhead shouldn't run joke wid Dread.*
> *Baldhead be careful, or you a go dead.*
> *Baldhead a go mash down Rasta City.*
> *At dawn tomorrow…*
> *It a go cause sorrow.*
> *It a go cause a clash.*
> *It involve cash.*
> *A clash for cash at Rasta City.*
> *…it nah go pretty…*
>
> *When Rasta rise, baldhead surprise.*
> *How Rasta rise?*
> *…Get a lif'.*
> *Everybody worldwide, start smoke spliff.*
> *Consciousness spread, Rasta get Dread.*
> *Income multiply, freedom for I.*
> *Freedom to travel.*
> *Freedom to sing.*
> *Rasta start to do everything.*
> *Baldhead look on and baldhead greedy.*
> *Baldhead claim Rasta move up too speedy.*
> *Baldhead feel Rasta should stay needy…*

Five thousand feet up in the mountains, IZion was listening. Ever since the day when he and Wire were the only two to escape death in the army ambush, he had been listening for news of a Rasta revolution.

> *Rasta live natural.*
> *Rasta live clean ... live by the vow of the Nazerene.*
> *Dread withdraw from the baldhead scene.*
> *Rasta cool out and wait until*
> *him start to see prophecy fulfill.*

Him read the Bible and the Bible says
Babylon crashing in these last days.
Baldhead depend on Babylon brain.
Him start feel hungry, him start feel pain.
Babylon falter, Babylon stall.
That nuh trouble Dread at all.
When baldhead frighten, him look round, and him see
the riches in Rasta ground.
When baldhead did have it, him never share.
When Rasta suffer, him never care.
Him seh Rasta peaceful and Rasta scatter ...
What Rasta feel is another matter.
Rasta strong, but holding back.
... waiting for baldhead to attack.

IZion was getting excited. All through the island there were youths like himself; on every hillside the bravest Rasta youth was planting food, smoking herbs, waiting and meditating. Immensely strong, they came of stock that had been through as ruthless a piece of genetic elimination as any in history, but the strength was scattered and the thoughts were like secrets within each individual's mind.

There was no central church for Rasta, no structures of any kind, no political affiliation, no priests, no titles. In the 1970s the vulgarities of the formal religions were nowhere near the centre of Rasta power. Rasta power was in the Bible. Rasta power was in the realisation that as black men in the West they were Africans above class and tribe. Rasta power was "Marcus" for pride and the symbol of "Selassie" for Pan-Africanism.

"Is this the beginning or the end?" asked Jahman.

"Now Rasta has more than words to defend," said Burru. Now, for the first time, IZion and those like him across the land, could pinpoint an event capable of pulling them together. If Red Roy took control of Rasta City, baldhead would reign supreme. Even

in the ganja trade, Rasta would have to bow to baldhead mafia—
the political gangsters and crooked police who had nearly killed
IZion once before.

*"If you coming, come now, don't be tame; better you die fighting
than live in shame."*

By the time the programme ended, IZion had left his hut to go
out into the night and dig up his gun. By midnight the mountain
valleys echoed with the sound of juke-boxes blaring music and
the roar of motorbike engines being fine-tuned. Weeping women
begged some men not to fight, and dry-eyed women watched
other men for signs of courage.

In heavy mist, before daylight, IZion set out for Burru's Beach.
Three others from his district travelled with him. By the time
they had gone ten miles, each rider had picked up a pillion
passenger. By the time they hit the main road, IZion was leading
a group of fifty Rasta fighters. By seven o'clock the highway
approaching the city from the west was clogged with Rastafarian
motorbikes weaving in and out, travelling at speed through the
morning traffic, the riders shouting war cries as they raced
along.

When Red Roy wheeled off the highway from the city with two
hundred fighters behind him, he didn't expect to meet more
than token resistance from the squatters. Rastas had always
professed and practised non-violence, even Wire did not go into
a fight wanting to kill, and Red Roy was sure that the Rastas
couldn't match his muscle. Protecting some trucks was one
thing; dealing with the combined force of every criminal left in
the city was another.

All of Red Roy's fighters were men who had been fighting

professionally since they were teenagers. Each one was strong enough to control their bit of territory and hadn't been challenged for years. The rush of adrenalin they felt when they were going into a fight was their favourite thrill, and because they enjoyed it and were practised and cool in the circumstances, they always won. Most had not been seriously challenged for so long that they had forgotten what it was like to be challenged at all.

Eddie Azani had caught Red Roy unawares, he hadn't dreamt Eddie would be a karate master, and he'd been distracted by the dog. But now Red Roy was armed the way he liked to be armed, and he was attacking in numbers that could take down the force that faced them with sheer weight. Now was his time to get even.

Eunice and Rupert, together with all the other women and children of the village, watched with horror as the approaching motorbikes seemed to fill the horizon, backed by a cloud of dust, aiming for the oasis of irrigated area in the parched scrubland. As Wire and the others who were going to defend Rasta City rode out to meet the baldhead forces, they felt nauseous with fear.

As they drew close to each other, the two groups of riders slowed and stopped, two hundred riders behind Red Roy on one side and not more than seventy-five behind Wire on the other. The noise from the nearly three hundred motorbikes was deafening, and the dust swirled through the crowd as the leaders rode to within earshot of each other. Although the heat of the sun was already intense, Wire felt bitterly cold. In ten minutes either he would be humiliated, or he would be dead. He felt fear closing in around him like a trap, but it was too late to turn back now.

When Red Roy was no more than ten feet away from Wire, all the engines around them throttled back.

"But wait," said Red Roy, "is dis de same Wire dat beat up my man and send im wid de facety message dat I mus 'dress back'? Eh? What happen? Yu come to tell me to dress back again?"

"We come fe reason wid you."

"What reason yu can give mi fe nuh bruk down yu backside, an everybady dat is in your camp, as a defyer?"

"So yu feel dis is fe yu property?"

"I come fe claim it."

"Is God land but we a use it."

Herman looked from Wire to Red Roy. The contrast was striking. Wire's hair fell in locks around his shoulders and down his back. Red Roy's hair was trimmed with the utmost care. Wire's voice was heated, emotional. Red Roy's voice was cold and sarcastic. Wire was thin and hard. Red Roy was heavy with muscle. The only thing they had in common was a mutual hatred and rivalry that went back to their first conflicts at fourteen.

"Dis a God land," said Wire again.

"How yu go keep it?" asked Red Roy. "Yu go blow yu horn like de ancient Israelites?"

When Wire saw the smile of contempt on Red Roy's face, he felt a flash of anger at being ridiculed that replaced the chill of fear with a hot flush of rage, and Wire reassessed his foe.

"Yu nuh need dis land," said Wire, "yu jus' come fe destroy."

"Destroy what? Yu can tek yu calaloo and zinc sheet when yu leave. Yu tink a few ragged-ass Rasta can stand in de way a progress?"

A surge of violence registered among Red Roy's men in the revving of engines, but there was another volume of noise that Wire was listening for. Where was IZion? He must have heard Burru on the radio the night before, the programme had been established as the main link between the centre of the smuggling operation and the suppliers across the island, and IZion should have arrived by now, but Wire looked and saw no help on the horizon. IZion was still too far away … Wire would have to stop Red Roy all by himself.

He saw clearly now that the battle couldn't be between Red Roy's army and his few followers; the battle had to be between Red Roy and Wire. The contest couldn't be a matter of physical strength alone; Wire would have to take the contest to a higher level.

"Yu shouldn't insult mi," said Wire.

"Why not?" asked Red Roy.

"Because yu might lose yu rass claat life," said Wire.

Before the words were out of his mouth, Wire had spun his bike and mounted it into a wheelie as he shot away from the crowd, who were as mesmerized by his riding as if they'd been at a show. The one thing Wire had always spent his money on was bikes, and he had the best, and he made it fly in a wide arc until he was just a ball of dust in the distance; a ball of dust that was turning. Suddenly out of the dust emerged Wire, heading back towards the invaders at a hundred miles an hour, headed for exactly that spot in the middle of Red Roy's line. Now Red Roy became aware that Wire on his Kawasaki was on a kamikaze run.

In vain, Red Roy tried to manoeuvre out of the way, but Wire hit him, and their two bikes made a marriage of steel and flesh and gas and sparks and explosion and noise, that consumed the lives of those two men, wedded in hatred since childhood.

With the explosion and death of both Wire and Red Roy, two hundred motorbike's wheels started spinning at once and a cloud of dust rose twenty feet into the air.

There were those of Red Roy's invaders who were so shocked by his death that they turned for home, but there were others who did not forget the spoils of war, and they started to join battle with the citizens of Rasta City, Herman among them. Within seconds, all one could see were hundreds of dark shadows darting and wheeling in the dust, so blinded by it that no rider knew if he was facing friend or foe, gun or machete, till seconds before the blow. Each man sought to identify himself with a scream, and the screaming, mixed with the noise of the motorbikes, came out of the dust cauldron as an unearthly sound for the women and children of Rasta City looking on.

As soon as they went into action, fear left the Dreads. From the first physical contact, they found out that the forces they had feared so greatly just a few minutes before had bodies no stronger than theirs, and their skill in killing had been obliterated by the blinding choking condition of the battle.

Many who'd been caught in it weren't fighting at all unless it was to fight their way out, and the dust formed into a cloud the shape of an erupting volcano as those who were trying to get away made wider and wider circles around the nucleus.

Caught in the middle of the madness, was Herman, father of Rupert, husband of Eunice, leader of the little band that originally escaped the city to build a dream at Burru's Beach. Coming towards him was an angry killer who had ridden out with Red Roy for the promise of blood lust. He looked like some animal coated in dust instead of hair ... only his eyes, shining through the dust mask, left no doubt in his mind that he had found the man he had to kill.

Herman had never had a fight in his life before that day, but when Wire led him into battle he fought like a man possessed. Almost as soon as the fighting erupted he had captured the revolver of a fallen baldhead and shot him in the leg before the other man's shots rang out. Now he had only the empty gun in one hand and a machete in the other. The killer from the city also had a knife and a gun, but his gun was still loaded. The knife was his favourite weapon. He was a kung fu fighter with three inches of steel clutched in his fist.

Herman saw that killer coming towards him, but he couldn't do anything about it, he couldn't get his thoughts together about anything, he could only think about Rupert and Eunice, and how it was funny that a snatch of tune Zack used to sing was running through his head at a time like this.

> Don't be afraid
> love casteth out fear;
> don't be afraid
> tho' the crisis is near ...

Herman knew that man was going to kill him. Herman wasn't a fighter, but he'd been seduced into a fight, and as a peaceful man of God, it seemed like God was going to punish him on the spot.

That's how he looked at it.

The killer didn't get away, for no sooner was Herman killed than IZion arrived with his men from the mountains. They slammed into the battle to scatter Red Roy's thugs in every direction, enacting a scene like some ancient historic desert battle in which the horses had been replaced by Hondas, Suzukis, and Yamahas.

The Rasta fighters from the hills were soon clear winners in the centre. As they peered through the clouds of dust they found that they were more and more surrounded by each other, less and less confronted with baldheads. The battle turned into a rout. The whole plain was covered with motorbikes kicking up dust, dodging boulders and cactus as Red Roy's remaining men headed back towards the city, riding for their lives.

The Dreads chasing their attackers quickly lost any lust for killing, and they started screaming with laughter and shouting insults after the baldheads as they drove them back to town.

Back on the battlefield, terrible pain had caught up with the wounded. Women came out from the village and started looking for their men. Children too were walking among the bodies, looking on with that childish tolerance for horror. Rupert was among the children.

"Herman, papa Herman," called out the child, as he walked along searching, "Papa Herman!"

Rupert's father had hushed him from the time before Rupert could remember. His mother had left the man with the infant slung across his shoulders, walking up and down in the night, wondering when the child's crying would cease. His father had fed him and bathed him and put on his clothes. He had listened to the child's stories, and told him of a new life. His father had carried him out of the fire, out of the city. He had built them a house and made them a bed, and grown food for them to eat. Herman had read to Rupert from the Bible and taught him how to kick a ball. He had given him a dog, rides on his motorbike, and swims in the sea. In a world where they saw other children being brutally beaten for not performing well as servants for their parents, Herman and his little son had lived as each other's true companions in life.

When Rupert saw his father, the child went into trauma. In later life, he would remember nothing before the instant in which he saw Herman's body lying on the ground, covered with flies, like the carcass of an animal which had been hit by a truck and left on the side of the road.

Chapter Thirty

When the oil ran out at the island's refinery, there was also no flour on the docks; no butter, or margarine, or cooking oil in the shops; no soap, no electricity, no pumped water, and very little kerosene. People started to stream from the city out into the countryside looking for friends and relatives, searching for small parcels of land that they had left behind, or that their fathers or grandfathers before them had left behind when they went to the cities to "better themselves". Now they were straggling back to the countryside very much the worse for wear.

On that fateful afternoon when Winston was threatened by asthma, he walked down towards the river till a big clump of bush blocked his way, and then he sat down to rest and restore his breathing to normal.

He sat with his elbows on his knees and the palms of his hands supporting his forehead, looking down. He didn't move for a long time as he concentrated on breathing out and breathing in, returning the flow of breath to his body with slow deliberation, turning over in his mind what he was going to do next.

Even when his breathing was back to normal he didn't move because he knew that when he looked up he was going to have to do the first thing that he saw had to be done, no counting the costs, no calculations of any kind except the labour of a man against some obstacle. The PhD had come back down to basics.

When Winston sat down, the clump of bush blocking the pathway had seemed like an impenetrable wall of solid sullen green, but when he looked up again, the sun had come out and the piece of bush was back-lit by the afternoon sun; there were dozens of different shades of green in it, Winston could very easily see where the bush was heavy and where the trunks and branches ran through the foliage that they were supporting.

As he walked towards the bush, it was obvious to him what his first stroke with the machete should be; it was to trim away some light vines around a branch that was holding up a big clump of bush on it. The cut was a high one, and as Winston drew back the machete to make the cut, he smiled as he felt himself moving into the position for serving a ball in a game of squash.

When he made the chop the bush parted easily. He realised the next chop was essentially a drop shot with the machete, the next one a volley. Suddenly he was chopping with a skill he had developed years before, his weight was in the right place, he was in no hurry, he was letting the machete follow through, and the bush melted away in front of him as though he was working on a great green sculpture, the light behind the bush showing him where to chop next even before he had finished the follow-through on the previous stroke.

Winston started to sing and dance with joy. No longer did he hate Michele, she had brought him to humility, and humility had set him free. Never again would he be blocked, never again would he have to sit and wait; this mountainside was big enough to absorb all his energy for a long, long time.

From the moment Burru felt the hand over his mouth and the gun on his spine on the night he was captured outside the radio station, he knew he must prepare himself for torture and death, but neither had come to him yet.

He was held in a small, airless, filthy room that served as cell and interrogation centre for army intelligence. They gave Burru his food, but otherwise they left him strictly alone. The guards seemed somewhat embarrassed by his presence. They had listened to him preach on the radio and they had agreed with what he had to say then. They thought of him as a preacher, as a man of God, and as much as possible they behaved as if he wasn't there.

When it came to torture, they got their fun out of someone else. They'd had another captive there for weeks and they beat him every night, sometimes just one or two lashes with a five-foot-long piece of plastic hose; sometimes they beat him for what seemed like hours on end. The torturers often saved the entertainment for the evening, as an after-dinner treat. It was something they waited till they were in a good mood to do, because they would laugh even louder at the victim when he jumped in pain, shrieked for mercy, went through a change of life before their very eyes. Cowards particularly amused them — half the time they didn't even have to strike a blow before their victims started to whimper and wet themselves with fear. After the laughter there was often a change of mood. The torturers often seemed to become emotionally involved with their victims in an almost sexual way. It seemed to Burru that the perversion in men like these was that total dependence turned them on. Instead of gaining satisfaction from the voluntary submission of a woman who was satiated with pleasure — they sought the tenderness of submission from other men as they grovelled and begged to be spared more pain.

The wretch who was beaten every night spent hours each day looking through the bars of his cell at the piece of rubber hose with which they beat him and which was left hanging where he could see it just outside his cell at all times.

As soon as he saw his tormentors approaching he would set up a piteous terrified pleading which goaded them to tease him with the promise of a reprieve, toying with him right up to the moment of the first lash. Then all the accumulated nervous tension would break from him in a scream. He would back, terrified, into a corner, begging them not to hit him again as they told him that if he screamed half as loud they would beat him twice as hard.

Eventually the screaming would stop altogether as his body went into a series of spasms and his mind was shaken loose from the torment in his flesh and bone, his swollen tissue and damaged innards; and they'd throw him into the cell to sleep till he woke up to stare at the length of plastic hose once more.

"Hey devil disciple," Burru used to call to the torturers sometimes. "You don't know that pain can reach you too? You know, one day you might just feel pain, and the next day it grow worse, and all of a sudden you start to suffer pain you can't bear, and a little later we hear you dead of cancer. Be careful!"

Burru knew that the torturers left him alone because he was a star and they were afraid of his faith, but he also knew that there was someone who didn't fear him or his spiritual power, and Burru prepared for the moment he would meet that man. He would not fear him, he would not fear for what he could do to his body because he had already prepared to put his mind with the Father and leave the structure with the killer.

Clearly the way to fight such a man was not with the body, particularly when yours was in his possession. No, the way to fight him was with the strength of the spirit, and that was what Burru was prepared to do. He knew that the spirit could protect the body from harm if it chose to do so, he came from a race of people who had been walking through fire for thousands of years, and the faith Burru derived from recalling his grandmother's stories convinced him that he could induce a self-hypnosis so strong that he would not have to bow to the devil.

It was Idi Morris himself who eventually stepped through the door.

"A long time I been trying to get to yu," said Idi Morris. Burru said nothing. "Because yu know something I wan know, and I intend fe yu tell me."

Burru smiled. "What I know dat yu wan know?" he asked.

"De night yu mek de broadcast," said Idi, "yu pull some man outta di hills. Who dem deh?"

"I nuh know," said Burru, dead calm.

Suddenly the palm of Idi's hand snaked out and slapped Burru across the face. The surprise surpassed the pain. Burru looked into Idi's eyes and read the rage building in him because Burru had not yet shown fear.

"Yu little bumbo claat yu! Yu tink yu can defy me?"

Again Burru said nothing. He had begun to prepare himself for the moment. His look towards Idi didn't change, but the general was working himself into a rage that would tear him apart if he didn't vent it on someone else.

He doubled up his fist and smashed it into Burru's stomach, then picked up a chair and smashed it across his head, then ... it didn't matter what he did then. He was putting pain into a corpse, the spirit of the devil was coupling with a cadaver.

That same evening, the Ayatollah Khomeini flew from Paris to Tehran, and the Cliffords were having dinner with a Greek ship owner who had done a great deal of business with the Iranians.

"What's the old man like?" asked Molly.

"He's a Saracen," said the Greek.

"Really, you mean he won't be content with getting rid of Palhavi?"

"Oh no. He could start a holy war."

"Just think of what Jimmy could do with that! He could go on TV and say *he's* very religious too, and *his* God has made *him* the most powerful man in the world."

"Think of what he could do with that in the Bible Belt!" said Hugh. "He'd be the biggest thing out of the South since Huey Long."

"They could have religious arguments on CNN." Laughed Molly. "Jerry Falwell versus the Ayatollah."

The Greek was laughing too.

"Ah, Molly, you joke," he said, "but is a serious situation."

"Oh indeed," she said, "and all because of that awful vulgar little man who has no more claim to the Peacock Throne than my chauffeur. Herbie knows him well and can't stand him."

"How is Herbie?" asked the Greek. "Did he get caught?"

"Herbie's fine," said Hugh. "He got out in time."

"So did I, thank God," said the Greek.

The day after Idi Morris murdered Burru, he called a meeting of his inner circle in Mark's old office to explain the policy of his government.

"Number one," said Idi, "everybady in dis country haffi realise dat dis a military govament, and nuttin so strange 'bout dat. Number two, dem haffi realise dat we not jokin. We waan find out who wid us and who against us, and dem dat against us a go dead. Number three, we waan every gallan a gas and every leaf a ganja fe store. In America wi a go mek dem unnerstant dat is a war against drugs wi fightin, because dem luv dat, but if dem nuh recognise mi regime an gi wi money fe cut it out, wi a go sell it rass an mek di money dat way because one way ar anadda we haffi survive, right?"

"Right," murmured the assembled company.

"Mi waan all a yu fe study how regime like dis operate all roun di world, educate yuself, find out how many a dem all over. Count how long dem remain in power. Check wat di top guy in dem regime tek fe dem recompense, an tink bout it, an come back an tell mi if yu for or against dis revolutionary guvament."

The brutality of Idi Morris' regime soon began to make itself felt throughout the countryside as his army proceeded to carry out his ganja reaping campaign. It was the only thing on the island that could be sold for cash, that, and maybe landing rights to the Colombians for the transhipment of cocaine, but that was still at the exploratory stage. While Idi proclaimed loudly that he was eradicating drugs, in fact there was no eradication of ganja, everything that was reaped was carefully stored; what was eradicated were the small farmers; their crops stolen, their women raped, their children traumatised.

Less than three miles from IZion, soldiers had invaded the fields of a friend of his.

"Weh di ganja deh?" asked Idi Morris's men.

"We nuh av no ganja," said the farmer.

"See ganja yah!" shouted one of the soldiers from the far side of the field.

"Yu liard rass!" The soldier hit the farmer across the face with the butt of his gun, breaking his jaw. "Weh de udder ganja field?"

The soldier was obviously angry enough to kill the young farmer, and his girlfriend screamed out, "Tell dem, nuh!? Yu willing fe lose yu life fe ganja?"

"Is nat ganja alone wi lookin fah," said the soldier. "Wi lookin fe gas tu."

But that *was* something that the farmer was willing to take further beating for rather than disclose.

In a mood of foul bad temper, the soldiers forced everybody in the yard to cut and load the entire crop of ganja, then they raped the two young girls and drove away.

Deeper and deeper into the countryside, the people would hear the rumble of approaching trucks and in a panic would grab whatever they could carry while running, and they would disappear into the bush, leaving their food and their possessions to be pillaged. Suddenly it seemed as though the entire island had been divided into two tribes, the attackers and the defenders, the town and the country, the grabbers and the growers, Babylon and Zion; as clearly defined as Yoruba and Ibo in Biafra, or the Xhosa and the Afrikaans in South Africa.

There were many in the army and the police, most of them loyal to Mark Bernard, who refused the opportunity to pillage and kill, but for every soldier or policeman who laid down their guns rather than bully innocent people, there were several outside the former forces of law and order who now joined the rampage.

When IZion heard the stories of pillage and rape he knew that it couldn't go on. He'd have to do something, and every night when he went to bed he prayed that he would receive guidance.

Burru, Wire, Zack, all mighty spirits without their own vehicle for expression in the physical world: they appeared to IZion in dreams and they told him that he was the only one left to lead the people against the wickedness that was sweeping the land; that they had come to help him and guide him, but that he was the one who would have to act, and one night when IZion woke up, he got up out of his bed and he went outside to look up at the stars, and he decided that next morning he would ride out and once more gather together the forces that he had led into the battle at Burru's Beach, but this time he would increase their strength a hundredfold. The moment had arrived when IZion must sharpen his machete, load up his gun, fit on his knuckle-duster, flick out his knife, gas up his bike, and ride out to avenge some wrongs.

Chapter Thirty-One

❦

Down by the river of Uncle T's abandoned cattle property, Winston made a clearing and set up a small tatu, stretching lino-leum sheeting over a framework made of sticks. The first night he slept well, and next morning he was up early, eager to start work. Winston didn't pause except to fall into short deep sleeps induced by hard labour, but hard labour at his own pace, hard labour under the shade of trees through which wind moved in waves of refreshment, hard labour taken gradually so that by the time the initial blisters on his hands had healed, he was impatient for the exercise that he had come to crave.

Within ten days he had started to look and feel so rugged in the bush that even if the car was discovered he felt that he could make himself pass as a surprised onlooker.

Far from being bored, Winston found that soon there wasn't enough time in a day to do everything he wanted. Far from being lonely, the small farmers who he had for neighbours became good friends who advised him on what to plant and how to prepare the ground, and who made him realise that the people who remained on the land were there because they wanted to be there, not because they were too stupid to make it in the city. Winston's talent for mimicry had allowed him to pass as a refugee from the city now terrorised by Idi Morris and his men. He told his new friends tales of travelling far, of working as a clerk in New York and London, of the girl he had fallen in love with and

342

the tragedy of his love for her; of his return to the island, of his search for the property of the man who his mother had always claimed was Winston's father. But Winston was no longer Winston, he was Jah T, in honour of the uncle whose land he had returned to.

"So who was your mother then?" the question was asked once or twice.

"She was a maid in Hodges Bay," said Winston; "seems like Mass T was jus' passing through."

As his confidence returned, Winston felt his mind turning back to the details of a plan for recovering the power that the family had lost.

He took out a road map and a pocket calculator and started to jot down the basic statistics that had been familiar to him for years—his father had compiled them for the British. Amounts of rainfall and water storage; acreages of land, fertile and marginal; markets for crops, traditional and potential; irrigation schemes and roadways planned a generation ago but never built; plans for tourism and communications and international banking and solar energy. The basic thinking didn't need computers, uninterrupted concentration was what was required at this conceptual stage, and before long Winston had set up a couple of wooden planks for a desktop and found himself working into the night.

Early on, a symbol of his resurgence appeared. Winston was sitting at his makeshift desk, and, as night fell, he lit his kerosene lamp, placing an eyeshade around it so that the reflection from the flame would fall on the paper and not reflect into his eyes. The circle of light spilled across the edge of the desk and onto the floor. He took out his calculator and a sheet of paper and was just about to start to work when he looked up to see, sitting at the very edge of the circle of light, a tiny starving mongrel puppy staring at him with huge frightened eyes.

"Well," said Winston, "who have we here?"

The puppy didn't move. It didn't wag its tail, it just sat looking at Winston with a desperate expression on its face.

"How you find me out here in the bush?" asked Winston. "You saw the lamp, ah? You must have seen the lamp, so I'm going to call you Aladdin."

Winston got up and put some food and water on the floor for this other refugee to eat, and still the starving puppy didn't move, but when he looked up from his work ten minutes later, the food was gone and Aladdin lay asleep in the dust.

Three days later the puppy's stomach had blown up like a balloon, and within a week he was a healthy happy little creature tied to Winston's heels by an invisible leash three feet long.

Nor was Aladdin the only creature associated with lamps that attached itself to Winston's routine. Each night, attracted by the warmth from the upward draft of the heat from the lamp, a lizard would position itself on the roof above the desk. Winston wasn't aware of it as he bent over his calculations, until his concentration was splattered with a burst of astonishment and laughter, as the lizard, with perfect precision, shat exactly into the middle of the bald patch on the back of Winston's head.

Each night Winston stared up into the heavens for ten or fifteen minutes at a time, any time he woke. It was so easy to see the movement in the sky in three dimensions once one had seen it in the cinema, and often Winston noticed pin dots of light, moving very fast, too fast for a plane he realised ... *they must be satellites* ... and somehow that made the whole spatial reality of the heavens impact even more on his imagination.

He mused on the theme of spiritual transmission; of how much mankind had gained access to the spiritual world. For one looked to the sky and saw nothing, yet one knew that it was full

of a million messages—TV, pictures, music, telephone calls—
and these messages were spiritual in that they carried emotion,
spiritual in that they were actual but intangible ... except through
electricity. In rainstorms, Winston felt like a primitive man
receiving the original messages from lightning. He imagined
how the message from electricity had run from first to last, had
started fire by striking a tree, and from there had gone on to
produce light, and heat, and transference—physical and mental;
how it had revealed its capacities for sound, pictures, memory,
and calculation; eventually collecting information to store, cross-
reference, and recall faster and in greater quantities than the
mind of any man. Electrons dancing on tape: the virtually
abstract, almost invisible, man-made model of the real big brain,
the one so vast and ethereal it could be discovered only through
revelation, up to now ... but now it was obvious.

Winston had always had dream highs, but now, in the bush,
he started to get high on physical speed as well, and he worked
all day long by sticking to the same principles in the field as he
used for working in his penthouse. He never worked so hard that
he got tired; he never rested so long that he got bored.

He expanded his menagerie with a hen and some chickens,
and he adopted a kitten. The animals amused and intrigued him
more than he would have imagined possible, and he was satisfied
with what they provided for his entertainment because he was
content to merely sit and watch, or lie down and listen to the
sights and sounds around him for hours on end. The notion grew
in him that if one were to consider how a god would relate to
man, one should consider how men related to the animal
kingdom.

So fascinated did he become with his immediate surroundings
that Winston hardly listened to the news. He could tell from the
items reported and from the tone of voice used by the news-
readers to report them that the radio station was not in touch

with what was going on. He realised that the only way to judge what was happening was with the evidence of one's own eyes, and what Winston was looking at got prettier every day. At first he was panicked at the thought of his batteries running out, but in fact, by the time they did, he hardly had time to listen to music anymore because he was so fascinated by his immediate reality. He was fascinated by farming, and, in the far future, he was planning the comeback of the Bernards.

It never occurred to him to expand his living quarters. He cooked over a fireplace of four large stones in one corner of the lean-to, and his two pots hung on a nail driven into one of the four posts that supported the roof of his hut. Inside his tatu he put together a bed of bagged leaves, the bags of varying sizes and densities so he could apportion pockets of softness to make a highly personal resting place.

Sitting on his bed, sharpening his machete or hoe, Winston looked out beyond the garden he had planted and beyond the trees to the river. He swam in the river so often he hardly ever needed to wash with soap, and he discovered that if he washed his plate and mug immediately after cooking and eating, he never had to deal with any pile-up of domestic chores.

As the crops grew and the animals became more and more affectionate, he became all the more comfortable in his solitude. Occasionally he heard news of nearby atrocities, of soldiers foraging in the neighbourhood, and of the dispossessed from the city who could do no better than steal, but these things never found Winston's hidden corner, and he was just beginning to think that he had escaped the consequences of the turmoil in the land, when he got the cut.

He was moving through a field from saplings to pumpkins to peas, checking them for insects and eaten leaves, occasionally stopping to smudge out an ants' nest or weed around a root, things he did in passing as he moved toward a new planting area.

He started work on a stony patch: his right hand holding the machete, his left hand using a crook stick to lift and clear the grass and weeds ahead of the blade so that the chopping was clean and precise. The bush started to gather itself into a roll that he pushed ahead of him till it grew big enough to mince into a pile that would turn to mulch when it rained. It was a clear day and hot, so he stuck to the shade, setting up a rhythm of work and rest that set his mind to dreaming.

He was proud of his survival, he was excited by the fact that he would be able to combine academic theory with practical experience at the most basic level, he was thinking that he would soon be ready to risk a visit to Michele again ...

As he chopped and moved forward, he cleared any stones in the way by picking them up and throwing them to one side. Sometimes he threw them around a tree trunk, sometimes he threw them along the line of a fence he had erected with sticks to protect his plants from stray goats; usually he was able to pick up the stones with one hand, occasionally he had to use two, always he checked for insects by turning over the stone and looking underneath before picking it up. As a child on this same property, he remembered when they would go out and look for scorpions so that they could catch them and put them in a ring of fire on the ground and watch them sting themselves to death, but he hadn't seen any scorpions since he started the clearing, and that fact, plus the wanderings of a mind set free from immediate worry, made him careless.

When he stepped on a loose stone, his ankle turned and the razor edge of the machete sliced a vein in his ankle.

He limped to where he had a shirt hung up, and holding it down with his good foot, he tore it into strips and managed to tie a tourniquet around his leg. When he flexed his foot it wasn't so painful that he wanted to stop working immediately, but later, when he washed the wound in the river and started walking back to his hut, it gave him some pain to walk on.

"Well Aladdin," he said to the puppy, "I'm living like a dog now boy, I have to cure myself the way you do. Trust in the Lord. Works for you doesn't it? How many thousand years did mankind live without taking drugs, eh? And they got through."

So saying he went to bed before sunset and he managed to sleep until the early morning hours, but when he woke then and lit a match to look at the wound, it had grown ugly, and his foot hurt him when he tried to walk on it.

By morning there were obvious signs of blood poisoning. Winston was sweating and he felt feverish, and he knew he had to seek some medical help, no matter how remote that help might be. Desperately, he started limping through the bush, forcing himself to move forward in spite of the pain. After walking for twenty minutes and stopping twice to avoid falling from a dizziness that was sweeping across him regularly, he got to the road that would lead him to the nearest town. There was no shade and the heat of the sun was merciless. Time and again he thought he was going to faint as his head swam with the effort that it took to force himself down the dusty road.

There was no traffic, only people on foot. Many were refugees. All had seen so many others in worse condition than Winston that they did not offer help so long as he could in any way help himself. When he eventually reached the clinic of the local doctor there were already at least twenty people waiting to receive attention. The doctor himself was not there, and the nurse told Winston that she had no antibiotics.

"You think this can kill me?" he asked the nurse.

"There's a lot of poison in your system," she replied, "but if your body is strong enough to fight it, you will pull through."

She had no serum for anti-tetanus injections, but she did have enough disinfectant to clean out the cut and bandage it with the strip of shirt that he'd had the presence of mind to bring with him for that purpose. The nurse had done what she could, but as he walked away, the pain from the wound had started to cripple one side of his body. He had waited for an hour and a half to see the nurse, and she had taken half an hour to do what she could for him, and by that time it was two o'clock in the afternoon.

Once again he had to face the five-mile stretch of road, dust, and cracked asphalt, which was giving off heat waves that made the landscape seem to swim, but luckily this time he got a lift in the back of a cart which dropped him at the turn-off for the dirt road leading into the property. When he got down from the cart he could barely stand. Every few minutes he tried to vomit up food that was no longer in his stomach, every hundred yards or so he had to stop and focus because his senses of balance and direction were being eroded by pain.

Very slowly he made it back to the old main house, and then he could go no further. He stumbled up to the top veranda where he had settled in when he first arrived, and there, his strength consumed with fever and pain, he slumped to the floor and collapsed.

The last thing Winston remembered hearing was the buzz of a mosquito which eventually settled on his forehead above his right eye. As the buzzing stopped and the insect prepared to suck his blood, Winston remembered thinking that he didn't have the strength left to swat it. He didn't have the strength left to move his body, and his mind didn't have the strength left to think; only his soul was left to dream, and Winston lapsed into delirium.

Aladdin whined and lay down with his paws in front of him, watching Winston, listening to him mumble the same thing over and over again, words that Aladdin didn't recognise.

"Michele, my body's in torment, my soul is in judgement," Winston murmured. "Michele, my body's in torment, my soul is in judgement," he said it over and over again, and as he said the words his brain filled with images.

When Winston passed beyond pain and into hallucination, it seemed to him that he was floating in the firmament of his own personal computer, lights blinking and counting, adding up the pros and cons of his existence on earth. A vision replayed as his sins were enumerated and his kindnesses accounted for, and then the calculation shifted to another gear. Now there were two main additions going on, on opposite sides, and Winston knew that the one on the left estimated his ambition, and the one on the right estimated his knowledge. The one on the left quickly filled up to the top, but the one on the right went only so far and stopped. There was something missing. Something Winston would have to know, would have to learn before he knew enough to fulfil his ambitions. The right hand column wouldn't hold, it started slipping, and as it slipped, the torrent of light from the left hand side poured over to fill the vacuum, and slowly, then faster, the lights started moving in a circle, creating a vortex, starting to flush Winston's life away into a howling black hole of oblivion ... his ambitions were too great for his wisdom. In his determination to survive and persevere and reach for power, in spite of all he'd been through and all he'd learned, there was still something crucial he didn't know. He'd failed the final test, and he prepared to die.

Chapter Thirty-Two

∞∞∞

Ever since he had driven out from the seaside cottage that day, Winston had been on Michele's mind. Every time she thought about their parting, a chill ran through her at the coldness of it. What glimpse she had had of Winston was of a man in shock. Winston, the man she loved, the one who was living, not the one who was dead. Had she been so self-centred in her guilt that she had not been able to acknowledge the completely unexpected and undeserved return of the man to whom she was married?

Her days started to fill with a new self-recrimination; she found herself worried about where he'd gone when she allowed him to drive away, and finally when her nights filled with nightmares about Winston drenched in sweat, delirious, she decided to act on her instincts and try to find him.

Michele literally had no idea where she was going when she left home to look for Winston, but as she walked along the route that he had driven, she put herself into his frame of mind and she knew right away that he would have stayed on the island. She knew he would have felt largely responsible for whatever had happened, and she knew he wouldn't run from the consequences. Eddie could leave because he had never pretended to guide events, he merely wanted to be one jump ahead, but Winston would feel responsible for the events themselves—it was a traditional Bernard vanity. Winston wouldn't run, there was too much of Edna and Arthur and Uncle T in him for that ... Uncle T! Winston would have had to hide, thought Michele, but he wouldn't just hide, he'd try to take advantage of the situation, try to use the time and circumstances for his own ends. He'd take advantage of the opportunity to see a side of life he had never experienced, but which he must now know would have to be at the very root of his plans since they were all going to have to start from scratch. He'd love the idea of putting his academic mind to a peasant's problems—that's what he'd do! Uncle T's property became her logical destination.

The trip across the island was an excursion into hell. The roads were empty of any traffic except for refugees on foot who were constantly, ceaselessly, begging.

Michele pressed on for two days until she reached a market town in the centre of the island. She had stopped to buy food when she heard a familiar voice behind her begging a market woman for something to eat.

"Where you come from?" asked the market woman.

"Rasta City," said the voice, "dem mash it up, dem kill mi 'usband." Michele spun around.

"Eunice!"

"Michele!"

"What you doing here?" asked Michele looking at Rupert and the baby, who both looked ill.

"Mi suppos fe meet somewan aan here" said Eunice, "how come yu walking?"

Michele laughed. "Everybody walking nowadays my dear," she said, but as she said it she heard the rumble of a truck approaching.

The truck, filled with soldiers, entered the market square and a flash of fear spread through the crowd.

A dozen soldiers jumped down off the truck as it stopped by the small gas station, and they immediately surrounded the man who used to pump gas when there was any to sell, and who still wore the shirt that proclaimed him as an employee of Texaco.

"Yu av any gas?" asked a soldier.

"No sah," said the attendant.

"Come, mek wi look," said the soldier, poking a gun into the man's belly and pushing him towards the inside of the building. "Fine de key an open de tank."

The other soldiers fanned out through the food stalls of the market, their guns at the ready, assessing what there was to eat, fingering the produce and checking out the girls in the crowd.

A corporal carrying a machine gun sauntered over to where Michele and Eunice were standing, and said "Good day."

"Good day," replied the market woman.

"What 'bout yu," said the corporal, looking at Eunice, "yu nuh seh 'good day' too?"

"I never know is mi yu was talking to," said Eunice, who looked towards Michele terrified.

"Yu travellin?" asked the corporal, looking at the bundle of clothes she carried. "Where yu gwine to?"

"Leave di girl alone, man," said the market woman.

"Leave di girl alone? A oo di rass claat yu tink yu a talk to woman?" He raised his booted foot as though to kick over the market woman's food stall, then turned back to Eunice. "I seh where yu gwine to?"

"Mi nah go nowhere" said Eunice.

"Why yu nah travel wid mi?" said the corporal, "yu nuh haffi walk, yu would get food, yu would get ..."

The baby started to cry.

"She nuh go nowhere wid yu, she nuh like yu style," said the market woman.

The corporal kicked over the woman's food stall, and poked her in the shoulder with the tip of his machine gun.

"Yu wan see my style? My style is a Rambo style, a tek-wat-yu-want style, an if yu facety wid mi: ah-kill-yu-rass style ..."

He grabbed Eunice, twisted her arm behind her back and marched her off towards the truck, pushing the scandalised country people out of his way. Eunice started to scream, the crowd starting growling with an angry murmur, and suddenly Michele found herself shouting: "Leave the girl alone!"

The corporal stopped to turn and look at her, and she shouted out again, "Let her go!"

The corporal, who was temporarily stunned by the tone of authority in Michele's voice, looked at her blankly for a moment, then asked, "A who yu?"

"I am Michele Azani Bernard," said Michele, addressing herself as much to the crowd in the market place as to the band of renegade soldiers, "I am the wife of Winston Bernard, the Minister of Finance, I am the sister-in-law of Mark Bernard, Minister of Security, I am the sister of Eddie Azani, who has given more cash to more poor people on this island than anybody ever, I am the cousin by marriage to Percy Sullivan the Prime Minister of the country, I am the producer for the Burru programme on Sun Radio, I was loved by Zack Clay when he recorded "Genocide" and took "Don't be Afraid" to number one around the world, and I say you are to leave that girl alone!"

Michele, even as she spoke, was conscious of giving a speech like an actress on a stage, and she was also conscious of winning over her audience. By the time she had said what she had to say, the crowd was stirred with a new spirit. Suddenly there was a focus of resistance instead of scattered terror, somebody had drawn a line and dared the hooligans to step over it, and, in a minute, that had become a line for the crowd to defend.

As this feeling of defiance spread through the market in general, there was one group in particular that was actually galvanized into action: IZion and a group of four other Rasta farmers who took orders from him had come to town to pick up Eunice and take her to their camp. She was a link with Rasta City—the shipment headquarters of the ganja that the Rastas had grown in a time of plenty—a link with Burru and Eddie and the town that IZion had failed to save because he'd arrived too late. IZion felt responsible for Eunice and had led a patrol out to get her. No patrols had ever previously challenged the army in the daytime, to do so would be to invite such a massive retaliation that everybody would have to flee for miles around when the army arrived to take revenge, but times were changing and as he moved forward through the crowd, IZion realised that the time had come to clash.

As he approached the corporal who was bullying Eunice, his men moved towards the three nearest soldiers, and in the next instant they all struck.

Before the renegade corporal could raise his gun, IZion had come up from behind and put a knife to his throat; before the other goons could react, IZion had grabbed the M16 from the aggressor and had it pointed towards them.

The crowd as a whole took the bullies by surprise, surrounding them with shouts of abuse and drawn machetes, looking towards IZion and Michele for instructions on the next move.

As he stood looking out at the crowd, IZion felt a strong spirit move in him for the second time. The first time had been in the battle at Burru's Beach—then he'd felt a direct connection with the ancient warriors of his line, the ones his grandmother had told him about, the ones who had never bowed ... and now here they were again.

"You want to know who *I* am?" shouted IZion, taking off his tam, shaking his locks loose, and mounting a pile of boxes to better address the crowd.

"I am IZion, cammanda in chief of di Rasta rebellion against Babylon, in charge of di army dat rise outta di mountains fe drive Babylon back to town. So give ovah yu gun."

Swiftly, as IZion's men took over the weapons and ammunition, the mood of the crowd turned form fear to anger.

"Mi nah bow to Babylon!" said IZion, "Mi neva bow to Babylon! Not even in de slave ship, mi jus keep quiet till when wi reach land and white man pay money fe mi and tek mi fe cut cane up by some mountain, an before im coulda dream to beat mi, mi gaan! Yes! Maroon! Ariginal rebel! Spirit intact! Fram dat day to dis I 'n I live as a free man, and dats undreds a years, so mi nuh av no slave mentality, and mi nah bow to Babylon, white or black!"

The crowd cheered and IZion continued, now looking at Idi's erstwhile raiders, "Yu waan to know I style? *Ital* style! So di whole a yu tek off yu boots."

There was an eruption of laughter throughout the crowd. In a second the violence was dissipated, and with the violence gone, the mood of the crowd turned to pity and disdain. Shorn first of their weapons, then of their wheels, and finally of their boots, the former bullies seemed pathetic, laughable actually, as, already limping out of town the soles of their feet bared to the ground for the first time in twenty years, many were seen to hop with pain when the first bites of the hot tarmac road hit them.

As Idi Morris's, men trudged away, IZion shouted after them that they should go back and warn the others in their army that there was another army in control of the mountains now. The war between IZion and Idi Morris had been declared.

When Michele left the village, she left in the army truck with an escort of six motorbikes, together with Eunice, the baby, and Rupert, safely aboard.

Part Three

Winning

Chapter Thirty-Three

∞∞∞

It was the puppy who first heard the sound of the truck when it was still half a mile away, grinding up the hill towards the house. By the time Michele climbed down from it, Aladdin was in the headlights, waiting to lead her to Winston. From the moment Michele started running through the dark to get to him in time, the fate of the Bernards was no longer a foregone conclusion as envisioned by Henry Lynch. On the contrary, and unknown to its enemies, the family was suddenly back in the power game.

The ganja trade was still in business to the tune of one or two flights a week out of the mountain strips controlled by IZion, and Michele was able to bring in the drugs that saved Winston's life that way.

For long hours as Michele sat at Winston's bedside, her mind drifted between Winston's present condition and plans for the future. Anything she had ever had to do with another man became a distant memory. She had known the moment she saw him across the room at the party in New York that he was the man she had been looking for ... then he'd hurt her, and she'd struck back. He'd tried to tell her then that there was more than the two of them at stake, and now she understood. Now she understood that he and she together formed a classic nucleus: for what she had, he lacked, and vice versa.

Once they combined forces, if they pulled together, what was it that they couldn't do? Reclaim control of the island from this old house in the bush? Of course! This time the links would hold. They'd get Percy back, get Mark back—they'd re-establish control, and this time they'd do it right, with the money that Winston had won for them in the first place.

Day and night Michele sat watching Winston for signs of recovery, willing the strength back into her husband's body. The prospect of making love with him again started to take hold of her imagination for hours on end, and she promised herself and she promised him that this time there would be no holding back. This time when they made love she was going to get pregnant. They were going to cement the nucleus once and for all.

She lay beside him, and waited. Finally, in the late afternoon, with the rays of the setting sun filtering through the window and across his face, Winston's mind surfaced from unconsciousness into pain and he opened his eyes to meet Michele's gazing down at him.

"Michele." His voice was weak but he made sure she could hear him.

"Yes."

"How did you get here?"

"I got a message."

"Will you stay?"

"Yes."

"How long?"

"Forever."

Winston closed his eyes and sank back into oblivion, a smile on his face.

As he slowly came back to life, it was Michele who helped him fight the pain, it was she who made the struggle worthwhile, for what was the point of planning other people's lives with a blank at the centre of your own life? To distract him from the agony of recovery, he let his mind float on memories of those first days when he had fallen in love with her, when he felt that if he could get her then his biggest fantasy would have been fulfilled, and if one's biggest fantasies are being fulfilled then *anything* seems possible. He closed his eyes and saw her ... he went right back to that love that his father had for his mother, Percy had for Ada, Mark for Vera—that finding of the other half, the other half that brings balance and lets life spin, setting up a centre for love and laughter and plans for good that deepen and spread ...

As the days passed, IZion began moving his centre of operations to the house where Michele was nursing Winston. For twenty miles around, motorbike patrols would pick up any movement in the area, and Idi's army was in such disarray that more and more it dared not move out of its fortified sanctuaries in the major towns, even in daylight.

The army and police had failed to find the supplies of gas that IZion had hidden in the hills, and what gas there was went ten times further in fuelling IZion's bikes than it did in moving heavy army trucks.

As they ran out of gas, ammunition, and food, the baldhead baddies took to fighting among themselves for what remained. Less and less did they dare to venture out to loot and forage for food, because the mountains were filled with farmers who could not only protect the crops they were growing, but who, far from being afraid, were attacking the bullies in retreat.

Round and round circled the wrathful hunters from the hills—picking up reports, taking down descriptions—and soon it was those in uniform who were terrified by the sound of approaching engines in the night as the avengers swooped down into corner pockets of Babylon.

Every drum beating in the distance became a message of terror for them, every sound in the night might mean they were surrounded by men with machetes who would pull them out of their beds and drag them out to face the judgement of those they had raped and wounded and robbed.

IZion told his forces not to render judgement. Instead they should leave the accused to the mercy of their accusers, and one village square after another filled with crowds surrounding killers who had not shown mercy and who could expect none now.

One night in a village in the hills nearest the capital city, the villagers, encouraged by the arrival of Ashanti and his patrol, crept up on the police station for the district in which they knew that a dozen raiders from the city were now sleeping.

Slowly they were awakened as random rocks landed on the zinc roof above them in the darkness.

In a panic, Idi's bullies were roused to realise that they were surrounded on all sides by a crowd invisible but terrible in size and mood judging from the noise that was coming out of the darkness around them.

The fall of the first few stones on the roof had escalated to a roar of stone on zinc, and the cries above that shouting, "Come out!" and "Judgement!", were terrifying to the men adjusting their uniforms as they scrambled out of bed.

A large bonfire was starting to flame, lighting the faces in the front ranks of the throng like some flickering vision of vengeance.

As Ashanti moved to the front, he raised his voice loud and clear to reach those now trapped inside their own stronghold.

"Yu are surrounded on all sides by dem who have come fe judge yu," he called to the men trapped inside the police station, peering through the slats in the windows. "Is useless yu fe shoot because right now we have more gun dan yu, is useless yu call fe help because nobady av gas fe come help yu, is only beg fe mercy yu can do now, so might as well you come out humble."

Inside the station there was a frenzied argument going on, but finally one of the trapped men wrenched the door open, and stepped out.

Nobody seemed to know him, and as he progressed without being stoned or beaten, others started coming out of the front door. Suddenly there was a commotion from around the back of the building and, amidst much shouting, three captives were brought out by four of Ashanti's men and about twenty farmers. In the crowd one man in particular was stirred by the sight of the three captives. Two days before they had invaded his place, and, when she refused to submit to rape, they had killed his wife. Now here they were, captive and at his mercy.

The farmer moved forward till he was directly opposite the soldier who had killed his wife, and without saying a word but with tears streaming down his face, he lifted his machete and cut the murderer's head clean off his body.

IZion was sickened by the report of the massacre that followed on the first chop. This was not his plan. IZion rode with a bible strapped on his bike, but many who'd joined forces couldn't be relied on to abide by the Good Book. His forces were growing too fast; there were many among them who couldn't resist behaving like conquering heroes when they had others at their mercy.

IZion rode to Winston for advice. This was a far bigger problem than he had ever faced before. Bullying Babylon in retreat was bad enough, but what if the country people decided to go to war on those coming out of the city as refugees? Then the bitterness from the city would infect the countryside as well, and the resulting hatred would poison the island for years to come.

"The solution is simple," said Winston, when confronted with the problem. "Set up food stands on the side of the road at the first roadblocks out of town. Everybody coming out of town must give up their gun. Anybody heading for the country as a refugee should be given food and helped on their way, anybody heading back to town can buy the food to take back."

"That's the right word, brother Winny," said IZion.

Of course it is! Thought Winston. He was back in the business of government again!

He'd faced his first crisis, and solved it. Now, not only would Idi's domain end very definitely at the edges of the city, the giving out of food would establish who was in charge throughout the countryside, and after food, medicine, and after that, communications and a plan for taking back the city.

Chapter Thirty-Four

Idi Morris sat in the king-size bed in the penthouse suite of the most luxurious tourist hotel on the island, and waited impatiently for his breakfast. His girlfriend, Joyce, lay carefully next to him. Idi knew what the problem was. They couldn't find the food! The tourists were gone, the industry had closed with no plans to reopen, and the larders had all been emptied within an hour after all electricity was cut off and storage became impractical.

For his visit, the hotel manager had managed to keep the hotel generator going until the night before—when a colonel had come in and taken away the last of the gasoline at gunpoint.

Everybody knew that to keep the general waiting for his breakfast was not only to make his stomach angry, but was to cast doubt on the most basic assumptions of his power: his ability to get a good meal on the island he controlled. It wasn't that the food was gone, it was being hidden! Visions of the measures he was going to take to make sure he got his breakfast wherever he was tomorrow were forming in brutal clarity in his mind, when the manager was ushered into the bedroom to see him.

The man, clearly, was terrified. Idi could tell, just by looking at him, that if there was an egg to be had within ten miles, he would have it in front of him right now.

Things were much worse than he'd realised.

Then into the room strode the colonel who had requisitioned the gas the night before.

Idi eyed him warily as he approached the bed, a look that Joyce, dressed as she was in her see-through negligee, recognised immediately—it was the look he had when he sensed enough trouble to want the trouble covered from behind.

"I hear yu bruk in and tek gas fram di 'otel last night," said Idi.

"Had to," said the colonel, "I have two hundred men down there without food or gas."

"Gas is somewhere," said Idi Morris, "is dem fe find it."

"Dem seh a wi fe find it; dem ready fe riot right now."

"Riot?" said Idi, "Listen Wickie, mi nuh waan hear nutten 'bout indiscipline wid yu men, adderwise I bruk yu rass back to sergeant so fas yu woulda figet yu was eva an offica."

"Wah mi a go tell de men?" said Wickie, "Yu nuh tell mi dat yet."

"Yu need gas, go an find gas, if ganja man av it in de hill, go an tek it weh fram im, an find yu way back to town. Wen I leave town, I mek sure mi helicopter has gas fe return."

"Dat good fe yu, but what about me?" asked Wickie.

"Yu af di gas yu tief fram mi last night," said Idi.

Within minutes Idi and Joyce were out of the bedroom and into the helicopter, whirring back to the capital city on the other side of the island—the only side they now controlled, if indeed the Rastas hadn't taken control of most of the southern parishes as well as in the north.

Ah, helicopters! What a balm for shattered nerves, and no sooner was Idi off and away than he returned to a theme he'd been harping on for days: there was a key to success in the business he was in and he had to find it. There were too many like him, on islands like this all over the world, who were by no means worried about breakfast, who had millions stashed away in offshore bank accounts.

For days, in answer to Idi's song, Joyce had repeated over and over, as in a duet, her advice that he should consult her friend who was in PR in New York.

"Duvalier, Doe, Amin, Bakassa! Wa dem men really av more an me?" said Idi Morris shaking his head.

"Yu ha fe talk to Valerie," said Joyce for the twentieth time in two days, "as soon as we land I gwine call 'er."

There was still one flight a day out of New York into the capital, and the next day Valerie was on it.

Valerie and Joyce had always shared a mutual respect. Valerie admired Joyce for her practical grounded approach to life, and Joyce admired Valerie for her style: afro and business suit. Valerie wasn't concerned with moral values, she was in a business that was paid to make her clients look good, and from that point of view, she merely saw Idi Morris as a considerable professional challenge.

"Look," she said to the general when they met, "this is a brand new team we have here. Nobody knows anything about you in America. You can be anything you want."

There was a long pause.

"I mean, have you at any time ever made a political statement of any sort on the record?" asked Valerie.

"Nah," said Idi.

"So you launch a press campaign to say you're against drugs and communism—"

Idi was looking at the sharp woman from Manhattan. Maybe she would know. It was a question that Idi had been asking day and night since he came to power, but either people pretended not to hear or they didn't know the answer to the question. Idi decided to try one more time with this woman.

He leaned forward, made sure she was listening closely, and then said, "Doe in Liberia, how im live? Duvalier? Nguema, Noriega, all dem guy? Dem nuh come fram nowhere more dan mi. Dem nuh av no oil. How dem survive?"

"They've got a deal going with somebody," said Valerie, "somebody's paying their oil bill and keeping them going."

"What kinda deal?"

"Depends. If you're dealing with the west, its business, and if you're dealing with the east, it's still business, but politicians do the business there, and in some places the army does the business."

"Like here," said Joyce, "dis a military regime."

"Like a hundred places," said Valerie.

"So suppose I approach Washington DC as a military man, what I have fe do fe get my deal?"

"I don't know, but there's a deal to be made, I know that. We have political consultants we can call on in the States. These people follow what's going on in every country, and, if they don't know, they find the people who do know until they give you the scoop. They're good, they're objective, they're impartial, you know what I mean? They cost, but they do give you the real story and then we can go to the next stage."

Valerie made it sound so easy, and in a way it was, because within one week of her meeting with Idi Morris, she was in Washington waiting for an appointment with Henry Lynch.

She waited in the foyer of Lynch's office for two hours before being ushered in to see him, and in that time the traffic she observed was phenomenal. Calls were coming in constantly, messages being taken rapidly. When staff crossed the hall they did so as fast as they could go without being ungainly, and some of them didn't manage that. Obviously Mr Lynch was a very busy man. Valerie had heard of him, of course, but he was a somewhat shadowy figure to her. She didn't know in detail how he'd got to the centre of things, but it was clear she was at the centre of something big while she waited to see him.

Lynch nodded as she approached his huge desk, and half rose, not so much to shake hands as to indicate that she should put her card into his hand.

He read it as he was sitting down again, and before she was seated he was looking at her and saying, "Yes?"

"I represent General Morris," said Valerie, feeling a secret thrill at the thought of being in what was obviously a key centre of power in Washington DC. "He has de facto control, as you know."

"Yes, I know, that's why I agreed to see you."

"The general feels you might have a mutual interest."

"And what is that?"

"The government of my client is prepared to renegotiate the tax that Winston Bernard tried to force on you."

"Well isn't that nice," said Lynch. He explained that within a few days he expected to be back in government so would no longer act as the attorney for the mining companies, but he gave Valerie the telephone number of the lawyer who would be able to negotiate, and within twenty-four hours Valerie was able to report to Joyce that Idi Morris had secured some powerful friends in his fight for power.

Shortly thereafter the Republicans won the election in the US. Henry Lynch was no longer on the sidelines, he was now once again part of the official power structure, and the confusion of the seventies gave way to a decade in which there was nothing whatsoever ambivalent about the realities of power in the USA.

Two weeks after the inauguration, IZion's main contact with the outside world came to say goodbye.

"This is my last trip back to the States," said Sedgwick, "next trip I stay here." He was sitting in an alcove on the edge of the lawn, in bright moonlight, the big house in the distance lit with candles. He was eating in company with Michele, Winston, and IZion who had brought him to visit on the back of his bike.

"May I ask why?" Michele sensed a series of problems that would arise without Barry's courier service.

"Change of direction. The Republicans aren't going to deal with the Caribbean the way the other lot did."

"I'm sure," said Winston.

"I have a feeling they'll get behind Idi," said Sedgwick.

"Surely not," said Michele, "the press—"

"Yes," said Winston, "he's right."

IZion looked intensely interested. If America came in behind Idi Morris, it would be very bad news for any Rasta.

"They'll ship him supplies in a minute if they can tell him what to do," said Barry Sedgwick.

"We 'ave to blow de bridges," said IZion, "if we blow four bridges, nuttin more dan a bicycle an donkey leave di city, is only helicopter dem woulda 'av fe use fe reach us. It woulda war."

"For that they would have to go to Congress," said Barry Sedgwick, "and that will cause hearings and give you some time, but you still have to move fast."

"How much damage will have to be done to the bridges?" asked Winston, "do you have to blow the foundations or can you just take out the middle?"

"We'll do as little damage as possible," said Barry.

"How do we know that we have no choice?" asked Winston.

"If the next time my plane lands and instead of me you see someone you don't like, blow the bridges, or you'll have Idi's army swarming all over you," said Barry Sedgwick. Michele looked at the American, who looked to Winston, who looked to IZion, who nodded.

"Seen" said IZion.

"I have explosives," said Sedgwick, "Ashanti knows how to place the charges."

"What's going to happen to you?" asked Winston.

"I'm going to retire. I want to get two acres overlooking the Caribbean with a stream running through the land and a reliable supply of good sensi."

Winston watched Michele in the light reflected from the dining table, she who had nursed him back to life, who had formed the centre again; but now sooner than expected, she was going to have to go away.

Barry Sedgwick's flight was the last one out, so now the plan had to go into action. There could be no more delay, the plan he had lain in bed and worked out in the finest detail to the week and day and hour and minute even; now the clock had started ticking for the countdown, and there would be no turning back. Now as he watched Michele's brown eyes flash with excitement, Winston knew that she heard the ticking too.

That night when they went to bed, Michele saw that Winston had recovered his strength, that his body had finally shrugged off the injury, that what pain remained could be ignored and, as she felt his body harden, hers turned to butter in the centre and a tingling excitement everywhere else.

Winston floated above her, beside her, around her, repeating the basic beat of the eternal embrace ... the rhythms he had first learned roaming the waterfront as a boy with Eddie and DeMalaga ... the moves they'd had to learn because they had to please if they weren't going to have to pay ... those moves had been second nature to Winston in the days of his sexual apprenticeship. But when he fell in love with Michele, it had been with her eyes not her thighs; with her mouth, her mind, her emotions ... her body as a delight had been overwhelming of *his* physical charms, and he'd forgotten the Paradise Street jukebox moves up until now, but now he wanted to make her gasp with surprise and moan with pleasure, he wanted to make her shake in extended and repeated extremity, and when she thought it was all over, he wanted to start again.

She lost the form of any woman in particular; her features swam from age to age, from generation to generation. As the poisoned chemistry of jealousy left his brain, Winston felt no need to behave himself, and he snapped back to those rude moves of the old days, when lust and love were indistinguishable.

For Michele, the movements of their bodies had become a cosmic dance, and she was a naturally gifted dancer ... they were both too high for personalities, too far gone for ego ... she felt as though ten spirits were using just two bodies to make love, and one of them happened to be hers ... she felt as though the force that travelled through both their beings was not theirs, it was a greater power surging through the connection that they'd made.

Chapter Thirty-Five

Michele flew to the Bahamas in Barry Sedgwick's Comanche at three hundred feet, skimming the surface of the sea to escape the radar for small planes approaching the US.

Before leaving home she had stamped her passport with one of the stamps that Eddie had bequeathed her for just such an emergency, so there was no problem with immigration.

In the Bahamas Michele called Eddie who sent her ten thousand dollars with which she went to Paris, booked into a pleasant little hotel on the Left Bank, had a long hot bath, a deep sleep, and then set out to find Percy.

As she stepped out into the Parisian night, she realised that her strategy had to be one that promised Percy even more fun than he was having here.

Percy was a born playboy. So far as he was concerned, anybody who didn't admit that having a good time in life was the most important thing was either a hypocrite or wasn't capable of having a good time in the first place—in which case they were obviously dangerous.. There was a kind of militancy about Percy's selfishness which was almost self-righteous, as though he was the last missionary left for good times in what was becoming an increasingly depressing world.

Percy was in fine form when they met for dinner. He had taken over the embassy, sold its lease and all but one of the cars, established a pleasant apartment on the Right Bank as his base of operations, and settled in for a life of political exile in the one city of the world which best understood such things.

At the height of his career, when old PJ was worth five million pounds and had enjoyed a French mistress after a visit to Haiti, he had set up foreign accounts enough to serve twenty years later as a considerable cushion for Percy's fall into the outside world.

He didn't have his own ponies in Paris, but Percy had been playing polo on mounts provided by those who'd been his guests in the Caribbean. He couldn't entertain on a large scale, but certainly he had been invited to the biggest balls of the past season as a man about town.

"Why would I go back?" he asked Michele.

"Because you can't say no, Percy."

"Why not?"

"Because the island's in chaos, it needs you."

"And whose fault is that?"

"I didn't say it was your fault," said Michele, "what I am saying is that you are the only one who can provide a legitimate elected government that Lynch can't bulldoze."

"Everybody let me down before ... Winston with all his big talk ..."

"Winston's going to win."

"How?"

"He has two hundred million dollars in Switzerland waiting for transfer as soon as he's back in office, and there is up to a billion in foreseeable earnings after that."

Percy looked at Michele anew.

"Hugh Clifford stuck by the deal and he's never stopped mining. When we get back, all the other companies will have to pay up retroactively."

It was at this point that they were joined by a stunningly beautiful African princess who was modelling in Paris, and the conversation shifted to clothes, cars, polo scores, and how much cash Africans of her acquaintance had stashed away in Europe. The profit from entire regional economies over decades of accumulation was the kind of money that impressed this lady, and as they dined and danced into the early hours of the morning, it became apparent to Michele that Percy too was mesmerized by loot on a continental scale.

After they'd dropped the girl home, they walked back and forth across the footbridge that spanned the Seine just west of the Île de la Cité, and Percy finally set out his terms. He wanted to marry the African girl. To do that he'd need a knighthood because she was from the West African ruling class and that was the least that would impress her family as a social calling card. If he did come back, however, and if he did get what he wanted for doing so, Percy could see clearly where he was on line for a lifestyle that, combined with the sophistication of his would-be wife, could establish him as the most glamorous black man in the world. He didn't actually come out and say so, but it was clear to Michele as they walked back and forth across the river, surrounded by what was, by deliberate design, the most elegant city in the world. The Americans threatened, but the French seduced ... how many millions of Africans were captive to the charms of Paris, Michele wondered ...

> *Parisian pum pum and vintage wine*
> *Chateaux and haute couture design*
> *rue de la Paix, Folies Bergére*
> *Citroen limousines that float on air ...*

How many deals concerning the future of the tropical world had been made beside this river, Michele thought, the flow of events as inexorably in one direction as the flow of the tonnes of cold, grey water?

How had they been able to get away with it for so long? How had they managed for centuries to enslave entire colonial populations by buying off their leaders with baubles?

The same way they'd captured Percy: with style.

"Is Mark back on the island?"

"Not yet."

"Can you get him back?"

"I certainly hope so."

"Well, that's a condition for my return, of course. I don't trust anyone else to take care of Idi Morris, and he'll have to do it before I put myself back in place."

"Any other conditions?"

"Yes. Before I go and put myself back into that nightmare, Winston is going to have to confirm to me that the money from Hugh Clifford is actually transferred into the Central Bank account, so we can start to run the place without having to go begging again."

"That's the whole point of Winston's plan."

"Just so you understand that it has to be there before I put myself at the mercy of my two dear cousins again. That's the deal."

Dawn had crept up while they spoke; suddenly ten thousand street lights flicked off all at once, and, as though it was their signal, the birds in the centre of the city started their morning song. Percy couldn't see further than the symbolism of the Eiffel Tower in the distance; it had been erected for no reason other than elegance, yet it towered above all else. That was as high as Percy wanted to go, but not Winston, not Michele. They wanted a world in which the centre was not always somewhere else far away from home, and although Michele had had to travel far to retrieve Percy, she'd got what she'd come to Paris to get, and as she said goodbye to Percy and started walking towards her hotel, she felt an inner glow of satisfaction that she was quite sure no bought bauble could ever bring.

Chapter Thirty-Six

∞∞∞∞

One week after he had returned to the States, Barry Sedgwick was called into a meeting at the CIA headquarters in Langley.

In the room there was a marine colonel and a man from the State Department, and as soon as he saw them, Barry realised he was dealing with a different type of guy altogether from the ones he'd reported to in the past.

Up to now, he'd felt no strain in dealing with Eddie and IZion on the one hand, and having an occasional chat in Washington on the other. But whereas before the atmosphere was friendly and he was treated more like an agent than a smuggler, now Barry was feeling more like a smuggler than an agent to the two men who faced him across the table.

One was named Elliot Bridgewater, political appointee in the State Department, trained by Henry Lynch and seasoned in South East Asia. The marine colonel's name was Alex West, another ambitious Henry Lynch alumnus. As they asked questions it became apparent that Bridgewater and West were regarding the army of Rastas in the mountains as the enemy, a force to be brought under control. It also became apparent that they had no qualms about backing Idi Morris to achieve that objective.

"Well I wouldn't do anything to help Idi Morris. I think he's the scum of the earth, besides which I actually like the other side, so..."

"You're talking about the wildest bunch of religious fanatics on record, known drug dealers," said West.

Barry Sedgwick didn't answer.

"We understand they're hacking people to death with machetes," said Bridgewater.

Again Sedgwick said nothing. He didn't want the questioning to go on, because it might lead to Michele and Winston and the fact that they were behind IZion. These guys obviously didn't know that, and he wasn't about to tell them. Winston and Michele and IZion would need all the time they could get to manoeuvre.

"We don't think that your friends are people we would necessarily like much, and I think your feelings about them are suspect to say the least," said West.

"So that's it," said Bridgewater, rising to finish the meeting, but not extending his hand, "no more trips for you."

"Good," said Barry Sedgwick, "because I don't want to work with you pricks anymore."

Three days after Sedgwick's last meeting with the CIA, IZion and ten of his men waited for Barry's plane at a landing strip high in the mountains.

"Dat nuh look like Barry plane to me," said IZion when it came into view, "Naw, dis one fatta," said his first lieutenant, Ashanti, the same Ashanti who had fought with Wire and survived to join IZion in the hills.

When Colonel West got out of the plane he was in jeans instead of his uniform, but even so he and the two men with him looked like they'd all got to know each other in the siege at Da Nang. There was a kind of swagger about them that was the opposite of the cool with which Barry Sedgwick presented himself.

"Weh Barry deh?" asked IZion.

"What'd he say?" asked West.

"He says 'where's Barry,'" translated one of West's two companions, who apparently understood the local lingo.

"Barry doesn't work with us anymore."

"Yu bring de tings Barry seh 'im wouda bring?"

"We brought cash instead. We prefer to deal in cash."

IZion was immediately suspicious.

"We preffa wha di cash can buy because nobady deal in cash much ere, an plenty a it counterfeit," said IZion, "so betta yu sen Barry come deal wid us."

"What'd he say?"

"He says no deal, he wants to deal with Barry."

"OK, let's get some pictures and get out of here."

The third man took out a camera, pointed it at IZion, and started clicking.

"Eh bredda!" shouted IZion, advancing on the photographer, "Mi neva tell yu to tek a snap, mi neva gi yu no permission ..."

Both West and the translator drew guns as they backed towards the plane, and the photographer kept working.

"Who di bumbo claat yu tink yu a giv di permission to?" shouted the translator. "Yu know a who yu a deal wid? Yu know wha cuda appen to yu if yu fuck wid dese man yah?"

"Man, jus get in yu plane an fly yah," said IZion, "a who yu want treaten? Ah jus buy a stinga and shoot down yu rassclaat like a bird, even if is jet yu come wid."

The three visitors got back in the plane, IZion and his men made no further move to stop them taking off, merely hurling curses after them as they taxied and took to the air again.

When they were airborne, West turned to the translator. "What did you say to him at the end there?"

"I said, listen you Rasta golliwog, if you shoot at us we'll come back in with the marines and helicopters and rocket ships and jets, and by the time we're through with your fucking little island, it will look like a piece of burnt toast!"

West laughed. "And what did he say back, right at the end?"

"He asked me if I'd never heard about the stinger."

West said nothing, but turned and looked out of the window. The stinger was a missile that could be fired from the shoulder of any peasant. But it was heat seeking. It could bring down a multi-million dollar jet. The Afghanis had already started using it to do just that to the Russians in the Himalayas.

Years later the individual explosions would still be remembered by name: ram, bam, and waddat!

With three strokes of well placed explosives, all of which went off within ten minutes, one bridge on every road leading into the capital was blown away. No truck, car, or any motor vehicle could pass for weeks to come.

Of the three roads connecting the capital city with the country-side, one ran through a narrow gorge for five miles, and in the middle of the gorge was one small bridge crossing the river. The second road ran out of town over the mountains, clinging to hillsides that could be blocked with relatively small blasts in dozens of places, and it too ran across a river on a very slender bridge. The third road could be blocked only by blowing up two pylons for the flyover of the central highway out of town, a job which required such a blast that it reverberated through the sleeping city five miles away to wake everybody up with a jolt, shouting: "Waddat?"

That blast was like a starting gun for the final struggle to survive. Everyone who could, set out to find relatives in the country, eager to escape a city that was being left to starve.

Looters were shot on sight by roving army patrols, not because the soldiers were protecting property, but because the army wanted the loot.

When they'd stripped the town bare and gutted the warehouses, Idi's troops finally reached the point where they only had each other left to prey on.

Chapter Thirty-Seven

When the news of the blown bridges reached Henry Lynch, it triggered an explosion of anger in him. No longer did he have the option of simply getting behind Idi Morris to control the island in a way that would not be noticed by Congress and the public at large. It was no longer a matter of some relatively small-scale assistance. The situation had escalated. Now they would have to repair bridges. Now they would need troops and heavy equipment. Now they would have to launch a major campaign to retake control.

"Those sons of bitches! If they want explosions we'll give them some that will blow the whole fucking little island off the map!"

Lynch, now surrounded by the trappings of official power, was sitting at the conference table in the conference cabin of his 707 as it crossed the Atlantic. Elliot Bridgewater was there and had just given Lynch the news, and Henry Kass had joined the flight in London in order to get an hour with him. It would be his only chance to see and confer with Lynch for the next two weeks.

"The trouble with supporting Idi Morris is that he's a hooligan," said Kass.

"Yeah, but he's our hooligan," said Lynch.

"Well maybe you can deal with him, but you'll have to have somebody on the spot to control him."

"We can deal with him, what's the alternative? An island ruled by a bunch of marijuana smoking fanatics? We have no choice but to back this guy."

"He's got a terrible image," said Bridgewater.

"He's got a smart PR lady," said Henry Lynch, "and this other bunch makes even Idi look good."

He picked up the photograph of IZion snarling at the CIA patrol, one of several pictures that Bridgewater had brought along with his report of West's mission.

"If we can't regain control through Morris and we have to go in there ourselves, why, these guys make it easy. Who would blame us for zapping a bunch that look like this?"

"They're massacring people in the countryside, we know that for sure," said Bridgewater.

Kass wasn't happy. He hadn't planned on being on a team with Idi Morris. He didn't fancy answering to the likes of Elliot Bridgewater. The British were one thing. He was used to them. The trappings of empire and all the fancy dress might be ludicrous, but at least they were polite. Now they had given over, the Americans would swallow up the island in their standard Latin American syndrome, barefaced, bare knuckled, crude ... Kass looked back and remembered how he had never supported independence; he'd warned everyone who would listen, but nobody had listened.

"What about public opinion?" asked Kass "Won't the US public object to an invasion?"

"No," said Lynch, "not after Vietnam, not after the hostage thing. The American public is tired of feeling helpless. They want to see us win a war, and it would certainly send the Sandinistas a message. It would send everyone a message in the whole region."

Lynch leaned forward and looked intently into the eyes of the island conglomerateur.

"We've got to do something to convince people that you can't fuck around with America," he said, "Southeast Asia, that's one thing. The fucking Iranians, you'd think that's as bad as it could

get. These people are on the loose in our fucking backyard!"
Lynch raised his voice again, but now he stood up as though
trying to calm himself before bringing the meeting to a close.
"The first thing this administration intends to do is send a clear
signal that this is an area in which what we say goes," he said.
Now he was calm again, enunciating policy, speaking in
measured tones. "We've done it before, we'll do it again whenever
things get out of hand."

"We're ready when you are," said Elliott Bridgewater.

Within twenty-four hours the pictures of IZion and Ashanti
threatening the camera and the world were put into a news clip
for TV which was duplicated many hundred times over and
distributed to stations across the globe. Simultaneously, in six
different languages, a newspaper article was being prepared
which would go to every paper with access to a wire service
anywhere in the world.

That took care of print and TV.

Now Lynch turned to the political aspects of the situation.

Michele first became aware of Lynch's media blitz to discredit
IZion on her way through London airport to catch a flight for
Nassau where she was due to meet Eddie.

She went to the newsstand and the papers had IZion's face on
the cover. She turned to the story on page three, and boarded the
plane in a daze of worry.

All the way across the Atlantic she pondered the situation.
Clearly Lynch was preparing to invade. Clearly this press blitz
was to justify the invasion to the public in the States and the
world at large. Clearly Michele had to move to counter Lynch's
press blitz. But how? He had unlimited resources, she had none.
On the plane she tried to sleep, she dozed for fifteen minutes
and woke to worry some more. All she had on her side was the

truth. IZion wasn't a bad guy, he was a charmer; one smile on TV would dispel the thought of him as a murderous fanatic. That was the message she had to put out, but who would spread it?

Should she try to at least mail out a still and an article to all the major networks and wire services from Nassau? She put aside the thought. Without explanation and follow up, they'd question the source. Again she tried to sleep, and one hour out of Nassau the thought came to her: Molly! Molly Clifford was the only person in the world who could save the situation.

Michele started out their meeting on an up-note by telling Molly of her success in getting Percy ready to return, but Molly's reaction was not as warm as Michele had expected.

"And what does Percy want out of it?"

"Only a knighthood."

"A knighthood! What on earth for?"

"He's going out with an African girl who's from a very wealthy family, he wants to marry her and run with that crowd. She'll marry him if she can take a title back to daddy."

"You mean the Banga girl?"

"Yes," said Michele.

Molly knew about them. Mines in West Africa. Three billion. Thugs. "Is that really all he wants? To be somebody's son-in-law?"

"He knows he can't make any real money out of politics, he knows Winston won't allow it, and Percy wants to live in the greatest possible style for the longest possible time."

Michele spoke of Percy's weakness as though she was stating a law of nature, something that Molly would accept, would take for granted, but instead Molly looked deeply offended. She looked as though she would withhold her help after all!

"Percy doesn't matter, Molly, he'll just be a figurehead. He's no problem. The problem is this press offensive that Lynch has launched against us. If there's no counter attack, Lynch's press is going to do us in. If we don't get our side of the story out, they'll invade." Michele looked to Molly for a response, but the older woman remained distant.

"Frankly," said Michele allowing an edge into her voice, "I wasn't expecting to have to sell you on the idea."

"Well I do really have to be sold, I'm afraid, because yes I can pick up the phone and call five people and get your story an airing around the world, and yes I do like you Michele, and I think you're charming, but I'm not really absolutely sure that Percy is necessarily a man that I would ask people to back."

"I'm not asking your help for Percy! I'm asking for your support of Winston, he'll be running things."

"Yes, quite." *She still doesn't get it, and I'm not going to help her till she does.* "Look, Michele, Hugh wants to help. He's taken a lot of flak for that I can tell you, and so do I want to help, but if Mark and Winston can't pull together and Percy's nothing but a playboy, is it worth it? Is the family serious?"

"Winston is serious, so is Mark, and so am I."

"Then what went wrong? One needs to know. What went wrong between Mark and Winston? What went wrong between you and Mark?" Molly paused to look Michele in the eye, "What went wrong between you and Winston?"

The question hit Michele like a slap. A hard one. She'd made it up with Winston! She'd put all that behind them! But for Molly Clifford it was still the key. Whatever happened, it had caused a civil war. Death and destruction. Molly wanted an accounting. She wanted an explanation. Now.

"Somebody has to take responsibility for what went wrong. Somebody should have held things together. Somebody is going to have to do it in the future."

"It was my fault." Michele stood up, trembling, not only making the admission to Molly but absorbing the terrible thought herself for the first time. "It was my fault," she said again, putting out a hand to steady herself against the edge of the sofa as she rose to move on to the balcony, to gulp some air, to get away from the cold blue gaze of Molly Clifford's eyes.

But Molly Clifford's eyes had softened as soon as she saw Michele buckle when the weight of guilt pressed down on her. Molly felt a great rush of compassion for Michele. It was as though the implications of the admission were so terrible that she had simply put all thoughts of the matter out of her mind, and now they were flooding back, and the weight of the guilt they carried was overwhelming. One *had* to take responsibility for something of that magnitude, thought Molly, one couldn't assume real responsibility again until it had been acknowledged and dealt with. And now that she saw it had, she moved gently to Michele's side and put her hand on her shoulder,

Images were tearing through Michele's mind: Winston's anger, Mark's humiliation, Herman's death ... they pounded on her with the familiar grief of Zack's last moment ... but that had been one man, this was hundreds ...

"Michele, it's never just one person's fault, everybody makes mistakes." Michele, still trembling with anguish, said nothing. "There's only one thing to be done about it," continued Molly, "you have to put things right, and I will help you if I can."

Michele turned without a word and went into the bathroom to wash her face. As she splashed water in her eyes and looked in the mirror, the thought occurred to her that Molly Clifford didn't have her power because she inspired fear, but because she inspired love, and when Michele emerged again, she went up to Molly and she kissed her and said, "It won't happen again."

"That's good enough for me my dear. I'll make the calls right now."

She called Rupert Murdoch, Jimmy Goldsmith, Gianni Agnelli, Katherine Graham and Bill Paley. She told them that she knew of the Rasta army on the island through the Bernards, that they were infinitely the best of the bunch on the island, that Idi Morris was a stooge of Lynch's, and that Lynch's campaign against the Rastas was to justify propping up a bad guy and possible intervention.

With just five phone calls and within an hour, Molly was able to guarantee that Lynch's message would not go out unchallenged, and that a fair hearing for IZion and the Bernards was required before Lynch would be allowed to obliterate them.

This was the league of inner circle power that Molly Clifford put within Michele Bernard's reach that afternoon, but she wouldn't have done it if Michele had failed a test for power that Molly had put in her way.

Molly would never have helped Michele if Michele had not been able to say: "It was my fault."

Once Lynch realised that the Bernards were behind IZion and the Cliffords were backing the Bernards, he knew what he was up against right away. He knew all about the independents, the ones who wouldn't take orders from the centre, the ones who would only play for their own team.

It was an old antagonism, the oldest in modern history, and this latest struggle between those who wanted to control everything from the centre and those who were determined to be de-magnetized from that gravity, was just the latest episode in the long history of struggle between the two factions.

Henry Lynch was captain of the team for central, hard-core, military/industrial/financial/technological/satellite co-ordinated, Wall Street rated, trans-party and trans-presidential inner-circle political power, versus those in the West who did not confuse monopoly capitalism with free enterprise.

Now that his president was in office, he was in no mood to be put down by a bunch of Caribbean locals, even if they were in league with someone like Hugh Clifford.

On the other hand, the likes of Hugh and Molly Clifford, Marc Gold, and the whole Bernard clan, were not prepared to bow to the likes of Henry Lynch.

Central power, historically, had always been chronically in debt, and the truly rich of the world had stayed that way by knowing when to jump the ship of any state which had bankrupted itself on power and glory. They'd been in the dollar since 1945 because the dollar was the only currency free to roam the world, the only currency you didn't have to beg somebody in authority to take abroad. But now that was going to change. Now, in 1980, central power had announced that it was plunging so deeply into debt that the dollar would be captive too, and those with the real wealth in the world were planning to switch, to make other currencies worth stashing in the traditional strongholds of the independently wealthy: Switzerland, Hong Kong, the Channel Islands, and, lately, Cayman and the Bahamas. The battle between central power and the independents in the Western World was at least as old as the Reformation, and for those who'd read their history, the outcome was by no means a foregone conclusion ... central power had always appeared too big to fight, but then so had dinosaurs.

Watching the news develop on TV, Mark realised that the build-up towards an intervention was gathering dangerous momentum.

"You can't be serious about supporting Idi Morris," said Mark to Frank Wood, in a last desperate meeting with his former friend and fellow officer. "If I had logistical support for five hundred West Indian troops, I'd clean up the situation in a week. There's no need to risk one American life on the island."

"It's not a military operation Mark, it's a PR operation. They're using the opportunity to send a message."

"What's the message? That you're prepared to support hooligans in the Caribbean?"

"That the Caribbean is our sphere of influence militarily. Period."

"And you think getting bogged down on one small island is going to prove anything?"

"They don't see us getting bogged down, Mark, they see us going in there and kicking ass. The public will love it. It's just what they want to see."

Wood's remark hit Mark with great force. It summed up in a phrase what he now realised he despised about this man he'd come to as a friend in an hour of need: arrogance combined with weakness.

"Well it happens to be my country we're talking about," said Mark as he got up to leave. "And if you think you'll just walk in there and kick ass and not get hurt yourself, you're an even bigger idiot than I thought."

At the door, Mark stopped and turned. "The first time I came to see you it was to ask for help. This time I came to offer help, and believe me you're a damn fool not to take it."

Molly's initial calls to the press brought one near universal response from her contacts' editors. They wanted to know more. They wanted to see for themselves. Twenty editors were prepared to send reporters to the island. They wanted a date of departure, and transportation in and out of Miami since there were no scheduled flights.

Michele called both Eddie and Max DeMalaga. She needed cash. She needed a producer. She needed a show. She picked a date three weeks later when everything would come together. The clock for the countdown was ticking more loudly than ever, approaching the time when the fate of the Bernard family would be decided for generations to come.

Eddie moved his boat to the Bahamas, hooked into a switchboard secured for him by DeMalaga at Lyford Quay, and arranged the charter flights.

DeMalaga started to coordinate the arrival of the world press.

Michele was back on the island, preparing the hotel where the media would be staying, getting the regional radio station on the air to bring normality back to the countryside, to explain to everyone what was going on and that all they had to do was stay cool.

Winston was planning the last three days of the next three weeks, down to the minute.

Mark Bernard drove the floor cleaning machine down another aisle in the shopping mall supermarket. It was three o'clock in the morning, and he was alone. That's exactly what Mark wanted. To be alone. To think, to analyse what went wrong. He was grateful for this job. It allowed him to work all night and sleep all day. It allowed him to avoid any contact with anybody, because ever since the betrayal by Winston he had barely felt like talking with even Vera or Sylvie.

He imagined his rage spreading to every corner of the empty shopping centre, absorbed in a million packets of stuff that house-wives bought ... expending his rage all by himself, accompanied by the roar of the machine.

After a while, as he made the same rounds night after night, he started to associate certain areas with changes of mood — frozen meats and the toothpaste section each had their thought associations — but tonight, after the meeting with Frank Wood, Mark felt that he was no longer in a rut, his mind did not run its usual course. Tonight, surprisingly, he was no longer bitter. He had a feeling that win, lose, or draw he was coming out of limbo: for three nights Michele's brother Eddie had been calling a friend's apartment and speaking to Sylvie on the only telephone connection that escaped Lynch's net. Mark Bernard knew what was going on.

Tonight as his machine swept into the zone where he usually had his dark thoughts about Michele, Mark decided that when he got back to the apartment he was going to return her brother's calls.

Chapter Thirty-Eight

᯾

Back on the island, the country was divided into two entirely different worlds, and the countryside, as controlled by IZion and Winston Bernard, was slowly struggling back to a sense of normality. Free from attack, the farmers had gone back to cultivation with a vengeance. Food was plentiful. So was herb. Gas was very scarce, so people just stayed put, but now without a sense of panic.

Eddie had had twenty thousand batteries flown in from Panama, so there was a spread of radio news throughout the island emanating from the second city—the centre of what had been the tourist trade when there had been tourists. Michele had made this the centre for her campaign of coordination and reassurance for the countryside from what had been the regional studio of Sun Radio.

Once again the station's signature was heard across the land; once again the familiar voices of popular deejays soothed their listeners with the promise of an eventual return to normal times.

Back at the big house in the bush, Winston kept pace. Although he didn't have electricity, he had a fully functioning office, set up to meet with the dozens of visitors who came to discuss how best they could use limited resources to provide food and water, and the distribution of what few medical skills remained on the island.

Night and day the old house buzzed with messages coming in and instructions going out, all bikes were ridden by IZion's army, all with gas supplied from the small coastal tanker which had arrived from Panama and that Eddie Azani had paid for in Nassau.

Even Aladdin had come of age and was ruling an animal kingdom based on the fact that scraps from the kitchen that fed twenty people a day could certainly provide for at least half that many cats and dogs.

Winston sat for hour after hour at his desk in the old house in the bush, planning the coordination of the comeback, budgeting the start up of government again, arranging payment for the feeding of IZion's army and food for the refugees, trying to gauge the transition period and the cost of providing for the press corps, and balancing these costs against the cash that he could get from Eddie. There were two thoughts that troubled him all during his waking hours, and, worse yet, when he was trying to sleep: what was Mark's reaction going to be to him when they met, and what was it he needed to know in the adding up of the final figures that he'd witnessed in his hallucination?

Michele floated down the gap in the coral reef, and slowly kept pace with a small shoal of parrot fish, giving herself over to the luxury of weightlessness and the thrill of colour. When she surfaced it was into a small cove, and in the distance were two yachts, one of sail, DeMalaga's, and the other an eighty-foot motor yacht, belonging to Eddie.

Both were there at Michele's bidding. Both were there because she had promised to bring the Bernards back together to fight for renewed control of the island, both were there because they could afford to be world class adventurers, and because the island, under the right management, provided them with unique opportunities for the expansion of their future plans.

DeMalaga considered that the key to making money was in his ability to guess where the taste of the musical world would move to next. He'd seen the cultural energy of his time move from Paris in the fifties, to London in the sixties, to New York in the seventies ... now he was watching it leave New York and he didn't know where it would go to next, but he was certain he'd be aware whenever it got there, because he was looking for that next location more than anything else in the world.

Certainly it would have to be a melting pot, a cultural crossroads. Certainly it would have to be a place which guaranteed freedom of expression. Hong Kong, Zurich, Cayman, and the Channel Islands — taken together their acreage was negligible, but they controlled the world of money enough to guarantee freedom for cash; why wouldn't this island be big enough for a base to broadcast to the world?

On every side DeMalaga could see where the whole thing was going to come down to a very few players in the satellite game, and they would all have their own agendas. Suppose they did manage to tie up the satellites? Suppose they reserved them exclusively for their own use so that unless you came out of a media colossus you would simply not find space on the airwaves. Now suppose those guys started to bore the audience that they'd captured because they were thinking more about corporate war than entertainment, and suppose that bored audience wanted to tap into something new altogether, then suppose the island had its uplink booked with Intelsat and functioned as a funnel through which all the blocked stuff from all over the world could be delivered to that starved audience? Well, those were some of the thoughts that had brought Max DeMalaga sailing into this cove, those thoughts, and the fact that he genuinely liked the Bernards ... and both Hugh and Molly were in on their side.

As for Eddie, over a lunch of conch salad and white wine, he, DeMalaga, and Michele discussed his situation.

"Can you imagine that having too much cash is my problem?" asked Eddie. "I used to dream of drowning in cash and now it's my biggest nightmare."

"Did you get it out of the States?" asked DeMalaga.

"Almost all," said Eddie, pointing downwards and looking around to make sure no one outside their immediate circle saw the gesture. "Thirty million," he said and laughed. DeMalaga laughed too.

"What the hell are you going to do with it? Just sail around and around till you die?"

"Sail where? The way these guys are moving when they search the fucking boat for customs, they'll ask questions about that much money, and if you can't answer in ten minutes they have your name in a fucking computer hunting you down all over the world. These guys do not want any money floating around that they do not control, more than a million dollars they pick up like a flash. The drug war is not about drugs, my friend, the drug war is about money because they don't want anybody else to have that much."

"Bahamas is OK," said DeMalaga, "you can always say you won the money gambling."

Eddie shook his head. "They're after Ledher and all those Norman Cay guys, and they're even going to go after the top man, so who knows?"

"What about Cayman?" asked Michele.

"They are descended from pirates, but they are very respectable," said Eddie, "and the Americans just arrested a bank manager who was passing through Miami. Barclays Bank! They wanted information on their accounts in Cayman."

DeMalaga himself banked in the Channel Islands. They had refused to let anybody see their books in three hundred years, but DeMalaga didn't say anything about that ...

"What about Panama?" DeMalaga asked instead.

"I hate those fucking cocaine people," said Eddie, "they're mad. This guy Noriega, who knows what a mad motherfucker like that will do? No man, the Caribbean needs a good port of call for a guy like me."

DeMalaga laughed. "With thirty million you could probably set up as a warlord in Beirut," he said.

"Where's Mark?" asked Eddie, changing the subject.

"He's coming in this evening," said Michele.

"What about Percy?" asked DeMalaga.

"He's standing by," said Michele.

"When will he meet the press?" asked DeMalaga.

"When Mark and Winston confirm they've got everything under control," said Michele.

"Once Percy's on the island, Lynch dare not invade, not if the press are here," said DeMalaga.

"That's the plan," said Michele, "but he's not going to do anything till he knows the money's in and Idi's out."

"Well, either the press will have that story to tell, or they'll be able to report on the invasion," said DeMalaga.

The telephone rang in Molly Clifford's suite at Brown's Hotel in London.

"Hello, Molly?"

"Hello Herbie."

"Yes, hmm, how about tea?"

"Yes. That would be lovely."

"Ritz."

"Yes."

"Five thirty."

"See you there."

Herbie was Molly's elder brother, and now that her father was dead, he was the rural earl. Herbie had not had a rural career, however. He'd been a great sport in his youth, and after doing well in the Second World War, he'd gone on to become a force to be reckoned with in the City.

A hundred years before, the Brits had made a deal for a few thousand rupees with the Al-Sabah in Kuwait because they suspected there was oil in the area. The only thing the Sheikhs were expected to do was welcome British battleships in an emergency and bank their money in London. It was a simple enough arrangement, made all the more attractive because anyone with a claim to Royalty paid no taxes in Britain. The only surprising thing was the quantity of the money that was forthcoming—at last count over a hundred billion dollars, pumped, as previously arranged, through the city of London's banking system. Herbie was a director of one of the banks that had been among the chief beneficiaries of the resultant cash flow ever since.

Molly met Herbie on the terrace overlooking Green Park. It was a lovely late summer's afternoon, and Herbie, still the man about town in London, wore a fresh carnation in his lapel.

They ordered tea, discussed the progress of the younger generation, and eventually worked their way around to the business at hand.

"How's Hugh?"

"Very well, though a bit worried about America I think."

"I hear they want to spend a trillion on arms in the next three years, bit thick when one considers there's no war on."

"They're going to have one in space, Herb. I'm not joking, that's what we hear. It's to be announced momentarily. In the meantime, they're making do with a little one against our friends in the Caribbean."

"Yes, dreadful mess." Herbie had owned a holiday house on the island for years. He was also a director of the telephone company, based in London, that controlled all the island's telecommunications. He shook his head. "We had to cut them off, you know. It got that bad."

"That's what I wanted to see you about ... I've decided to help Michele Bernard."

"I heard they were, ah, a bit wanking, the Bernards. Although, I liked their father ..."

"Well, I don't know. I do think they're the best bet, and they do have a plan, and you're part of it."

"Oh really," said Herbie, somewhat surprised. "How so?"

"They want the phones switched on again very precisely."

"How will we get paid?"

"You'll get paid as soon as they're back in business. The money's coming from Hugh, he'll guarantee it."

"Well, in that case just write out the date and time." He pulled out a slim notebook, with a cover of baby alligator skin fringed in gold, and handed it to Molly who wrote down the particulars and handed it back.

"Thank you." Molly smiled at her brother. "How's Irene?"

Irene was Herbie's mistress of twenty years standing.

"Oh, ever young. I can't keep up, I'm afraid. I feel a bit like that chap who said, 'the pleasure's momentary, the posture's ludicrous, and the cost's prohibitive'. So far as sex is concerned at my age, my dear, my prevailing attitude is to let sleeping dogs lie."

Chapter Thirty-Nine

⚭

During the flight down to the island, Mark said nothing. It wasn't that he was being unfriendly, it was simply that until he saw Winston in the flesh he had nothing to say.

The plane landed at eleven that night, Mark was met by Michele, and they were carried the fifty miles to Winston on the backs of motorbikes. Still, Mark had been unable to speak. All the way along the final stretch, up the old driveway, and through the darkness towards the old house, Mark remembered his uncle and those summers in the country all over again. He felt that even if he knew nothing else for certain anymore, he knew that he was in the right place at the right moment, because the first thing on the agenda of his life was now undoubtedly the confrontation with Winston. What was he going to do?

Was he was going to kill him? Forgive him? The most defining moment in his life loomed ahead in the darkness and he had no idea how he would handle it; then, just as the bike came to a halt and he climbed off, Mark had an inspiration. He would let the spirits of Uncle T and all the other old people judge his brother. He would let his mother and father, and his uncle, and all the others who, over all that time, had struggled to get them to the point where ... where ... where Winston had abandoned them—those spirits had made it known to Mark in Korea that they could render judgement—let *them* pass judgement on Winston now. If Winston had really betrayed them, Mark would kill him in a minute.

"Where were you when I needed you?" he said, advancing on his brother.

"I was out of it, Mark. I couldn't help you. I told you that in my note."

"Why didn't you warn me?"

"Warn you? You'd declared a state of emergency! You were in charge, you were telling people when they could go out into the street! You weren't listening to me Mark, you wanted me as a messenger boy to get money for you to spend on keeping everybody in line!"

"You're just like one of those people on a team, you pass to them but they're never there; you see a break, you call to them to pass to you, they don't even hear, they're busy dribbling around ... fucking around. You just disappeared! Just like that! Leaving me at the mercy of that idiot Percy and that son of a bitch DeCartret." Mark turned away from Winston as though he couldn't bear to look at him for another second.

"I'll deal with Michele, I'll even deal with Percy, but I won't deal with you Winston, because either you're a fucking idiot or you're a coward, and either way I don't want to have to have anything to do with you, you just left me to wander around looking like a fucking idiot ..."

"It was *your* plan! You must have known how to run it!"

Mark shook his head, stunned. "No, I didn't know how to run it. Not the side that you were supposed to handle, not the side that Michele was supposed to handle, I was completely dependent on you, completely!"

"Well, suppose we were in battle," said Winston, "and I'd been shot? Isn't that something you have to take in your stride in your business?"

Mark had come to a moment in life that he had not anticipated. He would either have to wreak havoc, or he would have to admit he was wrong. Desperately, he tried to get back to basics, to the decision he'd made as he climbed off the bike. Let the ancestors judge him! They were prepared to render judgement on Mark in the cockpit of an aircraft on the deck of an aircraft carrier, what judgement would they render on Winston now?

But when Mark looked at Winston again that night he didn't see the Winston he knew. This one held a machete.

"The fact is, Mark, that your plan failed and mine is a going concern, and, as to being a coward, I am going into my office to get the money that I need to put my plan into action whether you back me or not, so you can fuck off!"

"What do you mean?" asked Mark.

"I mean that Percy sent me a note saying he was not prepared to take over as prime minister again until the money that Hugh Clifford is holding for me is in and confirmed to him by the bank."

"How are you going to get to your office?"

"In disguise," said Winston.

For the first time since he'd seen his brother again, Mark focused on something other than his eyes, and realised that Winston had turned Rasta!

"Disguise!" said Mark, who suddenly felt a great urge to laugh as he thought of the reaction of the jury that he had called in on these family proceedings, and all he could think of was their shock at seeing Winston as a Rasta! His father, his mother, his Uncle T! Suddenly Mark did start to laugh, and once he started he couldn't stop because the laughter sprang from surprise and then from relief. Winston wasn't a coward, he knew what Idi Morris would do to him to get that money if he slipped into his hands, and if Winston wasn't a coward then he *could* be depended on this next time; and more important than that, much more important, Mark could love him again.

They talked till dawn, very little about themselves, almost continuously about the plan. Eventually they paused for breakfast and to walk in the garden just as the sun was coming up, and as they went across the lawn in front of the old house, Michele looked out and saw that Mark had his arm around Winston's shoulder

Chapter Forty

Back in the tourist capital, Michele started working a checklist the way she had done so often before in the theatre and on the campaign trail; sheets had to be washed with soap brought in by Eddie, food would have to be collected and cooked to last fifty people four days; staff had to be found and brought back into the hotel and local radio station; local telephone crew had to check that when the system was turned on again the line to the radio station was working. Percy was insisting on staying hidden until the call came through to confirm that Winston was in his office and the money was in the bank.

DeMalaga was handling the press, booking the charter to bring them in from Miami. Eddie was paying for a second load of oil in a small coastal tanker out of Panama which had already set sail, and he was bringing in a boatload of spare parts and medicine when he returned that evening from a quick trip to Cayman for the last of Michele's press party essentials.

Michele moved her headquarters from the hotel to Eddie's yacht as soon as it was alongside the yacht club jetty. There she was able to relax, have a drink, and look across the water to the city three miles away, which would be without light when night fell. A town that could only function in daylight. No fax, no telephone, no contact with the outside world except for a couple of yachts and a charter airplane, this was what they had to fight with against the armada at Lynch's disposal. Five or six good friends working against an army of bureaucrats, technicians, suppliers, and a communications network that covered the globe via satellite. It didn't seem like much of a contest, but Michele felt sure her side would win because she was going to tell their side of the story to the press, and the press was the equaliser.

All his life Mark had lived with the assumption that just under the surface of civilised society there was this angry bubbling mass, seething with resentment and a sense of revenge on the world in general and those who they saw as their oppressors in particular. An ugly, angry rabble, which, if let loose, would remind the world of Attila, Ghengis, the Huns, and the Vandals, the mob by the guillotine in Paris, and the sullen riotous criminal class that the British had tried to transport en masse to Australia. This was the portrait that Lynch had presented to the world of IZion, and yet here he was in front of Mark, smiling. Mark's sense of unreality increased.

Whatever he looked like, and to Mark he looked like the caricature of a savage, IZion controlled the island with an army, and Mark had none ... except the one that was shattered in the capital, the one he had to reclaim, but would not even survive to reach unless he was escorted by IZion's men.

"Pleased to meet you," said Mark, extending his hand to IZion on being introduced by Winston.

"Irie, brother Mark," said IZion, "dis ya a Ashanti, mi main warriah."

Mark shook hands with a guy whose locks fell to his waist, and who had an M16 cradled in his left arm.

"Now gentlemen," said Mark, "my main objective is to get back into camp and reclaim my command, clean out the army, turn it back into a disciplined force."

"Discipline who?" asked Ashanti.

"The army itself needs to be disciplined."

"Your army," said Ashanti.

"Yes."

"What about our army? You wan fe discipline us to?"

"If you're under my command, yes."

"Mi nuh under you command."

"No, not now. But when things get back to normal, there will only be one army on the island."

"Umhum," said Ashanti. He looked at IZion. IZion looked at Mark. Mark said nothing.

"What are you afraid of, Ashanti?" asked Winston.

"Mi fear your bredda gwine fix up him army an oppress us same way. Burn herb field, all dem ting deh. I nuh seh im nuh do it, but I nuh really feel fe help him, seen?"

Suddenly, and without warning, the alliance between Mark and the Rasta fighters was in jeopardy.

"Look, Ashanti," said Winston, "let me explain something to you. Tomorrow I've got to reach town, Idi has to be killed, the Prime Minister has to be reinstalled, and if it doesn't happen tomorrow it'll be too late. Nothing will ever get back to normal and Idi will rule."

"De herb is narmal," said Ashanti.

"What about cocaine?" asked Mark.

"Dat a steel drug," said Ashanti, "dat can go."

"What about smuggling?" asked Mark.

Now IZion stepped in. "Dat up to you," he said, "but herb mus' be free." IZion hadn't spoken until what he said was the final word.

The next day Mark started working with Ashanti and his men to spring an attack on Idi Morris. He planned to capture and kill him personally, it was as simple as that, but he had to get to Idi before Idi got to Winston.

Chapter Forty One

∞∞∞

The battery for the Jaguar was taken to the one gas station which had been reopened again to service the cars that would take the press around, it was charged and returned on the evening before Winston was due to leave for the city.

Winston got into the car, started it, drove it once around the driveway, and then parked it again.

As he got out of the car Winston saw Aladdin staring. The dog had discovered the car, but he didn't know it could come alive and he certainly didn't know Winston would be able to get into it and drive around, and as Winston saw the panic in the dog's face he felt a dreadful pang of remorse at leaving the old house in the country ... he'd arrived with every dream smashed, and he was leaving with the best chance he'd ever had for making them all come true.

As he walked around the garden with his little friend, through slants of golden late afternoon sun, he promised himself that he'd come back; that he'd buy the place from his cousins and bring up his children here. The old house had absorbed so much pain and still remained a happy place.

All that night Winston walked around the house and the gardens in the moonlight, going over once again the sequence of events that would have to be coordinated the next day. First, Winston had to confirm the cash to Percy, then Percy would declare that his legitimately elected government was back in control, and Mark would make sure that this was the case by taking out Idi. Michele would get the news out to the world at large that the island was safe for tourism once more, that things were back to normal. But first Winston had to reach his terminal; in the penthouse, in the city controlled by a psychopath.

He slept for three hours and woke at five, made himself a cup of coffee, and without saying anything but good morning to anybody, got in the car and drove off.

As he turned through the gate, he saw Aladdin running, desperate to know how this steel monster could have swallowed up Winston to carry him away, just like that. Winston wanted to stop and pick him up to carry him, but could he really? No, the city was starving, any army patrol would pick up a puppy for the meat. Winston accelerated, and the dust grew thicker, filling Aladdin's eyes and lungs as he realised that the car wasn't going to stop, it was going to hurtle on at incredible speeds seemingly forever ... out of his little world.

Winston drove fifty miles through the countryside, the roads empty except for donkeys and pushcarts, and the car was like good news announcing with a rush along the roadside that something was happening at last.

When he got to the main camp for IZion's army in the middle of the island's central mountain range, he parked the Jaguar and was picked up to ride pillion on a 250 trail bike with a Dread who was one of Ashanti's star scouts.

On the way through the camp he had a meeting with Mark. Mark had already tracked down several of his best men who'd scattered when Idi took over. They had been told who to contact as they crept back into the city, what objectives they were to secure as the real General planned to recapture the camp. Mark could take care of Idi, he was certain of that, but the timing was crucial.

"I should be at the hotel by five tonight," said Winston, "that's when we go public."

"I'll be there," said Mark.

Winston was taken at high speed for the next sixty miles to the point on the highway out of town past which Idi Morris' army could not venture.

Where the mountain road came to the junction of the highway into the city, a vast market place had grown up. This was where anybody coming out of town would get their first free meal if they were going to continue on into the countryside, but where anybody returning to the city would have to pay for food.

Had Winston not willed it, this place would not have existed, certainly not in its present form, but Winston drew no strength from that thought.

As he crossed the no man's land leading to the borders of Idi's domain, Winston felt as though he was advancing steadily into an ever deepening gloom.

The blown bridges had turned the area into a jumble of twisted steel and dust, and as they approached the city side of the boundary, Winston went from a world of green to one of dirty grey.

Gradually all paths through the crashed flyovers formed into three main queues, each of which led past a checkpoint manned by soldiers.

The soldiers were searching every bag, examining the food, taking some for the slightest excuse.

Suddenly there was an eruption of violence ten feet ahead of Winston in the line, and he saw a soldier grab a bag away from a man.

"Bumbo claat, watchya!" said the soldier, holding up some transistor batteries.

"Mi neva know battry is fabidden, baas," said the man.

"Oh yeah? Den why yu try fe hide dem den?"

"Mi neva try to hide dem, sah," said the man.

"Yu tek mi fe fool," said the soldier, "yu waan battry fe listen rebel radio."

"Tek de battry den, baas," said the man, "jus let mi go, mi a innocent man, so jus be nice an tek di battry an everyting cool."

The soldiers pocketed the batteries and waved the man on with a bored hand as he kissed his teeth.

"Tek aff yu hat," said the same soldier when Winston came up to him. The tam came off to reveal locks down to his shoulders.

"But wait, yu Rasta?" asked the soldier.

"No, sah," said Winston.

"Den how yu got locks?" asked the soldier.

"No sah, is jus a style, sah," said Winston, "mi neva know mi couldn't wear locks inna town, sah," said Winston.

"Yu look to me like one a IZion spy," said the soldier.

"No, sah! I is a lovin man baasie, I come to town because mi gal sick sah, believe me, please sah," said Winston, "I get a message dat mi baby muddah sick sah."

The soldier looked at him for what seemed like a very long moment.

"Believe mi sah," said Winston again.

"Mi nuh believe yu a rass claat, go an sit ova deh."

And Winston was moved over to join five other men in detention.

At the Pentagon, in the Canal Zone, at Guantanamo, the excitement was intense. Twenty Hercules, thirty helicopters, five destroyers, two aircraft carriers, the 82nd Airborne Division, the planes to carry them into attack ... everywhere there was noise at the level where one had to cover one's ears against it, the noise of movement, of excitement as engines of every shape and size were started and revved, as trucks and armoured carriers and bulldozers were all tested, armed, and loaded.

In the logistics department they hadn't had this much action in years, in every department of the military there was the certainty that whoever came out well on this one was going to rise on the ladder, and whoever fucked up would be revealed as unable to cut it when right on the edge ...

Everything was ready, the only thing holding them back was the President, and the only thing holding him back was pressure from the media to find out whether or not Percy Sullivan was, in fact, back on the island and in control, in which case intervention was out of the question.

Between the pressures from Lynch and from the people around Hugh Clifford, the President was restless, and in no mood to take a decision. He needed something to push him, and it was then that the calls came in from three concerned mothers. Their daughters were in a teachers' college that was located in the middle of the island. Were their daughters safe they wondered?

Suddenly, an obscure village, sleeping peacefully, high in the hills of the mountains' central range, became a focal point for fifty different planners in the overtime hours of an excited military in Washington DC.

Suddenly, plans were being made to fly in ten helicopters and a hundred men. The choppers would prep the entire area with firepower capable of thousands of rounds per minute.

LIVES OF STUDENTS AT STAKE! screamed the next press release to the worldwide media.

Nothing of Michele's press plan worked out as she'd expected.

Seven carefully selected magazine writers were to have been assembled in Miami and flown down to the island by Max DeMalaga, the plan was that they would meet with IZion to satisfy themselves that he wasn't a drug-crazed terrorist, then they would meet Percy and be witness to the fact that the legitimate elected government of the island was back in control; they would be entertained, taken around to the degree possible given the gas shortage, and, ultimately, the hope was that they would be impressed enough to go and write articles in influential magazines as witnesses to what was actually going on on the island.

It was to have been low key, controlled by Michele almost as if these people were there as her personal guests; but Lynch was moving faster than anybody suspected.

By the time DeMalaga had left Miami, he had had twenty calls from reporters who had not been invited but who wanted a ride on the plane.

They were not aware of Michele or IZion or any nuance of island politics. They wanted to get onto the island in time for the invasion. These were not sympathetic editorial types, these were hard core news junkies, looking for action.

During the course of the next twenty-four hours, fifty more world press arrived. Everything from polka-dot bow ties to Banana Republic bush jackets, jamming the hotel bar, calling for cold beers. That was test number one for normality anywhere in the world. Michele had foreseen this, but had underestimated the ice she ordered. Thank God there was a breeze blowing, she thought, maybe they wouldn't notice the lack of air conditioning.

That night, the ice in the bar replenished, she put on a floorshow after dinner, and then introduced IZion to the crowd.

"You've heard a lot of wicked things about this man," said Michele, "but I would like to introduce you to him as the one who saved this island from rape and plunder, and who has been wrongly accused in the international press in order to justify intervention."

The faces at the tables that were turned towards her remained impassive. For most of the reporters assembled, intervention was the story they'd come to get. That's why they'd chartered planes to get here. That's why they had loaded up with tape and film and battery driven portable typewriters—they were all there to get pictures and write stories that would result in the biggest possible headline: WAR!

IZion stood up and they clapped in a polite kind of way.

"We are happy to answer questions," said Michele.

"Who do you represent?" asked a reporter.

"The government of Percy Sullivan, the elected leader of the country," said Michele.

"Is he here?"

"He's on the island but he isn't here tonight."

"Why not?"

"He's planning to meet with the press after he's addressed the nation tomorrow."

"Do you think that will stop the invasion?" asked a TV journalist who turned a bright light on Michele to record her answer.

"Invasion?" asked Michele. "What invasion?"

"Well you may not be aware of it, but in the States, at the top of the news, is a story that the island is in chaos, that American lives are in danger ..."

"Where?" asked Michele, incredulous. "Where are American lives in danger?"

"Is there a teachers' college in the interior?"

"Yes ... but there's been no problem there."

"That's not what we've heard," said the man from the TV crew as they snapped off their lights.

"Do you expect us to say to the American public, 'you can go back there and you'll be safe?'" asked a travel writer.

"Not yet," said Michele, "not until the government is back in the capital and things are back to normal, but in the meantime I think it's worth knowing that the countryside is not at the mercy of outlaws, or—"

"When do you expect a return to normal?" asked a political journalist.

"Some time very soon."

"I'd like to ask a question of IZion," said the man from *Newsweek*.

IZion, blinded by the light, turned in his direction, blinked.

"What is your basic ideological orientation?" asked the journalist.

Michele translated for IZion. "They want to know what ism you belong to," she said.

"Mi nuh deal in ism schism."

"Are you religious then?" asked *Rolling Stone*.

"Yes. Dat a di root ... just do God work, put down evil and keep a clean heart."

"What the fuck is this guy talking about, I can't understand a word he says," complained a man from *The Wall Street Journal*. "He could be the Ayatollah of the Rasta Caribbean, for all we know," said the man from the *Miami Herald*.

It's strange, thought Michele, that IZion—courageous, truthful, having saved the island from a monster—had no credibility at all with the foreign press. It was apparent that they would only be impressed by Percy. Percy who had no power to do anything except make Winston risk his life before he would accept the burden of government again.

Soon the consensus was clear. The press wasn't interested in IZion. The overwhelming majority of them were only interested in the invasion, or in Percy's appearance, because only that could stop it.

DeMalaga saw the panic in Michele's eyes, and went over to her as the press briefing broke up.

"We've got to keep them busy," he said.

"Yes, but how?"

"Make sure the drunkards get drunk, the lecherous get laid, the dancers dance."

"I'm worried about Winston. I can't get him out of my mind."

"I'll handle it. Eddie and I."

"Thank you, Max."

By ten o'clock about half the crowd had gone to bed, *Playboy* and *Rolling Stone* were gambling, *Vanity Fair* and *Paris-Match* were on the dance-floor, and CNN was setting up and testing their equipment, with Eddie beside them to make sure they got through with everything more or less under control.

DeMalaga's thoughts returned to normal. He was enjoying all this, but there was something missing. Everybody was looking for a story out of an event that was costing millions to stage, and he still hadn't focused on what it really meant to him in practical terms.

There were fifty ways of reporting what was going on, and *someone* was going to shoot an interview or write a piece or take a photograph to sum up the whole thing, and whoever that was was going to make a fortune. Who, wondered DeMalaga, which of them on the island that night would win that particular contest?

And could he spot the winner?

After dinner, thinking along these lines, DeMalaga noticed a lanky young girl who had been watching IZion and taking photographs. She'd noticed something about IZion. When he scowled he looked very ferocious indeed, but when he smiled he looked like an angel.

DeMalaga noticed that when the rest of the crowd had drifted off, she joined IZion, Ashanti, and the others who were gathered around a chillum they'd set up out on the terrace by the sea.

DeMalaga watched the girl and he saw what she was seeing. He asked around to find out whether IZion was a singer. He discovered that not only was he a singer, he was going to sing at a groundation with his entire army the next morning at dawn.

DeMalaga arranged the transportation, went over to the group, introduced himself to the girl photographer, told her of the photo opportunity at dawn, and put her on the back of a bike. They rode thirty miles up into the hills, where she slept on a clean bed in a small hut for three hours.

It was the sound of singing voices that awoke her. Two thousand of them. Grabbing her camera, she went out into the pre-dawn light to see an entire hillside covered with IZion's people, facing the sunrise, singing.

Lost in a sea of images, the girl shot three: one of him stern, one of him joyous, and one of the size of the crowd on the hillside.

Those photographs ran on the covers of eight different magazines in six different languages, sold literally thousands of copies in newspapers around the world, and adorned the front and back covers of the album that resulted.

Those photographs were destined to be the only trace left of that entire press corps airlift ten years later, and there were at least a million of them lying around as record covers for a lot longer than that.

Chapter Forty Two

∞∞∞

With the help of IZion's army, and of IZion himself who never left his side, Mark moved much faster than he had anticipated. Within a day of rounding up fifty reliable men from his own force while he was in the rural camp, he had moved to the edge of the city and had started sending for his key men within the main camp.

Sergeant Wilson arrived at eleven o'clock that night to find Mark and his platoon in a large abandoned warehouse in the first village on the way out of town and into the mountains. All that night they planned the attack on the army camp that would return it to Mark's control.

Wilson wasn't worried now that Mark was back. He knew that Idi's army was in a state of virtual mutiny. Men who hadn't been paid in weeks didn't mind so long as they could plunder the countryside. But now that they were besieged in the city, and everything there had been plundered out long ago, they had only each other to prey on.

Nevertheless, a bungled attack was the last thing that Mark Bernard had in mind, and the plan took till midday the next day to finally fall into place. By that time Winston should have been in his office, but Mark had seen no sign of him, and dared not start the attack on Idi for fear that Winston was a hostage.

Hostage, no. Captive, yes—for although Winston was as yet unrecognised, he saw the day dawn through bars.

He'd been trapped in a new security measure instituted by Idi just the day before. There was no warning, but here he was, sitting on the ground of a prison enclosure hour after hour. He didn't feel tragic about it, he didn't feel outraged, more than anything else he felt absurd about the situation; that some goon in this room really had the island's future at stake, that it could be as arbitrary as that. Well, Winston thought, obviously he didn't *deserve* to get through ... the fates had rejected his application for the top spot.

The screening process, as it had dragged on through the night and into the next day, was revealed as a two stage identification parade for everybody coming into the city who was regarded as suspect. The first identification parade involved calling the person who the captive gave as their contact in the city. The second panel was made up of captives from IZion's army, and they would be forced to identify anyone they recognised.

Winston racked his brain to think of someone who was poor enough to justify his disguise ... Missa D! The bell captain for Winston's hotel. Privy to the plan, cool in a crisis, Missa D was an inspiration, and as soon as he arrived, Winston shouted out to catch his attention.

"Missa D, Missa D!" called out Winston to the man who had never called him anything but 'sir' in his life. "Missa D!"

The old man turned to see a version of his boss that he would not have imagined possible, even in this crazy world that had developed ever since the Bernards stopped running the country.

"You know this man?" asked the guard.

"Missa D yu don't remember mi, sah? Winstan, mi usu stay down by di hotel, mi tell di man dat mi come a town fe look fe Sarah, yu dawta, and dem nuh believe mi, sah."

Thank God Missa D took the cue, told the policeman he would vouch for Winston, and was told to come back the next day after the captives had been put through the second panel.

All that long night the processing continued. Those already captured and identified as Idi's enemies were moved down the line of the captives yet to be tested. A flicker of recognition was enough. Winston was well known to the men of IZion's army. What chance was there that among those searching for new recruits into the hell of Idi's prisons wouldn't be someone who would identify Winston Bernard as the one who IZion himself had taken instructions from.

By three the next morning, as the panel approached Winston, he realised that there *was* a man in the line who knew him. He saw him coming across the room. The man had not seen him, no captive was supposed to look at another until a guard was looking at them both eyeball to eyeball down the line, so the guard could pick up any sign of recognition no matter how small. Then the beating would start till the information was out, all of it, lists of family, friends, contacts, locations; wrung dry of every last drop of information, he would be left with just enough life in him to inform on others, the endless cycle dragging on day and night in the huge filthy enclosure where Winston sat trapped like an animal sent to slaughter.

As he sat there, awaiting his fate, he was not at all hopeful of deliverance, because he knew that he had not solved the final question, the question of the hallucination, the question he had to answer if he was to be worthy of controlling the penthouse, if he was to be the man responsible for over two million other people. There *was* no reason he should make it if he didn't have the answer. That was his last thought as the man who knew him came closer, stopping, looking, certain to register recognition when he looked into Winston's eyes, the man was moving into his vision ... and in that second Winston closed his eyes to pray, and when he opened them again, the other captive had passed on, having registered nothing ...

By the time Winston was released on Missa D's surety, twelve hours had passed. He hurried the old man along as soon as they were out of sight of the police station.

"Everything alright at the hotel, D?"

"Yes sir."

"You seen Mr McFadden?"

"Him nuh come down, but mi see him inna di window yessaday marnin."

"Alright. D, get him a message that I'm back."

Outside, the hotel looked closed, but when Winston came into the lobby he could see that the place was clean and had not been looted. McFadden had used the interim cash to good effect.

"Emergency generator tested?"

"Is OK, sir."

"Fuel supply for how long?"

"Four day, sir."

"Never found it huh?"

"Neva find nutten."

Winston placed a hand on the old man's shoulders and squeezed gently to show his appreciation.

"Well done, D," he said.

He walked all the way up to the penthouse because the elevators would require the main standby generator and Winston wanted only enough power to run his office. When he reached it and flicked a switch, a bright green dot appeared on the stereo system and the row of terminals opposite Winston's swivel chair.

Hardly daring to hope, Winston proceeded to the phone. It worked. There was a dial tone! It had been there since yesterday when he was supposed to make the call ...Winston put the phone back down and sat for a moment to collect himself. After a year in the bush without it, he had electricity again! Electronic speed! He took a few moments to absorb the acceleration, then he went and sat in his chair and began the process of arranging the transfer of the two hundred million dollars from Switzerland into the account of the government Central Bank across the road. It was a routine he knew by heart, but he couldn't concentrate. His mind kept slipping, his head started whirring with the sound of the hallucination, he started to feel the warning constriction in his throat. Winston staggered up from the swivel chair and went into the bedroom to lie down. As he moved towards the bed, he suddenly glimpsed himself in the mirror — filthy from the journey, in the clothes of a very poor hill farmer, with a beard and hair like a Dreadlock who had lived more roots than anybody but the true believers; he asked himself a question when he saw his image in the mirror, and the question was: *how often would a guy looking like you get to punch those buttons?* And the answer came back, *Never again ... that's why you have to get it right!*

Get it right?

Winston was in effect in a state of prayer, seeking guidance, and a picture formed in his mind of the words on a paperweight that he had once given to Michele.

Nobody needs advice, came the answer, *everybody needs information.*

The pressure on Winston's throat eased, and his brain seemed clear enough when he next looked up from the edge of the bed and saw himself in the mirror.

He got up, went to the cupboard, took out some clothes and laid them on the bed. Then he took off his old clothes, and had a shower. After that he got some scissors, and he started to cut his beard, standing and looking into the bathroom mirror.

Everybody needs information.

Obviously he couldn't approach the swivel chair in the middle of his control centre till he knew what that meant in practical terms. He looked at the time. It was a quarter to four.

He kept cutting. First his beard, then his hair.

Information. That meant he should run an open system. A totally open system. He himself, whatever the temptations, whatever the pressure, should hold no information secret ... should undo all the protections that those in power all over the world had always been addicted to.

So simple as to seem naive, but so basic as to be absolutely obvious. Why then had it never been tried before? Because of greedy, self obsessed little men who hadn't risen to the opportunities that power offered them. What thrill could mere money buy that would compare for Winston Bernard with the thrill of playing it straight? What sense of accomplishment could wealth bring him that would compensate for having to hide any expenditure he might make of public funds? If he wanted personal cash, all he had to do was to go out and make it, but that was a cheap thrill compared to the one he contemplated, Because what he was after was the fusion of an *ideal* with reality. What Winston was after was a future in which he did not *need* the protection of secrecy because he would live in a world where there was nothing to hide. They all started out that way and they all sold out—for what? Some cars? Some homes? Some women? He already had what he wanted of all those things. What he wanted was something more.

Two million people, all with their own ambitions, plans, energy; it was true, they didn't need advice, they did need information! If he opened up the system and let the information flow—and *only* he could do that—they would make their own plans, they would unleash their own energy. And what was the energy of one man compared to that? The standard response for those in power had always been to try to make as many people as possible carry out one plan, but that was two million carrying the energy of one. Winston wanted the opposite. He wanted to be one man unleashing the energy of two million!

It wasn't that Winston didn't want power. It was, rather, that he recognised that there were two classes of power: one which *did* involve the energy generated by ego and one which required that ego be relinquished altogether. The first lifted one to the heights, but then a shift was needed from climb to cruise. Because, having reached the peak, it was as fatal to keep climbing as it was to go forward in the wrong direction.

Anybody who'd ever watched powerful men close-up knew that their power would increase the more they humbled themselves, that hubris was fatal. History was full of nothing much else but the warning that those who forgot always perished, and drama since time immemorial was full of the stories of their forgetting. It had been easy to forget in the past, but to forget now ... to attempt to restrict the possibilities of the universal knowledge available to him to fit the dimensions of his own mind, his own ego ... obviously a fuse would blow. Clearly in Winston's generation the ultimate power would demand the ultimate humility. Then the lesson of his deathbed finally came. Now that he was finally central to everything, he himself must become nothing, as egoless as a terminal in his computer systems.

He had to open the tap so that the information would flow to everybody. For the first time anywhere ever in the tropical world, Winston would run a political system as it was designed to run in the first place. He would be the first to recognise the triumph of communications over politics, of information over myth. That was it. That was all. That was the *real revolution*. It seemed so simple. It seemed so obvious. Yet it had never been tried. Winston picked up the phone and made the call to Hugh Clifford.

"Ah, you've arrived, good," said Hugh Clifford, "I wondered where you were. Are you OK?"

"Yes, here I am," said Winston, "everything's fine."

"Congratulations," said the old man, "I'll make the calls."

First he would call Marc Gold; then he would call Percy and Michele and confirm that the money was on the way. They had won!

Both Winston's call to Hugh Clifford and Clifford's call to Marc Gold were picked up by the NSC, DEA, CIA and DIA. The calls were relayed immediately to Henry Lynch in the back of his limousine in Washington, and Lynch immediately told the information agencies to monitor all money transfers into the island.

"Goddammit!" he muttered.

"Turn around," he said to the driver, "take me back to the office."

By the time he had got there, Elliott Bridgewater was waiting for him.

"Do you have Idi Morris's number?' asked Lynch.

"I'm told he never leaves the camp," said Bridgewater.

"Get him on the phone, and when you do, tell him this ..." Lynch started writing out the message.

When Idi Morris heard the phone ring in Mark's old office, he nearly jumped out of his skin.

"Is waddat?" he exclaimed.

"Is de phone!" said Joyce.

"Tree months dat don't work."

"Somebady mussi pay di bill."

"Hello, General Morris?" said a voice when he picked up the phone.

"Who dis?" asked Idi.

"This is a friend with some information you should have," said the voice from overseas, "Winston Bernard is back in the city."

"Weh?" asked Idi.

"He's at the Central Bank," said Bridgewater.

"Who is dis?" demanded Idi again.

"He's got two hundred million dollars that's just come in, Idi, and if you capture him you can capture the money too," said the voice.

In the past twenty-four hours, Mark had checked for Winston at the penthouse four times. He had slept there for the three hours of rest that he'd snatched during the night, inbetween meetings with the scraps of his army that were coming in to report for instructions as they heard of Mark's return.

For at least five hours, Mark had had everything in place to begin the battle for taking back the camp, but suppose Winston was Idi's captive inside it? If Winston hadn't made it to his office, where the hell was he? He *must* have been captured, thought Mark, but had he been recognised?

By the end of the afternoon, Mark was steeling himself to go and look for his brother one last time at the agreed rendezvous, dreading the moment when he would call out Winston's name and there would be no answer. Deliberately not letting his hopes get too high, Mark sent for his bike and rider, determined that this would be his last attempt to make sure that Winston was safe before going after Idi.

There were lookouts posted at every exit from the camp, and as the sun was going down, Mark got a report that Idi had broken out of the camp. The lookout for the southeast gate had seen him in Mark's Mercedes, loaded with bodyguards, as he drove through the exit and turned right. He was driving fast.

"Which direction did he take?" asked Mark.

"Downtown direction," said the scout.

Mark jumped onto the back of IZion's bike.

"Hotel Caribe!" he shouted.

As the bike tore through the empty streets, Mark imagined Idi's lead, he imagined him arriving three minutes ahead of him, he imagined him protected by his six guards with machine guns, he imagined him bursting in on Winston ... all with a three minute lead.

When the bike pulled up to the side of the hotel, however, Mark didn't see the Mercedes in front, he saw it across the street parked by the front door of the Central Bank. That's what the man from Washington had said, "the Central Bank", he didn't know that Winston lived across the street in the hotel. He didn't know he had duplicate computer terminals there and an extension of the governors official telephone line. And so the man that Idi Morris crashed in on was Alistair McFadden, and the fatal three minutes was regained.

Up in the penthouse of the hotel opposite, Winston had wandered out onto the terrace to watch the sunset. His body had registered the lodgement of the two hundred million, as an advance on a billion already in the pipeline, with a multi-billion dollar flush of pure joy which had left him in a state of sublime relaxation.

He'd won!

The money had come in. The press conference would be called, the address to the nation would go out, and tomorrow everybody would wake up to a world in which everything had started to work again. *That* was the reward Winston wanted.

Percy was the one who needed recognition: to be loved, to be known, to have his image spread as far and wide as possible. But Winston wanted no public image whatsoever. In his business, publicity only indicated that things were not going according to plan. Relaxation and precision, that was what was required now. Relaxation so he wouldn't turn into a human computer; precision so that he wouldn't fumble.

Winston's thoughts turned to Michele ... he walked over to the trampoline on the terrace, tested the stays, then he climbed up onto the edge and looked down into the net.

He looked out at the afterglow of the sunset, stretched his arms wide, and, with a laugh, flung himself into the air.

Winston had been a champion on the trampoline as a kid; it had been the one sport that Mark couldn't beat him at, and he'd kept a net ever since, whenever he had the space. It had been while he was teaching Michele how to float in the air that he had first started making love to her ... so long ago ... when tonight was just a distant fantasy. Now the youthful governor of the Central Bank flipped and fell and rose again, twisting up and over above the throbbing of the springs. He let his mind drift on about Michele as he choreographed the celebration in bed of *this* triumph when he and she got back home again.

"Backside, watchya," said Idi Morris when he looked out across from McFadden's office and saw Winston. Like a fish caught in a net was what Winston looked like to him, and he was out of the door faster than he'd come in.

The afterglow was nearly gone by the time Idi Morris and his men had come down and crossed the road.

The entire forecourt of the hotel was in deep shadow, and when he heard the approach of Idi and his men, Mark had no trouble avoiding the beams from the headlights of his car.

Idi had six bodyguards, Mark was alone, but as he saw Idi make his move towards the hotel entrance what he did next came as easily to Mark as if he were in a dream. His voice came out of the darkness in a shout of anger and authority so intense that it froze every man in place.

"Sergeant Morris!"

Suddenly, the boss was back. There wasn't a man who had ever served under Mark Bernard who would obey Idi Morris in Mark's presence. One was an impostor and one was a real general, and as Mark emerged from the shadows, all of Idi's bodyguards shrank back, leaving Idi to stare with terrified eyes at the gun that Mark Bernard was aiming at his head.

"You presumptuous bastard," said Bernard, just before he squeezed the trigger to blow out Idi Morris's, brains.

In that very moment, when IZion witnessed Mark's execution of Idi, when Winston was flipping on his trampoline, and Percy was entering the TV studio to the stand-up applause of the international press ... Michele watched from the control room and she felt the baby kick for the first time ...

Macmillan Caribbean Writers

Look out for other exciting titles from the region:

Crime thrillers:

Rum Justice   *Jolien Harmsen*

Fiction:

The Girl with the Golden Shoes   *Colin Channer*
The Festival of San Joaquin   *Zee Edgell*
She's Gone   *Kwame Dawes*
Molly and the Muslim Stick   *David Dabydeen*
John Crow's Devil   *Marlon James*
This Body   *Tessa McWatt*
Walking   *Joanne Haynes*
Trouble Tree   *John Hill Porter*
The Voices of Time   *Kenrick Mose*
Brother Man   *Roger Mais*
The Humming-Bird Tree   *Ian McDonald*

Short Stories:

Fear of Stones   *Kei Miller* (shortlisted for the 2007
   Commonwealth Writers' Prize)

Poetry:

Poems of Martin Carter   *Stewart Brown and Ian McDonald (eds.)*
Selected Poems of Ian McDonald   *Edited By Edward Baugh*
   (shortlisted for the 2009 Ondaatje Prize)

Plays:

Bellas Gate Boy (includes audio CD)   *Trevor Rhone*
Two Can Play and Other Plays   *Trevor Rhone*